DUNCAN SWAN

MONSTRE

VOLUME ONE

D1500515

SUPER
HOOT
PUBLISHING

MONSTRE

For information about this title or to order other books and/or
electronic media, contact the publisher: Super Hoot Publishing
superhootpublishing@gmail.com

Duncan Swan asserts the moral right to be identified
as the author of this work.
www.duncanswan.me

Cover design: Blow
Source Art: Fiona Darwin
Interior Design / Formatting: Pikko's House
Section Headers / Front Matter: Andrew Swainson
Editors: Clayton Bohle, Crystal Watanabe

Paperback ISBN: 978-1-7345740-0-5
eBook ISBN: 978-1-7345740-1-2

To all the peacocks who just gotta fly.

CERN
The European Organization for Nuclear Research
Meyrin, Switzerland

REESE

Dr. Reese Richards was a numbers guy.

When it came to math, Reese was gifted, bordering on afflicted, sitting somewhere on that delicate edge of amazing and utterly fucking incompetent. Consumed by his work at the expense of everything else in life.

Exercise had never been much of a priority. An elevated heart rate was an unpleasant experience, something to be avoided, like going to the dentist or getting injections. Which meant his weight was a problem, his fitness non-existent.

And after six flights of stairs, Reese wasn't running anymore; he was pretty much crawling, wheezing for air, dragging himself up by the railing.

The front of his shirt was stained with vomit and drenched in sweat, and each step was agony.

He could feel his muscles burning, his legs shaking, his heart hammering away in his chest. The overworked organ slowly unraveling as it pumped nothing but acid through his veins.

"Evacuate!" an androgynous voice screamed as the fire alarm howled in the enclosed space. Then again, but this time in French, then Italian, German, then back to English. Like a broken record, a continuous screaming loop, its shrill blasts echoing and ricocheting off the drab white walls while orange lights flashed high overhead.

Someone raced past him. A gust of wind, then another, fast, taking the steps two at a time.

Reese only saw the backs of their heads, their white lab coats flapping like capes behind them.

"Wait!" Reese shouted.

They didn't stop. They kept going. Too quick, too dark to see their faces.

"Wait for me!" he screamed as he listened to their footsteps fade. But they didn't turn around, didn't come back. They didn't give a shit, and, with a sick jolt, Reese realized he was running out of time. His vision was already crawling with black, and he was starting to get dizzy, wheezing and coughing with every step, choking on air thick with smoke, air that stank of molten metal, burning plastic and human hair. Air that was getting hotter. He could almost feel the hungry flames licking at the back of his neck, and Reese looked over the side of the railing to the ground far below.

It was like putting his head into a furnace. Hot, burnt air scorched his face and roasted his eyes, but through the pain and the tears Reese could see thick smoke belching into the bottom of the staircase and, beneath the smoke, the flickering orange glow of flames.

Oh God...

It was gaining on him.

Reese pulled his wide eyes away and forced himself to keep going, looking straight ahead, willing himself to move faster, chanting the same words over and over in his head. *Left foot. Right foot. Breathe.*

Another blur passed him, then two more in quick succession, almost knocking him over as they went.

"Help me!" he shouted at their retreating backs, his hand reaching for them. "Please?" he whimpered. "I don't want to die."

He shook his head. *Not like the others. Not like that.*

The ground vibrated beneath him, a small earthquake that knocked him to his knees. A reminder of the big one about to hit. A reminder of the readings he had seen on his computer screen before the world went mad, before up became down, before he was unable to do anything but watch all those people die.

He'd been inside the CMS Observation Room. A tiny, poorly ventilated room located three hundred feet below ground. A room filled with tired, frustrated people, hot computers, and the smell of old coffee and stale sweat. It was cramped and uncomfortable, but Reese had always found the view more than made up for the claustrophobic conditions.

The Observation Room gazed out into an enormous man-made cavern. A cavern wrapped with green steel girders like the ribs of some giant beast, while silver pipes and electrical conduits snaked down the walls like veins and arteries, carrying liquid helium and enough electricity to supply a small city. All of which fed into the heart of the facility, the CMS, or Compact Muon Solenoid.

One of two large general-purpose particle detectors built on the Large Hadron Collider, or LHC, which together formed part of a single enormous machine. A machine that stretched over 25 kilometers, sat astride two borders, cost eight billion dollars, and had taken thirteen years to build. A machine designed to smash hydrogen atoms together at nearly the speed of light, theoretically creating microscopic black holes, dark matter, and clues to extra dimensions in the tangled mess left behind.

The CMS itself was just one small part of the LHC. A *small* part that weighed 14,000 tons and stood six stories tall. It was an absolute monster of a machine, and it was broken. Again.

Reese was almost starting to think the damn thing was possessed. Ever since its second and final year-long hiatus and power upgrade, it had been plagued by issues. Debris in one of the magnet modules in March. A leak in one of the liquid helium containment chambers in May. It had overheated and broken down again in June. And now this. Whatever *this* was.

Reese picked up the walkie-talkie lying on the table next to him.

"Sometime this year, gents," he said with a tired sigh before taking his thumb off the button.

"Hold on to your panties, Reese," came Dr. Connors's flustered reply, followed by a hard click and the soft static-filled hiss of the empty carrier wave.

Reese bit back his retort. He held on for another fifteen minutes with nothing to do but watch Dr. Connors and O'Malley through the window in front of him, forced to wait as the men slowly strapped themselves into their safety harnesses before finally climbing onto the yellow scissor lift parked at the base of the CMS.

Only once they were clipped in did it start to rise into the air, its hazard light flashing and alarm beeping until they came to a jolting stop three stories above the ground.

"How about now?" asked Reese impatiently, his eyes flicking from his computer screen to all the technicians standing around the base of the CMS. He looked up at the two men on the platform sixty feet away, his stomach rumbling at the delay.

They'd been working away at this new issue for hours already, all day really, and yet they were still no closer to finding the cause of the problem, and, quite frankly, he was over it. So was everyone else in the room behind him. They'd already lost months of testing, and it now looked like they were going to lose their Friday night too, but they didn't have a choice. They needed to work out why the CMS was spitting out gibberish. Nonsense readings on his computer screen that continued to get bigger and bigger. Readings that made no sense, especially considering the LHC was shut down.

They shouldn't be seeing anything. Never mind the constant bombardment of electrons, muons, and charged hadrons the CMS was "supposedly" detecting as they traveled through its multiple layers.

To Reese, the readings almost looked like random noise, energy discharges without rhyme or reason. At least until he'd looked closer and found a pattern, which was strange. But it wasn't a software issue; he knew that much. He'd debugged the code three times just to be sure, and he still couldn't find anything wrong with it.

It has to be the hardware, he told himself.

In the meantime, Reese could do nothing but wait for the bumbling Brit and his Irish intern and watch as all the technicians scurried about in the room below him, their fluorescent vests and hard hats catching the light as they gradually dismantled the outer layers of the CMS, slowly working their way deeper and deeper.

His walkie-talkie spat out a short crackle of static.

"How's it looking now?" Dr. Connors asked.

Reese picked up his walkie-talkie. "Still the same, Connors. I'm getting nothing but garbage up here. Either you've got a wire crossed somewhere or one of the interns is playing a practical joke on us."

"Got any other bright ideas?" asked Connors.

"Yeah, I'm almost starting to think this is a job for Sherlock Ohms."

Reese let go of the button and sat back, proud of himself, smiling at his own engineering joke. He looked away from his computer screen for a moment to see that the two men were far less impressed, shaking their heads. Then they exploded into a fine pink mist.

Reese jerked backward, his eyes wide as bits of Connors and O'Malley splattered against the window in front of him. Clumps of hair and slivers of bone, glistening red and dripping wet. Stuff that used to be two men.

Someone screamed, and Reese looked out the window through the dripping mess. And then his brain simply stopped working.

Something was hanging in the air sixty feet away, where Connors and O'Malley had been standing.

It looked like one of those plasma globes he'd had when he was a kid. But bigger, a dark black sphere wrapped in blue iridescent lightning and purple coronal discharge, maybe a foot across, floating fifteen feet above the ground with nothing holding it there.

Lightning arced from the sphere to the ground with a buzzing crackle. Another one reached out, like it was alive, probing its environment. Lightning lanced into the walls, burning through metal girders and chewing into concrete before it raked across a series of bright red canisters along the base of a wall.

The coolant system, Reese's brain identified.

Liquid helium, highly pressurized and supercooled.

But not anymore.

He had just enough time to realize what was going to happen next.

The gas expanded like a bomb. A wall of solid white air moving faster than he could blink, flash freezing as it went.

He watched ten people die that way, frozen solid in an instant, before the window in front of him imploded and he was picked up and thrown across the room, screaming, his arms flailing, the world spinning end over end before his head met concrete.

Reese came to lying on his side, surrounded by a cold white mist, his ears filled with a hollow ringing.

Am I dead? he wondered, but then he blinked. His eyelids felt like they were made out of sandpaper. He coughed and felt his throat seize, ice-cold air burning his lungs as he sucked in a startled gasp.

He blinked again, still seeing nothing but smothering white, so he rolled over, letting out a moan as he pushed himself to all fours, small shards of glass and slivers of cold steel cutting into the palms of his hands.

Reese stopped.

He was staring at someone's foot. It looked like a man's shoe, expensive, polished black leather with a silver buckle and a navy-blue sock. But above the sock was nothing but splintered bone and torn flesh, the ragged edges dark red and crusted with hard ice.

Reese screamed. He pushed himself to his feet, his ankle twisting beneath him as he stumbled on something soft.

He looked down to see Dr. Evans blinking up at him through a river of red, his face covered in blood from a nasty cut on his forehead.

Dr. Evans said something.

Reese saw his mouth move, but all he heard was a constant high-pitched whine.

Dr. Evans said something again.

"What?" Reese shouted at him, shaking his head and taking half a step toward him, stumbling again as the floor trembled beneath him.

He looked over his shoulder, out the empty space where the window used to be, and he forgot all about Dr. Evans.

The ball of lightning was gone, and there was a chunk missing from the CMS, like something had taken a bite out of it, the sharp edges of severed metal glowing white hot. Even from this far away, he could feel the heat radiating off it as molten steel and plastic dripped to the floor.

He looked up to see the steel girders around the room glowing red and beginning to sag as a shower of sparks cascaded down from above, throwing out flashes of light that bounced off the frost-covered wall before disappearing into a thin layer of white mist that hugged the ground.

Reese took a numb step toward the missing window, shuffling forward in a daze as shattered glass crunched underfoot.

He peeked nervously over the edge just in time to see the CMS try to eat itself, watching with uncomprehending eyes as it crinkled and folded like an empty can, and 14,000 tons of metal, concrete, and frozen body parts simply vanished. Crushed to a point smaller than a pinhead in an instant.

It didn't make a sound, but Reese felt it. A hard punch in his guts and a deep thump that traveled through the ground and into his brain like a steel spike.

He fell to his knees screaming, his hands clamped to his ears as a furious wind roared out through the shattered window, rushing to fill the vacuum left behind, sucking papers, bits of shattered plastic, and dust with it. He felt the wind roaring past him, clawing at him, pulling at his clothes, sucking the air from his lungs.

He rolled onto his side, his hands still pressed to his ears, mouth open in agony, his eardrums feeling like they were going to burst, like his head was about to explode, and the lights overhead blew out in a shower of sparks.

The Observation Room was plunged into darkness. Darkness filled only with screams and panicked shouts before the emergency lights kicked on, the fire alarm started wailing, and thick white foam came shooting from the twelve blowers lining the cavern's walls, attempting to drown all the fires that had burst into life around the CMS.

That's when it finally sunk in. That's when things finally *clicked* in Reese's brain, and it wasn't the screams that did it. It wasn't the howl of the alarm, the orange flashing lights, the severed foot, or the bits of glass and chunks of cold flesh lying around him. It wasn't even the frightened woman with the blood-splattered lab coat pulling at his arm.

It was the cracked computer screen lying in front of him. His computer screen. The one that had been showing him all the gibberish numbers, only now he knew they weren't garbage. Now he knew it wasn't just a glitch or a practical joke. And if he believed the numbers he had seen, then it wasn't random either.

It was an energy spike, part of a pattern, and patterns repeated themselves. And the numbers on his computer screen had told him the next energy spike would be bigger. Much bigger.

That's when he pushed himself to his feet and started running.

The ground shook beneath him, an angry groan that seemed to make the whole world tilt to the left, and Reese stumbled. His foot missed a step, and he threw out a hand against the wall to steady himself.

He looked at his watch, confused, watching the second-hand tick by, doing the numbers in his head. He did them again, still getting the same answer.

"Shit," he wheezed, pushing himself off the wall and leaving a bloody handprint behind.

It's accelerating. The cycle was repeating itself, but it was shortening. The time between energy spikes was halving with each repetition, like a half-life, which meant the next spike would hit in five minutes, not ten like he'd first thought, then two and a half minutes, then a minute fifteen, and so on and so on, down to zero.

Add that all up and he had ten minutes. Ten minutes until time ran out, and Reese didn't want to think about what would happen then. He didn't want to be here to find out either, but he still had so *far* to go.

He glanced up, head tilted back, burning eyes seeing nothing but more stairs, stairs filled with smoke and flashing lights, and he felt time slipping by. Seconds ticking by so loudly he could almost hear them.

I'm not going to make it, he realized with despair. But Reese started climbing again anyway. He didn't have a choice; he couldn't give up yet.

Instead he tried to think of less frightening things as he climbed. Harmless little things that also used a countdown and didn't end in death, rattling them off in his head. Egg timers. Microwaves. Alarm clocks. But Reese's thoughts kept coming back to a bomb, and if his numbers were right, which they always were, and if the energy spikes kept growing the way they had, then when time ran out it was going to be big. Like nuclear big.

I'm going to die, Reese realized. He let out a strangled sob and looked straight ahead, still climbing, still chanting the same useless words over and over in his head.

Left foot. Right foot. Breathe.

Three long minutes later, Reese rolled himself over the last step, flopping onto his back with an exhausted groan. His eyes closed, and he ignored the shrill scream of the alarm. He ignored the strobing orange glare on the other side of his eyelids, seeing only moments of darkness and a red tracery of veins.

He couldn't get up. He couldn't move another inch. It was all he could do just to keep breathing, gasping for air as his pulse roared in his ears, and he felt his heart miss a beat. A stuttering lurch in his chest that made him twitch and grimace as a burning pain crawled down his arm.

Reese's eyes snapped open, his sweaty hand clawed at his chest, and for a split second he was struck by a new thought. *Is this what a heart attack feels like?*

He would have laughed if he weren't so damn scared.

Until today, Reese had never once thought about death. Not in a practical sense. Not with any real immediacy, even though his doctor had tried to warn him. Death had always been an abstract concept, an end occurrence. Death was just another case of probability, a chance of one in one, and it would happen when it happened. Reese had never really given it any more thought than he gave to breathing. Old age is what he'd thought would get him.

His doctor had told him it was more likely to be from heart

disease, or more specifically a big, fat heart attack, a 1-in-2.5 chance. A "Twinkie complication" the doctor had called it.

Morbidly obese was the more politically correct term, and Reese knew all the signs were there: his sleep apnea, type 2 diabetes, and circulation problems. He had to use a brush on a long handle to clean his back in the shower, and he'd gotten one of those fancy toilet accessories installed in his bathroom—the one that sprays water up your ass after you're done dropping off the kids. Reese liked it, simply because he couldn't reach around to wipe it himself anymore.

The doctor had said that if he kept going the way he was, he'd be lucky to see the other side of fifty. At forty-five, Reese had ignored him. Cognitive bias, it's called.

He had assumed his body would continue to work because it always had, and he'd concentrated on other things instead of his health, predominantly his work at CERN, being part of the CMS experiments, looking for the Higgs.

For Reese, finding the "God" particle had only been the beginning. The first step in what he liked to think of as a long journey to find the rest of Him, and with half a terrified wheeze Reese realized he might be seeing God a little sooner than he had thought.

So he lay there, forty-six years old, probably not going on to forty-seven, staring at the ceiling, staring at the orange lights flashing above him, sucking in breath after breath, his lips tingling and going numb, finally ready to acknowledge that he might have let himself go. Just a bit.

A shadow fell across his face.

Reese blinked up at a silhouette, a head haloed in light looking down at him like an angel.

Am I dead?

He raised a hand to block out the glare, confusion clouding his oxygen-deprived brain before a face swam into focus.

Dr. Jaime Stevens looked down at him, breathing hard, her face flushed from exertion, her lab coat stained with dark soot and bright splotches of blood.

Reese looked at her dumbly through the haze of smoke, looked to where her hands rested on her hips. To where her chest was rising and falling with every breath. Her chest… Reese caught himself staring.

His eyes snapped back to her face. "Uh…"

Part of him knew that now wasn't the best time to be looking at her tits, but it was a small part, numb with shock and pushed too far.

"Get up!" she shouted.

Her mouth moved, but he didn't hear her. Reese found he was staring again.

"GET UP!"

"I can't," he mumbled.

She leaned forward, and, when he did nothing but blink back at her, she grabbed a handful of his hair and pulled, grunting with effort as she dragged him to his feet.

Reese had no choice but to follow, howling through the pain, pushing himself to his knees before grabbing onto the railing with both hands, his legs shaking as they strained under his weight.

"What…?" he forced out, gasping for air between the tears, dizzy from the head rush. "What was that for?"

"I'm saving your life! Now move!" She grabbed him by the back of his collar and propelled him forward, faster and faster, somehow managing to keep him upright as she pushed him down the corridor, using him like a battering ram through the emergency exit doors and out into the warm evening air.

Reese had just enough time to look up, just enough time to see the sun starting to set out west. Just enough time to see the sky glowing a beautiful pink, thick black smoke vomiting out of the roof behind them, before Jaime was screaming in his ear again.

"Right! Turn right!"

Reese turned right, away from the building and out into the parking lot. Straight into madness.

They ran past screaming people, past fire trucks and ambulances, past flashing lights and wailing sirens. They ran past men in yellow fire-retardant suits with oxygen tanks on their backs dragging thick red hoses. He saw people crying and bodies lying on the grass.

Reese wanted to tell her to wait. He wanted to warn them all that it was too late, that they all had to get out of there, but the next thing he knew Jaime was pushing him through the back door of a waiting SUV, its engine revving and its horn blaring.

Reese made eye contact with a frightened little girl in the back before Jaime rammed her shoulder into his ass and pushed him inside. He fell across the backseat. The car started to move, and Reese began dragging himself in, grunting and cursing, clawing at the fabric as Jaime hauled herself in on top of him, clambering over him as the car picked up speed.

His legs were still hanging out the open door as they raced out the front gate.

They were seven kilometers away when they ran out of time. When the countdown in his head hit zero and the sky was filled with a blinding pulse of white light. Then another and another. When CERN and everything within half a mile was vaporized.

They were doing nearly 160 kph when the blast wave caught them, and yet it made it look like their car was standing still. The wall of destruction picked their SUV up and flung it from the road like it was a toy.

Reese remembered the sensation of flying, of spinning through the air. Then nothing.

He'd woken up some time later to pain, so much pain, clouds of dust, and the smell of burning. And for the second time in an hour, he'd been very much surprised to be alive at all. But since then he'd been thinking. First about his broken leg, then about brain damage and repetitive head trauma, and lastly about CERN.

His leg meant he wasn't going anywhere, so Reese had all the time in the world to think. He had a thousand questions tumbling through his head, but none of them were helping. None of it made sense. None of the answers were good, or even possible. And he had no one to talk to about it either, not since the rest of the survivors from their car crash had abandoned him to head west on foot to try to find help.

But that was two hours ago. They hadn't come back, night had long since fallen, and Reese didn't know what to do.

They should have been back by now, he kept telling himself, starting to panic, feeling cold and alone, sitting in the dark with a hard rock digging into his back, and trying very hard not to cry. Not that there was anyone left alive to care. At least not to the east of him, not if he did his math right. Not for twelve kilometers, maybe.

It was likely that CERN, the Large Hadron Collider, and Meyrin were gone, maybe even Geneva, wiped off the map like they'd never been. A hundred thousand people now nothing more than radioactive dust floating high above his head.

Somehow their work at CERN had created a bomb, or a black hole, or something that behaved a little like both.

To be honest, Reese didn't know what it was, and that terrified him even more. Nothing known to man gave off energy like that, nothing behaved like *that*. He shook his head. It wasn't possible for them to have created anything like that at CERN anyway.

They'd even had to go to court back in 2008 to prove it. Before they were allowed to turn the LHC on, before more than a thousand of the smartest, most qualified people on the planet were able to conduct even a single test, Reese and his fellow colleagues had to prove that their experiments weren't somehow going to destroy the world in the process.

In his eyes, it had been like trying to explain common sense to an idiot. That they had just as much a chance of making a black hole big enough to be a threat as they did of clapping their hands and making the moon explode, or of waking up tomorrow to find that gravity no longer worked. It was unrealistic and impossible.

Plus the stupid thing wasn't even turned on! he raged silently. *Then how?*

He had no answers, so Reese concentrated on numbers instead, pulling them from memory. Likely, unlikely, simple numbers, probabilities, comparing them, ranking them in his head, concentrating on the numbers instead of all the dead.

The chance of dying from cancer: 1 in 5.

A falling coconut: 1 in 250,000. Being struck by lightning: 1 in a million. A plane crash: 1 in 11 million.

The numbers didn't mean these things couldn't happen, just that certain events were less likely than others, which brought him to his current predicament. One event he could account for, but two?

The chance of dying in a car crash: 1 in 8,000.

Nuclear facility meltdown: 1 in 10 million.

Admittedly, not an ideal comparison, but a nuclear meltdown was a good proxy until he had more data, and 1 in 10 million would do as a minimum at least. Combining the two gave him a probability of 1 in 80 billion.

When he put it that way, he was 80,000 times more likely to be struck by lightning. *Impossible numbers.*

And yet it had happened. First the explosion, then the car crash, and he'd survived both. One hell of a fat tale. *Just like me.*

Reese started laughing, then he started crying. He couldn't help it, chest shuddering, snot bubbling from his nose, and why not? He was cold, injured, and apparently going into shock. That's probably why he was thinking about probabilities. *Wasn't it?*

His body was slowly shutting down. The fear, pain, and exhaustion were getting the best of him. His blood pressure was dropping, and not enough oxygen was going to his brain, which meant it was getting harder to think, to concentrate, and he was starting to get dizzy.

Reese understood shock; he'd read enough about it to recognize the symptoms. He'd just never experienced it firsthand before, and he was having a tough time being rational about it, which by all the books and articles he'd read on the topic was perfectly normal.

But reading and experience are two different things, and until this point in his life he'd been pretty heavy on one and pretty bare on the other. Which is probably why he was pretty heavy in life, too. "Butter Cup" is what the kids in school used to call him, a derivative of Reese's.

Coz he's twice as fat and half as sweet.

Reese shook his head, trying to get their voices out of it.

Yup, definitely going into shock, he acknowledged glumly, wiping his nose as wet sobs escaped his blubbering chest, while each pathetic wheeze reminded him just how full his bladder was.

"Pull your shit together, Reese," he mumbled to himself, but he couldn't. Butter Cup only cried harder, and thanks to his broken leg he couldn't move, couldn't relieve himself. He couldn't even roll over to take a piss. He just had to sit there and hold it.

Hold it as the pain in his bladder grew worse and the air got colder. Cold for the middle of summer, cold even for autumn, like they were heading straight into winter. Cold that seemed to be coming from where CERN used to be. A cold wind that had draped the world around him in frost, freezing his breath on the air as it set his teeth to chattering and his fingers to aching.

But as bad as the cold was, the darkness was worse.

There was no moon overhead, no stars anymore. Only a featureless black nothing. There was no light at all, not down here, down in this ass crack of a gully, off to the side of the road and enclosed by trees. Not since that cloud of ash had rolled by overhead and swallowed up the sky.

It made it seem like there was simply nothing above him and nothing around him. He sat in complete and utter darkness, cave black, tomb dark. A void with nothing in it but him, the wind, and its haunting sound as it whistled through the trees, licking at his skin, sucking away his heat, stirring the hairs standing up on his arms. A wind that made the leaves rustle somewhere high overhead, making strange noises in the forest around him, low moans and creaks that echoed in the dark. The sounds scratched at his nerves. They drove him mad, but that wasn't the worst.

The worst was his leg.

His leg hurt. It ached. It screamed at him like it had been cut off at the knee.

Reese turned on his phone. He couldn't help himself anymore, mashing the Home button with his thumb and wasting even more of the remaining battery.

The screen appeared as a brilliant rectangle, a blinding light floating in the dark. Reese blinked, then blinked again, trying to see through the glowing purple afterimage swimming in front of him.

He turned his phone so he could see the hideous swelling, an ankle turned a dark shade of purple, the skin around it mottled and bruised, fat blue tendrils snaking up his calf. He turned his phone so he could see the rest of his leg. His leg that was bent wrong, knee turned one way, foot the other, shin deformed where splintered bone pressed against pale, hairy skin. Reese shuddered; the sight made him want to be sick, but he had nothing left to throw up. Most of it already decorated the front of his shirt, stinking of bile and half-digested chicken schnitzel.

And the pain! *Oh God, the pain.* Pain that was pounding and pounding with each beat of his heart.

Reese groaned, though it was really more of a moan, maybe a

mewl, gritting his teeth. Shivering while clammy sweat turned his stained white shirt see-through.

He turned his phone, shining the light away from his leg, banishing the cloying dark in a small circle around him as he used his phone like a flashlight and a shield, peering over the edge, his wide eyes searching the dark. Wide eyes that looked up to see flakes of ash drifting down lazily. Flakes of ash that caught the light as they fell, smelling of fire, stinking of smoke and sulfur, maybe even cooked meat. But that had to be his imagination. *Didn't it?*

Reese looked to his right, to where he could see the reflection of smashed headlights, their SUV flat on its back like a dead bug and pressed up against a tree.

Its black paint rendered it nearly invisible amid the darkness, but he could still make out its mangled shape, a door torn off and its chassis bent, the SUV reduced to a lump of twisted metal, its body panels crumpled and scratched. It was even missing a wheel.

There were footprints all around the wreck. Scuff marks left behind in the churned-up dirt, a trail of them leading up the hill, out of the gully, back up to the road. And then gone.

Reese looked back at his phone, turning it to face him. Its light illuminating his sweat-lined face and his red cheeks, bunched up beneath quivering, frightened eyes.

He turned off his phone, and the darkness rushed back in like some creature swallowing him up.

He felt another small sob escape his lips. He felt the shame and fear warring within him, and beneath it a simmering anger, a small, pathetic flame of resentment that sputtered fitfully in his mind.

Cass and Jaime. This is their fault. Their fault that he had been abandoned.

He knew it was irrational, but he didn't care. He was past caring. They had left him with nothing but a shit, useless space blanket that barely covered him. Oh sure, he could cover his legs or his chest, but not both. *One size fits all, my ass.*

So Reese covered his legs, the silver blanket crackling and crunching like tinfoil, and he wrapped his arms around his chest. He rested his arms on his stomach, resting them on his vomit, his phone clutched tightly in his slippery hand.

And he waited, cold, frightened, and very much alone.

CASS

Jaime stumbled, and Cass felt her fingers dig into his shoulder. They dug in hard, and Cass opened his mouth to say something, but then he looked at Klaus, and then his eyes flicked to Lena, and the words died in his throat.

He had no right to complain. Not while Klaus shuffled along behind him like that, his face a burnt mess and quite possibly blind. Not while all those dead people drifted down above their heads, nothing more than little pieces of ash and radioactive dust.

Cass shook his head. He had no right to complain at all. At least he was still alive. Bruised, but alive.

But fallout will be an issue later, he acknowledged. Surface detonations were bad for that, especially when it decided to rain and all that radioactive dust and swirling ash fell back down to Earth.

Not to mention the radiation we've already received, he added glumly, coughing and wiping his eyes as clouds of dust and smoke drifted across the road.

At least the wind was in their face, being sucked back in by the sudden low pressure above CERN, trying to fill the vacuum left behind as all that superheated air rose into the sky, but he knew it wouldn't last. They might be okay for now, but the wind could change direction any moment, and there was a limit to how much radiation the human body could take.

If it was in the 100 to 200 rad range, they'd be okay. They'd get sick, of course—nausea, vomiting, abdominal pain. It wouldn't be pleasant. They would think they were dying, but they would live.

If the dose was in the 200 to 1,000 range, the outlook got steadily worse. More than 1,000 rad and they were already dead, their bodies just didn't know it yet.

The problem was that the longer they kept walking through all this shit, the worse their chances of survival, and Cass couldn't see an end to it. There wasn't a tree or building left standing, no people, nothing but scattered fires and columns of smoke, charred and splintered trees lining the sides of the road. Their shattered trunks glowed white in his flashlight, like jagged teeth, as though the four of them were walking into the mouth of some giant beast.

Cass glanced back at his group, his ragtag bunch of survivors. The "lucky" ones.

Not counting Reese, they were maybe the only people from CERN who had made it out alive, and they had been nearly seven kilometers away at the time, driving west, driving fast, across the border and into France. Or at least that had been the plan before the world ended.

Cass figured the explosion must have been equivalent to something just under a megaton. Any bigger or any closer, and they'd all be dead, squished to a pulp, their flesh cooked, the blackened skin peeling from their backs. And then there were all the cars they were walking past, flattened, twisted pieces of metal that looked like they'd gone through a trash compactor. He didn't even bother to check for survivors; the bodies inside were too crushed for that to be a possibility.

Cass shook his head. It could just as easily have been them, should have been them. The fact that they were still alive was nothing short of a miracle.

The scientist in Cass was a little more pragmatic, attributing it to the fact that they were just far enough away to survive the initial thermal burst, and the car had absorbed most of the blast wave that followed. It was almost as though the blast wave had caught them in the Goldilocks Zone. Not too hot, not too cold. Just right.

Everything after that was pure luck, because when that blast wave did catch them, the only difference the extra distance made was that it meant they didn't die instantly. The blast wave just picked them up and sent their car tumbling through the air before gravity took over again and tried to finish the job.

He didn't know how they'd survived. Especially Reese. The lucky bastard wasn't even strapped in. But one thing was certain: they all owed Reese their lives. Somehow he had known what was happening, or what was about to, at least.

"Drive faster!" he had shrieked, spittle flying from his mouth, staring at his watch like his life depended on it, giving them just enough warning to get away in time.

Afterward, when he'd pulled Reese from the car and Reese had stopped screaming long enough for him to ask how he had known, Reese had only shrugged, his fists clenched into balls and his eyes glazed over with pain, saying that he'd recognized a pattern in the numbers.

Cass didn't have the faintest idea what numbers Reese meant, and he hadn't had time to ask, but he swore that if he made it out of this, he owed Reese a beer. *Whether the guy wants it or not,* he added as an afterthought.

Reese wasn't exactly the most social of creatures. He was American like Cass, and a nuclear physicist, with a Dr. in front of his name, but that was where the similarities ended. Cass was from New York, a registered Democrat, an avid runner, and black. Meanwhile, Reese originated from somewhere in the Midwest, weighed over 300 pounds, and lacked almost any social graces and any pigment. And whereas Cass could make friends with almost anyone, Reese stayed in his office most of the time, and he seemed to prefer the company of computers to people. Some of them even called him Moby Dick behind his back—some mythical white whale no one ever saw but everyone knew existed.

Cass felt bad about leaving Reese behind, but realistically there wasn't anything else he could have done. Carrying Reese simply wasn't an option. He was just too damn big.

Cass flicked his flashlight across the ground behind him, shining its light on Jaime's and Klaus's feet, going no higher than their knees, low enough to not get it in their faces. Definitely not in their eyes. He didn't need to do any more damage, and he didn't need to be a doctor to know it was bad enough already. He looked at Lena, Klaus's daughter, her face pale and terrified, thirteen years old and guiding her blinded dad like some seeing-eye dog, and Cass felt his worry grow.

He wasn't equipped to deal with this, none of them were, but they were all depending on him, and Cass was worried he was going to fail them.

He looked over his shoulder at Jaime, at her hand gripping the fabric of his shirt, holding onto him because she had to, because, thanks to sheer bad luck, she was just as blind as Klaus.

Cass reasoned that the two of them must have been looking almost directly at the flash when it went off, except Klaus had come off a little worse. He'd been the one driving, which meant CERN had been on his left when it blew up, and perhaps his window wasn't as heavily tinted, or maybe his window had been open.

Either way, the flash burns he'd gotten were the worst by far. It looked like the left side of his face had been pressed into a grill. Cass guessed second degree burns, possibly even third, and it was getting worse by the minute, skin blackened and charred, blisters filling with fluid.

Jaime, on the other hand, had been lucky, if you could call it that. She was sporting nothing worse than a bad sunburn, her skin red and angry but unmarred. She said her sight was slowly coming back too, that she was starting to see more than pure white. Klaus's sight didn't seem to be coming back at all, and that was a problem.

Best case scenario: Klaus's face took the worst of it and saved his sight.

Worst case scenario: permanent retinal burn.

He might never see again, and there was absolutely nothing Cass could do about it. Even basic first aid was beyond him. They had no painkillers, no water to run over the burns, and no ambulances or hospitals in sight. They were in the middle of nowhere, with nothing but fields and shredded forests to either side. The two nearest towns were already behind them, Le Crét and Péron, and they were burning, twin firestorms only a few kilometers apart, flames licking hungrily at the sky while the sound of explosions carried on the wind.

No help there.

The only option they had was to keep walking, but Collonges up ahead didn't look much better. Four kilometers to go and Cass could already see a soft orange glow on the horizon, which had him worried. Collonges was too far from the explosion. They should have been fine. *So what's burning?*

He shook his head. *One thing at a time.* The only thing he should be thinking about now was getting Klaus to a hospital. A proper hospital, somewhere equipped to deal with burns, which meant specialized, which meant big. *Which meant where?*

Bourg-en-Bresse?

It might just be their only chance, but it was too far away. There was no way they'd make it on foot, and he hadn't seen a single headlight in the last hour. Maybe a chopper or two in the distance or high overhead, but no ground traffic, no emergency vehicles, no flashing lights. No red and blue. And Cass knew this road, the

D884. He'd driven on it enough times across the border into France to know it like the back of his hand, and there was nothing out here but forests and empty farms. After the blast wave, even less.

He gave the smoke vomiting into the sky behind them another frightened glance, seeing a black haze spreading across the night sky.

So much ash, he thought. Ash that used to be trees and cars and buildings and people, and Cass realized again just how lucky they had been. It could just as easily have been him reduced to atoms or blinded with his face looking like cooked steak. But he didn't want to think about that.

He just put one foot in front of the other, flashlight held out like a magic staff, like he was Moses parting the dark with his measly little Maglite. Jaime, Klaus, and Lena shuffled along behind him while he worried about Klaus, about all of them, but feeling especially guilty about leaving Reese behind, and feeling angry for feeling guilty.

Just hold on, Reese. I'll come back as soon as I can. It wasn't personal. He had tried to tell Reese that. "Blind or a broken leg, which would you prefer?"

Reese hadn't said much after that. Cass had taken that to mean he agreed.

He turned to look back at Klaus, forcing himself to speak. "You guys okay back there?"

Silence.

"Klaus?" Cass asked, a little louder.

Klaus didn't answer. Cass didn't expect him to. The last time Klaus had spoken was an hour ago to say he couldn't see anything at all. And that it hurt. He hadn't said a word since, and his lips remained pressed together in a hard white line.

Cass knew he must be in agony, but the guy didn't make a sound. He bore it silently, his head hanging low as he was led by the hand like a small child.

Lena just stared straight ahead, hanging on to her dad's hand so tightly it looked like she thought he was going to float away right before her eyes.

Cass couldn't really blame her. Stranger things had already happened today, and it was a lot to process for a thirteen-year-old. *Fuck that, it's a lot to process for a 38-year-old!*

But still, he felt bad for her. Talk about the wrong day to come to see her dad's work.

"Jaime? How about you?"

"I'm okay, Cass," she said, giving his shoulder a squeeze, telling him she was hanging in there.

"How are your eyes?"

She hesitated. "Hard to tell. Getting better… maybe? I can see something at least, I think. Is there a fire up ahead?"

Cass nodded. "Yeah. I think it's Collonges. You can see that?"

"Kind of. It's brighter." Another pause. "How far do you think we need to go?" she asked, her voice hopeful.

"To Collonges? Maybe five kilometers? But it doesn't look good. Not if we can see it from here. The next nearest town after that is Léaz, or Bellegarde-sur-Valserine, I think. But those are still over ten kilometers away. So at this rate…"

At this rate they'd be walking all night.

"Well, shit," said Jaime.

"Yeah," Cass agreed, looking up and tracking the cloud's progress as it arched high overhead.

In the last hour it had already raced far ahead of them, no longer satisfied with just Meyrin. The moon was hidden somewhere behind it now too, and the light from the stars was slowly fading.

It looked like a black curtain was slowly being pulled across the sky, and Cass realized if it kept going like that soon there wouldn't be any light at all. No moon, no stars, just the orange glow of a thousand fires and his shitty little flashlight. Maybe their phones, until those died too, and briefly Cass wondered how Reese was doing, how he was coping with his leg and the dark and the cold.

He felt the sting of guilt again for leaving him like that, but, once he had dragged him out of the car, merely the suggestion that Cass check his leg had reduced Reese to unintelligible noise.

Cass had shrugged it off. Reese was in shock; he wasn't thinking straight, but Cass didn't have the time for an argument, and they had far more pressing concerns, so he'd left him behind. Concentrated on getting as many of them as far away from Meyrin as he could.

But a broken leg was a broken leg, and Cass would have wanted something done if their situations were reversed. They could at least have rearranged Reese somewhat. Straightened it out, splinted it, maybe?

It might have helped with the pain at least, but Reese's refusal meant he was going to be left like that for an indefinite period of time, probably a long time, and in a lot of pain.

He'll be fine where he is for a while anyway, Cass told himself. *A broken leg like that won't kill him.*

And if he was honest with himself, they were making much better time without him, and they still had a long walk ahead of them. Even if Reese hadn't broken his leg, Cass had no illusions as to his endurance; they would have had to leave him behind at some point anyway. They had walked for kilometers already, single file, step by step. No way could Reese have done that.

Cass was amazed Reese hadn't died from a heart attack already.

REESE

Reese felt for his phone again, his cold hands fumbling with it in the dark.

He turned it on, and the screen lit up like a second sun, but this time he looked away. This time he was prepared for the glare. He was learning, and Reese smiled, proud of himself.

He knew he was wasting the battery. He knew it, but he couldn't stop himself. Any semblance of self-control had long slipped from his grasp. About an hour ago, about the same time he had pissed himself. When lightning had flashed overhead, splitting the darkness in two with thunder so loud it sounded like a bomb going off inside his head.

He'd screamed as everything was illuminated in an instant. Bleached trees loomed closer, glaring white. Like dead things jumping forward, ghostly gray and twisted, bark wrinkled and folded, branches like reaching arms and clawing fingers.

But that had been an hour ago, and the warmth and the relief of his emptied bladder had long since vanished, leaving him with nothing but the shame and pants that were still wet, now cold and clinging to him. Humiliated, he could only cry harder.

The occasional flash of lightning mocked him, made him twitch, and he listened as the thunder rumbled and retreated through the sky while the flashes left ghostly afterimages in his eyes.

Reese looked at his phone, 9:59 p.m., four hours since the accident. Three since he'd been abandoned. *What's taking them so long?*

He wiped at his mouth, grimacing at the sour taste of vomit, a taste that he couldn't seem to get rid of no matter how much he spat.

Reese looked at the time again, 10:00 p.m. Battery down to thirty-five percent. Still no signal, not even a bar. He took a deep breath. *You aren't afraid of the dark, are you?* he asked himself as he turned off the screen.

But he was, and as the darkness came flooding back in, swallowing him in its jaws, Reese went back to shivering and crying in the cold silence.

Time passed, an hour, maybe two.

It was hard to tell unless he checked his phone, his thoughts growing increasingly disjointed and sluggish.

It's the shock, Reese told himself. *And the cold.* They were one and the same, but it was the shock that would eventually kill him. He was pretty sure of that. He'd read somewhere that the sudden release of adrenaline could cause a heart attack. A chance of one in…

But Reese didn't know the number anymore. Even his numbers were leaving him as his brain shut down, abandoning him to the dark and the pain. The pain that had reduced him to a blubbering wreck. The fear that had him twisting and turning at every sound and slow creak, blind eyes peering into the dark in desperation. His frantic eyes wider than an owl's, staring into pitch-black nothing until he saw spots floating in front of him.

He turned on his phone again, his breath misting before him in the glow as the air turned to ice on his lips, and his eyes watered in the cold breeze.

12:14 a.m., battery down to twenty-four percent.

Then Reese heard a sound.

It took him a moment to place it. Gentle at first. Just a soft chirp, but ugly, a raspy oscillation on the wind. *Cicadas?*

The sound seemed startling after the silence. *Does France even have cicadas?*

Reese didn't know. He didn't care.

He looked at his phone again, 12:15 a.m., battery down to twenty-three percent.

He turned off the screen and rubbed his arms, trying to generate some heat. The blanket crackled as he jiggled, his leg reminding him loudly that was a bad idea.

Reese leaned back against the rock behind him. He closed his eyes and listened as one cicada became two, his own private choir. The sound was distracting, familiar almost. It was something at least, and his mind craved the input, anything besides the dark.

He pulled the space blanket closer, shivering constantly now, listening to the noise, trying to guess the species, or at least the family.

He frowned. *Do cicadas sing at night?*

He only remembered them during the heat of summer amongst the green fields of Iowa, sun beating down and the trees stirring in the breeze. Never at night. *Crickets, then? Do crickets even sing?*

There are other species. Katydids, maybe?

The sound grew louder. It bounced through the trees like an echo. Like they were talking to each other.

Reese listened as the sound built, coming in waves, slowly at first, gently, like he was listening to the sea. As though a storm was blowing in, the waves getting bigger. The sound grew fuller, deeper. And loud.

It became a shrill screech, like feedback from a microphone too close to a speaker, and Reese shrieked. His eyes snapped open, and he dropped his phone. He felt it bounce off his stomach, heard it bite into dirt, and then he was moving, moaning, leg screaming, his hands sweeping across the ground, frantically searching for his phone. His one source of light. His safety blanket. His fear rampaged out of control before his fingers finally slid across cold, hard plastic.

It didn't sound like cicadas anymore. It sounded like a threat, like a rattlesnake about to strike. *Bad noise, bad noise, bad noise,* Reese's instincts screamed.

His thumb hit the Home button, and light was born. He waved his phone around him, the trees casting long, dark shadows that spun away, and the noise grew louder.

It reverberated inside his skull. He could feel the vibration running across his skin, feel it thrumming in his ears. Like the buffeting of wind through a car window.

Reese winced as he put his hands over his ears, emitting a small groan of agony as he tried to duck from the noise.

He heard another sound. Something new.

Reese dropped his hands, ears straining over the constant shrill squeal.

He heard it again.

A twig snapped, a loud crack that echoed in the dark. And Reese realized he wasn't alone.

There was something moving out there. Something big. And whatever it was, it was coming closer.

CASS

Cass came to a stop in the middle of the road.

"How about a break?"

He wasn't particularly tired, but he didn't want to push Klaus too hard. He was surprised Klaus was still walking; a lesser man would have given up long ago.

Not Klaus. Klaus was the kind of guy that did marathons for fun. Fit, accustomed to pain. But Cass noticed that he was slowing down, drenched in sweat, and his feet were starting to drag.

"Jaime?"

Jaime, on the other hand, was doing much better. Her vision seemed to have returned in the last hour, not completely, worse on the left, but enough for her let go of him and take a few steps back in the line so she wasn't stepping on his heels anymore.

Jaime nodded. "Sure."

Cass looked at Lena, her hands clenched tightly around her dad's arm, knuckles white as she guided him forward, hiding behind him, somehow doing both. But the close contact seemed to be helping, keeping her focused, giving her a purpose.

"Lena, why don't you find your dad a spot to sit? How about..."

He looked around, pointing his flashlight at a grassy patch on the side of the road. "Over there?"

Lena nodded once in the gloom. "*Ja.* Okay."

Cass looked at his watch. It was nearly midnight. They'd been walking for almost five hours, put some decent distance between themselves and CERN. The trees were still standing this far out. Things were almost starting to look normal again. Except for them. They looked like ghosts, like all those people after the Towers came down. Shell shocked and stumbling along. All covered in gray dust.

So he told himself a short stop now would be okay.

Klaus looked like he needed it, and Reese would be fine by himself for a little longer. The scientist in him acknowledged that if fifteen minutes really made a difference in terms of radiation exposure, then they were as good as dead anyway.

Cass looked up at the cloud above them, a vast black stain pressing down on the earth, huge twisting forks of blue and purple lightning branching and crawling across its surface as thunder boomed. It seemed to be moving faster too.

He knew that had to be a simple trick of perception, but even accounting for the angle it covered more than half of the visible night sky. And it felt wrong somehow, like no mushroom cloud he'd ever seen. It was the purest, most unsettling shade of black, almost like ink. And when he looked to the southeast, whenever they topped a slight rise, he could still faintly see the orange glow of whatever was left of Meyrin on the horizon, a funeral pyre burning in the darkness.

As for how, as for the explosion itself, Cass couldn't explain it. There was nothing at CERN that could have gone nuclear. They didn't have enough fissile material to light a fart. It was impossible; the physics wouldn't allow it. It was simple math; two times two didn't suddenly equal 1,000.

Maybe Reese had a better idea. So far Cass had nothing, and that worried him, but right now he had bigger problems. The road ahead of them remained dark and empty.

There were no fire trucks racing toward them from neighboring towns, no police cars, no ambulances. Nothing. Which was simply wrong. It didn't make any sense. *Where is everyone?* It was like they'd all run away instead of coming to help.

He turned his flashlight at random and noticed something in the bushes.

A rusted letter box, overgrown with vines, with the number 320 written on its side in faded red. He had completely missed it before, and it was by pure chance he spotted it now. But it didn't look promising. The path next to it didn't look like a driveway, it looked like an access road, narrow, overgrown, loose gravel with poorly maintained borders. Still, it was worth a try, and he had fifteen minutes to burn.

"Mind waiting here with the others while I go see if anyone's home?" he asked.

"Sure," Jaime said, confused at first before she followed his gaze.

Walking down the road was like walking into a cave. The trees pressed in close, their branches intertwined overhead. The gravel crunched underfoot, and his own breathing sounded loud to his ears.

He walked for a good minute before he stepped out in the open again, trees falling away to either side as the road poured out into a dirt clearing.

It didn't go anywhere else. The road ended in a rusted red gate and a wood post fence that disappeared into the dark to either side.

Cass lifted the catch and swung the gate open, turning his flashlight left and right, playing it across the corrugated iron sheds that lay before him, their fronts open to the air and their insides filled with farm equipment. He smelled diesel and manure. He saw trailers and shelves full of boxes, bags of fertilizer and large oversized tools he couldn't even begin to name. But no people. No lights. And no help.

Disappointed, he turned to leave, flinching as the night was banished in an explosion of light as lightning struck to the east of him.

Cass looked up, counting in his head. *One, one thousand; two, one thous—*

Thunder boomed. So close he felt it thump in his chest, so loud he thought he would go deaf.

"Fuck me!" he swore, his ears ringing, cowering from the noise and giving another wary glance to the dark sky. *That was way too close,* he thought before turning and hurrying toward a barn the lightning had illuminated in the distance. He could still see its ugly yellow outline glowing on his retina.

Up close the barn looked even worse; it looked old and half forgotten. Its green paint was flaked and beginning to peel, it was even starting to lean.

Cass pulled on one of the doors before it came to a jarring stop, padlocked chain drawing taut. He pulled harder, forcing the opening wider, pressed his cheek to the gap and peered inside.

His flashlight glinted off glass, blue paint, and the high top of a silver grill.

"Jackpot," he said, seeing the hood of a truck gleaming back at him.

Now to get in there, he thought, stepping back to examine the door and chain before he walked back to the sheds.

He needed a tool—an axe or a crowbar.

He found a pruning saw instead.

Luckily the door was ancient, the varnish poorly applied. The wood had been exposed to the elements for years and was well past starting to rot. It took him less than a minute to make the chain redundant by simply cutting around it. Job done, Cass pulled the doors open wide and stepped inside. But as he walked around the truck, he got a better look at it, and his spirits sank.

It was a Ford, a flatbed with steel dropsides, some model he didn't recognize. And it was old, more rust than metal. It belonged in a junkyard or a museum. It didn't even look like it would run.

He tried the handle, and it wasn't locked.

Of course, he thought. *Why lock it? No one is his right mind would ever want to steal this piece of crap.*

He opened the door and climbed into the driver's seat. A seat that might have once been covered in brown pleather, but now had nothing more than a few remaining flakes clinging to the edges, exposing the pitted yellow foam beneath. It was filthy inside too, and the car smelled old and polluted, reeking of diesel and cigarettes and manure.

An unlocked car in a locked shed. *Maybe they left the keys in the truck?* Cass shined the flashlight around inside, breathing through his mouth and mumbling, "Keys, keys, keys."

They weren't in the ignition, and the glove box was empty except for yellowed papers and old maps. The ash tray held nothing but cigarette butts, and the side compartments were full of junk.

"Great," he finally said, frustrated but not worried. Not yet.

A rule of thumb with cars: when trying to steal them, the older the better. Anything pre-mid 90s was fair game. No real antitheft devices, no immobilizers. Not complicated ones, at least. Any electrical engineering undergrad could do it. Hell, anyone with Google and half a brain could do it these days.

Cass shifted forward, gripping his flashlight between his teeth and reaching under the steering column to pull off the console. Then he stopped, remembering an old movie trick.

He raised his hand to the sun visor, paused for a second, and pulled it down.

A set of keys landed in his lap.

"Ha! Son of a bitch!"

He put the keys in, held his breath, and turned.

The starter motor came to life with a sick, grating purr. The whole truck shuddered, and a thick cloud of black smoke belched from the exhaust. It filled the back of the barn, rising up before curling in on itself like a wave, swirling down over the truck and flooding into the cab through his open door.

Cass gagged. "Holy shit!" he wheezed, his eyes watering as he choked on the thick fumes, scrambling to put the car in gear and wincing as the gears meshed with a loud crunch.

REESE

The roar of the cicadas cut off like someone had flicked a switch, and the forest went silent. Silent in a way the animal part of Reese recognized, and some primal part of his brain started lighting up like a Christmas tree. Instinct kicked in, and warning bells started screaming in his head.

Run, they said.

But Reese didn't move, he didn't even budge. He couldn't. He just sat there, his lips trembling, his heart racing as his shaking hands waved his phone around him.

"Hello?" he called, his voice high and desperate.

"Hello? Anyone there?" he asked again, his heart thumping in his chest.

"Cass? Cass, is that you?" Reese shouted, his voice shaking, almost hysterical.

"Cass? Stop being an asshole," he called, and his voice cracked. He coughed to clear it, but he was starting to hyperventilate, and it was making it hard to breathe. The cicadas started singing again, but there was something wrong with the sound. It was moving, coming toward him, and Reese realized it wasn't cicadas.

It never had been.

"Cass?" he whimpered.

He heard branches bending and cracking as something pushed through the bushes to his left.

Another sharp crack rang out, this time from another direction, and Reese swiveled to face it, eyes starving for light, his pupils straining to dilate, his ears filling with clicks and a chittering hiss.

It wasn't Cass. Reese knew this. Cass would be coming down the road in an ambulance, lights flashing, siren wailing, headlights blinding and brilliant. Cass would be coming with paramedics, a stretcher, warm blankets, and morphine.

Cass wouldn't be coming from the trees. Cass wouldn't be making *that* noise, and there were two of them. He could hear them, clicking to each other as they circled him like sharks.

"Hello?" he stuttered, feeling his stomach drop away as the trees shook, wood splintering and crashing as something big raced through the undergrowth, grunts filling the air.

Reese didn't even see it.

It was as if the darkness simply jumped forward and bit him. Just a puff of dirt at the edge of his phone's light before something slammed into him from the side.

The force of it yanked him around, his phone spun away from his nerveless fingers, and a bright flash of light exploded in his brain as his head snapped back against the ground. His mouth opened to scream as a maw of teeth bit into his ruined leg, clamping down hard. Reese's mouth stretched wide, wider still, and the bones in his leg shattered.

He sat up screaming, his hands clutching at whatever was latched on to his leg, hands sliding off something cold and hard and wet. He heard its jaws crunching and grinding as his blood sprayed in the air and on his face.

Reese screamed and screamed.

CASS

The truck trundled out of the shed, its engine revving hard, a worrying knocking sound emanating from deep within its guts. It sounded like it was dying.

Cass figured only three of the cylinders were firing. *It might just be the spark plug.* But it might not, so he brought it to a stop in the middle of the enclosure, the brakes making a high-pitched squeal that echoed in the darkness, and he listened to the engine as it threatened to stall.

"Don't you fucking dare," he warned it.

He turned on the headlights and twin beams weakly illuminated the fence posts in front of him.

"Really?" he said. "My flashlight is brighter than this!"

He shined it out the windshield just to prove his point before flicking on the high beams. At least those worked.

Satisfied he could see, and that there were no engine warning lights showing, Cass lifted his foot off the clutch. He gave it some gas and drove out of the clearing, through the rusted red gate, and onto the dirt track, truck swaying and rocking on shot suspension before gliding out onto smooth asphalt.

He stopped in the middle of the road, turned on his hazard lights, put the truck in neutral, and pulled up the handbrake. He tapped the gas needle just to make sure it wasn't stuck and left the engine running, worried that if he turned it off now, it might never start again.

Jaime walked up to his window, stuck her head inside, and looked around.

"Where did you find this piece of junk?"

Cass shrugged. "Well, it was this or the Ferrari, and the Ferrari only carries two..."

"Going back for Reese?" she asked.

Cass shook his head, looking down, his hands still on the steering wheel.

"I don't want to push our luck with this. Something's wrong with the engine. Might just be a spark plug... or maybe it's the timing belt. But it might be something worse, and the last thing we need is to go back all the way we came and have it die on us. I'll find us a hospital first, drop you all off, then get a better car and head back for Reese."

Jaime nodded, then she stepped back to let him out.

He walked over to Lena and Klaus sitting on the grass, huddled close together.

"Hey, Lena, I got you a belated birthday present. What you think?"

"I think you can keep it," she answered in slow but almost perfect English, her nose crinkled up in distaste, but with the smallest ghost of a smile on her lips.

"Okay, Klaus, we're off," Cass said, "I found us a fine bucket of rust to ride into town. You wanna ride shotgun?"

Klaus extended his right hand blindly, and Cass pulled him to his feet.

"Lena, you and Jaime can ride in the back."

Lena smiled. Clearly the thought of riding in the back of an open-air truck sounded novel to her. Cass used to think the same when he was thirteen.

He watched Lena climb up first, Jaime a second later. The two of them settled down behind the cab while Cass got Klaus seated, pushing his head down so he didn't brain himself as he climbed in.

"What smells like the manure?" Klaus asked in his heavy German accent. Not that he was judging. Klaus spoke five languages; Cass spoke English and bad Spanish.

"You're sitting in it," replied Cass, glad Klaus was finally talking.

"Oh," Klaus paused, sighing and shifting slightly, as if it was the final straw.

Cass walked around the front and climbed in.

"Still beats the walking," Klaus said to himself before going silent again.

That it does, thought Cass as he eased the truck into first and gave it some gas. They crept forward, truck shuddering and rattling before he dropped it into second and they slowly gathered speed, the rattling lessening as the revs increased.

He nudged it into third and kept an eye on the temperature gauge as it began to climb, letting out a relieved sigh when it stopped. They were running hot, but they were running. It seemed to run the smoothest in fourth gear, just on 50 km/h, red needle bouncing up and down. Not quick by any means, but he was happy. They were making progress, and it was better than nothing. Plus, Klaus was right. After walking for five hours, it felt like they were practically flying.

They drove in silence for twenty minutes before Klaus started talking, slowly at first, his voice low and hesitant.

"Cass?"

Cass glanced at him before turning his attention back to the road. The truck had an annoying tendency to veer to the left, and it was taking all his concentration to keep them straight, fighting the pull of the steering wheel as it vibrated in his hands. "Yeah?"

"What just happened?"

Cass wanted to laugh, but he squashed it down and shook his head instead. "Which part?"

He looked in his rearview mirror. He could just see Jaime and Lena, their backs to him and their heads close together.

"All, the explosion," said Klaus. "How? It does not make the sense. And where is the police?"

"I don't know," Cass said. "To be honest, I was expecting the army to be here by now."

He risked a quick look at the radio, trying to familiarize himself with the layout before he leaned forward and turned it on.

The old head unit lit up, and a faint white glow filled the cabin. He turned up the volume and flicked through the stations—AM, FM, twisting the knob across the whole range—and getting nothing but static. The white noise sounded loud in the cabin.

"I'm getting nothing on the radio."

"EMP, *ja*?" asked Klaus.

Cass was quiet for a moment, thinking it through.

"No," he said, his voice growing more certain as he continued to talk. "Our phones still turn on. EMP would have fried them for sure. I can understand the power being knocked out, even the civilian networks being down. But we're far enough away from the physical damage, and the emergency broadcast system would be hardened, so we should be hearing that at least. And the range… a ground detonation would mean the EMP wouldn't reach much further than sixteen kilometers anyway, and anything on the other side of a hill would be fine." Cass nodded to himself. "I think it's our radio that's the problem, this piece of shit is probably just broken."

"But then why no one come? We walk for hours and nothing."

Cass looked up. There was only a narrow strip of stars still visible ahead of him and complete darkness in his rearview mirror, as though the world was slowly being consumed behind them.

"I think they're staying away on purpose. I mean, not to be a dick," Cass said, "but you should see the ash cloud coming from CERN. It's fucking impossible. Maybe that's why we haven't seen anyone? Maybe they think it was an attack?"

"An attack? Is not an attack. With what? And who would attack CERN?"

"I don't know," Cass continued. "But the police should have been here by now, or the army. Hell, half the world should be here by now and they aren't. There must be some sort of no-go order in place, and only the French military can enforce something like that. At least on this side of the border."

"So what now? You have plan?" Klaus asked.

Cass shrugged. They weren't exactly spoiled for choice. "We keep going. We get away from here, find a hospital. Somewhere big enough to…"

Klaus nodded. They were both thinking the same thing. Somewhere big enough to deal with an injury like his. Maybe big enough to tell him there was nothing they could do.

"Got idea where?" Klaus asked after a while.

"Now that we have a car, yeah. Bourg-en-Bresse. It's where I've been aiming for anyway. It's the only real option. Big enough population and a pretty decent hospital if I remember correctly, but it's further away. And that's if I can even find it in this crap," he said, peering ahead.

Klaus nodded again, going quiet as he settled back in his seat, and Cass concentrated on the road, his eyes occasionally flicking to the dark cloud above and the narrowing band of stars still visible on the horizon, like a mouth slowly closing with them still inside it.

REESE

Everything was pain, an electrical storm thundering along his spinal cord and into his brain.

His reflex response was to try to pull his leg away, playing tug of war with whatever was clamped on the other end. Whatever it was, it was strong. And it was winning.

Reese felt a sharp tug. Something tore, and the pain got worse. Too much for his mind to process, thalamus drowning in sensation. The circuit breakers in his mind flashed, fused, and died as parts of his cortex lit up like the sun, trying to work out where the pain was coming from, trying to form a response. Comparing it to his past memories, flipping through the catalogue of old grazes and sprains, his entire lifetime of experience analyzed in a split second as his overwhelmed brain tried to identify this new sensation.

What did it hurt like? What did it hurt more than?

His brain failed him. This was something new.

He was being eaten.

Reese's mind attempted to process the idea. It failed again, and the jaws pressed shut with a click. He heard a soft pop as ligaments snapped and nerves were severed, and in a second his leg was gone with a wet tear.

Time slowed to a crawl.

Reese clutched at his thigh, pulling it toward him, still screaming, watching blood spurt from the stump below his knee. He watched his leg being carried away by something the size of a dog with too many legs. He watched it with wide, uncomprehending eyes, seeing white bone and ragged red flesh hanging in strips.

He sucked in a lungful of air to scream, and something hit him from the left. It hit him hard. His head snapped to the side, and he felt his ribs crunch, his scream cut off with a surprised wheeze.

Reese was pushed across the dirt, away from his phone, its screen still shining as he was wedged up against a tree, pinned there by an immense weight. He felt something sharp slide into him, and Reese convulsed. He smelled dirt, he tasted blood. He felt it grip and pull. He felt it tear him open.

Blood filled his mouth as he felt it push its head into his guts. Reese gagged on it, unable to breath, unable to scream, coughing out a spray of red, a pathetic cough reduced to a wet gurgle as his lungs refused to work. He tried to stop it, tried to push it away, his soft, ineffectual hands patting at its head like a pet. *NO, NO, NO, NO* repeating in his babbling mind like a broken record as his hands were brushed aside, numb fingers catching in his wet intestines.

Reese tried to look at it, he tried to lift his head, but nothing happened. He just stared wide-eyed at the white branches high overhead, still visible in the soft light of his phone, as the world began to fade.

It felt like he was falling backward down a long tunnel, slowly at first, his body becoming weightless, falling faster, the pale branches above shrinking away as his retinas were starved of oxygen. Black edges crept in, darkness spreading, the roaring in his ears dying away, filled instead with a hollow hum.

Reese felt its head pull out, he felt his body twitch one last time, nothing but a numb piece of meat as the thing came away with half his guts in its mouth. Then it stopped, red ropes of his intestines dangling from its huge jaws. And it turned to look at him, its head cocked to one side, almost like a bird. As though it was surprised he was still awake.

Then his phone turned off, and he didn't get to see the end.

CASS

They made it to Bourg-en-Bresse in the end.

Somehow that bucket of rust didn't give up on them, didn't break down, didn't fail. It just kept going and going, carrying them out of hell, joining the tail end of a stream of traffic—the first people they'd seen in hours—driving through two checkpoints, past people fleeing on foot, past men in gas masks with guns, past flashing yellow lights and red flares burning on the road, and past convoy after convoy of trucks. Trucks full of soldiers, all heading in the opposite direction. For the border, for Meyrin and the mess they'd left behind.

Better late than never, Cass thought as the trucks roared past, clouds of black smoke spewing from their exhaust pipes.

He even tried to stop and ask for help at the first checkpoint just outside of Bellegarde-sur-Valserine, but the soldiers weren't interested. They wanted the traffic to keep flowing, they wanted the roads clear, but mostly Cass figured they just wanted the civilians out of the way, because when he got out of the car to ask for help the mood turned ugly, real fast. There was shouting, threats were made, guns were pointed.

So he got back in the truck and kept going, worrying more and more about the distance growing between them and Reese, worrying about the time that had already passed, constantly checking his watch as five hours became six, then seven. The back of his truck quickly filled with people who'd been walking, until they didn't have room for anyone else. And Cass realized he had made a mistake.

He should have gone back for Reese when he had the chance. Instead, he kept driving. He didn't have a choice. He couldn't turn around, not now, not when they were so close. Not with this many people depending on him. He tried to smother the rising panic he felt, and he watched as the road got busier and busier. Like some invisible boundary had been crossed or a decision had been made, because all he saw was soldiers and people running away. A line of red taillights stretching ahead of him while the army trucks whizzed past his window, their headlights blinding in the dark.

He glanced up as the air above their heads slowly filled with helicopters and jets. First a trickle, then a flood, aircraft flying low as the cloud continued to grow. Its black mass flickered with lightning, pulsing with flashes from deep within.

Cass wished he'd paid more attention to it at the time. But he'd been far too busy watching the road to look up. Too worried about Reese to admire the view, and far too busy trying to navigate the chaos that was Bourg-en-Bresse.

The city itself was a nightmare. There were soldiers everywhere, roads blocked by police cars, their lights flashing as detours popped up left and right. Big, glowing arrows trying to control and direct the flood of traffic coming in.

Great in theory, but in practice the roads simply couldn't cope with the numbers, and their pace slowed to a walk, then a crawl, and pretty soon they stopped dead. Plumes of car exhaust glowed red as they rose into the cooling air in front of them.

Cass could hear engines idling, the crash of thunder in the distance, and somewhere up ahead someone was shouting.

"Now what?" he said in frustration, looking at the gas needle hovering on empty.

And as if on cue, it started to rain. Fat, heavy drops that splashed across the windshield. First a few, then more, then a steady downpour as the skies opened up.

"Shit!"

Cass turned to look over his shoulder, out the window in the back of the cab.

Jaime was looking back at him with wide eyes, holding a moldy piece of tarp she must have found over her head with Lena tucked in next to her.

"Everyone okay?" he said, loud enough to be heard over rain hammering on the roof.

Jaime just shrugged; she looked miserable. Then she pointed ahead, and Cass turned to find the cars in front of him had moved. They moved again, and the gap widened.

He turned on the windshield wipers, but they did nothing more than smear the rain around. He lifted his foot off the brake, and they crept forward. The traffic kept moving, gathering speed, then it turned right, then left. A cop with a glowing baton waved them down a side road into a mess of residential streets with odd names. Then another cop waved them down another road, and Cass understood.

"They're directing us out of the city…"

"Problem?" asked Klaus.

Cass glanced at him, then looked away quickly. He didn't like what he saw.

"No," Cass answered, leaning forward, peering through the rain, looking for a way out. *There.*

"Hold on!" he shouted.

Cass yanked the wheel to the right, and the truck lurched out of the line of traffic, climbing up over the curb, around a barricade, and down another road.

He heard shouting. Someone shined their flashlight at him, and he saw shadows running toward them. Cass stamped down on the gas, and the truck surged ahead. He took the first left he could, then the next right, and he promptly got them lost.

He spent the next ten minutes driving around in circles before he saw a sign for the hospital, more thanks to luck than anything else. He dutifully followed the blue arrows until he saw a three-story building blazing with light before him, its parking lot filled with cars. Closer and he could read the sign out front. *The Medica France.*

Cass had never felt relief like that in his life before. He almost laughed, grinning like an idiot as he drove them in, his hand mashed down on the center of the steering wheel, the horn blaring as he skidded to a stop in front of the entrance. Feeling a weight lift off his shoulders as the doors opened and hospital staff came running, arms raised over their heads, trying to shield themselves from the rain. The scientist in him was still screaming about the fallout, but he didn't care. *We made it!* He almost couldn't believe it.

Cass wasn't religious. He didn't believe in fairy tales, but right then was the closest he'd ever come to saying thanks to the invisible Flying Spaghetti Monster in the sky.

Things moved quickly after that.

The nurses took one look at Klaus and ran back inside for a wheelchair, getting him out of the car while everyone else spilled out of the back, desperate to get inside and out of the rain. Then Cass explained the situation as best he could. He kept it simple, telling them only what they needed to know. They'd left someone behind, he was hurt badly. And they needed to go. Now. Before it was too late.

Two paramedics on standby offered to take him. So they all

jumped into an ambulance, a man named Gerard on his left, a woman named Helen on his right, and Cass sandwiched in the middle.

They had an easy run out of the city, the first real sign that their luck was finally changing. The ambulance's lights were like a free pass, cops opening up roadblocks to let them through, and Cass felt a small measure of confidence returning.

I'm coming, Reese.

He tried not to look at his watch as they drove—eight hours since they'd left Reese behind, another two hours before they would even be close to him. A long time to be alone and injured. But there was nothing he could do but wait, so Cass watched the road instead. He saw a tour bus packed with people. He saw soldiers in the streets. He saw a cop with a flashlight turn to watch them drive past, probably the same one from before, looking wet and miserable as the rain came down heavier and heavier.

They made it another two blocks before any thought of rescuing Reese went straight out of Cass's head.

About the same time as the power failed, the city went dark, and something big came through the windshield in a spray of glass and noise.

The next thing he knew, he was covered in blood, someone was screaming, and he was staring at what was left of Gerard. Half of him, really. Just his legs, a mess of torn purple entrails, the white nub of his severed spine, and his right foot still stamped down on the gas, steering wheel twitching left and right all by itself.

Cass looked up, blood in his eyes, cold wind and rain pelting his face, and he had just enough time to brace himself before they drove into the back of a car at sixty kilometers an hour.

He woke up with something on top of him, something heavy and warm and soft; dead weight. He touched it, and his hands came away sticky and wet, so he moved, and something touched him back. He tried to push it away, and his hands got tangled in thick, slippery coils. That was when Cass realized it was what was left of Gerard.

He pushed the legs off with a horrified scream and rolled sideways, crawling through still-warm intestines as he pulled himself out of the overturned ambulance, grunting and cursing and panicking as he wriggled out through the missing windshield, scrambling on his hands and knees across shattered pebbles of glass until he remembered how to stand. Part of him wondered where the other paramedic had gone, remembering her screams just before they hit. Part of him wondered what the fuck had just happened and why his head hurt.

Nothing was making sense, but then he heard a noise. Something other than the rumble of thunder, the pouring rain, or the constant, maddening wail of the ambulance's horn behind him.

It sounded like cicadas at first, like static, crackling and echoing all around him, getting louder, deeper, static turning into harsh clicks, clicks speeding up until it sounded like there was a dial-up modem screaming inside his head.

He covered his ears, grunting in pain as the sound burrowed into his head.

"*Qui set lá?*"

The clicks stopped.

"*Qui set lá?*" came the voice again, a woman's voice.

The paramedic. Helen, Cass realized, letting his hands drop.

He heard her take a step, and the clicks came back. They sounded closer.

"Hello?" came her voice again, a little softer, a little less certain this time. "Anyone there?"

The ground shuddered. Sharp, hard impacts as something heavy moved toward her voice.

Cass turned to follow it, his eyes going wide as he caught a glimpse of something big scuttling through the dark, something enormous, pale skin glistening wet. He saw a massive head with a hunched back and too many legs.

Then Cass was running, already ten feet away, her awful scream like a starter's gun inside his head.

He wasn't sure where he ran. He wasn't thinking clearly. He simply ran to get away from the noises behind him, her scream getting higher and higher until it cut off with a wet blurt. The noises that came after were worse, like a butcher hacking away at a piece of meat.

He fell over, his legs refusing to work properly, but he pushed himself back to his feet and kept going, and through the pouring rain and the blood in his eyes he saw a light. So he changed direction and aimed for it, hearing screams all around him now, what sounded like gunshots, people dying, and he kept running, too afraid to look over his shoulder, imagining something behind him getting closer until it was breathing down his neck.

DAY
89

Liberty Road
Five miles south of Scotts Hill
Tennessee, USA

TRACE

From where he was parked it was easy to see. It stood out. Ugly and wrong. A sharp line that cut deep into the green heart of the field like a wound, green flesh parted, dark soil exposed to the air while crows swarmed above it like flies drawn to shit. The air filled with the buzzing clap of their wings and their ugly, greedy screams.

That's what had first drawn his eyes, and then his ears. The crows, dirty scavengers calling to him from the road. Talking to him long before he had seen all the abandoned cars and bicycles that lined its edge. Laughing at him long before he had seen the path leading out into the field, and then the path had started speaking to him all by itself. A path that screamed *wrong*.

Not because it was on private property, or far from town or the next nearest house. No, it was wrong for one simple reason: there were too many footprints going into that field, and none coming out.

Trace could see that with a single sad glance. And the path ran straight as an arrow, no deviation, no meandering, no hesitation. It was efficient and deliberate, and it was impossible to miss. Like a smudge on his eye, a cataract, or sun damage, maybe. And no matter how much he blinked, no matter how much he wanted it to disappear, like a scar it simply wouldn't go away, it wouldn't heal.

So Chief Trace Colter of the Tennessee Highway Patrol did the only thing he could. He did what he had spent most of his life being paid to do. He got out of his patrol car, and he followed it. One slow step at a time.

There was no rush. *Not anymore,* he reasoned, and, frankly, he needed the time to think. And when he was done thinking, when he was finally honest with himself, he needed the time to prepare. Sara had tried to warn him.

"It's bad," she had said, sounding choked up over the radio, sounding like the world had come to an end a little earlier than expected.

He could see her waiting for him now, her small shape standing out in the field like some ineffective scarecrow. Her arms at her sides, her flashlight pointed at the ground, not even trying to keep the birds away.

Trace waved at her. Sara didn't wave back.

So he took it slow, walking along a path in what would normally be a fallow field. Empty and unseeded, overgrown with obnoxious weeds, yellow flowers, and green grass. Once full with the promise of rest and rebirth. But now…

Now the long grass was flattened, flowers crushed. The blades broken, some dead, some dying, a little less green, slowly turning brown. Dark soil disturbed beneath, ugly. He tried not to look at it. He let his old eyes wander instead, lifting them to either side of him where the grass still rose as high as his knees, still alive, still green and vibrant, mired in mist, morning dew still clinging to its blades in defiance before the day's heat arrived.

Trace looked back over his shoulder as he walked, looking east, past the line of abandoned cars, like a funeral procession parked nose to tail on the side of the road. He looked past his patrol car, its lights flashing, red and blue strobing in the gloom, and Trace stopped, turning to watch the sunrise. Another bad sign of things to come.

It was 6:30 a.m. on a Tuesday morning in September. Normally at this time of year, the sun would have been up half an hour ago, and yet it was only just beginning to climb above the dark storm cloud he could see on the horizon. And behind that somewhere was the Cloud itself.

A wall of darkness blowing in off the North Atlantic, its leading front touching the ground like a curtain, purple lightning crawling along its edges. Looking like one of those incredible dust storms he'd seen on the Discovery Channel. So big it altered global weather patterns. So dark it blocked out the sun. So thick it killed radio signals. It was Armageddon, steamrolling the world at a walking pace, and in three weeks it would be here.

Trace tried to put it out of his mind. There was nothing he could do about it, and worrying never solved anything anyway.

He tried to concentrate on something else, watching the light glint off cold metal, thinking about all the fuel in those abandoned cars' gas tanks.

He watched the sun struggle into the sky. He watched it finally pull itself clear of those clouds, its light defeating the darkness, slowly replacing it with brilliant red, red tempering to orange in a heartbeat, then dipping to warm yellow the next.

Trace closed his eyes as he felt the first touches of warmth on his face, and he breathed in. He tried to take in the moment, he tried to commit it all to memory. He wanted to remember all the colors before they were gone for good. He wanted to remember how the sun tasted on his skin, knowing it was only going to become rarer over the next few weeks, and then… never again.

He breathed out and opened his eyes.

The warm yellow light was already gone, replaced with the clinical white glare of a morgue, cold, harsh light beating down on the earth, exposing the dirty evidence. But that was good; it made things easier to see, or clearer at least, and where his day was headed he was going to need all the light he could get.

And as Trace stood in the middle of that field, his feet rooted to the ground like a tree, he felt every one of his sixty-six years catch up to him in a rush. He felt every old wrinkle and new line of worry prominent on his brow. He felt every lazy beat of his well-worn heart, the soft stuttering rush of his pulse, and the arthritis in his knees. He felt his eyes burning in their sockets, dark circles beneath, red and dry behind his glasses, but mostly he just felt exhausted, hung over, and sleep deprived. Disturbed days followed by disturbing dreams, leaving him drained and half dead.

Trace wiped his forehead with his sleeve, catching a whiff of his own scent.

Shit. When was the last time I took a shower?

Sleep, real sleep, and a shower, that's what he needed. Not that he would get either one anytime soon. He still had a job to do, at least in his head.

He hadn't been paid in months. He knew he'd never get paid again. But Trace had been a cop for so long he didn't know how to be anything else; and if he wasn't a cop, then what was the point?

So Trace set his shoulders. He stood up a little straighter, and he turned his back on the rising sun, turning to face this morning's grisly task. He was here to look at dead people after all.

It's what he was good at.

He passed the first ones a few yards later.

A young couple, their bodies carelessly tangled in the grass. Mouths yawning open, pupils dilated, black pits staring at the sky, dried vomit and blood running down their chins.

Their faces said it all. *Wait! I made a mistake. I don't want to die anymore...*

He imagined they had meant to die together in each other's arms. He imagined they had thought death would be quick and painless. Romantic, even.

Fools.

It looked like they had suffered instead. Long, drawn out, messy deaths, and now they were starting to rot and bloat.

He passed more bodies. He passed Charles, a friend.

A dead friend, he corrected himself.

An old man like himself, but wiry, thin where Trace was thick. Gray-haired with a kind and weathered face, a lifetime of laughter etched in his wrinkles.

Charles looked like he was dressed for church. Beige suit and blue tie, but the image was a mess. His white shirt untucked, face turned purple, pants full of shit.

His wife lay next to him. Nancy. Her Sunday best all twisted and ruined with grass stains. Hair matted and clumped, the left side of her face pressed into the ground. Her mascara had run; she must have been crying at the end, and Trace found he was now too.

It was hard seeing them like this. People once filled with such hope and strength, their memory tainted with the bitter stench of vomit. He was going to miss them.

"Safe journey, my friends," he said, dipping his hat to them, waiting for more words to say, closing his mouth when nothing came, trying to ignore the smell. Trying to remember instead countless nights spent talking out on their porch, countless nights spent sitting in soft silence, watching the world go by, watching the traffic. The lights that traveled from east to west, and then west to east again. A cigar on his lips, a cold beer in his hand, maybe too many sometimes… an unhealthy indulgence. A coping mechanism. One he had needed in the dark years after his wife's death. One he had been abusing since his son's.

That one had been worse. No casket, no burial. Just an email from France. Scanned image attached, a letter of dense, hurried, smudged handwriting.

"Hi, Dad," it had started on the first line. By the second one he was having trouble reading it.

He still had it in his left breast pocket. Printed it out when printers were still a thing. A reminder. Next to the last picture he had of them all together. Jen in the middle, his arm around his wife's waist, when the cancer was only just beginning to gnaw at her bones. James on the other side, his arm around his mom's shoulders. James looking big and healthy and strong. So proud in his blue dress uniform.

Jen had died five years after that picture was taken.

James had come home for the funeral, on special leave from the Marines. It had been a cold, wet day in November. Trace remembered the rain hammering down on her casket, how gray and dull the world had looked without her in it.

The rest of the day was a blur. He remembered arguing with James. He'd just buried his wife. He refused to bury his son. He wanted James to quit, before it was too late, before he came home in a body bag or in bits or not at all.

James refused.

Trace had lost his temper. He'd said things, things he couldn't take back. So had James. They were much the same in that way, stubborn and proud.

James had left, and he hadn't come home again. And as the years rolled by, they spoke less and less, and then James had been sent in under the Cloud, and Trace hadn't heard from him since.

But it was Day 89 now. Time had rolled on. The Cloud had kept growing, and, alive or dead, Trace knew it didn't really matter. He would never see his son again.

He walked past the Andrews. A beautiful family, a perfect family. *Less so now*, he thought as he felt something break inside his chest.

He had known it would happen. He'd tried to prepare himself.

He just hadn't known it would be so hard. Forced to watch it all end. Just like it had in New York, and Boston, and everywhere else along the East Coast. When people started giving up. When suicide had overtaken heart disease as the leading cause of death.

He pulled his eyes away from Luke, the dad, all curled up in the fetal position. The mom, Rachel, lay next to him with burst blood vessels in her eyes and flies in her mouth.

And Sam.

Trace had to do a double take to make sure the boy was in fact dead. The five-year-old was still sitting upright, legs crossed, but his chest didn't move, and his dead eyes only looked down at the mess in his lap.

And then there was Katy, once beautiful Katy. Only eight years old. Her hands clenched like claws and her bloody, messy mouth still screaming.

The kids didn't deserve this, Trace raged inside his skull. He'd been to both their Christenings. He had watched them grow up. Now he was going to have to put them in black zip-up bags.

He almost missed a step, remembering the smallest body bags were always the heaviest. He frowned, struck by another thought. *Do we even have any left?*

Trace kept walking. A slight stumble to his step as he fought for balance, for a reference point in a world turned upside down.

Bodies, familiar names, and well-known faces were on either side of the path now. A sad reunion of dead friends scattered through the grass. Trails snaking away as though some had tried to run, and maybe they had, right at the end. When the first ones fell over and started twitching. When harsh reality caught up to naive intention.

But they hadn't gotten far. The farthest runner seemed to have hit the dirt fifteen yards out, plowing into the ground like he'd tried to plant himself.

Where did they even think they were running to?

He stepped over more vomit. He stepped over Bryan.

The path widened, then opened into a large, flattened circle, grass pressed down, trampled flat in an area nearly ten yards wide, and it was littered with bodies, plastic cups, and one-gallon jugs of some red fluid.

He counted nearly twenty corpses. Trace concentrated on the number, recognizing the faces, trying to push down the names that kept filling his mind. He had a job to do; coping would have to come later.

Ha, coping.

He kept walking, weaving between them, stepping around their twisted shapes, trying not to look at the young faces. Little faces all locked in pain, trying not to hate their parents close by, failing at that too.

He wondered exactly what type of pesticide they had all decided to drink. A toxicology report would have told him, right down to what year it was made and where, but that wasn't going to happen. Neither were the autopsies, not anymore, which left him with nothing but an educated guess. *Probably Roundup, or maybe Atrazine?*

It usually was. Living surrounded by so many farms meant it was incredibly easy stuff to get ahold of. And without Google to answer every question, people were stupid and uneducated.

Thirty years as a cop in LA, and Trace thought he had seen all the ways a person could kill himself. The last three months had proven him wrong, and, in terms of ways to go out, turns out drinking pesticide is about as slow and nasty a way as you can get.

It was too slow. Too inefficient, for lack of a better word.

First there was a fever as your body tried to fight the poison, then an increased rate of breathing as your blood oxygen levels fell, vomiting followed by uncontrollable muscle twitches as the nervous system shut down. Then diarrhea, convulsions, the inability to breathe, unconsciousness, and finally—mercifully—death.

It's also highly acidic, hence the mess. The effects inside a person were like they had swallowed a bomb.

Trace hoped they had cut it with something else, painkillers or sleeping pills. But judging from the expressions frozen in their faces, it didn't look like it.

"Hi, Craig. You too?" Trace asked.

Craig didn't reply. His mouth was too full of flies to say anything.

"Trace," said a voice.

He looked up to find Sara still watching him, still waiting for him. Eyes slightly wide and clearly shaken. Trace nodded.

Time to get to work.

Sara was the one who had called it in.

She'd been out on patrol when she came across all the abandoned cars and bicycles on the road. She'd seen the trampled grass leading out into the field, and so Sara had gone for a walk.

Trace imagined some part of her regretted it now, and he noticed a slightly fresher patch of vomit a few feet away, still wet, this one minus a body.

Trace looked back at Sara as she talked into her walkie-talkie. Her pale white face, her shaking hands. The too-loud voice and the eyes that didn't look down.

Trace shook his head. *Poor kid.*

Before the Cloud, the most Sara normally had to deal with was drunk underage youths, the occasional bar fight, or the rare domestic, maybe a runaway dog on a slow day. Trouble, *real* trouble, was rare here, and with a population of less than a thousand nearly everyone in Scotts Hill had known each other, and town gossip had proven to be a much better deterrent than jail time ever was.

Trace looked down at Karen while Sara kept talking.

He'd always liked Karen. Pretty, a little quiet. Reserved, but nice, and lonely like him. She had always greeted him, always had a smile for him.

Trace didn't like this new look on her face. He wanted to close her eyes, but something made him pause, something about evidence, about leaving the bodies undisturbed. Some now meaningless bullshit.

What does it matter anymore?

He knelt down. The smell of her perfume mixed with the sour stench of vomit. He reached forward, his hand resting on her brow, her skin tinged blue, cold and clammy beneath his touch.

Trace closed her eyes, said a quiet goodbye, and stood up.

Coping comes later, he reminded himself.

Trace knew he should be calling it in, asking the few remaining cops still out there for help, an extra pair of hands, but he already knew what they would say. No one had the head count, or the fuel, anymore. They were on their own.

He watched the emotions jump across Sara's face as they told her the same, cheek twitching like she had Tourette's. Shock, confusion, disbelief, a flicker of anger, gone just as quickly as they appeared.

"You okay, Sara?" he asked, even though he knew she wasn't.

"No one's coming," she said, shoulders slumped, her hand dropping to her side, her voice quiet.

Trace nodded.

The bodies lying at their feet would be left out here for the birds and stray dogs.

Sara kept talking. "They said there's a lot of traffic heading our way. Everybody is running west."

Sara looked to him, then to the empty road.

There was no traffic, not yet, not for a few more days. Then the roads would be full of strangers, the entire population of the eastern seaboard, 112 million people all trying to go the same way. A flood of people heading inland and beyond, all heading west, like rats abandoning a sinking ship.

The fact that there was nowhere to run to anymore didn't stop them from trying. And saying it had caused a traffic jam didn't do the chaos justice. The country's roads had choked to a standstill, most of them nothing more than parking lots now. So people had started walking, and the fastest ones were almost here, a wall of people washing in across the US like a tsunami.

Trace knew that's when the real trouble would start. Trouble like this town had never seen.

"What's going on, Trace? Why this? Why now?" Sara asked, looking at Craig before tearing her eyes away.

Trace bit back his instinctive response, the fatherly instinct to slap her on the back of the head.

Be gentle, he had to tell himself. *But is it simple naive youth, or does she choose not to see the truth?* He couldn't tell.

"This is it. People are giving up, Sara," Trace said, looking toward the dark cloud somewhere over the horizon. Still too far off to see the lightning that sparked along its edges, but he had seen enough of it on the news to know it was there. When there had still been power for something as luxurious as TV.

"We have three, *maybe* four weeks left."

"And this is how they're dealing with it?" she asked, bewildered, spreading her arms wide.

"One of the ways."

"And the kids? Sam? And Katy? How can anyone do that?"

Trace didn't say anything. What was there to say? It wasn't the first time he'd seen dead kids. It wouldn't be the last, either. But still, the Andrews had been the quintessential family. Sam and Katy always underfoot, always smiling; everyone had loved them. Good kids, sweet kids.

Now the maggots would get a taste too.

"So that's it? It's over?" she asked.

Trace just shrugged. It had been over for some time. The last few weeks had made that painfully obvious.

"You don't think we can win this?"

"Win this?" Trace frowned. "Sara, we can't win this. You know that. We've just been holding on a little longer than most. Hell, we did better than I expected."

His head tilted to the cold corpses littering the ground.

"These poor bastards just didn't want to wait any longer. And who's *we*? The armies couldn't stop the Cloud, the 5th and 6th Fleets didn't even last a week. All they did was slow it down."

And they'd had tanks. And bombs. And planes. They had turned most of France into green glass, and it still hadn't done them any good. It hadn't done his son any good.

"But why? Who chooses *this*, Trace? They could have gone west at least, run away."

"Run where, Sara?"

"To Colorado, to NORAD. You heard the radio same as me."

Trace shook his head. NORAD was a fairy tale. A relic from the Cold War, an early warning missile defense system. Nothing more.

Sara was clutching at straws, like one of those people who still believed in Santa Claus or the Easter Bunny.

Not that he hadn't heard the chatter. Talk of frantic activity all across the country, massive constructions projects going up left, right, and center, NORAD being one of them, talk of trucks coming and going, lights burning 24/7, that they were expanding the complex, turning it into a modern-day Ark. Somewhere safe to ride out the approaching storm.

A nice story to tell the kids at bedtime, maybe, but that's all it had been. Make-believe.

"That's nothing but a rumor, Sara," Trace said slowly. "There's nothing there. And even if it's true, you saw what was happening before the power went. These poor bastards didn't run for the same reason we all chose to stay here. It's not safe out there. Remember?"

"Oh, come on, Trace!" said Sara. "You're saying it like there's no point anymore. If that's true, then why don't we join them and put a gun to our heads and get it over with? Why bother doing anything?"

Trace shook his head. "That's not what I'm saying."

"Then what? I can't accept that!" she said, pointing at Karen, her eyes red. "But I can't just sit around and wait for that damn cloud to get here either. We have to do something, anything..."

She looked at the Andrews, pointed at Sam, the little boy still sitting up. "I have kids too, Trace. Can you imagine if that was Peter? Or Stacey?" Her voice wobbled. "I couldn't do *that* to them. I refuse." She shook her head. "There has to be another way, somewhere we can go."

Trace grunted.

There wasn't, not realistically. Sure, they could run west like every other idiot, but the West Coast wasn't a destination. It was a dead end. There were no ships waiting to carry them further when they got there, and in another couple of months there'd be nowhere left to sail anyway.

"Trace? You listening?"

"I'm listening, Sara. I don't have an answer for you."

"So what do you suggest we do? Roll over and kiss our asses goodbye?" Sara looked away. Trace pretended he didn't see her wipe a tear from her eye.

He just shrugged. He had to admit when he was beaten.

"Well, screw that!" Sara spat, taking a step toward him. "I say we make a run for it. All of us. Drew, yourself, and anyone else willing to come. I don't care, let's just go. Get away from this!"

She pointed east, at the clouds on the horizon, or maybe she was pointing at the corpses. He wasn't sure which.

Trace looked at her, frowning. "Run where, Sara? NORAD?" He tried to laugh, but it died quickly, a sick wheeze lost to the wind.

"Why not?" Sara demanded. "What have we got to lose, Trace? If we stay here, we're dead for certain, but out there... out there at least there's still a chance."

For what? Trace almost asked. But then he remembered who he was talking to: Sara, the only person who could stand in a field full of dead people and still believe in miracles.

"Fine, then," Trace said, rubbing his face with an exhausted sigh. "Hypothetically, say we did it. Say we left here. How far do you think we'd get? I have less than a quarter tank of gas left in my car, and I doubt we could get much from all those back there." He jerked his thumb over his shoulder.

"And ignoring gas for a moment, do you even know which route to take? We don't even know which roads are still passable. What if the road is blocked? We'd have to backtrack. And at some point we're going to end up on foot. With two kids in tow. We can't change our minds halfway. Food and water will be a problem. And even if we somehow made it, what makes you think they'll even let us in? I'm pretty sure we're not on the guest list."

Sara waved him off. "I know all that, Trace. I'm not an idiot. But look around you. Look at all these people. This place is dying. We can't help them; they don't want our help. We've tried our best here, really, we did," she said, forcing herself to point at all the bodies around them. "But I can't just give up like they did. Not while I still have some fight left. Neither can you. Do you think James would have just given up?"

Trace opened his mouth to deny her, but nothing came out. That was a low blow, bringing up James, but she was right. *Goddamn it.*

James wouldn't have given up, and neither could he. Not while he was still breathing. He owed his son that much. But running away would never work. Leaving here was suicide, same as all the people at their feet, just slower. He knew that.

He wondered if Sara did too.

"Okay," he said, defeated.

"Okay," she repeated, as if she hadn't really heard him. "Wait. What? You'll do it?" she asked, eyes going wide as if she had expected more of an argument.

Trace shrugged. What difference did it make where he died?

"I'll talk to Drew first. But, in the meantime…" he held up a hand to stave her off. "In the meantime, go home, Sara. Go home and talk to Ian. And if you still want to do this, then let me know, and meet us back at the station in three hours."

"Why the station?" Sara asked, watching Trace pull out his own walkie-talkie.

"Because we'll need a plan. And guns and ammo and the spare gas masks. I'll get Drew to meet me here first with a siphon and some jerry cans. We'll meet you there once we've gotten all the gas we can out of those cars."

"When do we go?" Sara asked, her eyes looking through him, and Trace could see her mind already racing far ahead.

"If we're ready… and I mean *if*, then first thing tomorrow morning, once the sun is up and everything is packed. If we're going to do this, then we need to move fast."

Before I come to my damn senses.

CLAY

Clay saw the Jeep coming for miles.

Sunlight glinting off its windshield as it bounced and swayed across the road. Fat rubber tires and soft suspension soaking up every dip and fold of the land, its big engine purring, eating up the miles of asphalt.

He didn't know the man driving. Never seen him before in his life; he was a nobody. A nothing. But he was alone, he had a Jeep, it seemed heavily loaded, and its engine was still running, which meant it had that next-to-impossible thing to find.

Gas.

And then the Jeep stopped on the side of the road, the driver climbed out to take a piss, and it all became so impossibly easy.

So Clay didn't hesitate. It would be a shame to waste the opportunity, and on his next breath out, between one steady beat of his heart and the next, he pulled the trigger.

There was a deafening crack, his rifle kicked, and a fraction of a second later the man's head blew apart in an explosion of red. His brains neatly excavated in the afternoon air, a pink puff of mist that used to be an identity, now vapor drifting on the wind.

And just like that, the Jeep, the gas, and whatever else was in it were his.

The stranger's body took a little longer to agree, standing upright in surprise, dripping empty hole where his eye used to be looking accusingly back at Clay for a brief second before the corpse toppled sideways.

Clay inhaled. He lifted his eye from the scope, pulled the walkie-talkie to his face, pressed transmit, and spoke into the mic.

"He's down. You're clear. Go."

There was static, a short click. Clay heard laughter. Another crackle of static.

"Nice shot!" said the voice on the other end. "Dumb bastard must have been looking right at you."

More laughter. The sound of an engine starting. Another harsh click, then quiet again.

Clay looked back to the body lying in the road, remembering the man's head turning mid-stream, looking west, almost directly at Clay. Worried eyes looking at something above Clay's head, his pale face catching the fading orange glow of the sunset just before the bullet drilled through his head.

And Clay wondered if maybe he had somehow known his time was up, or maybe he'd seen the reflected flash of Clay's scope. Maybe he had been watching the sunset. Or maybe it was simple boredom as his bladder emptied itself onto the gravel at his feet.

All irrelevant now anyway, Clay told himself.

He found it hard to care anymore. The first few kills had taken that ability from him, and in the months since then it had become almost easy, like breathing, automatic. He barely had to think about it.

It's nothing personal, he kept reminding himself. *Just survival.*

Clay shuffled on his elbows to try to ease the cramp in his neck before he reloaded and sighted back down the road. He skipped over the Jeep with its Nashville plates, passing over the two shapes on the red motorbike that broke from the woods, its back wheel spewing a spray of dirt and torn grass behind it as it raced toward the Jeep.

He scanned the woods to either side, looking for any unwanted guests. Not that he expected any more company. The stranger was the first traffic of the day, likely the last as the sun set and the light started to fade.

But he would stay here, even after nightfall. Just to be sure. Same as the day before, lying silent and still, watching the road, rifle pointed down it while the "boys" hid in the woods off to the side, waiting for some unlucky bastard to stumble into their trap.

The usual plan was for the motorbike to chase their prey into a roadblock they had set up a mile further along the road. They had it down to a fine art now. Everyone had their job to do, a part to play.

Clay preferred being up here, out front. The way he saw it, there was less of a chance for him to get shot at, which happened occasionally when whoever they were chasing into the roadblock realized they were trapped.

But wouldn't you know it? The poor bastard with the Jeep had saved them all the hassle.

Unlucky for him. Lucky for us, thought Clay. It all came down to perspective, really.

He shook his head. *Idiot.*

Clay had never thought of himself as a smart man—street smart, yes, good with his fists—but as for book learning, he didn't have much of an education. He hadn't even finished high school, but he would have assumed any idiot would know not to stop on the side of the road for a piss. You don't stop for anything, not anymore. You pissed in a bottle if you had to. It was common sense as far as he was concerned.

So he didn't feel too guilty. The stranger was a moron. Clay had probably done him a favor, giving him a quick death. Better than the alternative... The men waiting at the roadblock would have played with him first. Used him for target practice.

Unless it was a woman. Then the games they would have played would have been very different, and Clay shivered at the thought.

He'd made it a rule to shoot the women first, if he could, and if no one was watching. It was kinder that way. He'd seen that after the first one.

He lifted the scope higher, tracing it along the edge of the highway, looking out east, trying to see the smudge of dark cloud just over the horizon, wondering when he'd see it, wondering how long they had left.

The Commander said a month, said he was good with his numbers. Clay didn't believe a word that came out of his mouth. But he supposed he should be grateful. If it wasn't for the Cloud, he'd still be rotting away in a cell.

Bad luck he was even there in the first place. Bad luck he'd been born to a drug-fucked mother. Clay didn't even know who his father was; his mother certainly didn't. She'd been so high most of the time she'd hardly ever known what day it was, never mind who she'd turned tricks for that week.

All Clay knew was that his dad must have been a giant. His mother was a shriveled little thing, like a twig. And Clay was big, six foot five and 295 pounds of bone and muscle. The way he saw it, he had to have gotten it from somewhere. But that had only been the start. Bad luck had seen Clay fall in with the wrong crowd, picked for his size. He'd joined a gang, spent some time in juvie for assault, and once he'd gotten out he hadn't gone back to school. What was the point? Not like his mom gave a shit, and school was hard. The words never came out how he thought they would; they came out backwards or not at all. So Clay had dropped out and fallen in with an even worse crowd, gone pro. Held up a few stores, robbed an armored car or two, started ram-raiding ATMs. Made a career of it. And for the first time in his life he'd had money, and at thirty years old Clay finally thought his luck had changed.

But then they'd hit that bank and all his bad luck had come back with a vengeance.

A security guard had decided to go Rambo instead of lying down like he'd been told to, and bad luck had seen fit to pair Clay with a trigger-happy idiot for a partner. Even worse luck had seen the security guard catch a bullet in the mouth.

Fifteen fucking years he'd gotten for that. Three of which he'd spent rotting away in El Dorado, but then the Cloud had come along, and it's hard to keep a prison going without guards or water or electricity. So here he was. Out early on bad behavior. Until the Cloud came to finish him off at least...

The Commander said they'd all survive if they just stuck to the plan. They just had to do as he said. Follow orders. And that with the gear they were lifting off every idiot that fell into their net, they extended their own lives another week.

Clay didn't believe him. Even he knew the math on that one didn't add up, and he had no doubt the Commander would cross them all the first chance he got. The way Clay saw it, once a deserter, always a deserter. Besides, it's what he would do if their positions were reversed. *Nothing personal. Just survival. And common sense.*

So Clay was working on his own plan. Nothing flashy, but he was doing it quietly and carefully. Hoarding food and gas, hiding the food in a tree, collecting his daily ration of gas, never enough to go more than ten miles on his bike. He'd siphon out a mouthful, leaving just enough to still get around if he went easy on the throttle. Relying on his legs the rest of time. Then he hid the stolen gas in two 5.3-gallon jerry cans buried in the ground, no markings to give them away, no signs, no X marks the spot, nothing that could connect it to him.

That was something else he had learned, long before prison had tattooed it into his brain: don't trust anyone and always have a backup plan.

Clay turned his attention back to the Jeep. The boys on the

motorbike had reached it by now. One was in the driver's seat, the other was pulling shit out of the back.

Clay swore and pulled the walkie-talkie to his face again. "What the fuck are you doing?"

He waited until it was clear they weren't going to answer.

He tried again. "You think this is a joke? You want me to let the Commander know you're going through *his* stuff?"

The one in the driver's seat lifted something to his face and Clay's walkie-talkie hissed.

"Gonna snitch on us, Clay?"

"Commander's orders," Clay said, "You can take it up with him. So cut the shit or you can lube up that little asshole of yours for the fucking of your life."

The one in the driver's seat lifted his other hand and pressed it against the windshield so Clay could see one finger standing taller than the rest.

"See this, Clay? Go fucking rotate on that."

Clay kept his finger off the trigger and counted to three before he did something stupid.

The two boys were all talk. White trash brothers, dirty little runts with inflated egos, and they forgot Clay was the one with the rifle. But their daddy was in tight with the Commander, buddies from high school or some shit. So these two little 'tards were special, untouchable. At least out here.

On the inside they would have been broken in on their first day. Thin white dudes with no gang affiliations, no pals in prison, and no fighting skills? They wouldn't have had a choice.

Punks, as they were called after their first gang rape; they'd probably have ended up as someone's bitch. They would have learned to take it, make all the right noises. Clay imagined they would have learned to enjoy it. Simple survival again. Amazing what people will do to stay alive.

"Your funeral," was all Clay said.

He clicked off the button and started moving the frequency dial on his walkie-talkie to another channel.

He lifted it to his face, and he waited.

Technically he really should be calling it in. But he wasn't a complete fool. Rat them out and he'd wake up with a knife in his guts. He had to be careful. It's not like he could sleep with one eye open all the time.

It was an empty threat, but it still seemed to do the trick because the one pulling stuff out the back started throwing it back in.

Clay watched them slam the doors shut, and he watched as the Jeep pulled off the shoulder and start driving toward him.

He pressed down on the transmit button.

"Clay to the Bench."

There was a pause.

"Report," came the one-word answer.

"Turnover made. Running backs on their way home with the ball. Open up a hole."

Clay watched the other one run back for the motorbike, jump on, and rock it back off its kickstand before he raced to catch up with his brother in the Jeep.

"Copy that. Clearing a path."

The Commander loved his code words—fancied himself a bit of a football authority, too—that and he didn't like the idea of radio chatter. Too worried about people listening in. Eyes in the sky, he said.

Paranoid bastard, but it meant everything had to be in code. Subterfuge, the Commander called it.

Not a word Clay had ever used, but he liked the sound of it. It sounded smart, and he was happy to play along. It kept the Commander happy, and that was important.

Clay had met the man three times.

The first was when Clay joined their group. It was that or starve. The second was when he'd stopped a car on the road, one that had been loaded with weapons. And women.

He had to deliver it and the two girls inside it personally, girls crying for their dad and brothers, or maybe their boyfriends. Clay hadn't asked. He didn't want to know. But they'd left the three men on the side of the road with their pockets emptied and bullets in their heads.

But as they say, the third time's the charm. That was when he learned what necklacing was. Something the Commander had learned in Africa. Something he'd brought back home with him.

The Commander had made everyone line up and watch as three idiots who'd been caught stealing food had tires filled with petrol draped around their necks. Then they were set on fire.

Clay had never heard screams like that. He never wanted to again.

So a happy Commander was a good Commander, and, the way he saw it, the more distance between them the better.

That was another lesson he had learned in prison.

Keep his head down, do his time, and get out. And Clay was finding his new life outside to be much the same. It was a dog-eat-dog world out here. The Commander was simply the biggest dog around, and a rabid one. It's why he'd let the boys drive the Jeep in by themselves. It's one of the reasons he preferred to camp out here on the road on his own. The way he saw it, the less attention he brought on himself the better. Less of a chance he had of fucking up and catching alight.

TRACE

Trace was tired.

And sore. His knees ached, he had blisters on his hands, and his back was a mess. He was covered in dirt, and his boots were caked in mud. But they'd buried the kids and covered the adults in a layer of dirt, and that was the closest to a funeral those twenty-five fools were going to get.

Then, once Drew and himself had emptied the abandoned cars of their gas, they'd driven to the station in Lexington, met up with Sara, and taken what they'd needed. Then they'd spent the rest of the day arguing about what came next, debating the "smartest" way to do this.

It meant it was late when he got home, and dark and quiet and cold. No lights. No electricity. No hot water. No one waiting for him.

He didn't bother taking off his shoes. What was the point? He hadn't cleaned the house in months. Not like he had any visitors. Besides, he was so stiff and sore from flinging dirt and dragging corpses he couldn't bend down to undo the laces.

He made his way through the foyer, past the stacks of firewood and milk cartons full of captured rainwater, into the living room, tracking dirt across the carpet. He navigated more by memory than sight, feeling his way along the wall until he stopped in front of the fireplace. He patted at the mantel until he found the matches, lit one, and leaned forward with a groan to start a fire.

He waited for the flame to catch, fed it some more wood, then he turned around and fell into his chair with an exhausted sigh, and he just sat there. The first time he'd stopped moving all day. Watching the fire spread, an orange glow filling the dark room, flames growing taller as the room began to warm.

But sitting still wasn't a good thing. Because Trace started thinking, and too much thinking was bad. There was no one to talk to, no one to keep his mind off things.

So he grabbed the bottle on the table next to him and the glass next to it, pouring out the gold liquid until it licked at the rim.

He lifted it to his lips, opened his throat, and knocked it back, grimacing as the cheap whiskey burned his throat, grunting as it hit him in the chest like heartburn. Then he poured himself another glass and knocked it back just as fast.

Trace poured a third and raised it to the fire.

"Here's to coping."

Being a cop had its perks, having access to the evidence lockers being one of them—lockers full of booze that had been lifted off underage kids, enough to fill a bathtub, enough to drown in if he wanted.

Trace knew he was an alcoholic, but knowing and caring were two different things, and Trace didn't care anymore. He'd stopped caring a long time ago. Hard to care when you had nothing left to live for. Sixty-six years old and his whole life had come down to this? Wife long gone, son probably dead, and now it was just him, sitting in an empty house, alone, in the middle of nowhere. What for? What was the point?

Trace shook his head.

It was never supposed to end like this.

He never wanted to be here in the first place. Moving to Lexington had been Jen's idea, not his. A last chance, an ultimatum really; he had to choose, the job or her, before it killed him.

But Trace had been a cop for so long he didn't know how to be anything else. Sitting still wasn't in his vocabulary. If he stopped working, he'd drop dead. Jen had known that.

Chief of Lexington had been the compromise. That's what marriage was all about, wasn't it? Meeting halfway.

So they'd moved halfway across the country, as far from LA as they could get without ending up in New York.

They'd started fresh, started to patch things up, at least with her, but then she'd died, he'd messed things up with James, and he'd been drifting ever since.

Trace looked at the dead TV in front of him. He looked at the pictures on the walls and on the mantel.

Then he drained the glass, put it down, felt at his right hip, pulled his Glock from its holster, and placed it on the table next to him. Close by in case he needed it. His security, or, if he was honest with himself, a way out when he got desperate.

Then he reached for the bottle and his glass again, and, as he had done every night for the last three months, Trace drank himself to sleep.

CLAY

Six hundred miles to the west, Clay was counting his steps. He hit thirteen and stopped walking. He was completely alone, standing in the middle of a small clearing. He turned his head to check. Dark trees all around him, full moon hanging overhead, shining down on him like a floodlight.

He looked ahead. Then he looked over his shoulder, and he drew an invisible line between him and the tree behind him, extending it between his feet and out in front of him until it hit another tree.

He looked to his right and drew another line—from the tree with the broken branch, beneath his feet again, and to his left. Invisible lines crossing at right angles beneath him.

All lined up. He bent down and started clearing away the dirt with his shovel. Careful not to disturb the ground around it. Careful not to make a mess. He dug a hole a foot deep, and then he slowed down, testing with the edge of the shovel, exploring, scraping away dirt. He hit something hard, heard it scrape against the shovel, saw a flash of orange plastic. He dropped the shovel and knelt down to brush away the dirt with his hands.

In the ground in front of him were his two orange 5.3-gallon jerry cans. His escape plan, and a work in progress. The one on the left was full, two and half months of hard work. He left it alone, but he dug around the edges until he could grip the handle of the one on the right. Then he lifted it out, only three-quarters full, its contents sloshing around inside.

He put it on the ground next to him, brushed away the dirt from its lid, twisted the cap open, and Clay was hit by the smell of gasoline. He'd always liked the smell. So he breathed in deep.

Then he took the bag off his shoulders, undid the zip, and pulled out a 10-ounce water bottle filled with a tannish yellow fluid—half his day's gas ration. He undid the cap and poured its contents into the jerry can. He screwed the cap back on, lowered the jerry can back into its hole. He scooped dirt back on top, packing it around its sides, compressing it down. Then he stood up and stomped on it with his boots to make sure it felt like just another patch of dirt.

Almost there, he told himself. Everything was falling into place.

He hadn't been caught yet. All he needed was another week, maybe two. All he needed was another gallon. He could do that. He had to. The way he saw it, he didn't have a choice.

His Yamaha YZ250 dirt bike had a 2.1-gallon gas tank, with a top speed of 75 mph. It wasn't a street racer. Speed wasn't the point—torque and off-road handling were—but its range was its weakness. A full tank would get him maybe eighty miles on the flat; 10.6 gallons would give him 400 miles, if he went easy on the throttle, if he kept the RPMs low...

Throw in hills and the mileage would drop, and that was the problem because standing between him and LA were the Rockies. But that was a problem for later.

He bent down, picked up his shovel and backpack, stood up, and started walking.

But he didn't go straight back to camp. He walked in a big loop, counterclockwise. Like he was patrolling the perimeter, marking his territory. Another habit he'd picked up on the inside. Pacing back and forth. He stopped a few more times, doubled back, kicked up some dirt, dug another hole, took a shit because he needed to and to muddy the trail.

Then he made his way back to his tent up on the hill, in the trees, away from the road and out of the wind. Home sweet home. He had a mirror nailed to a tree, a little table and two mismatched chairs, odds and ends he'd collected over the last two months, pots and pans, creature comforts.

He dropped his pack next to his tent. Got a fire going, rolled out his sleeping mat, laid his rifle across his pack, ate his daily ration of food. Then he lay down next to the fire, crossed his feet, put his hands behind his head, and settled in for the night, gazing up through the gaps in the trees, watching the stars, watching the Milky Way.

He'd never seen it before, not until he came out here. There were no stars in Miami, not like this.

He'd never even left the city before. Not until he went to prison, and then the only thing he'd seen at night was the pitted ceiling of his cell.

By the end of his first year he'd counted every hole in the tiles—3,399 of them. By his second year he'd started naming them. In his third year they'd moved him, and he'd gotten to start all over again.

But that was all behind him now. He was a free man. Prison was nothing but an ugly memory. Clay let out a slow breath, and he started to relax.

Today had been a good day. He'd done his job, his plan was slowly coming together, he was warm, he had a full belly, and he was still alive.

The way he saw it, it didn't matter how much longer for. Didn't matter what he had to do to keep it that way. He tried not to worry about the future too much. Prison had taught him that too.

Why worry about what he couldn't control? It was pointless, a waste of energy. He'd just have to figure it out as he went. He was okay with that. He was a survivor, and, the way he saw it, every new day was a gift.

And with that thought, Clay closed his eyes and drifted off to sleep with a smile on his face.

DAY
1

72 Allée du Furet
Bourg-en-Bresse
France

MASON

"Mason?"

Someone was shaking him.

"Mason, wake up…"

The words slipped into his dreams, and something with too many teeth hissed his name.

"Mason."

Mason came awake with a start.

"What?" he mumbled, tired and groggy. He hadn't slept well; it didn't really feel like he had slept at all.

A storm had rolled in during the night, unusual for the middle of summer, but the sky had been rumbling for hours, thunder booming overhead, windows rattling in the wind, flashes of lightning fracturing the darkness outside. It must have blown down a few trees, too, because through the thunder and the rain he'd heard police sirens all night.

But it was quiet now, except for Claire's breathing. With a tired sigh, Mason opened his eyes to find the room draped in soft shadows as a pale blue light shone from the screen of Claire's phone.

He pushed himself up on his elbows, resting his head in his hands as he rubbed the sleep from his eyes.

"What time is it?"

"Seven."

"Huh?" He turned, his legs tangling in the sheets as he reached for the light.

"Seven," repeated his wife, voice slightly shaken. "They don't work."

"Huh?" he said again. Confused, he flicked the switch, then flicked it back. Nothing.

"The power out?" he asked, flicking the switch again. Still nothing.

"I don't know. Listen, something's wrong. I—"

"It's just a power failure," he said, cutting her off, already lying back down, trying to get comfortable. "Storm must have brought down a tree across the power lines. It'll be fine," he said, eyes closed as he patted her arm, trying to placate her, but mostly just trying to go back to sleep.

"No. Listen to me! Something's wrong… It's not just the power. The phones are down, and I heard noises earlier. Mason, it's seven a.m. Do you hear me? Seven!"

Mason sighed. "So what? It's the weekend. Sleep in while you can."

"No, you aren't listening, Mason. Look outside!"

Mason cracked one eye open, just a sliver. He knew he wouldn't get back to sleep unless he at least humored her.

He looked out the window and his eye opened wider, the sliver becoming a crack. It was pitch-black outside. He opened his other eye and it was still dark. He hadn't really cared earlier, still half asleep, but now… now his brain began picking through the information sinking into his thawing mind.

"Are you sure your phone is right?" he asked, rolling over to look at her.

"I'm certain. I looked at yours too. It's seven a.m. Same as my watch."

Mason felt the hairs on his arms stand up as a slight unease crawled up his spine. He was well on his way to getting worried, and wide awake now too.

"Where's the sun?"

They faced east. One of the best aspects of their house, of this room at least, was waking up to the sunrise. It should be nearly blinding out there, glorious orange light filling the sky, clouds tinged with red, glowing pink. Instead, nothing but a black abyss showed through the half-opened curtains, like they were at the bottom of the ocean. The world outside drowned in ink.

Their bedroom door burst open, crashing against the wall with a bang.

Mason's head snapped around to see a wide-eyed slip of a girl running across the room.

She jumped onto their bed. "Maman!" she shouted. "Mom!" The bed shook as Jessie crawled across the covers, climbing into Claire's lap, little arms wrapping around her mother's neck, pulling herself in tight.

"What's wrong?" asked Claire, worried, trying to see Jessie's face, sharing a look with Mason, trying to calm Jessie down enough to get an answer out of her.

"Jessie? What's wrong?" she asked again, hearing nothing but Jessie's frantic breathing. "Jessie?"

"There's something outside my window," Jessie said in a whisper.

Two hours later, Mason was in the kitchen looking out the window, seeing the dim outlines of people huddled together in the street, moving in pairs or standing still. He watched as their flashlights cast sweeping beams through the misty air and falling ash, catching each other in their light for a second before the darkness rushed back in to claim them.

Mason shivered, and it wasn't just from the cold.

The middle of summer and yet a thin layer of frost clung to everything, coating the grass in white as clouds of vapor swirled in the air and ash fell from the sky. Ash that stank of sulfur and something else, something metallic and bitter. Like every breath he took was rusting on his tongue.

The ash itself was like a haze—incredibly fine, almost like powder—and it was getting into everything, settling on everything. Even with all the windows closed and curtains drawn, it was still getting into the house, blowing in through the cracks in the doors, billowing up through the vents in the floors, stirred up by people's feet, and brought in on their clothes. It left hanging clouds wherever you walked and dull gray halos glowing around the candles in the living room.

He looked down at the little battery-powered radio in his hands, his flashlight held between his teeth as he tried to get it to work. The bowl of cereal he had forced himself to eat only half finished and already forgotten.

Mason was confused. Even with the city's power out, the radios and cell towers should be working. They had to be. They even had their own backup power supplies for when the grid went down. That was the whole point: an emergency broadcast system was meant to work no matter what. But there was nothing except a harsh static hiss across the entire frequency range. AM, FM, every station he tuned in to was nothing but white noise. No announcements, no emergency broadcast, nothing but silence and static, and the silence was worrying the retired soldier in him. A little voice of warning in the back of his head getting louder with each passing hour.

He looked over his shoulder to Claire sitting in the living room, looking relaxed and calm, her face lit by the dim yellow glow of a candle.

They made eye contact, a brief smile passing between them, but the smile never reached Claire's eyes, and he knew then it was all an act. Claire was the type of person who could put on a brave face like it was makeup.

At least we have candles, Mason thought as he watched the shadows dance across her face. Some houses along the street didn't even have that, but Mason liked to be prepared for just about anything, and as a result they currently had six of their neighbors and their scared, sniveling children huddled together in the living room, clustered around three candles on the coffee table. The children were too young to know what was wrong, but old enough to feel the fear and uncertainty in the air. And then there were all the people out in the streets, walking around aimlessly, staring at each other stupidly. As if that would somehow fix it.

He knew the real reason they were out there walking in circles. Fear.

No one had any idea what was going on, no answers, no confidence, no believable lies to offer each other or their families. *No fucking clue at all.*

So helplessness and fear kept them in the streets for now, walking up and down, shining their flashlights into the quiet dark, like children poking a dead thing with a stick. Fascinated, curious, but ultimately useless.

Claire said something to one of the other parents, got up, and Mason watched her walk through to the kitchen to come stand by his side, a small candle cupped in her hands.

"Any luck?" she asked, nodding at the radio in his hand, flickering yellow light dancing across her face, her eyes drowning in shadow.

He shrugged, then shook his head, took the flashlight from his mouth, and hefted the useless lump of plastic in his hand.

"Nothing, and that shouldn't be happening. I don't get it."

Claire looked away, out the window. Watched the people

outside, watched the falling ash that was getting thicker and thicker with each passing hour, like they were slowly being buried in it.

"Claire?"

She didn't seem to hear him.

Mason reached out, cupped her chin, and turned her face back to him.

"It's all going to be okay, Claire, I promise," he said, making her look at him, repeating himself when she just blinked back.

"How do you know? How can you say that? How is this even happening?" she asked, stepping closer, putting a hand on his arm and letting some of that fear and panic leak out in her voice, all the emotions she kept hidden from Jessie. "What the hell is going on? What are we supposed to do?"

"I don't know, but we'll get through this. We'll figure it out, okay?"

Claire nodded once, but he could see she didn't believe him, and the fear remained.

Mason looked at Jessie in the living room, glad to see a small smile on his daughter's lips before he turned back to Claire and put the radio down. The damn thing was a waste of time anyway.

"How is she?" he asked, trying to distract Claire, feeling bad for neglecting them and having nothing to show for it.

"She's better now. She knows something is wrong but is treating this as an adventure more than anything else."

Mason shook his head. He wouldn't exactly call this an adventure.

For the first hour after he had woken up there had been no sound but the wind and the rumble of thunder. No dogs barked, no birds sang, there was no noise but people. Worried voices growing louder while others called out the same names over and over and over.

It had taken Mason a while to realize why. They were looking for their pets.

There wasn't a single animal left on the street. It was as though they had all run away. Just the occasional soft chirp of crickets remained, the dumb things apparently just as confused by the dark as the rest of them were.

There were no lights on anywhere in the city either. At least not in the view he had of it. It was completely dead out there, no stars, no moon, and no sun overhead. It was as though the world simply stopped at the end of their street. If it weren't for the jets flying overhead, Mason could almost imagine they were the last people on Earth.

He could count ten of them in this one narrow slice of the sky alone, jets tracking through the darkness in perfectly straight lines, their red, white, and green navigation lights flashing, all heading in the same direction, all heading for the Swiss border to the southeast.

He couldn't imagine what the ash must be doing to their engines, but their exhaust plumes were enormous, and the constant stream of them made it look like they were watching a meteor shower.

There had been some cars on the streets earlier too. Driving slow, up and down, doing laps. Maybe people looking for help, maybe people who had decided to leave, but he hadn't seen any in a while. There was no sign of the police, no fire trucks, no emergency services. He'd been hearing sirens occasionally, when the wind changed direction, but they were far away, and they'd been blaring for hours.

In the meantime, people stayed indoors, curtains drawn, huddled inside their houses, frightened and confused. All waiting for the sun to appear, for some sort of an explanation, for someone to tell them what to do.

"What are you thinking?" asked Claire.

Mason shrugged. "We need more information, but I get the feeling we're not going to get any answers just standing around here.

I think we've waited as long as we can." He put an arm around her, pulling her close, breathing in her scent, borrowing strength from her as much as she did from him.

"So what do we do?" she asked.

He squeezed her once before stepping away.

"I'm going to go outside and see if I can round up some volunteers to go into town. If the police won't come to us… then we'll go to them. Surely they'll have some idea of what's going on."

"Wouldn't we have heard something already?" Claire asked.

Mason shrugged. "I don't know. I would assume so, but it depends on what's gone wrong. And even if they wanted to let us know… I don't think they can. Something is screwing with the radio. But there has to be a working phone line and some power somewhere, and someone is still out there," he said, nodding out the window to the blinking lights tracking through the sky.

He couldn't make out their markings, but the jets were flying too low and way too fast to be anything other than military. The occasional helicopter trailed behind them, rotors thumping, the whispers and conversations in the living room drowned out until they had passed.

"Surely someone must be in contact with them," Mason said. "And I imagine they have a much better perspective from all the way up there, some idea of how far this goes, what we should do. We need to know if it's safe to stay here, or if we should leave. And if we need to run, then we need to know which way first."

Claire nodded, and Mason turned to leave, but she grabbed his arm.

"Come back soon, okay?" she said, almost pleading, as if she thought he might not come back at all.

"I'll be back before you know it," he promised, giving her a quick kiss before he grabbed his jacket and stepped out into the cold.

"Mason," they said together.

"William, Alec, Thomas," he replied, nodding to each in turn, mere outlines in the dark, flashlights gripped in their bony hands. The neighborhood watch. Grumpy old men with too much time on their hands, but tonight that was proving handy. Tonight they were his eyes and ears.

Lightning flashed overhead, flickering pulses that illuminated the cloud above, its black mass seeming to roll outward in waves, like ripples on a pond.

He'd never seen a thunderstorm like it in his life, lightning coming almost like clockwork. And there was so much energy in the sky; even the air was charged. He could feel the static electricity building up on his clothes, hear it crackle as he moved, feel it tugging at the hairs on his arms and head. Not a good sensation to have with all that lightning exploding overhead.

The men flinched when the thunder boomed again, crowding together and shuffling a little closer toward him, worried wrinkled faces looking to his.

Mason had always found that strange.

Even without the uniform, minus the medals on his breast, six years out of the service and these men still treated him like a soldier. Some trick of psychology, he assumed. People always looked to the soldier in the group when there was trouble, especially when they were afraid. *Or was it that age-old human need to be led, to leave the tough decisions to someone else?* He wasn't sure, maybe a bit of both.

This was well out of their general experience. Well out of his own too, but the dark was threatening, and threat was very much his territory. At least that's how they probably saw it. They knew his past, so these three men looked to him now, waiting for him to tell them what to do.

"Strange day we're having, wouldn't you say?" asked William. *"Non?"*

"Dammit, Will. It wasn't funny the first time or the second.

Give it up already," said Alec, his voice flat, his patience clearly worn thin.

"You tell everyone?" asked Mason, ignoring their bickering.

"Oui," said Thomas. "As many as we could. They should be coming now."

Mason nodded, watching as a few more of those stalking the street began to wander closer.

He waited five minutes, until it looked like no one else was coming. Some twenty people in the end by his quick count.

"Good morning, ladies and gentlemen," he started, barely recognizing a quarter of the faces there. Not that he was surprised. It wasn't the friendliest or most inclusive of streets, even in the best of times.

"Can everyone hear me okay?" He waited for an interruption. "Everyone speak French?" He waited again, but no one stopped him. "Good. So for those of you that don't know me, my name's Mason. I live over there." He pointed behind him. "Now, introductions aside, I'm going to state the obvious first, and then move on. Clearly something has gone wrong. The phones are down, the power is out, and the radios are getting nothing but static. And in case anyone hadn't noticed it yet, the sun seems to be missing."

No one laughed, and Mason kept talking.

"Now, the question is what can we do about it? We've all been waiting for help to come to us, but it doesn't look like that is going to happen any time soon."

Someone started grumbling in the back. "Who the fuck died and made you king?"

"No one," Mason said. "You're welcome to take over if you want."

No one else said anything.

Mason let the silence hang, long seconds ticking by until it got awkward.

He nodded. "Okay. So help doesn't seem to be coming to us,

and we don't know what's going on out there, but we can assume it's bad. If the police could help, I'm sure they would have already. The fact they haven't means they must be busy, and it means we're going to have to help ourselves."

He looked around the group, waiting for another interruption, but no one said anything. They were all waiting for him to speak.

"Here's what I'd like for us to do. Let me know if you have any suggestions or other ideas. I can't think of everything. But first, I need to know if everyone is in this together. Until help does arrive, we're going to have to work as a team. I'm not going to ask much, but if we all help out it will be easier, quicker, and safer for all of us."

Mason tried to look at everyone in the group, bottom-lit faces looking back at him, eyes hidden in darkness, turning his head slowly until they all at least nodded or shrugged back at him.

Good enough.

"First, I need some volunteers, enough for two carloads, and someone willing and able to go for a drive."

"Why?" asked a huddled shape in the back.

"What's your name?" said Mason, following their voice.

"Bernard, bu—"

"Because, Bernard, if help won't come to us, then we're going to have to go to them. We need to know what to do. If we need to leave, then we need to know which direction to go, and we can't make that decision until we have more information. I know some of you probably want to leave right away. But where will you go? We don't know which way is safe, we don't know what's causing this or how far it stretches. Leaving without a plan could only make things worse. So we need to be careful, we need to think this through first. That means I need people to go into town, find the police, and get us some real information. Who's willing to do that?"

A couple of hands went up around the group.

Mason smiled. "Good, thank you. Now remember, it's dark out there. You'll also be navigating from memory and street signs. None of the radios or phones are working, so I'm guessing GPS isn't an option either. You still okay with that?"

Their hands stayed up.

"Okay, you five wait until I'm done with the rest," he said, looking at each of them before turning back to address the group as a whole.

"I need a few more of you, people willing to go for a short walk, just once around the block."

Ten more hands rose into the air, a few hesitant ones as they looked at each other, mostly men in their twenties or mid-fifties. Mason assumed they were probably the ones that had nowhere to be and just needed something to do.

"I want you to go door to door. Anywhere you see people, really. Walk in pairs, walk to the end of the block, then split up and walk one block in opposite directions. Then head back here. I want you to talk to whoever you can. Keep calm and tell them what we're doing. Let them know we're here. Give them my address. And give them clear directions. Remember, nobody has Google Maps anymore. But most importantly, if you can, I want you to gather everyone sitting by themselves and bring them to my house, and Alec's… if you don't mind, Alec?"

Alec shook his head, then raised his hand and waved to the crowd, not sure of Mason's plan but happy enough to follow his lead.

"Now, I'm not saying force them. If they refuse to come, or if they're happy where they are, then leave them. Some will want to stay in their own homes. That's fine. But try to explain the situation, and this is it in a nutshell: right now, we're down to candles and flashlights, and we don't know how long whatever this is will last. We don't know when the lights will come back on. So the more people we have in one house, the less light we need and the less light we waste, which means the longer it will last. Plus, it makes it easier to keep everyone in the loop, especially if we have to leave here in a rush. Got it?"

More nods.

"And tell them to bring warm clothes, blankets, and whatever supplies they can pack. Having us all together also means it's easier for help to find us when it gets here."

"You really think help is coming?" asked someone, sounding skeptical.

"Who said that?" asked Mason.

"I did. Me, Paul."

Mason followed the voice.

Paul looked like he was in his mid-thirties, clean shaven, well dressed.

Mason pegged him as an office worker, an accountant, maybe. Something safe and boring.

"Of course help is coming, Paul. This isn't the end of the world. It might just be taking longer than we'd like," answered Mason. "But whatever has happened is obviously worse or more widespread than we're accounting for," he said, pointing to another jet as it flew overhead. He waited for the sound to fade before he started talking again.

"Clearly some sort of response is already underway, so I'm assuming the police have their hands full. And emergency services always takes a while to get its ass into gear. So for now, it's up to us. Now, who hasn't got a job yet?"

Another five or six hands went up. Paul was one of them.

"I need someone to organize us a convoy. Paul, that's going to be you, if you don't mind?"

Paul's eyes narrowed. He knew he was being manipulated, but he nodded slowly anyway.

Mason smiled at him. "I'm going to leave you in charge of sorting it out. Now if everyone is okay with this, we're going to need some of your cars. We need large sedans, SUVs, or station wagons—people movers. Who owns something like that?"

A few raised their hands, a few mumbled.

"Your cars are going to be our backup plan. If it turns out that we need to leave, for whatever reason, then I want to be able to get as many of us out of here as quickly and as calmly as possible. If you're willing to help, then I need you to talk to Paul once we're done. Give him your name and how many people you can safely fit in your car. Then go home, drive your car back here, and line them up in the street outside my house, nose to tail, and lastly, leave the keys in the ignition and make sure you turn the lights off. We don't need any flat batteries. Yes?"

More nods.

"Paul, I want you to get a headcount once we've gathered everyone we can. Make sure we can fit them all in. If we need another car, find it. Ask around, assign passengers, keep families together, and pack the cars. No wasted seats. I don't want any confusion or dawdling, and I definitely don't want anyone left behind. Got it?"

Paul nodded. "Oui."

"Everyone happy? Everyone understand what you have to do?"

More nods, more puffs of steam.

"Good. Get to it," he said, clapping his hands, and they all scrambled to comply, flashlights bouncing away into the dark. Some turned to talk to Paul, while the rest paired up and started walking toward the nearest houses, where the warm flickering light of candles shone through drawn curtains.

Mason turned to look at the five who still remained, his volunteers willing to go for a drive.

A rugged up couple in their mid-forties wearing matching North Face jackets and three youths. One girl. Two boys, not quite men, late teens, maybe early twenties. Back from university for the weekend probably. One big, one scrawny.

"Sorry, what are your names?" he asked.

"Jean," said the girl, her cheeks rosy with the cold. She looked nervous.

"Vince," answered the boy next to her.

"Michelle's kid?"

Vince nodded.

Mason turned to look at their friend.

"Fabian."

Mason took him in with a glance. Fabian looked solid and heavy, like the prop in a rugby team. He even had the ears for it.

Mason nodded now that he had them placed in his mind. Boyfriend, girlfriend, and the unfortunate third wheel.

"Nice to meet you, I'm Mason."

"Anya," said the older woman when Mason looked at her.

"Francis," said the man next to her, stepping forward to shake hands.

Mason smiled and nodded. Pleasantries aside, he turned back to face the youths.

"I need you three to go to the police station. Do you know where it is?"

"I do," said Fabian, sounding embarrassed.

Mason didn't bother asking why. "I want you to see if anyone is there, find out what you can, find someone in charge, ask them what we should do, and then come straight back here. Think you can do that?"

They nodded.

"Do you have any questions?"

They shook their heads.

"You sure?"

They nodded again.

"Get going, then," Mason said.

He watched them hurry away, wondering what he was sending them into, and secretly hoping real help was on its way, and soon.

Then he pushed the concern away, turned his attention to Anya and Francis. He gave them almost identical instructions, just a different destination.

He told them he wanted them to go to the hospital instead, the Medica France. Hospitals had backup power generators. The whole city might be out, but the hospital's lights should still be on. They might have a working radio, maybe a phone line. A direct line to the outside world, doubling their chances of finding someone with some idea of what the fuck was going on.

CASS

Everyone outside was dead.

All those people in their cars, all those soldiers in the streets, the two paramedics from the ambulance. All gone, past tense.

Jaime, Lena, and Klaus might still be alive. *Might.* But even if they were, they had no idea what was out there. Or why he hadn't come back. He had no way of warning them either, and the hospital would have been a soft target. All those people trapped inside, all those windows. All that glass…

So they were probably dead too. Reese certainly was. Cass had no doubt about that anymore. Nothing was moving out there. Nothing human, at least, which meant he was all that was left from their little group. He had to accept that now, and the guilt hit him like a kick in the ribs.

He closed his eyes and let his head sink to his knees, but he couldn't seem to cry for them; he was numb inside, empty. He shook his head, tried to snap himself out of it. He didn't have time for guilt. Guilt was a wasted emotion, it was pointless. It wouldn't bring them back. It wouldn't change anything. He couldn't feel guilty. *Not now, not yet,* he told himself. Besides, there was still so much to do, and he needed a clear head to do it. And he had tried. He had to remind himself of that. He had done everything he could.

Not that it had made even the slightest bit of difference in the end.

The lights flickered, and Cass glanced up at them warily.

Dim, line-fed lights hung from the fire sprinkler system above his head, their power cables looped and hanging off the crossbeams before slithering down the wall to his left, across the floor, out the door, and all the way back to the generator he could hear stuttering in the garage.

The lights flickered again, a gentle hum tumbling in the air for a moment before the generator's rhythm kicked back in and the lights blazed back to life. Fat bulbs housed in metal cages cast a yellow glare on all the people huddled beneath, and Cass waited for them to fail again. He waited for it to go dark one last time.

Part of him imagined it was like they were on life support. Part of him imagined they were that guy beeping away in some sad, forgotten corner of a hospital somewhere. Only still breathing because of a machine, and he couldn't help but wonder when it would happen. *When do they pull the plug? When will someone put us out of our fucking mis—*

A shadow fell across his face, and Cass blinked, coming back to himself.

He looked around the room in a daze, barely registering the faded posters on the walls, ads for oil changes and car services and discounts on new tires.

His new home and prison for the last twelve hours, the Norauto gas station. A tiny little building crammed with people just like him. Those who had somehow slipped through the gaps. Some from the tour bus he'd seen, families with kids, a few mechanics who'd already been inside at the time, a couple of cops, and anyone else who'd been close enough and fast enough. Some fifty people.

His eyes skipped over the dead flat-screen TV in the corner

and instead followed the two men who had walked in front of him wearing dark blue uniforms and yellow badges on their chests, cradling shotguns in their arms like babies and pistols on their hips.

The one in the lead glanced at Cass, and their eyes met.

Léon was the elder of the two. Somewhere in his early forties, maybe a bit older. It was hard to tell. He looked a little rough, a little worn, and a little overweight. But he seemed to be the one in charge around here, so Cass nodded at him.

A meaningless gesture, but Léon smiled at him anyway, as though everything was going to be okay now, like this was all just a silly mistake, a misunderstanding.

But Léon's smile wasn't convincing. He looked pale, with dark bruises beneath his eyes and a stain on his shirt. One that looked a lot like dried vomit.

Cass looked away. He looked down and noticed his own shirt was unbuttoned, untucked, and covered in blood. He had cuts all over his hands and his pants were torn and stained with grease, and Cass realized he looked just as bad as Léon, maybe worse. So Cass looked up, and he smiled back. Even if it was a lie. He figured the guy needed it.

Someone had said Léon had a family out there. Two kids and a pregnant wife.

They're probably dead by now, thought Cass. And he could tell by the look in Léon's eyes that he thought it too, and Cass's smile faltered. He looked down again, and he tried not to think about Jaime and Klaus and Lena.

He turned his mind to the problem at hand instead: how much longer would the lights stay on, and would they be able to finish the bus in time? It was all that mattered now.

The bus was their one way out of this mess, their one and only escape plan. It was the reason for all the noise coming from the garage, the harsh whine of a pneumatic drill, steel saws cutting, grinding, hammers banging on metal as men worked around the clock. First to repair, then to retrofit the only vehicle capable of carrying this many people to safety and sunlight. *Anywhere but here, really.*

But the longer it took to finish, the more the cloud above their head seemed to grow, the darker it seemed to get, and the more fuel the generator rumbling in the garage consumed keeping the lights on. The longer it took to finish the bus, the less fuel they would have left, which meant the less distance they could cover in it, and no one had any idea how far this madness had spread.

So time was short, but they couldn't rush it either. They needed the bus to be perfect. They needed to turn it into a homemade tank.

Going outside in a normal car was suicide. One look out the window was enough to tell him that, and if they wanted to make it out of here alive, if they even wanted to pretend they might, then the bus was their only ticket out.

The real problem was that nobody even knew if all the armor they were adding would be enough. Maybe it would barely slow those things down. Maybe it was too much. Could the bus even carry that much extra weight?

The other option was to do nothing. To sit tight and wait to be rescued. If they didn't take the bus they could stay here for days. But what then? What if no one came? What happened when the lights failed? No. He shook his head, harder this time. They couldn't afford to wait.

He turned his attention back to Léon and his partner, Michael, watched the men as they moved through the room, checking the blocked exits, the makeshift barricades and boarded-up windows. Their eyes looking down before every step, careful not to step on a leg or a hand.

There were twenty people in this one room alone and a little over twenty in the next. All crammed in on top of each other, in the corners and away from the doors and as far from the windows as they could get. Floor space was limited. Lying down wasn't an option, so people slept sitting up or not at all. They leaned on each other, rested their heads on their knees or on each other's shoulders, their eyes closed. Others had their eyes wide open, staring at nothing.

The lights flickered again, and Cass looked to his right, to the only door that hadn't been welded shut and the semicircle of bare linoleum in front of it. The empty space like a shrine to the mountain of furniture piled high in front of the door, desks and chairs and computer monitors, anything heavy that wasn't bolted down.

They hadn't welded the door shut just in case someone else needed to get in, but no one had come screaming and banging on it in hours, and he doubted anyone else would, which made that door the biggest risk to their safety.

Cass sat up straighter, rubbing the back of his neck and yawning until he thought his jaw would break. He looked at his watch.

It was Saturday morning. He hadn't slept in almost twenty-four hours. He was beyond exhausted. But sleep wasn't an option. He couldn't sleep if he'd tried. He didn't know how anyone could with those things just outside. He could even hear one now, sniffing and grunting as it walked past the window to his left. He could feel the tremors that ran through the ground beneath him with each heavy footfall, hearing the slow stuttering clicks it made as it circled the building, looking for an easy way in.

He looked at the boarded-up window again, seeing the steel rods welded across the frame, the burn marks on the walls from where the welding torch had spat sparks and molten metal. The bars themselves looked flimsy and insubstantial. And he'd seen how strong those things were. What they could do to cars.

And to people.

So what are they waiting for? Why haven't they come for us yet?

The only reason he could come up with was that they didn't like the light. Or maybe they knew some of the men inside were armed. But that suggested a level of intelligence that scared him even more.

He leaned back against the wall, trying to ignore the crying that floated on the air, trying to ignore the sound of people coughing, trying to listen for more sirens or screams outside, and, with a start, he realized he couldn't hear the thing outside anymore.

He listened harder, hearing the wind howl as it clawed at the building, whistling as it slipped through the tiny air vents in the walls above his head. Vents that were crusted with black ice as the ash poured inside, swirling around the lights, settling on everything, sticking to their skin, getting in their eyes and burning.

Cass resisted the urge to rub them. Rubbing them only made it worse.

He ran his finger along the floor, fingertip coming away black like he'd wiped it in soot.

Just what is this stuff, anyway? He rubbed it between his thumb and forefinger, feeling it grate and grind like sandpaper. It smelled strange too, like ozone, that smell you got after a short circuit or an electrical fire.

The garage door opened, and Cass looked up as five men escaped the frantic activity inside, gasping and coughing as they walked past, the stink of burnt metal and exhaust fumes clinging to their clothes.

My turn. Cass looked at his watch one last time before he wiped his hands on his pants and pushed himself to his feet.

That was the other reason he couldn't sleep—he didn't have the time. He still had work to do. Another forty minutes working on the bus before he got another twenty minutes off. Otherwise he'd be overcome by the fumes, and carbon monoxide poisoning was insidious. You didn't even know you were being gassed. You got confused, disorientated, and then you just went to sleep and didn't wake up.

They couldn't leave the generator outside, nothing with an electric pulse could go outside anymore. So they had to keep it running in the garage, its exhaust venting through a hole they'd cut in a wall. But it wasn't perfect. The pipe leaked, and the air inside the garage was hot, hazy, thick with fumes and stirred up ash.

It meant the men working inside had to work in shifts.

He passed Léon in the hall, gave him another empty smile, and then Cass was at the garage door, pushing it open, stepping through and looking at the monstrosity taking shape before him, seeing smoke and blinding white light, sparks flying. Feeling the heat on his face, hearing the boom of steel sheets being hammered flat across the bus's windows as its white paint slowly disappeared beneath steel bolts, messy welds, and char marks.

The lights flickered again, the gas metal arc welder sucking juice from the generator, spitting out a blinding white glare and silhouetting the Frankenstein creation slowly taking shape before him.

It wasn't the largest of buses, about the size of an airport shuttle. Nothing much to look at to start with either, but now... Now it looked nasty and dirty. Like one of those old Russian submarines.

And as Cass gazed at their desperate escape plan, he realized he had never known hope could look so ugly.

MASON

"Mason?"

He turned at the voice, or more its tone.

William stood on the other side of the screen door, inky darkness peeking over his shoulders, his hat held in his hands, twisting it like he was breaking a duck's neck, but Mason wasn't watching William's hands. He was watching his face. More specifically, he was watching William's eyes, and William's eyes were telling him he had something important to say. Something that he couldn't mention, not here. Not where people could hear them.

"Will?" asked Mason.

He had stepped into the kitchen to escape the press of bodies in his living room, but trouble seemed to have found him anyway.

"You got a minute?" asked William softly, his eyes wide. Alarm bells started ringing in Mason's head.

He nodded, picking up his flashlight before gesturing for William to lead the way. He took one last look into the living room, his eyes sweeping the room, looking for Claire, giving her a single, slow nod, his lips pursed. *Trouble.*

Be careful, her eyes pleaded.

He winked. *Always.* Then he turned away and followed William out into the cold. He gave the screen door a nudge and let it swing shut behind him as he fell in next to the old man, their breaths misting in the air, solid clouds of white vapor streaming past their heads as they walked. The frozen grass crunched underfoot, sounding like they were walking on glass, and Mason realized that the crickets had stopped singing.

Their chirping had become so constant he had almost tuned it out, and now in its absence he couldn't help but feel a little unsettled as his flashlight picked out footprints in front of him. Dark outlines like bruises in the white frost as they walked across his front lawn, cutting across the path leading to his front door.

He looked up and realized it was starting to snow, and it was at that moment Mason knew the world had truly gone mad.

"What is it?" he asked, turning to look at William.

William shook his head, just a faint impression of movement in the dark. "We aren't sure." He shook his head again. "Better if you see it first. Better if I just show you."

Mason frowned, looking up as Paul hurried across the street toward them, carrying a lantern above his head, the glowing tube throwing out a diffuse sphere of light all around him, like he was walking in a bubble, dancing across the white frost.

Mason saw other people jogging away through the dark, heading up the road to another house.

"Cars are good to go," Paul said as he fell into step on Mason's right.

"*Merci,*" said Mason.

He'd been watching them getting ready for the last hour, and Paul had done a good job. He had six SUVs lined up in the road, one blue, one red, two silver, one green, and Mason's own boring white Toyota Rav4.

White hadn't exactly been his first choice, neither had Toyota, but it had been on special, ex-demo… and, well, money was tight.

But they were ready, parked nose to tail, lights off. Just how he had asked. There in case they needed them.

"Everyone knows which car they're going in, and we still have space for another three people," said Paul.

Mason nodded. He was happy with the numbers.

Between Alec's house and his own, they had rounded up nearly thirty-five frightened neighbors, and they now also had a mountain of water bottles, candles, batteries, and flashlights. There was a system, there was less waste, there was cooperation, and with it a small sense of calm. But most importantly, the fear had receded somewhat. Not completely, but enough for now. People were talking and almost smiling again.

Another trait of human frailty he had used for leverage. People felt safer together, but William's very palpable fear and worry was quietly poking holes in that illusion.

The man was terrified.

"What's up?" asked Paul, picking up on the mood.

"Don't know," said Mason. "William?"

William didn't answer. He just pointed to five men standing in the dark, all the way at the end of the road, their flashlights all pointed at the same thing. An empty patch of frost-covered grass at their feet and a row of dark trees just beyond.

Mason's warning bells stopped ringing and began to peal, loud and insistent. Three of the men were armed. They looked like hunting rifles or shotguns. Long barrels, too dark to see what kind.

Two of the men turned as they heard them approaching, while the others kept playing their flashlights across the trees.

"Okay, enough with the fucking secrecy. What's the problem? And why are you armed?" asked Mason sharply.

The men shuffled to either side to give him an unobstructed view of the ground in front of them.

"That's why," said William, his voice quiet in the cold, pointing to a flashlight lying on the ground.

"And that," said William, pointing to a discarded double-barreled shotgun and spilled red shells.

Mason looked at the gun. What the fuck is going on?

"And that," said William finally, shining his flashlight on a wide splash of red—blood, a lot of it—scuffs marks, and deep gouges in the dirt where something had been dragged away. Mason followed the bloody smear with his flashlight. Followed it until it disappeared into the trees, seeing strange marks to either side.

"Any idea who?" Mason asked, rounding on William.

"Claude. That's his gun. We go hunting together."

"You go looking for him?"

"Are you mad? I'm not going in there," said William with a sharp shake of his head before looking at the trees.

Mason frowned. "When was the last time anyone saw him?"

William shrugged, the four other men standing in the group looked at each before they turned back to Mason. "Maybe fifteen minutes…? We haven't been walking down this far."

Mason looked around the clearing. He turned back to the street. Most of the houses behind them were dark and empty, but a few still had light shining through curtains and out of open windows. Those that had preferred to stay by themselves. The closest one was less than fifteen meters away, almost directly across the road from them, house glowing like a giant paper lantern.

Mason pointed his flashlight at it.

"You ask them if they saw anything? Heard anything?"

William shook his head. "Nothing. Whatever it was, it was quiet, and it was quick."

"Do you know what he was doing down here?" asked Mason, watching the trees. "Why'd he have a gun anyway?"

"Tracking," they said as a group.

"Tracking?" repeated Mason, thinking he had misheard.

The men nodded. Mason could almost smell the worry wafting off them.

"Tracking. He must have seen the tracks and gotten his gun," said William, louder, more certain this time.

"What are you talking about?" asked Mason.

The men didn't say anything, they just turned and shined their flashlights on a different patch of frozen grass with a distinct set of marks.

Footprints, realized Mason as he looked closer. But strange ones, almost like footprints left by a bird. *Though it would have to be the biggest fucking bird on the planet,* Mason thought. The footprints were enormous, bigger than dinner plates.

The tracks wandered down the side of the road, weaving across the frozen lawns, angling in toward the houses with light shining inside. And next to the tracks were Claude's tiny footprints, still crisp and clear, yet to be covered by the snow that was starting to fall heavier by the minute.

He'd been following something all right. *Or had it been following him?* Either way, whatever it was, he had walked right into it. His footprints ended in the torn-up grass and blood.

"What the hell kind of animal makes tracks like that?" asked Mason.

"No animal," they said as a group, clutching their weapons a little tighter.

Mason looked at them, but they didn't seem to have anything else to offer.

Paul stepped past him, bending down to touch one of the footprints. "What do you mean no animal? What the hell is it then? Bear?"

"A bear is an animal, Paul," said William softly, shaking his head in amazement. "These aren't from a fucking bear."

"So what, then?" said Paul, looking at the trees.

William crouched down, pointing, his fingers tracing along the edges of the marks. "I think its four legged, maybe, kinda like a bear, but I think these are the back feet."

"You think?" asked Paul.

William shrugged. "That's what I'm saying, I don't know what leaves marks like this. It's all wrong. But see here? See the depth? It's heavy, big. Real big. But look here," he said, standing up again and stepping away to point to a slightly different set of marks. Three impressions, but more like round ovals and less like a foot. No claw marks either, but deeper, like they'd been driven into the ground.

"I think these are its front feet. See how they're even deeper? It's definitely carrying more weight at the front. I'm guessing big shoulders, big head. Like it's walking on its knuckles. You ever seen gorilla tracks? You ever seen how they walk?" William hunched himself over in an imitation. "It looks like that, at least to me…"

"So?" asked Paul, still not following.

William stood back even wider, and he pointed his flashlight from one track mark to the other, from left foot to right foot, starting at the ones closest to them and gradually moving away, like it was placing one foot down at time, as though it was padding away from them. Track marks to each side of the red smear where Claude had been dragged away.

And when William did that, Mason could almost see it. A faint impression as his brain filled in the missing pieces and his imagination did the rest. He felt something in his guts squirm because, if he looked at it that way, then this "thing" was five feet across. This *thing* was enormous.

"Fuck. That," said Paul, dragging the words out.

Mason turned to look at him, and he could tell Paul saw it too. He could see the fear in his eyes.

William was right, this was no damn bear. Going after it would be a mistake, and now he understood the guns. He just didn't know if they'd make a difference. Shoot something this big and all they were going to do was piss it off. Mason took a step forward, bent down, and picked up the shotgun, putting the discarded shells in his left jacket pocket before he unlatched the break action and cracked the shotgun open.

It wasn't loaded. Claude hadn't even gotten that far.

"We need to be moving back to the houses," said Mason, standing up quickly and loading two shells into the side-by-side breech. "Now! Quickly, gents," he said before he snapped the shotgun back together with a solid crunch. Then they were moving, a tight group walking fast, their flashlights all pointed outward, beams washing across the houses to either side and shining into the dark gaps in between.

"What do we do now?" whispered William next to him.

"We get everyone inside, keep them away from the windows. We lock the doors, and we sit tight."

"Any idea what it is?" William asked.

"No."

The fact that he didn't know didn't concern him. It was a threat, and judging by the blood splashed across the grass, a very effective one. That was all he needed to operate on. The rest was automatic. *When in doubt, retreat.*

He was also starting to have very real concerns about the two cars he had sent into town. He'd expected them back a while ago, but the road remained dark and empty. And with a growing sense of dread, Mason realized they might not be coming back at all.

It was right about then that the screaming started.

CASS

Cass stumbled from the garage, gasping for air, trying to breathe, the din escaping from the room fading until the door clicked shut behind him.

He put his hand out against the wall, hearing the muted thumps and feeling the vibrations beneath his fingers as the frantic work continued on without him.

"Est ce que vous allez bien, monsieur?"

Cass stared at his feet, fighting the surge of bile in his throat.

"Est ce que vous allez bien?" said the voice again, slower this time, and Cass realized someone was talking to him.

"Huh?"

He looked up to find Michael looming over him. Big, with wide shoulders and a thick neck. Twice Léon's size, half his age, and with none of the hair. More like a bouncer than a cop. And his shaved head glistened with sweat.

"What?" Cass said.

"Are you okay?" asked Michael in English.

"Fine. I'm fine," wheezed Cass, waving him off. But he didn't feel fine at all, he felt like he was about to decorate his shoes.

"Here," said Michael, bending down. He grabbed Cass's arm and draped it over his shoulder before he half-carried, half-dragged Cass down the hall like he weighed nothing.

Cass didn't try to resist; he couldn't. He just concentrated on staying upright, putting one foot in front of the other until he felt cold concrete at his back and Michael told him to sit.

He sank down to the floor with an exhausted sigh, sliding down the wall until his ass hit carpet and he couldn't fall anymore.

Almost there, he told himself as his head started to clear. *Just a little longer until the bus is done.*

He stared up at the lights burning in the ceiling above his head.

"Salut," said a voice.

Cass looked down to find a woman kneeling in front of him, her concerned eyes looking into his.

She said, *"Parles-tu Français?"*

Cass shook his head. "English."

She nodded, and Cass could see her switching gears.

"I'm Elayne," she said. "What's your name?"

"Cass."

"American?" she asked.

"Guilty," he wheezed.

Elayne smiled, and Cass tried to smile back. He liked her instantly. She seemed kind. An older woman, brunette, slowly gathering wrinkles and going gray at the temples. Cass figured she was either too proud or too indifferent to dye it. She wore no makeup, no earrings, no jewelry on her hands except a plain gold wedding band.

"How are you feeling?" she asked.

"Like crap."

He had pegged her as a nurse. The blue scrubs kind of gave it away.

He figured she must have been on her way to work the night

shift, or maybe already on her way home to bed, when everything had gone to hell.

"Let me have a look at you."

Elayne took his right arm and turned his hand until it was palm up, her movements slow but firm. Used to dealing with difficult people, used to getting her hands dirty. Her fingers came to rest on his wrist.

Cass could feel his pulse thumping against them, beating hard, beating fast.

"How long were you in there?" she asked.

He turned his head, lifting his watch to his face and staring at it dumbly, his eyes slipping off the silver dial before he wrestled them back. 12:15 p.m., if he was reading it right. The hands kept moving and blurring together, but if it was 12:15, then he'd been in there for more than an hour. Closer to two. Far longer than he should have. He knew that. He knew it was dangerous, dumb really, and now he felt sick. He could barely breathe, like there was a steel band wrapped around his chest, squeezing, tighter and tighter, and when he coughed it sounded wet.

"How long, Cass?" she asked again.

"An hour," he lied.

Elayne shook her head. "Too long, Cass. You're going to have to stay out here for a while. You need to rest."

"Can't. Have to finish. Have to go back," Cass said.

Elayne let go of his wrist and frowned at him. "If you pass out on us, you're no good either. You understand?"

Cass closed his eyes and nodded once.

"Good," said Elayne. She touched him on the shoulder. "Have a break before you go back, okay? Try to get as much fresh air as possible."

Cass wanted to laugh. Instead, all he did was cough in her face.

What fresh air? The air stank of diesel and fumes, thick with dust and smoke. He could see it swirling around the lights, almost as bad out here now as it was in the garage, and Cass knew he couldn't sit here. Sitting out here didn't achieve anything.

Inside that garage he could still make a difference. Inside that garage he was useful, needed, all his electrical engineering experience coming in handy. Circuit diagrams and math equations scrawled across one of the walls. Lights being installed in parallel in case they lost one. Calculating voltage drops across the different resistance ratings. Running the power from several spare car batteries they had bolted under the front seat. Building in a redundancy system.

He needed to get back in there. It was already taking too long, working with tools he hadn't used in years, under shit conditions, with people he couldn't understand. No. The longer he took meant more delay for people waiting on him, more time lost. The longest he could stay out here was another twenty minutes, maybe, but even that was pushing it.

"How are you, Elayne?" Cass asked, changing the subject, trying to turn her attention away from a pointless argument.

"I'm fine. It's you I'm concerned about. You feeling okay?"

She put a hand to his forehead.

"Just hot," he said, trying not to cough in her face again. "No air conditioning in there, you know?"

Elayne shook her head. "You have a fever."

No, I have radiation poisoning, Cass thought. *And it's going to get worse before it gets better.*

"Elayne?" called someone from deeper in the room.

Cass's head swiveled to see an old woman with her hand up. She looked like she was in her seventies. She looked worried and thin, just skin and bones. The old guy next to her looked even worse; he was breathing too fast and his color was all wrong, lips turning blue, eyes unfocused, skin like paper with a sunken face. As though all the life had been sucked out of him and just the husk remained.

"Excuse me," Elayne said. She got up and tiptoed her way across the room, weaving between the people on the floor.

Elayne crouched down next to them, turning her attention to the old guy, picking up his hand and turning it over, the same way she had Cass's.

She said something. The old guy nodded, and Elayne let go of his wrist. She touched him on the shoulder and said something else, something meaningless, Cass imagined. Something to put them at ease.

Elayne smiled. The old woman smiled back, and Cass saw her relax. The old guy nodded again. He saw their lips move, and Cass filled in the gaps.

You're doing well, Elayne said with a smile. *We'll be out of here soon.*

But to Cass, the old timer didn't look good at all. He doubted he'd survive the night.

A small part of him doubted any of them would.

MASON

They burst into action. Mason quickly outpaced William and the older men. Only Paul kept up with him, the two of them running toward screams that didn't even sound human. A single piercing sound full of pain, like a dog getting hit by a train, a meaty hit, and then the sound of flesh tearing and bones breaking.

He heard another scream, the sound muffled, coming from inside a house down the road, and people started pouring out into the street, stumbling to a halt, their heads all turned toward the noise.

He shouted at them, waved at them to get back inside, but nobody listened. They just stood there, gawking like idiots, getting in his way, forcing him to weave between them.

Mason heard a gunshot. He saw the muzzle flash, curtains glowing bright white in the dark like a photograph.

He kept running, his legs pumping, shotgun cradled against his chest, Paul only a step behind. They were almost at the house, the screams coming from inside were louder now.

Another gunshot rang out, glass splintering, gunshot drowning out the screams, and Mason saw a shadow thrown against the curtains. Man or woman he couldn't tell. *BOOM.*

Three shots, he had counted. He didn't know what kind of gun it was, just that it was loud, with a slow rate of fire. Could be a shotgun or a hunting rifle. Either way, it didn't seem to be working.

He heard a high-pitched shriek, muffled by distance and the walls still between them.

BOOM. Something else flashed against the curtains. It looked wrong, moved wrong. He didn't have time to wonder why, he didn't slow, but he heard others behind him gasp.

BOOM. The shape moved again, hunched and twisted, and Mason heard another scream, a man's voice, desperate. His scream became a gurgle.

The whole street turned and ran, tripping over each other in their rush to get away.

Mason surged up the steps to the patio two at a time, his boots thudding on the wooden deck, his heart in his throat, running straight at the door, yelling in fear, in anger. A primal attempt to sound bigger, scarier, meaner. He sucked in one last breath and launched himself at the door, left foot anchored, right foot driving through like a battering ram. Only idiots used their shoulder.

Wood splintered, and the door flew open, crashing against the wall, its stained-glass inserts detonating, small fragments bouncing off his face as Mason kept moving, and his training took over.

Breaching a room was all about speed. Number two through the door is normally the first one shot, once the shock is over and reaction times kick in. It's better to go first, better to be fast. Luck plays a part too, both good and bad.

Mason slipped.

His legs disappeared from under him, eyes going wide in surprise, ears filled with clicks, his arms flailing. The back of his head cracked against the floor and a white pulse flared behind his eyes as pain lanced through his skull. His flashlight spun away from his nerveless fingers, his shotgun smacked against the ground, and something heavy blurred through the air above him. It passed through the space he had just been in. The air seemed to vibrate in front of him and his ears filled with a high-pitched screech.

Something clawed at him and Mason screamed. He rolled with it, his mouth wide, clutching his chest, his hands catching in torn clothes and wet flesh. He looked to his right, just in time to see the kitchen window explode out into the garden as a blur jumped through it.

He could hear people at the front of the house screaming, shouts of alarm ringing out, shouts getting closer. But inside, it was quiet, just a ringing echo in his ears and a strange gurgle coming from behind him. Mason rolled over with a groan, pushing himself to his hands and then his knees, hissing through his teeth, fumbling for his shotgun, using it as a crutch, pushing himself to his feet, grunting as he felt a pain spreading across his chest. He swore as the pain doubled him over and threatened to take him straight back down to his knees.

"Fuck me," he wheezed, blinking against the black clouds gathering in the corners of his eyes.

He forced himself to breathe, sucking in air, black edges receding until he didn't feel like passing out anymore.

He turned his head and saw a pair of twitching feet, heels drumming on the floor. Paul was flat on his back, hands clutching at his neck, gurgling with nothing but a ragged mess of flesh where his throat used to be.

Paul's feet stopped moving, and Mason knew he was dead. He stared at Paul's corpse until he heard boots thumping up the stairs behind him and the rest of the men burst through the door. They skidded to a halt when they saw Mason, eyes going wide when they saw Paul and the puddle beneath his head.

William bent down, but he stopped himself halfway, hand in midair. There was nowhere left to even check for a pulse.

"What the fuck was that? Did you see that? Did anyone else

fucking see that?" shouted one of the other men that had followed them in. He peered over William's shoulder, taking a step back when he saw Paul. "Holy shit!"

Mason didn't answer. He was looking at his hand, fingers dripping red where he had touched it to his chest. He looked down at the blood soaking into his shirt, flesh parted by a six-inch gash, muscles pulled to either side.

"Shit," he said, putting pressure on it. Pushing harder when it didn't stop bleeding.

"Shit," he said again.

The house grew still, filled only with the labored breathing of frightened, winded men. And a smell. The sharp odor of something raw and rank, something burnt. Like meat that had been cooked in diesel.

William shined his flashlight on Mason, and Mason looked down at the trail of blood he had slipped in. Red smeared across the floor, splattered across the walls. His eyes followed it back to its source, thick and dark, pooling beneath a headless woman's body. *Whose house was this?*

His mind working slowly as he looked at the corner of the living room, where a man lay crumpled and twisted, as though he had been trying to protect what was left of a pair of legs. *A child? A little girl*, Mason realized when he looked closer.

The man's guts trailed across the floor behind him, as though he had tried to crawl away after being eviscerated.

Mason turned; it still hadn't clicked. Not until he looked at the fireplace, not until he shined his flashlight on the family photographs.

He looked back at Dan's body, the dead man with his guts hanging out. Then to Erin's, his wife, minus her head, and to what was left of their daughter, Céline. He had no idea where the rest of her was.

Mason turned and threw up—a wet splatter of curdled milk

and brown cereal—across the floor, just a little more mess.

He leaned on his gun, grabbed his knee to steady himself.

"Mason?"

"Get everyone in the cars!" he hissed and spat.

"Mason?" one of them asked again.

"Now! We leave now!"

No one moved.

"GO! Fucking move!"

That got them going, men jostling each other in their haste to all fit through the door at the same time.

William stepped forward and grabbed Mason under the arm, walking him out of the house and helping him down the stairs. The two men stumbled to a stop when they noticed a faint orange glow seeping into the air to the west of them.

Fire, thought Mason. Something was burning out there, and whatever it was, it was going up fast. The sky was getting brighter and brighter.

The dark was interrupted by an enormous explosion. The whole night was suddenly bathed in blinding white light as a huge fireball belched into the sky, curling in on itself as it climbed higher and higher, getting darker, orange turning black as the fireball ran out of fuel.

The shockwave hit them a couple of seconds later; it knocked people to their knees, shattered windows, and set off car alarms all down the street, their indicators flashing yellow as the sirens wailed.

"What the hell was that?" shouted William, trying to be heard over all the noise, the screams, the rumbling echo.

Mason didn't know. He shook his head, still seeing the afterimage of things flying through the air.

"You okay?" asked William.

"Can you drive?" Mason said, leaning on him, feeling woozy, black edges growing in the corner of his eyes.

I need to stop the bleeding.

"You okay?" asked William again, his voice full of panic.

Mason shook his head. "You're going to have to drive, Will. I don't think I can."

It was taking everything he had just to stay on his feet.

CASS

He felt the ground shudder beneath his feet as bits of burning metal soared through the sky like missiles, trailing smoke as they spiraled back down to Earth.

"*Merde!*" Léon shouted as he pushed in on Cass's left, his voice nearly drowned out by the rumbling roar outside and the screams behind them. People trampled each other in their rush to get away from the windows while only a few stepped closer, like Léon and himself.

"*Baise-moi!*" Léon swore.

Cass agreed.

"Fuck me!" was right. The explosion had scattered flaming debris a mile wide, and where the explosion had been, a whole city block was burning.

Léon grabbed the walkie-talkie clipped to his left shoulder, tucking his chin to talk into it.

Cass heard more French and less swearing this time.

"What happened?" demanded Léon, dropping into English and turning back to look at him. "Did you see anything?"

Cass shook his head.

The fire was already spreading, jumping from building to building, growing impossibly fast. Something big had gone up, something highly flammable.

Fuel truck? Another gas station?

Léon grabbed his walkie-talkie and spoke into it again.

More French. Faster this time, a little more desperate, then in English.

"This is Officer Léon Perrin at the Norauto service station on Boulevard Charles de Gaulle. Please copy if you can hear me. Can anyone hear me? Is there anyone out there? Over."

"Aidez-moi!" screamed someone behind them.

They both spun, thinking the worst, thinking those things were inside, but all Cass saw was a room full of petrified faces staring back at him. He looked down and noticed the old couple on the ground. The old man wasn't moving, and his wife was kneeling at his side, shaking him by the shoulders, screaming in his face. She looked up, turning to the room, frantic.

"Elayne!" she cried when nobody did anything but stare.

Léon turned his back on her, back to the orange glow outside, still muttering into his walkie-talkie.

Cass pushed himself away from the window.

Watching the fire solved nothing. Whatever was happening outside was already over; it was out of his control. The only thing that mattered right now was the bus and whatever else happened inside these walls. And right now, there was someone who needed help.

Elayne appeared on his left, pushing her way through the door and the people trying to go the other way. Away from the screams and the bodies they could see lying on the floor. Those who had been stepped on or knocked down, people groaning and hugging trampled fingers to their chests.

He could feel the panic building, and he knew they needed

to control this soon or it would become a stampede. One with nowhere to go.

"Léon!" he shouted, trying to be heard above the noise.

Léon glanced over his shoulder.

Cass jabbed two fingers at his own eyes before he pointed at the press of bodies trying to get out the door. *Do something!*

Léon looked at all people pushing and shouting. He looked at the people rolling around on the floor, and he pushed away from the window with a tired nod.

Cass turned to find that Elayne already had her fingers pressed to the old guy's neck, feeling for his pulse and finding none. She leaned closer, putting her ear to his mouth.

"What can I do?" he shouted. He heard another series of explosions, these smaller.

Elayne shook her head and grabbed the front of the old man's shirt and ripped it open, sending buttons spinning away across the floor.

"Heart attack," Elayne said matter-of-factly. She turned to the group of people huddled in the corner and shouted something at them in French.

She had to say it twice more before one of the men pushed himself away from the wall and forced himself out the room.

The old guy's wife reached forward and grabbed Elayne's arm.

The only word he understood in a sentence of unintelligible French was "Elayne." The rest was just noise, words tumbling over themselves in the rush to get out of her mouth. He could see her pulse fluttering in her temple, her skin so thin he could see the red and blue veins beneath.

Elayne said something back before she leaned over the old guy, tilted his head back, checking his airway before her fingers pinched his nose shut. She cupped his chin with her other hand, put her lips over his, and breathed out, forcing air into his lungs.

Cass watched his chest expand like a balloon, ribs pushing

through pale skin dotted with gray hairs and a long red scar that split him from sternum to belly button.

Open-heart surgery, Cass figured, and he felt the old man's chances slip even further.

Elayne breathed out again, then she sat back, putting her hands on his sternum. She began to pump, arms locked, bending from the hips, using her own weight to drive her hands down into his chest.

One, two, three, four, Cass counted. All the way to thirty, steady, no rush, no panic. Just calm experience at work. The old man's chest denting and bouncing beneath Elayne's hands until it looked like it would cave in, hard enough that Cass thought she was going to break his ribs.

Elayne leaned forward to breathe into his mouth again before she switched back to pumping, her lips moving as she counted beneath her breath.

"What can I do?" asked Cass again.

Elayne shook her head. Her mouth opened to say something, and that's when the old guy's wife decided to join him on the floor.

You have got to be kidding me.

"*Merde!*" swore Elayne, caught between the two of them with only one of her.

"Do you know CPR?" she shouted at him, lifting her head to scan the room like she was waiting for something.

For what? A defibrillator? It's the only thing that would make a difference at this point. *Would they even have one here?* Maybe they had to. Maybe it was law, or whatever passed for workplace safety around here.

He'd read a statistic somewhere on that once, the survival rate of heart attacks without defibrillators, some frighteningly low number, but he couldn't remember what it was. *Reese.* Reese would know, no doubt. He used to love pulling out these random bits of useless informa—

"Wake up! Do you know CPR?" she shouted at him again.

"Yeah," he said, moving closer.

"Take over from me! I'll take care of her. You ready?"

Cass nodded.

"Okay," said Elayne, still bouncing up and down. "He needs air in four, three, two, one."

Cass leaned forward, his own heart beating fast enough for two people, trying to remember lessons learned in calm conditions, under bright lights, and in air-conditioned meeting rooms.

He pinched the old guy's nose shut, covered his mouth with his own, and then he realized several things. CPR on a real person is not the same as a plastic doll. It isn't a test. There's no score out of 100 or a certificate at the end. It's not like in the movies. You do it or they die, and he had never understood the mentality of people who wouldn't help. He'd never been the type to just stand by and watch. So he ignored the sour taste of bile and the bitter tang of blood in his mouth. He didn't even stop to think about it. He just concentrated on breathing out. One hard, full breath, lifting his head to suck in more air, then another, watching the old guy's chest expand out of the corner of his eye.

Cass sat back. He put one hand down on the old man's sternum, the other on top of it, and he began to pump, up and down, arms straight, using his legs and his body weight to do most of the work. He counted to thirty in his head, feeling the ribs buckle and flex like he was giving CPR to a bird. The bones were thin and brittle beneath his hands, like they were made out of air. Cass crushed the worry down. *Better a broken rib than dead.*

He let himself get lost in the repetition. He let the process take over, counting in his head, leaning forward, pinching the nose, cupping the chin, tilting the head back. And he breathed and he breathed, again and again, counting to thirty, and again, until the sweat dripped from his face and his arms burned, hearing his own ragged breathing, the old guy's body rocking back and forth beneath him, muscles slack and dead.

It's not working, Cass realized, seeing Elayne's frantic efforts next to him. But he kept going. Rule one of CPR: don't stop, even if it seems hopeless.

Then he heard a new noise. But it came from outside. It sounded like cars, the roar of the engines getting louder, and he was nearly knocked over as everyone ran for the windows.

Cass leaned over the old guy's prostrate body, trying to protect him as best as he could. He caught a knee to the side of his head, then someone stepped on his leg. He saw someone else step on the old man's hand, and he heard bones snap.

Idiots.

He didn't care what was happening outside; it wasn't important. And just like the fire to the north of them, whatever was happening outside was already over. Because whoever was in those cars was as good as dead.

They just didn't know it yet.

MASON

Mason could feel the heat through the windshield. Fires so hot the road was starting to melt in front of them, black asphalt bubbling like tar as row upon row of houses went up in flames to either side of them.

"Don't slow down!" Mason shouted when he felt William's foot ease off the gas. "We have to get away from this!"

William nodded, leaning forward, his knuckles turning white.

Mason was pushed back in his seat as they accelerated, their headlights turning the smoke blowing across the road into a wall of shifting gray, reducing their visibility to less than three car lengths.

They were driving blind, but they didn't have a choice; slowing down wasn't an option. They were only just staying ahead of the fire, and if they slowed down now they might get trapped between the fire and whatever killed Paul.

"Which way?" shouted William.

"Take a right at the end of the street. Take us south."

Mason grunted as William yanked the wheel to the left, swerving around a mangled car that emerged from the glowing haze, its doors ripped off and windows shattered.

Mason gripped his door handle tighter, his left hand pressed to his chest, shotgun clamped between his knees as he tried to keep pressure on his wound, unable to tear his eyes from the road as smoke poured in through the car's air vents, thick black smoke that stank of burning wood and plastic.

"Take the 1075 all the way round town, then a right onto the Jules Ferry. We need to get on the D1083. That will take us to Lyon."

"Why Lyon?"

"Becau—"

William yanked the wheel to the right, missing another car by inches, and Mason was thrown to the side.

He heard Jessie scream behind him. He felt his seat belt bite into his chest, and the pain took his breath away. He saw nothing but darkness and stars, his ears humming as little white dots swam in the air in front of him.

Mason sucked in a ragged breath as he watched them fade.

"Sorry!" shouted William, and Mason blinked, turning to look in his passenger mirror, counting all the headlights chasing them.

Five. Still five. Good, he told himself. They hadn't lost anyone. The cars behind were still following their lead, weaving from side to side as they dodged all the obstacles in the road—barricades, bits of metal, shredded cars.

Mason glanced down at his chest, gritting his teeth as he peeled away the blood-soaked cloth, grimacing as his flesh parted like wet lips. He saw the white of his ribs smiling through the gap, and Mason knew that nothing short of stitches was going to fix that lopsided grin.

"Shit…"

It was bleeding again, and another wave of dizziness washed over him. It felt like he was in a tunnel, colors muted, light fading, noises echoing and bouncing around him.

No! He fought it, concentrated on staying awake, concentrated on his breathing, concentrated on the road ahead.

"Why Lyon?" shouted William again. He wrestled with the steering wheel, making short, sharp movements left and right.

Mason pressed his feet into the floor, trying to stop himself from being thrown around. *Why Lyon?*

Because Lyon was south, and they couldn't go north. Something big had exploded up north, and Mason didn't want to go east. The cloud above their heads seemed to be coming from there. So south it was, and then west.

"Because the Mont Verdun Air Base is in Lyon," he said. "If there's going to be any military response, it will come from there."

Plus, all the other roads seemed to be blocked off, and he didn't have a better idea.

Mason fumbled for the lever on the side of his chair, his numb fingers skipping off it once before he found it again and pulled it up.

He had quickly discovered a shotgun wasn't ideal for aiming inside a car. Not one-handed, not when the car was moving so much. Not when every movement ripped his chest apart, and not when the gun had a barrel nearly three feet long. So he leaned his seat back like he was going to take a nap. He held the shotgun across his chest and aimed it up at the window.

"It's clearing up!" shouted William.

The engine growled, and they surged ahead, finally pulling free of the fire and blinding smoke, and from his new angle Mason watched it grow dark outside. He watched the red glow of the fires die away, no longer all around them, just a warm orange glimmer to either side before dimming to yellow somewhere far behind them, their headlights reflecting off flakes of falling snow and ash like they were flying through space. And Mason noticed something else.

A star bigger than all the rest, growing brighter, expanding fast as they picked up speed, and Mason realized it was the Carrefour gas station and, next to it, the Norauto service center.

Its lights were on, and for a split second, through one little window, Mason got the briefest glimpse of people. Their faces pressed to the glass as they watched them drive past. Then they were gone.

William took the next right and they were on Jules Ferry Boulevard, racing past a line of abandoned cars, their headlights still on. William took a left at the end of the road and they were on the D1083. Almost home free.

Mason turned to look behind them, but his eyes met Claire's instead, and time stopped.

For a brief moment it was just him and her, a little bubble sucking them away, Claire's wide eyes looking into his, her face pale and afraid in the reflected light of the car's dash. He wanted to tell her it was going to be okay. He wanted to reach out and touch her, but something hit them from the left and the bubble popped.

It hit them hard, two separate impacts, like a one-two punch, and the SUV shuddered. And then they were hit again from the other side. The right rear passenger door buckled inward, and glass sprayed through the car. Mason heard Claire scream as the curtain airbags deployed above her head.

William flinched away from the noise, tugging the steering wheel to the right and aiming them straight at a tree.

"Fuck!" William yanked the wheel in the opposite direction. He overcorrected, and the SUV swung back to the left, its high center of gravity pulling it off balance, swaying on soft suspension, tires squealing as the back kicked out. And then it all went to shit.

"Papa!" Jessie screamed behind him as they began to fishtail.

Mason ignored her. There was nothing he could do but hang on.

William spun the steering wheel back, battling to regain control as the car bucked and swayed, his arms straining.

Fuck, fuck, FUCK!

"Daddy!"

Something came through his window in a spray of glass. An

arm, Mason realized, its flesh pale white and pulsing black, swirling snow sucked in after it as it reached for him. Curved black claws as long as his hand, like meat hooks.

He unclipped his seat belt and threw himself sideways, and its claws caught nothing but air.

"MASON!" screamed Claire.

"Get down!" Mason shouted as its arm slashed right, claws tearing through the back of his chair.

It roared in frustration and pulled its arm out, and for a single heartbeat Mason saw nothing but blurring snow and empty darkness before its head came through the hole. Thick, knotted veins standing up on maggot white flesh. And teeth. Mason saw teeth. Row upon row of serrated knives glinting as its lips peeled back.

Oh, God, what is that?

It forced its way in, clinging to the side of the car as they swerved across the road, clicking and chattering as it kept pushing, but its head got caught on the edges of the door frame, and it got stuck.

It grunted and snarled, metal groaning as his door deformed. The thing's head slid forward another inch.

"MASON!"

Mason pulled his shotgun up. He jabbed the twin barrels in under the thing's chin and pulled both triggers.

The face disappeared in a spray of lead and shredded flesh as blue blood splattered across the windshield. It sprayed in his face. It got in his eyes, in his mouth. Mason gagged on it. He tried to spit it out but vomited instead.

"I can't see!" screamed William, frantically wiping the windshield in front of him, the car filled with a thin blue mist and the stench of rotting meat. "I can't see, dammit!"

The SUV swerved to the left and Mason was flung against his door, its hard edge caught him in the side while his head whipped through the empty window.

He saw darkness. He saw ground. He felt freezing air tearing at his face as white snow and trees whizzed by, so close he could hear the *thump, thump, thump* as their trunks tore past his head.

The SUV changed direction and Mason found himself back inside, his face numb from the cold and his ears filled with screams. He felt the car roll beneath him as it swung to the right and lifted slightly off the suspension.

"Mason!"

They're working together.

He could almost see them, gray blurs rushing out of the dark, throwing themselves at the SUV with angry snarls.

They're trying to tip us over, he realized with a sick lurch as the SUV lifted up on two wheels. He felt gravity pulling at him, felt himself sliding sideways as the car teetered on the edge. All it needed was another tap, a nudge.

The car behind them simply beat them to it.

He saw it pass that point of no return. And then it began to roll, slowly at first, a casual flip, a pirouette, like it was dancing. It kept going, headlights spinning, getting faster, going airborne as it spiraled off a bank. He saw someone's body ejected through a window, rag-dolling end over end before disappearing into the dark. The car began to come apart, still spinning, shattered glass flying, body panels and dirt flung into the air before it slammed into a row of trees with a hollow crunch.

The attack on their car ceased. The blurs peeled away to either side, calling to each other as they went, strange shrill clicks fading away into the dark.

William yanked the steering wheel to the right and brought their SUV back down on all four wheels with a tortured smash.

"Go!" Mason screamed, pulling himself back into his seat, his heart thumping as he started to reload, spent shells popping up as he cracked the shotgun open. He pulled them out one at a time, brass ends hot, his hands shaking, numb fingers not responding. He slid a new round home, reached for another. The car swerved to the right, and he dropped it. He felt it roll past his feet.

Mason pulled another shell from his pocket.

Don't fucking drop this one, he told himself, and he forced himself to go slower. He slid the shell home, snapped the shotgun closed, aimed it back at the window, and he waited.

He could hear the roar of the engine, the howl of the wind, Claire screaming his name, Jessie crying, and he could hear William's wife praying loudly in the back seat.

Mason ignored them, tuned them out. He needed time to think. *What do you know of your enemy?*

They're big.

What else?

They're fast.

What else?

They're invisible.

No, but nearly. Think harder Mason.

They're wearing camouflage.

Good, slow, but you got there in the end. What else?

We got ambushed.

So?

Those things were waiting for us, just beyond the fires.

So why is that important? Think, Mason. What are you missing?

His brain began picking through the pieces, clutching at straws, connecting the dots.

We only got attacked as soon as we were in the dark.

And?

Mason turned to look at Claire as understanding struck him like a lightning bolt.

"It's the light!"

Claire looked at him like he'd gone mad.

"The light! Turn on all the flashlights. Shine them out the windows."

"Why?"

The car bounced, and Mason hissed as he lost his balance again. "No time. Just do it! Now!"

She nodded, and Mason looked at William's wife.

"Yvonne! Lights!"

She ignored him, eyes squeezed shut, hands clamped together hard enough to bend steel.

"Yvonne!" Mason screamed at her.

Yvonne's eyes snapped open.

"Turn your flashlight on!"

Mason looked back at his window, his breath misting before him for a second before it was sucked away. He risked a glance to his left through the dark, blood-splattered windshield, and he saw an orange glow ahead of them. Fire.

Another one?

He could see the tips of flames licking hungrily at the sky, only a block away, coming up on their left and coming up fast.

Mason pointed ahead. "Go faster, Will! Aim for that!"

"Daddy!"

He looked at Jessie. She reached for him, her little hand desperately trying to touch him.

Mason looked away. *Not now.*

"Give me another flashlight!" he said, wedging his in his headrest, aiming it out the window and into the darkness.

The car swerved again.

Mason grunted. The shotgun was getting heavy, or he was getting weak. Either way, the barrel dipped, gravity dragging it down until it was pointed at the door.

He groaned, pain tearing through his chest as he dragged it back up, his ears filling with a low hum as the world dimmed.

Mason sucked in a breath and looked behind them, seeing Alec's BMW right behind them, counting the cars still following. *Only three? When did we lose the other one?*

He saw lights blossoming within, flashlights turned on, aimed out of the windows, beams stabbing out into the dark on every side as the idea caught on.

"Go! Go! Go!" Mason shouted, turning back to the front.

Hard, hollow thuds slammed into the side of the car, and they lurched to the right.

"They're back!" screamed Claire.

Something hit them again.

The SUV started to vibrate, steering wheel shuddering violently in William's hands, and Mason heard the *thwup, thwup, thwup* of a flat tire.

"Mason!"

"We're okay! We're okay!" Mason shouted, fumbling with the shotgun, losing his balance as the car shuddered again.

"PAPA!" Jessie shrieked.

"MASO—"

It came through the back window, mouth wide open. Air filled with glass and shrill clicks. It pulled itself over the back seat, cut through Claire and Jessie like it was made out of knives. It crushed Yvonne's head with one hand. Ripped out William's throat with another.

And as it came for him, all Mason saw was its teeth.

DAY
91

217 Summers Street
Lexington
Tennessee, USA

SARA

Sara pulled the curtain to the side, peering outside to see the night sky turning the softest shade of indigo, twinkling stars fading one by one as dawn's light slowly painted over the cold darkness of space.

"They're here."

Trace's Ford Explorer sat out in the middle of the road, silent and still, lights still on, engine turned off. His repainted car was almost invisible beneath two cans of black paint.

The original paint job of Trace's Tennessee HP state-issued Ford had posed a bit of a problem. It had screamed cop, and that wasn't a good thing to be anymore, but it was the perfect car for the job. All-wheel drive, terrain management, heavy-duty brakes. And it had a 3.5-liter twin-turbocharged EcoBoost V6 instead of the more common naturally aspirated 3.7 liter the rest of the Highway Patrol drove.

It was big and fast and fuel efficient, and it could stop on a dime. Perfect, they had all agreed. Just the wrong color.

So last night they'd gone about disguising it, and now, beneath all that black paint, it looked mean and nasty, just another patch of darkness. "The Batmobile," as Drew had christened it when they were done.

She could see the two men sitting inside easily enough though, dome light on above their heads, one side of their faces lit by its faint glow.

"They coming inside?" asked Ian from their bedroom, his voice muffled by the walls between them.

Sara watched a moment longer, frowning before she let the curtain fall back.

"Doesn't look like it."

Trace and Drew weren't moving. They didn't even seem to be talking. Drew was staring straight ahead, and Trace still had both hands on the steering wheel, like they were glued to it.

Sara walked out of the living room, taking a right into the hallway.

"Ready to go?" asked Ian, his boots tapping on the wood floor. He held a small kerosene lamp in his left hand, its yellow light filling the hallway as he walked toward her.

She nodded. She even tried to smile. Ian's smile wasn't convincing either.

Are you sure you still want to do this? his eyes asked her as his hand came to rest on her hip.

And for a moment Sara almost said no. She almost chickened out. But she kept her mouth shut, bit back the terror. She buried it deep, and the moment passed.

Ian gave her a quick squeeze and he kept walking, stepping around her, stopping to blow out the lamp, placing it on the table in the foyer, then bending down to pick up two bags off the floor, slinging one over each shoulder before turning to face the door.

Sara watched him come to a stop. She watched him grip the handle, breathe in once, and with a big breath out he pulled the door wide open and stepped outside. And just like that, they were committed.

She watched him walk toward Trace's car, her husband blending in with the gloom until it was just his hands and the side of his face that she could see, white and pale in the gathering light before he disappeared around the back.

They'd thought about it a lot over the last two days. Standing out, blending in. Camouflage, mostly for the car, but also for themselves. Even the roads they were going to take and the bikes they needed to bring for when they ran out of gas.

They had spoken about how far they thought they would make it before that happened. The problems they might have along the way. Everything from this point on was about going unseen and avoiding people. The fewer people they ran into, the fewer chances of something going wrong.

They'd been planning and preparing for two days, and yet Sara still had this terrible feeling that they were forgetting something, that *she* was forgetting something. So she hesitated, her eyes bouncing from one dark room to another. Looking at the pictures hanging on the walls, the home they had built, all the memories they were leaving behind.

They had all the gear they could feasibly carry. She knew she wasn't forgetting anything physical, but that terrible sense of unease refused to leave, and she had the sinking sensation that no matter what they did, no matter how well they had planned, something awful was going to happen out there.

In fact, the planning and packing had taken so long that it wasn't until nine p.m. last night that they had even gotten around to working on Trace's car. They had unbolted the cage from the back and stripped the red and blue light-bar from the roof before scraping off the stickers and decals. But they had left the gun rack and comms station between the driver and front passenger seats, as well as the bull-bar on the front and the antennas on the roof.

"Bull-bars are a bonus," Trace had said. "You never know when you might need to ram something."

They had painted the car last.

Sara looked down at her hands. She still had black smudges and hard, dried drops of paint from where she'd gotten sloppy, dark smudges against the pale white of her skin, paint she didn't have the time to wash off.

She caught herself staring at them, noticing how her fingers were shaking slightly, just a tiny tremor.

Please, God, she prayed, closing her eyes. *Let this be the right thing to do.*

Sara opened her eyes again, took a deep breath, and bent down to pick up her AR-15 from where it was leaning against the wall. She grabbed one of the bags they'd packed for the kids and followed Ian out into the retreating dark, walking quickly across the dead grass of their front lawn, kicking up puffs of dirt beneath her boots as the birds started to wake up all around her. She wondered how long it would be before the Cloud drove them out too.

She opened the left passenger door and dropped the bag in the footwell.

"Morning, boys," she said, leaning in and laying her AR-15 across the back seat.

Sara stopped dead, struck by a familiar but almost forgotten smell. Her head turned to follow her nose.

"Is that...?"

"Coffee?" answered Drew, turning to look at her, a fleeting smile on his lips, the flash of teeth barely visible through his beard.

"How?" asked Sara, staring at him.

She hadn't had coffee in months, she couldn't even remember what it tasted like. *But the smell.*

Drew shrugged. "I've been saving a jar just in case. Want some?"

"Just in case what?" she asked, dumbfounded. She held up her hand and shook her head. "Never mind. Thank you, Drew, yes, I'd love some. Just let me get the kids loaded in first."

Drew nodded, fleeting smile filling out, grinning wide. He almost looked like he was enjoying this.

Sara didn't know whether to be surprised or not. More than half of the gear and food they would be using was his. It was almost as if he had been preparing long before it had all gone so wrong, and not for the first time did she send up a silent prayer of thanks that he was coming with them.

Drew was a godsend, a country boy down to the bedrock, but in the best of ways, solid and calm. A little older than her. Forty-five, forty-six? Sara couldn't remember. But single, solitary, never divorced. Never even married. Drew had no family. He was one of those guys more comfortable by himself, on the empty highway or in the forests of the Midwest. He had chafed at having to sit and push pens around a desk, but out there that was going to be a bonus. Out there Drew was going to be their very own woods guide.

"Morning, Sara. How're the kids?" asked Trace. He sounded tired, and he had deep bags under his eyes. Sara wondered what time he'd gone to bed, wondered if he'd slept at all. Wondered if he was even okay to drive.

"They're good. Stacey's up. Peter is still asleep, though. I was going to wait until everything was packed before I got him."

"Need a hand?" asked Drew, shifting in his seat.

"No, we're good. Thanks, Drew," she said, watching Ian walk back out of the house, a bag on each shoulder, a bag in one hand and his shotgun in the other. Like it was a contest amongst all men about who could carry the most.

"Back in a minute," she said, patting the roof of the car before stepping away.

Sara poked her head into Stacey's room.

A single small candle sputtered in the corner, its flame throwing out shadows that danced across the wall.

"You dressed?" Sara asked.

"Do we really have to go?" asked Stacey, her eyes wide with her hands clasped in front of her. She looked nervous, and it was only her mouth that moved.

Sara stepped further into the room.

"We already spoke about this, Stace. Are you ready?"

"What about the monsters?" Stacey said softly, stalling, looking at the ground as Sara knelt down to give her a hug, wrapping her arms around her and pulling her close.

"We're going somewhere safe, somewhere they can't get us," Sara said, rubbing Stacey's back, closing her eyes as she breathed in Stacey's smell.

"Promise?"

"Would I lie to you, honey?" she asked, fighting to keep her voice level.

Sara felt a gentle sob leak out of her daughter, felt Stacey burrow into her shoulder.

"Stace... I need you to do something for me, okay?" Sara said, giving her a squeeze before leaning back so she could see her daughter's face.

"What?" said Stacey, rubbing her eyes.

"Will you look after your brother for me?"

Stacey nodded.

"I mean it. I need you to watch Peter like a hawk. It's dangerous where we're going, and I might be too busy to keep my eye on him all the time. Can you do that for me?"

"Yes."

"And don't talk about the Cloud or the monsters where he can hear. If you have a question, then ask me when Peter's asleep. I don't want him to be more afraid. Got it?"

Stacey nodded.

"I need you to protect him, Stacey. Can you *promise* me you'll do that?"

She nodded again, and this time with the most serious look Sara had ever seen on a nine-year-old's face.

"Promise," she said.

"Good," said Sara, giving Stacey a kiss on the forehead before standing back up. "Trace and Drew are outside. I'm just going to go get your brother. Go jump in the car in the meantime, okay?"

Stacey didn't move.

"No dawdling, Stace. We need to go," Sara said, already turning to Peter's room.

"Can I bring my books? Please?" Stacey called, waiting until Sara was already halfway down the hallway.

"One," said Sara over her shoulder. She couldn't say no. She'd allowed herself one small concession too—a tiny photo album. A dead weight in her backpack, but one that she couldn't imagine leaving without.

She pushed open the door to Peter's room, flicking on the small flashlight in her hand, pointing its beam at the ceiling to give herself a soft white glow. Bright enough to see the small sleeping shape on the bed in the corner. She pulled the covers back and slid her arms under her little boy, pulling his warm body to hers as she lifted him up, his hair smelling of four-year-old boy and two-day-old shampoo.

His head rested on her shoulder as she walked. *God, he's getting heavy,* she thought, his legs hanging at her sides, his arms swinging across her back with each step.

He woke up halfway to the car, turning to look at her with bleary eyes.

"Shh. It's okay, Peter. It's okay, go back to sleep. Put your head on my shoulder, that's a good boy."

Sara kept walking, the sun rising higher and higher, poking its head above the horizon, bathing the land in glorious orange light, reminding them all it was time to go.

Since the power had gone out, there were no electrical lights out there anymore. And with the gas shortage, no traffic, not in the way there used to be, and that meant no driving at night. A human eye can see a candle from thirty miles away, so driving at night was a quick way to end up dead. Driving with the lights turned off wasn't an option either. Even with their pair of THP-issued night vision goggles, they might not see a roadblock or spike trap until it was too late.

The night was going to be about hiding and staying quiet. No lights to give them away, not even a fire, not unless they were desperate. Or 100% sure they were alone.

Their clothing was focused on keeping them hidden too. They were all wearing camouflage or hiking gear in the most neutral color they could find, and they had face paint for later, when they ended up on the bikes or on foot.

Drew said mud and charcoal would make a decent replacement if they ran out. He said if he had some cream, he could make some just using food coloring and water. Sara reckoned he just wanted to show off.

But as she got closer to the car, she could see Drew and Trace staring straight ahead. She followed their eyes but saw nothing but empty road, and she wondered if their thoughts were as dark as her own.

TRACE

Trace was thinking about the THP Special Ops Aviation unit based out in Nashville. He was thinking about how it had four pilots and one mechanic, five Jet Ranger helicopters and one Huey UH-1H.

Had, as in past tense, because those pilots and their machines were long gone. As soon as the Cloud had smothered Europe, as soon as the reality had hit home, those pilots had taken themselves and their families, and they had gone west. Any spare seats went to the highest bidder, leaving the rest of the Tennessee Highway Patrol with one thumb up their ass, waving goodbye with the other.

Now Trace was about to do the same, but he didn't have a helicopter or a million bucks, and even if he did the only pilot in the group was Drew, and he hadn't flown anything bigger than a kite in years.

Instead they were on the ground, about two months behind the curve with no realistic plan. Nothing more than head west, west to Colorado Springs, to NORAD, chasing after a rumor.

Trace glanced at Drew, who was staring straight ahead, lost in his own thoughts. The same ones he was having. He could tell by the frown.

Trace looked back to the road in front of them, a darker smudge amid the gloom that seemed to stretch forever.

They had figured that if this was going to be a long shot, probably the last one they would ever take, then it may as well be a big one, like out of the park big. Because if they wanted to survive, if Stacey and Peter were going to live, if they even wanted to pretend they might, then they needed to get them underground, down deep. Somewhere airtight, with light, power, and clean, breathable air. They needed to get to a bunker, and that meant NORAD. But that meant ignoring one obvious fact: even if it was real, even if it was everything they hoped it could be, they wouldn't be allowed in, not in a million years. Anything else was wishful thinking. But that was Sara for you.

There was nothing he could do about it, though. Nothing he could do but try to keep them safe for as long as possible. Besides, it's not like he had anything better to do.

"Morning, Stacey," Trace said as she walked toward the car, lifting one hand off the wheel and giving her a soft little wave using all five fingers.

Stacey waved back at him shyly, the flash of her white teeth like a little ray of sunshine in the dark.

Trace could see her mom in her. She had the same elfin face, the same light build, the same sapphire-blue eyes. Stacey would have grown up into a heartbreaker one day. *But now?*

Trace knew she wouldn't live long enough to see her tenth birthday.

Stacey climbed in the back, a fat book clutched against her chest, a pillow under her left arm. Quiet until Drew asked her what she was reading.

Trace smiled.

For a man who'd never had any kids of his own, Drew was surprisingly good with them.

Trace watched Ian turn to lock the front door behind him. Trace doubted Ian even realized he did it. *Habit, maybe?* Simple habit ignoring the fact that Ian would never be back here again. None of them would.

"Good to go?" Trace asked when Ian got closer.

"I believe so," Ian answered, coming to a stop by Trace's window with a worried frown on his face. "So…," he said, hesitating, leaning closer, like they were sharing a secret. "You sure about all of this, Trace? You reckon it's going to be okay out there?" he asked, tilting his head down at the road ahead of them.

Trace frowned back at him.

Okay? Is he serious?

It wasn't *okay* out there. It hadn't been *okay* for quite some time.

But he didn't say that; he just shrugged. "I don't know, Ian, but we'll do our best, I promise you that," he said, nodding to Drew next to him.

"Thank you. You too, Drew," Ian said, putting his arm through the window to grip Trace's shoulder. "I prayed for God to watch over all of us last night. To keep us all safe. You too, Trace."

Ian said the last part softly, like he was doing him a favor, as though Trace's lack of faith was an affliction, some embarrassing disease that Ian could wish away.

Trace's hands tightened on the steering wheel, skin going white across his knuckles. *God?*

Cancer had taken his wife, and the Cloud had taken his son. "God" appeared to have been absent for both. Trace had little reason to believe "He" would show up now simply because Ian asked nicely.

"Thanks, Ian," Trace said flatly, turning to look away from him. He let out a slow breath and tried to tame the twitch above his left eye.

"Well, this is going to be fun," said Drew.

"What?" asked Trace.

"Nothing," answered Drew, his face deadpan.

Trace frowned at him.

"We good to go?" Drew asked, talking over his shoulder and avoiding eye contact.

"Almost," said Sara, her AR-15 in one hand as she loaded a thirty-round magazine with the other. She tapped the bottom to make sure the rounds were seated.

"Now I'm good."

"I'm in," said Ian, climbing in on the right.

"You ready, kids?" Trace asked, trying to put more cheer into his voice than he felt.

"Ready," said Stacey.

He looked in the rearview mirror and could just see Stacey's eyes poking out from the nest they'd made in all the gear. Peter was silent, covered in a blanket and already asleep. Trace wondered how long that would last. Two kids trapped in a car all day was a recipe for disaster.

Sara climbed in on the left, car rocking gently, and Trace was reminded again just how overloaded they were and why the distance was going to be a problem. And 1,236 miles was a big problem to have.

That's how far it was, start to finish, from here to Colorado, and they weren't going to make it.

The average distance a Ford Explorer could cover on a single tank, per advertised, under cruising highway conditions, *perfect conditions*, was 460 miles.

Even with all the gas he and Drew had siphoned from the abandoned cars two days ago, they only had what amounted to two full tanks. Under "perfect" conditions that would take them as far as 920 miles. But they weren't heading into perfect conditions. They would be driving the back roads, avoiding the highly populated areas. They were going to be hard miles, slow miles. Their fuel consumption would be shot to shit, and, quite simply, at some point they were going to run out.

The bikes strapped to the roof would help, but, even so, that meant sticking to the roads, and that carried its own risks. But that was a problem they'd have to worry about later.

"How about you? You ready, Trace?" Sara asked, closing her door with a hollow thump.

Ready?

He shrugged. He supposed so. Either way they were out of time.

By Day 120, Colorado would be gone, smothered by the Cloud. By Day 130, LA would be the last place you could see the sun. By Day 135 it would be all over, the Cloud would have covered the whole of the US.

They had twenty-nine days to get from Lexington to Colorado. Four weeks to cross a country that had lost its mind. And they would be walking or biking nearly a third of it.

"On your marks," he mumbled to himself, feeling like he was at the starting line, already far behind, already weighed down and tired. Old adrenaline thumping in his veins, waiting for the starter's gun. Or the guillotine. He didn't turn his head to see which.

And at 7:02 a.m. on a beautiful Thursday morning in September, Trace turned the key in the ignition.

They covered 130 miles that first day, taking the 412, going around Dyersburg, then across the Mississippi into Missouri, avoiding Hayti and Caruthersville on the other side by driving around them.

It took them ten hours, creeping along, coasting to a halt every couple of miles to scope out the road ahead. Drew would lean forward with his binoculars to make sure they weren't driving into any nasty surprises, scanning the civilian, emergency, and police radio frequencies. Listening for anything that wasn't static.

Every now and then—only once they were sure they were

safe—would they let Peter and Stacey out of the car to stretch their legs or pee.

They talked most of the way. Idle chatter, something to keep their minds occupied. Drew and Ian talked about sports and teams that didn't exist anymore. They played games with the kids. Sara had even brought a CD with a bunch of songs for Peter.

After the fourth time on a loop, Trace had all the songs memorized. After the seventh time listening to "Let it Go," he started to go insane.

He had also quickly rediscovered that a grown man could only play "I Spy" so many times before it made him wish he was deaf. And blind.

But their luck held, and their first day on the road passed almost without incident. At least until Peter decided to throw up all over Sara, himself, and most of their bags.

Ian and Sara cleaned up as best they could, but they had to drive the rest of the day with all the windows open and the sour stink in their noses.

Stacey was quiet for the most part, talking softly to Sara or keeping her nose buried in a book. But Trace never once saw her turn the page, and occasionally he would catch her looking at him in the rearview mirror.

"You okay, Stace?" he asked the second time he caught her staring.

Stacey nodded, her face red with embarrassment, and she looked away, out the window, giving worried glances to all the abandoned cars lying on the side of the road.

Trace figured she wanted to ask him something and was gradually working up the nerve. He knew she'd spit it out eventually. The shy ones always did, it just took them longer, and he was happy to let her do it in her own time. So when she kept watching him later, he pretended not to see it.

Trace brought the car to a halt seventeen miles southwest of Kennet, still in Missouri, somewhere on the 412.

There wasn't a single car in sight, no glint of sunlight off windshields behind them, and nothing but the sun way out ahead of them, slowly sinking toward the horizon.

"Why are we stopping?" Ian asked, leaning forward as much as he could without waking up Peter, who was sleeping between Sara and himself. A plastic bag was clutched in one hand, just in case Peter decided to repeat his earlier party trick.

"I figure we should find a place to stop for the night while the sun is still up. Here looks good," said Trace, looking at his watch.

Ian looked to either side and shrugged. "If you're sure…"

Trace was. It was five p.m., almost on the dot. Sunset wouldn't be for another two hours, but they still needed to set up camp for the night, and he didn't want to be caught out on the road or stumbling around in a field when darkness fell.

Problem was they had only driven through Kennet in the last hour, a city that once had a population of 11,000. Less so now, but still… far too many people had seen them arrive, and far too many had watched them go.

He needed a safe place to hide them for the night, just in case someone decided to follow, and he thought he just might have found it.

They were stopped in the middle of a four-way intersection. The roads going north and south were bare dirt, access roads. South was farms and north was farms. Both directions looked empty, brown fields and blue skies. Both directions looked exactly the same to him.

So Trace turned the wheel hard to the left, stepped on the gas, and they went south.

In his experience, when people were faced with the choice, a fork in the road, they tended to turn right. Especially if they're right-handed, and nine-tenths of the population was right-handed.

Secondly, when people are being chased, they tend to head north.

Why?

Simple. The way most people are taught to think of the world is to associate north with up. That's how a map is orientated, and someone once told them that *up* was an advantage, so heading north became an advantage.

Moral of the story? People are stupid and predictable, nine times out of ten.

It was the other ten percent that worried him.

He drove another half a mile, going past some scraggly bushes and a dirty pond before pulling off the road and coming to stop beneath a copse of trees. A windbreak planted a hundred years ago, or perhaps all that was left of whatever forest once grew here before man showed up. Either way, it was going to be their home for the night.

Trace killed the engine and sat back with a tired sigh as the doors opened up behind him and everyone climbed out.

He sat there for a while, listening to the birdsong outside, feeling the soft, cool breeze blowing in through his window, carrying with it the smell of dirt and decaying vegetation. A cool breeze that stirred the trees above his head, their leaves slowly changing color, turning to golds, reds, and yellows as the countryside headed into the last fall it would ever see.

Trace opened his door and climbed out, taking his AR-15 from the gun rack and slinging it over his shoulder before he walked around the back to help Drew unpack.

He stumbled to a stop.

Peter was running through the field, squealing with delight as Ian chased him, only a step or two behind. His arms raised above his head, lumbering along in some childish pantomime of a stupid monster.

The irony wasn't lost on Trace. Turns out monsters were anything but slow, and anything but dumb.

And it made him remember James. It made Trace remember his own son. It made him remember all that wasted time, all those mistakes he could never take back.

Trace shook his head.

James's birthday had been a month ago. He would have been thirty-eight, ten years older than Trace had been when they had him, but Trace knew James would never get married or have a family of his own now. He would never grow old, and Trace would never get a chance to say sorry. It was too late. What's done was done, and with a small shock he realized that having Stacey and Peter along for the next few weeks was the closest he was ever going to get to being a grandfather.

He didn't know how to feel about that.

So he forced himself to turn away, and he concentrated on something else. Their progress, and he was happy with it. Granted, 130 miles wasn't far by anyone's standards, but today had been a trial run, a test of teamwork. Today had been about setting up a system, a semblance of a plan for when things went wrong, having the kids practice lying on the floor when told. They'd discussed how they were going to coordinate their fields of fire for when, not *if*, they were attacked. Because as soon as they had left Lexington, they had become targets. It's why they hadn't left before, and it's why they were all armed to the teeth.

Drew, Sara, and he each had their THP-issued .357 Glock Model 3 sidearms, plus three Bushmaster AR-15 semi-autos. They were wearing bulletproof vests under their windbreakers, and even Ian carried two guns, a Remington Model 870 Express pump-action shotgun and a Beretta 92F.

The shotgun made Trace nervous, though. Shotguns and kids were a bad mix, especially when the shooting started. But if Ian actually needed to use it, then Trace figured they'd already lost and he was probably dead.

Two hours later and Trace could see Ian's shotgun resting against a tree, close at hand while he got Peter tucked into bed.

They had packed a little blue tent for the kids, and with Ian's flashlight on inside it, it glowed like a giant nightlight. Trace could see Ian's shadow moving across the wall.

Idiot.

He was just about to yell at him when the light went out. Trace shook his head.

Then Drew stepped in front of him.

"How're you doing, Chief?" Drew asked, lowering himself down to sit next to him.

Drew felt at his left jacket pocket, pulled out a crumpled pack, and offered Trace a cigarette.

Trace shook his head. "Those things will kill you, you know?"

Drew gave Trace a knowing smile, then watched Trace pull out a cigar of his own.

"Drink?" Trace asked, shaking a little hip flask he kept for emergencies.

He'd packed his "medicine" and cigars right alongside all the canned food he still had. He wasn't worried about the extra weight; it wasn't much considering how little he still had.

Drew hesitated before taking a swig and passing it back. He coughed, his face turning red as he thumped his chest.

"Jesus, what is that? Lighter fluid?"

Trace chuckled at his discomfort.

Drew turned his face as he cupped his hands and lit his cigarette.

"So... what do think we're going to run into out there?" Drew asked, making small talk.

Trace frowned. Drew knew what was out there, he didn't need

Trace to spell it out. He was asking the question out of politeness, an agreement that they both recognized the problem at hand: Some of them were going to die, probably all of them. Long before they made it anywhere near Colorado.

He opened his mouth to reply.

"Um... Sir?"

He turned at the voice, and Stacey stepped around in front of him. She was dressed in lilac pajamas dotted with blue flowers. She still had her hiking boots on though, and Trace could see Sara over her shoulder, striding toward them, arms swinging, the expression on her face very much that of a prison guard hunting down an escaped inmate.

"Yes, Stacey?" he replied, smiling, wondering how long she had been evading her mom.

"You ever killed someone?" Stacey asked, quickly taking it to a darker place.

Drew coughed again. It sounded like he was choking.

"Stacey! You can't ask that," Sara exclaimed, outraged. "Say you're sorry."

"I'm sorry," said Stacey. But she didn't look sorry. She looked relieved, like she had been holding the question in all day.

Trace nodded. "It's okay, Stace."

"No, Trace, it's not," Sara said. "That's enough of you for one night." She grabbed her by the arm and pulled her away. "I've told you twice already, young lady. Bedtime!"

"But…"

"No buts. Bed. Now," she said, leaning forward and giving her a gentle nudge to get her moving.

Stacey turned around, shoulders slumped, and walked back to the little blue tent like she was heading toward a firing squad.

"I'm so sorry about that, Trace," said Sara with a soft shrug and helpless eyes.

"Relax, Sara. It's fine."

Drew and Trace sat in silence for a while, even after Sara had left.

"So…," said Drew, almost casually. "Have you?"

"Twice," said Trace quickly, softly.

Drew glanced at him. "Mind if I ask how?"

"It was back in LA. Twenty years ago now, some shitty drug bust gone bad. Some low-life idiots whacked out on coke thought they were bulletproof." He shrugged. "Who really knows what goes through their heads sometimes. Anyway, I yelled police, they shot at me, I shot back. They missed, I didn't."

Trace lit his cigar, tasting it on his tongue before expelling the smoke into the dimming sky, watching the sun set in front of him, feeling the darkness racing up from behind. Without power, without city lights, without the reflected glow of light pollution blinding the sky, night came quickly and utterly, stars bursting into brilliant life above him. Billions of them coldly watching man go extinct far below.

"What was it like?" Drew asked, showing the first real sign Trace had seen of being afraid.

"What was it like?" Trace paused. "To be honest, I don't really remember. I didn't really have time to think. They went for their guns, and I went for mine. One died instantly, two in the chest." Trace tapped his breast in pantomime. "I got the other guy in the neck, and he bled out waiting for the paramedics."

"H-how was it… after?"

Loaded question, thought Trace.

"After? Depends what you mean. I got put on administrative leave, did some gardening, went fishing for a few days, and I tried not to think about it too much. They were dead, I wasn't. I got to go home to my wife and kid. That was good enough for me."

They sat in heavy silence for a while.

"How far do you reckon we'll make it before we run out of gas?" Drew asked, changing topics like it had never happened.

Trace leaned back, looking to where Sara and Ian were setting up their tent for the night.

He turned back to Drew. "Not as far as we hoped. On the first tank… maybe the other side of Harrison? Today chewed up more than it should have. We need to be going faster to get any decent mileage. But even on the second tank, I don't think we'll make the 35, not unless we get lucky or find more gas along the way."

"More gas?" repeated Drew. "I've got more chance shitting a gold brick tomorrow. Every car we've passed so far has been sucked dry."

They were pretty easy to spot, too, cars stopped in the middle of the road, facing west, fuel latches ripped open. Some with bullet holes decorating the windshield and decaying bodies still inside. They didn't let the kids see those.

"You eaten?" asked Drew, stubbing out his cigarette.

"Yeah, tuna. Tuna tonight, tuna every night. At the rate I'm going, I'm not going to have to worry about the Cloud. The mercury poisoning will get me first."

Drew chuckled.

That was another problem they'd have to deal with—food and water and rationing. They didn't have much and where they were going there was even less.

They'd looked at the maps, tried to plot a route. Drew had figured their best chance was to try to make it to the 35, or as far as the car could go, then ride the bikes along the 400, which ran parallel to the 70 as it snaked along the Arkansas River, which meant water if they filtered and treated it properly. Plus, it was off the main thoroughfare and hopefully avoided most of the people.

But water was only half of the problem. He still didn't know what they were going to eat once their supplies ran out. They'd done the math, counted calories. Four adults and two kids, then throw in high activity levels, cold weather, and heavy gear…

They had enough food for two weeks, three at a stretch. Dry-packed and canned goods, Drew's supply of MREs, vitamins and supplements, the bare essentials. The whole food pyramid. Which was just as well.

The fields they were driving past had been left untended for months. It was the wrong season too, and, considering the plague of people that had already traveled through the area, there wasn't really anything left.

Drew got up and went to turn in. He had the watch from four to six and wanted his beauty sleep.

"Night," Trace nodded as he left, and their first night out on the road passed mostly without incident.

Peter had a nightmare and woke everyone up at two a.m., screaming about the things trying to get into his tent.

Trace finally managed to go back to sleep sometime around three. He pulled his sleeping bag around his ears, listening to Sara hush Peter back to sleep, telling him there was no such thing as monsters, that he didn't need to worry, that he was safe.

Trace fell asleep listening to Sara lie.

SARA

Sara woke to the sound of rain.

She lifted her head to see everything outside draped in mist and dripping wet, but it was dry and warm inside their tent, and she tried to forget why they were here. If she did that, she could almost pretend they were on a family camping trip. Like the good old days, before the Cloud. And the madness.

The idea was so tempting that Sara almost burrowed back into her sleeping bag. Instead, she forced herself up onto her elbows and turned her head.

Ian was still asleep next to her, lying on his back with wet hair plastered to his face. Trace and Drew were already up; she could see them loading their gear into the car.

Sara gave Ian a gentle nudge, then another, a little harder. He opened his eyes and looked at her.

"Morning, handsome," she said softly. "Time to go."

"Already?" Ian groaned.

Sara smiled back at him, and Ian nodded, closing his eyes with a sigh before he pulled one arm free of his sleeping bag, then the other, pushing himself to a sitting position. "You sleep okay?" he mumbled.

Not really.

She shrugged. "I suppose."

She must have lain awake for another hour after she had gotten Peter back to sleep, listening to the wind, listening to Ian breathing, thinking.

"When did it start raining?" Sara asked, reaching across to brush the hair off his face. "And why are you so wet?"

Ian looked confused for a moment before he smiled at her. "Ah, a little after five."

He patted his hair. "I set up the tarp to catch some of it. But I was trying to do it in the dark, so it took me a little longer than it should have."

Sara nodded, looking out into the field as it continued to rain. The sky above was full of fat gray clouds, their edges stained a pale purple and slowly getting brighter as sheets of water blew across the field, driven by the buffeting wind.

She didn't know what they had once farmed here, but all it contained now was puddles of water, dark brown mud, and their clear plastic tarp, pegged out in a neat little square with a little blue bucket placed beneath to catch the run-off.

Catching rainwater had been one of the first things they'd all learned to do.

Once the power failed, the pumps stopped, and they lost water pressure. Their taps ran dry. The city's sewerage system packed in and everything backed up. Then it overflowed and started to stink.

After a while you didn't even notice the smell anymore. Besides, by then they were far more concerned with being thirsty, and people did strange things when they got thirsty. Desperate things.

Murders in Lexington had no longer been about money, but more about whether people thought you were holding out on them. Food, fuel, or water—it didn't really matter, and the violence had only gotten worse as time wore on. But with water suddenly scarce and getting rarer, they were forced to improvise.

The town council rediscovered the old well, and they drained the town pool. It was clean too, once they had filtered out most of the chlorine. But there simply wasn't enough. Beech Lake wasn't the safest to drink from either, but lots of people did, and lots of people got sick. Lots of people died.

Rainwater was the safer option. You didn't have to go anywhere to get it, which meant minimal contact with other people, and all you really needed to collect it was a tarp, rope, trees—if available— or tall posts. But the Cloud had been screwing up the weather patterns for months, and rain had become increasingly rare and unpredictable.

Today was the first time it had rained in over a week, and one glance at those clouds told Sara it wasn't going to stop anytime soon. They would be able to collect enough rain to see them through for a few days at least, maybe a week. She looked at the sky and closed her eyes. *Thank you.*

Ian yawned, unzipping his sleeping bag so he could climb out. "Ready for day two?" he asked.

"As long as you're next to me," Sara said, opening her eyes and smiling up at him, holding out a hand so he could pull her to her feet.

They got going quickly after that.

Sara woke Stacey and Peter, got them dressed and fed, bundled them into the car while Ian packed up the tent, their gear, and nearly six gallons of rainwater. They hit the road at eight a.m., traveling the same as the day before, just faster.

They drove past more abandoned cars than she could count, doors flung wide while discarded possessions and garbage littered the road for as far as the eye could see. They drove through dead towns and ghost towns, and at one point they drove over ten corpses lying in the middle of the road, like they were bowling pins. Like someone had gotten a lucky strike and hit them all at once. But considering they were all lined up in a neat row, Sara figured it looked more like they'd all been executed.

Ian covered Peter's eyes and told Stacey not to look. Not that it was necessary. The bodies had already been driven over so many times that they looked like nothing more than roadkill, just flattened lumps of dry, discolored meat. It was only the clothes that gave them away.

They passed through Imboden, Hardy, Salem, the lot.

Halfway between Salem and Harrison, Trace said they were starting to run low on gas, the fuel gauge needle hovering around the quarter tank mark.

They kept going for another thirty minutes before Trace found a side road that looked safe. They drove down it until the highway was hidden from view and decided to stop there for the night.

She and Ian made camp while Drew and Trace emptied one of the three full jerry cans into the gas tank.

It wasn't until nine p.m. that Sara finally crawled into her sleeping bag for the night. She pulled it up around her neck, pushed her back into Ian's side, and closed her eyes. Then Ian did for her what she'd just done for Stacey. He pulled her close, wrapped his arms around her, and held her close until she stopped crying and fell asleep.

The next thing Sara knew it was three a.m., and Drew was touching her shoulder, waking her up to take her turn on watch.

Six hours later and they were back on the road. Sara was staring out her window, watching the country roll by, almost hypnotized by the yellow and brown fields blurring into one as the Ford ate up the miles.

She watched the countryside slowly change color as they drove further and further west, trees getting smaller, slowly losing their leaves. Farms and fields came less frequently, just the occasional square of yellow and brown corn fields. Corn too rotten to eat.

They drove in silence, no sound but the hum of the tires on asphalt and Peter's soft snores from where his head lay in her lap. The bodies the day before had shaken everyone, and after three days on the road nobody had anything left to talk about anyway.

She looked down at her sleeping boy, glad he was asleep, glad for the small break. One hand on his head, softly stroking his hair.

"Mom?" Stacey whispered in her ear.

"Yes, Stace?"

"I'm hungry."

"I know, Stace, we all are. You'll just have to wait."

"How much longer? When do we get to Colorado?"

"Not long, Stacey, but we're going to be riding our bikes next. You'll miss the car then, so enjoy it while you can."

Stacey mumbled something and went back to watching the road behind them, leaving Sara alone with the thoughts she'd been trying to avoid all morning. They had less than a tank left.

After today they would only have two, maybe three more days of driving. After that they were on their bikes, or walking, and she knew that's when the real problems would start. And as Sara looked at her family, she was unable to feel anything but dread.

It wasn't until just after noon that they noticed a fire burning to the north of them. A fire that seemed to be spreading, a column of smoke that separated into two, then three. Several separate fires. Sara didn't think that was an accident.

"Trouble," Drew said, binoculars glued to his face.

Trace brought them to a halt in the middle of the road, but it wasn't just the smoke that made him stop, or Drew's remark. There were cars blocking the road, and people clustered around them.

A few turned to look back at them, but most were watching the dirty smoke coming from where Sara assumed there was a town.

"Mom? What's happening?" asked Stacey, leaning forward over Sara's shoulder.

"Not now, Stace," Sara said, opening her door a crack in case she needed to get out quickly.

"Are we safe here?" asked Ian, turning to look behind them.

"Dad? Who are they?" Peter said loudly, pointing ahead.

Sara leaned forward to get a better look, taking the binoculars from Drew.

She counted two cars, a Greyhound bus, and nearly fifteen people walking around outside, and they were all armed. Not that she expected anything else.

"What do you want to do?" Drew asked.

"Don't know," said Trace, letting his own binoculars drop to his lap. "I don't think they're a threat. I think they stopped because of the fire. But we'll wait here and see what they do first."

Trace turned off the engine to save fuel, its soft rumble dying away. Sara opened her window, letting a cool breeze in that carried with it the soft, stuttering thump of explosions.

"Someone's fighting," said Drew.

"Who?" asked Ian. "The army?"

Trace shrugged.

"Peter, Stacey, come here," Ian said quickly, pulling Peter from the back. "Peter, we're going to play a game."

"But—" began Peter.

"No buts. You're going lie on the floor for as long as you can, okay? And I'm going to time you."

"No!"

"Tell you what, Peter, I'll make you a deal. If you can stay down longer than Stace, then I'll buy you any toy you want when we get to Colorado. Okay?"

"I want Batman!"

"Batman it is, then. But no complaining, and you can't come up until I tell you. Okay?" asked Ian.

Peter mumbled something that sounded like a yes.

Sara smiled at him. Bribery. *Genius.*

Ian shrugged back a guilty apology, but she had already forgiven him the little white lie.

"Come on, Pete," said Stacey, looking at Sara before she slithered through from the back, dropping into the footwell. "I bet I can go longer than you."

"Nuh-uh!" exclaimed Peter, squirming out of Ian's arms and onto the floor.

Good girl, thought Sara, turning her attention back to the cars in front.

They waited another twenty minutes until the people up ahead came to some sort of a decision. They all got back in their cars and started moving again.

Trace followed about half a mile behind them, never getting any closer, but never letting them out of sight either, and for the next hour they became something of an informal convoy, tolerating each other but never letting their guard down either.

Just another sign of how times have changed, Sara thought.

Europe had simply fallen too quickly for the changes to happen, too quickly for the madness to take hold like it had here. The fear and distrust. But once France fell, the rest went down like dominoes. Germany, the UK. The whole of Europe was gone in two weeks.

It had taken another sixty days for the Cloud to hit the East Coast of the US, eighty days before it swallowed up Maine. More than enough time for the entire country to blow its brains out. And with ninety-seven guns for every hundred people, it had made for quite a mess.

Their paths split just outside of Springdale, Arkansas. The strangers turned south, while they kept going west on the 412.

Sara told Stacey and Peter to wave goodbye to the boy leaning over the back seat watching them, and then they were alone again.

Sara thought the strangers might be aiming for Mexico. Drew said they were probably trying to get on the 40 before aiming for Oklahoma, but neither of them could think of what else might be down there. And for a cruel second, she wondered if maybe they knew something the rest of them didn't.

They covered 205 miles that day, 180 miles the day after that, going around Joplin and then aiming for Wichita. Empty fields and farms rolling by endlessly to either side that lulled them into a false sense of security.

They were fifty miles out of Wichita when they ran into their first ambush.

TRACE

His mirror exploded. He heard the impact, then the gunshot. Trace flinched away from the noise and the slivers of glass that sprayed against his window.

"Fuck me!"

"Motorbike behind us!" Sara shouted, and the car filled with something halfway between a sound and a pulsating pain in his ears. An unending *thrum, thrum, thrum* as she opened her window.

Trace heard Stacey shout something. He heard Peter scream, sounds smothered as Ian grabbed them and pulled them down, pushing them to the floor before lying on top of them.

"Where is he?" Trace bellowed before the crash of gunfire drowned out his words. He felt several more hard metal thuds eat into the car. He felt one bite into the doorframe right next to his head.

"Right behind us, a hundred yards. Coming fast!" Sara screamed as she leaned out her window, pushing her AR-15 ahead of her. The painful thrum in his ears faded somewhat as she plugged the hole.

Trace opened his own window, the echo died away, and the car filled with a roaring wind instead. He glanced sideways to see Drew following Sara's lead, climbing out his window and turning around until he was half out of the car, holding on with one hand and leaning against the roof so he could fire behind them.

Trace put his foot down, engine growling, nose rising as they accelerated, eyes dropping to check their speed, looking up. Eighty, ninety, one-ten, needle climbing, 120, 125, 130, maxed out, engine screaming.

"He's still coming!" Sara shouted.

He heard her returning fire, a staccato rush of explosions just behind his head.

"*Where?*"

"Left side! Left side!" screamed Sara. "Seven o'clock. Shit!"

Trace heard glass shatter, then he heard a wet thunk and someone grunt in pain.

He looked ahead, road dipping down toward a river overgrown with trees. *A great place for a roadblock,* his brain told him. *At least that's where I'd wait,* thought Trace, and they were being herded right toward it.

His eyes desperately started searching for a way out.

"Hold on!" he yelled, taking his foot off the gas and tapping the brakes.

Trace yanked the wheel to the right. The car skidded for a second before it plunged off the road, getting lighter as they dropped down a low bank, the suspension crunching as they bottomed out. He heard Sara grunt in pain, and Drew yelped as he almost lost his grip.

Trace mashed his foot back down on the gas, and the SUV surged forward across a stretch of grass, straight through a low wooden fence and into a corn field.

He lost sight of everything, the road, the bike behind them. He couldn't see anything but gray sky peeking down from above and a wall of brown in front of them, a blur of sickly corn stalks whizzing past to either side, rotten husks and leaves smashing across the windshield, hard impacts echoing inside the car like they were driving through a hailstorm.

Drew pulled himself inside, covered in vegetable juice and bits of corn husk. Trace glanced at him, his jaws clenched in pain, his face pale and splattered with blood. He couldn't see where he'd been hit.

"You ok?" Trace shouted.

"My arm," Drew said, turning in his seat to look behind them. "Are they still following us?"

"I can't see them," Drew hissed, peering out the back window. "Wait! Got 'em! Fifty yards, coming hard!"

Sara started shooting again, and Trace caught a glimpse of *them* in the rearview mirror. Two men on a red dirt bike. He lost them again as they exploded out of the field.

He spun the steering wheel and the car slewed to the left, tires digging into dry grass, pulling them through a gate and out onto a narrow dirt road bound by trees, thick trunks blurring past with a rhythmic whoosh.

He watched the needle start to climb again. Fifty, seventy, eighty, the car's suspension soaking up the beating they were getting.

Trace heard several more hard thuds and then a wall of sound, bullets coming fast. *A full auto,* Trace realized just before the back window blew out in an explosion of glass and bullets tore through the car.

Drew swore as Trace felt them rip past his head, sucking away sound and leaving him deaf in his right ear as a staggered series of holes appeared in the windshield.

"How close are they?" he bellowed.

"Thirty yards! TWENTY," shouted Sara.

Trace angled the car to the right. He saw the motorbike pull to the left, about to race up alongside them. He lost them in his blind spot, but he could hear them, the motorbike's engine roaring, a high-pitched *braaaaaap* getting louder.

"Sara, get inside! NOW!"

Trace drifted to the left, trees getting closer, motorbike racing for the narrowing gap.

My turn.

He stamped down hard on the brake, mashing it into the floor, and the nose dropped.

Heavy-duty brakes, AWD, traction control. Perfect car for the job; it could stop on a dime. Even on gravel.

Trace flung his door open, and he let momentum do the rest. He let it yank the door out of his hand and swing it wide like a clothesline.

The rest was physics.

The motorbike tried to brake, it tried to weave past, but they were going too fast with nowhere else to go. They hit Trace's door hard, nearly ripping it from its hinges. The man driving was crushed against it while his passenger was catapulted through the air. The motorbike dropped away to the side, skidding across the ground before its mangled handlebars dug into the dirt and sent it cartwheeling into a tree.

Trace kept the brake pedal flat to the floor, and they came to a halt in a cloud of rolling dust.

Trace looked at Drew.

"You okay?"

"I'm okay," said Drew, eyes wide, his right hand clamped around his bicep as blood welled up between his fingers.

"Everyone else okay?" Trace shouted, trying to be heard over the screaming coming from the back. "Ian! Is everyone okay?"

"We're okay! We're good!"

"Sara?"

"I'm okay!"

Trace unclipped his seat belt and climbed out of the space where his door used to be.

"Sara, on me," he said, taking his Glock from his hip as he

stalked toward the two figures lying in the dirt.

He pointed his gun at their heads, smoothly pivoting between them, but they weren't a threat. One clearly had a broken leg. Trace could see him clutching the ruined limb as he screamed, and the other one wasn't moving at all. He just lay there, holding his chest as though he was trying to cover up the dent where his ribs had caved in.

Trace moved closer, and he was surprised by how young they were. Two white kids, early twenties. They looked like they were brothers, similar faces, same build, same coloring, and dirty.

"Sara," Trace said, pointing at the one with the broken leg. "If he so much as moves… shoot him."

Sara nodded, and Trace bent down to pick up one of the men's rifle from the ground.

An AK-47, and well cared for. Clean, well-oiled, and in a far better state than the two men, even more so now. Looking closer, Trace could see it had been modified back to full auto. *Illegal,* his cop mind noted. *Clever,* the pragmatist in him added, hefting it in his hand. *And mine now.*

He slung it over his shoulder.

"Drew!"

"Yeah?"

"Siphon the fuel out of their bike. Get Ian to do it if you can't. And be quick about it, we need to get out of here."

"On it."

Trace could hear the kids still screaming inside the car.

Trace stepped closer, crouching down next to the one with the caved-in chest. He pressed his gun into soft flesh until he could feel broken bone grating beneath the barrel.

Trace put some weight behind it and the man groaned, but he didn't wake up. His eyes remained closed, and Trace could see pink foam bubbling from his lips.

Punctured lung?

Trace patted him down with one hand, stopping when he reached his left hip.

He pulled out a handgun, a Glock 19. Trace checked the safety and put it in his left jacket pocket. He kept going, finding a spare clip for the Glock and a walkie-talkie. They both went in his right jacket pocket. The rest of the man's pockets were empty.

Trace stepped away and walked over to the other one, coming to a stop a few feet away.

This one was still awake. He'd stopped screaming and was watching Trace warily as he approached, jaws clenched, his face white with pain.

Trace looked at his leg. He could see the white of bone poking through torn flesh and cloth. It was a nasty break. The kind of break that required a tourniquet. And surgery, but the man on the ground wasn't going to get either. Especially not from him.

Trace shook his head. "Doesn't look good."

"Help me," the man said, lips trembling, spittle gathering in the corners of his mouth as he tried to stop the bleeding with his hands.

"We had kids in the car. Did you know that?"

The man didn't say anything.

"What's your name?"

The man didn't say anything.

Trace nodded once before he bent down and pushed the barrel of his gun into the man's head.

"Name," Trace said again.

The man held his breath. Then he went very still, and his eyes remained locked on Trace.

"Ray," he said softly.

"See? That wasn't so hard. Now I've got your attention, Ray. And just so we're clear, I'm going to pat you down, and I'm going to take whatever you have that I want. And if you so much as sneeze, I'll pull the trigger. You follow? Blink once if you understand."

Ray didn't say anything, but he blinked just fine.

"Good," Trace said. He tapped him on the forehead with the barrel before patting him down left-handed.

He found two spare mags for the AK-47, another sixty rounds, and a knife he didn't need. That he threw into the bushes and only then, only once he was happy the man was disarmed and completely harmless, did he step away.

"Wait!"

Trace frowned at him. "Wait?"

"You can't leave me like this."

"Says who? As far as I'm concerned, Ray, you can go fuck yourself. And as for your brother over there, he isn't going to wake up again."

Ray glanced at the still shape farther down the road before his eyes looked back to Trace. He didn't say anything, but Trace saw a flicker of something in his face. Fear and then hate, and Trace smiled back at him.

"Ready?" he called over his shoulder.

"We're good!" shouted Drew.

"Let's go," Trace said to Sara, walking to the car backward.

He put his Glock back in its holster, climbed in through his ruined door, put the car in drive, and he waved goodbye to Ray with one finger as he drove around him, his mangled door kicking and dragging across the ground.

CLAY

Clay pushed down on the kickstand with his left heel and killed the engine.

He slung his right leg off his dirt bike and started walking, his rifle across his back, his Glock held out in front of him.

The black SUV was gone, but he wasn't taking any chances. He wasn't a complete idiot, so he went slowly, cautiously. He walked in the last ten yards, scanning the trees to his left before he looked at the men on the ground.

He stopped five feet away from the nearest one. Cletus.

It looked like Cletus had caught a bowling ball with his chest and the impact had forced all the blood into his little head. His face was bright purple, there was blood in his mouth and dried trails of red running from his nose. He looked like a burst berry leaking jam.

Clay walked past him. Dumb fuck Cletus was dead, but Ray was still alive. *White trash kids with white trash names,* thought Clay as he nudged Ray in the ribs with the toe of his boot.

"Hey, fuckhead, why'd you chase it?"

Ray opened his eyes and looked up at Clay, his face ghost white and going gray.

Clay looked at the splinters of shin bone poking through Ray's pants, looked at the puddle of blood beneath him.

Ray stared up at Clay, his mouth open to say something, and then Clay realized Ray's chest wasn't moving anymore.

Clay just stared at him, and the reality of the situation caught up with him.

"You stupid, dumb fucks! You stupid, stupid fucks!"

He swore. He felt sick. He saw red. He had a moment of sheer panic.

So he kicked Ray's limp corpse until he felt better. Then he took a breath, and he let it out. He brushed the hair off his face and went into damage control.

He started looking for their weapons. He checked their pockets, empty. He couldn't find their spare ammo or the radio either. He noticed the fuel cap from their mangled motorbike was missing, and Clay knew he was wasting his time.

"You fucking idiots." He turned to look back at Ray. "You got yourselves robbed as well? And where the fuck were you going? Where the fuck were you chasing them to? There's nothing down that way!" shouted Clay, pointing north.

But for once, smart-ass Ray didn't seem to have much to say. He just stared at Clay with that confused look on his face. So Clay kicked him again, just because he could. After that he pulled out his walkie-talkie, and he started planning what he was going to say, pacing back and forth, thinking hard, because right now Clay had a big problem.

Cletus and Ray might have been white trash, but so was their daddy, and their daddy was best friends with the Commander, and that made their dad like a king around here. Which meant Cletus and Ray were white trash royalty, as close to princes as this place had. And Daddy wasn't going to be happy. No, sir, Daddy would be pissed. Daddy would want blood, and someone to blame, and that wasn't good news for Clay, not good at all. *Think, Clay, think.*

Running away wasn't an option. It was too soon. He wasn't ready. He knew he wouldn't get far. They would catch him eventually, and when they did, they'd make an even bigger example out of him. They'd cut off his hands and his feet, use tourniquets to keep him alive, or maybe they'd make him eat his own dick. Something nasty. Or maybe they would try something new. So no, running away wasn't an option, not yet at least…

Clay changed the frequency dial on his walkie-talkie and noticed his hands were shaking.

Play it cool, he told himself. He had to be clever about it, make sure he covered his own ass.

He took a breath, pressed transmit, and started talking.

"Home… Uh, we have a problem."

There was a three-second delay.

"Clarify."

"The running backs fumbled the ball."

"Copy. Where is it?"

"Gone. Out of bounds. Heading north."

"Where are the running backs?"

"Out of the game."

"Clarify."

And that's where it got tricky. Clay swallowed. He didn't know how to say the next part in any sort of code.

"Uh. They're dead."

"Where the fuck were you?" spat Taimus, his yellow teeth flashing as spittle flew.

Clay tried not to breathe. Cletus and Ray's old man's breath stank like shit, like his teeth were rotting. Clay doubted he'd ever brushed them a day in his life.

Taimus stabbed his finger in Clay's face again, and Clay resisted the urge to grab it and snap it off. It's not like he hadn't done it before, and to bigger men. But Clay didn't move, he didn't even blink. He kept his face blank, and he kept his mouth shut. No teeth display, no aggression. He ignored the sweat crawling down his back, and he kept his eyes on the Commander. They were in his tent now; this was his house. His rules. The way Clay saw it, as bad as Taimus was, the Commander was worse. He called the shots around here. The decision would come from him, and the King would have to be fine with it.

"Well?" said the Commander. "Answer the man."

"I was in position," Clay said. "They went too early. The Ford saw them coming and left the road. They followed it, and I lost sight of them. By the time I got there it was already over."

Technically true. He'd watched through his binoculars to make sure. No way was he risking his life for those two morons.

Taimus lunged at him. "You should have done something!" he screamed, his hand bunched into a fist as a fat vein throbbed in his forehead. His face went from red to purple, and for a second Clay was reminded of Cletus.

"I did," said Clay. "As fast as I could. They were already dead when I got there. Nothing else I could do."

Also technically true.

Clay kept himself very still. He didn't shrug. He didn't apologize. Saying sorry would mean he was responsible, and he wasn't. Those two dumb fucks had got themselves killed all by themselves. He just couldn't say that to their old man.

There was a pecking order everywhere in life. Prison had taught Clay to see it easier, how to read a bad situation. When to talk, when to shut up, when to go out arms flailing, when to wait.

And right now, he needed to wait. He needed to stay calm, needed to see which way the wind was blowing before he decided to take a piss.

So Clay just took it as Taimus raged, resisting the urge to wipe the spit from his face. He kept his eyes fixed on the map behind the Commander's desk, a map dotted with important-looking pins and marked with red pen, and he waited until the King stopped screaming at him long enough to catch his breath.

The Commander stepped forward in the gap. He put a hand on Taimus's shoulder, pulled him away, leaned in close, and said something in his friend's ear. The King went very still.

It was a long conversation. Clay could see the Commander's lips moving, talking softly.

The Commander stopped. Taimus turned to look at Clay, then he spat on the floor and walked out of the tent.

Clay didn't know what that meant. He assumed bad. It normally was, and he started sweating even worse, getting that dry mouth, like he needed to spit too. But he knew that would be a bad idea. So he waited as the silence dragged on and on, waiting for the Commander to say something.

But he just stood there, watching Clay, looking at him like he was a bug and not a 295-pound man, and Clay knew he was in deep shit.

"Sir, I didn—"

"You've created something of a problem for me," the Commander said, cutting him off.

Clay opened his mouth again.

"Don't talk," said the Commander.

Clay shut his mouth real fast.

The Commander turned away and went to sit behind his desk. Something they'd brought back to camp for him, special-like, a gift. Picked it up from one of the houses they had raided a couple of weeks back.

It was a huge, grand thing, made of old oak and polished until it shone. It must have weighed a ton, too, and it looked ancient, like something that belonged in a museum or on a plantation from the slaving days. Either way, Clay thought it looked ridiculous inside a tent.

"Those people you let get away. You're going to find them. And you're going to bring them back here, alive. Or I give you to Taimus. We clear?"

Clay nodded. "Yes, sir."

"I'm going to send you with a couple of my boys. Sergeant Roberts will be in charge; you answer to him."

Clay nodded again, letting out the breath he'd been holding. "Yes, sir."

He kept waiting as the Commander started going through papers on his desk.

The Commander looked up at him.

"You're still here?"

Clay didn't know what to do.

"Get the fuck out. Now!"

Clay left with his tail between his legs, but he left alive, and he chalked that up as a win.

Clay ducked out of the tent, trying very hard not to look like he was running. He picked up his backpack and rifle from the ground, slung the bag over his left shoulder, his rifle over his right. He turned to walk away and found Sergeant Roberts blocking his exit.

"Going somewhere?" Roberts looked him over, not bothering to hide the contempt in his voice. "Grab your shit and fall in. We're leaving now. To fix your fucking mess!"

Clay just shrugged. He didn't say anything, didn't bother arguing, didn't rise to the bait. What was the point?

Roberts was a dick, a little man in a dirty uniform with a short-shit complex. He had a high-pitched voice, and he seemed to like the sound of it.

"Wonderful," spat Roberts. "I got lumped in with the fuckin' Neanderthal. You speak English?"

Clay smiled lazily. He could have snapped Roberts in half. He towered over him, but Roberts had that one thing he didn't:

friends, a lot of friends, and that made him untouchable. So Clay just shrugged again and motioned for Roberts to lead the way.

He followed Roberts through the middle of camp, one half of which looked like it had been made by someone with OCD. The dark green army tents on his right-hand side were straight as arrows, neat and orderly, no rubbish, no mess, even the grass was cut. Fifteen tents in total, five rows of three, six soldiers to a tent. Some had solar panels on the roofs and basic air conditioning.

The King's side of camp was another story entirely. It was as though a fair had come to town, or a hurricane. No tent was the same color or shape, there were crossed wires and ropes everywhere, and not a straight line in sight. Filthy tents housing only half the number of men but scattered over twice the area. There was rubbish and shit everywhere, and their half of the camp stank of piss, like the King's men couldn't be bothered walking the hundred yards to the latrines.

Clay was just waiting for them to get sick, another reason he camped out near the road by himself. He didn't feel like spending his last few weeks on Earth with his pants around his ankles, shitting himself to death.

Roberts veered off the path, aiming for one of the bigger tents on the King's side, his boots slipping on the trampled grass and mud. He didn't bother to check if Clay was following. Roberts seemed to think that walking in front meant he was in charge.

Clay had a different opinion—a rule, really. Never turn your back on someone; it makes you vulnerable. There's no way to see an attack coming, no way to defend against it, and turning your back on someone is a good way to end up with a knife in your kidneys, especially if they don't like you, and the kidneys were a good target. Low on the body, close to the surface, no protective layers, no ribs in the way, and with something like a fifth of the body's blood supply running through them. You wanna kill someone? That's one of the spots you aim for. You go for the neck, the kidneys, or the arteries in the groin. Lots of blood flow. Hard to stop once they're severed. Messy, but quick; a man would bleed out in minutes.

They picked up four more men along the way, two soldiers and two of the King's men, but none too high up the chain. Shit kickers, basically. No one would miss them if they didn't come back, and Clay found he was smiling again. Today was turning out to be a good day. It had stopped raining, the sun had come out, Ray and Cletus's deaths hadn't stuck to him. He still had all his limbs. And his freedom.

Clay hoped they got to take one of the trucks they were walking toward, that way he might be able to lie down in the back and sleep. Another thing he'd learned in prison—close your eyes and time goes faster. For a second, Clay even fantasized about taking the Commander's chopper. He'd never been in one before. He didn't even know what type it was, big and painted matte green, parked next to the line of trucks and sitting high on its trailer with its rotors folded back along its body and orange plugs in its air intakes. Parked just behind it were six Hummers and twelve APCs, their cargo of ammo and weapons and gas masks unloaded long ago and carried down into the facility behind him.

That facility was the whole reason they were all here in the first place.

It was the whole reason for the ten-foot-tall barbed wire fence that wrapped around the entire compound, almost a perfect square with sides two miles long, and it was the whole reason for the small hut at the end of the camp that sat across the only road into the place. A guardhouse, complete with a boom gate, road spikes, and a big red sign with white letters: *Restricted area. Government property. No trespassing.*

They were sitting on top of an old Cold War relic, a nuclear missile silo. The nukes were long gone, but the facility was still functional, or had been just before the world ended. The Commander had made very sure of that before he'd helped himself to his base's armory and hit the road.

But he hadn't stopped there. The Commander had a vision, a "plan" as he kept telling them. They just had to do as he said. Follow orders.

So that's what they'd been doing, and Clay could see they were slowly turning this place into a fort. Erecting a smaller razor-wire fence within the original boundaries of the compound, laying a minefield between, rigged with searchlights and trip wires. Meanwhile, inside the second fence they were building garages and watchtowers connected by covered tunnels and walkways.

And every day the King's men returned to base with the Commander's shopping list of building supplies and equipment: heavy-duty earthmovers and forklifts and trailers loaded with steel pylons and concrete barriers.

When the Cloud came, the idea was they would all scurry underground and shut the blast doors behind them. It was airtight, self-contained, and had enough food, water, and fuel stockpiled to last two years. The Commander hadn't been specific on just how old the food was, or how many men he had accounted for in his calculations, but there were a lot of men up here, and even more of the King's men out on the roads.

Clay smelled a rat.

He'd been inside. He'd spent a whole day moving equipment inside like some glorified pack mule.

No way they could all fit, and he had no doubt that when the time came, he'd find the door slammed shut in his face. He was almost tempted to try and make his escape now, ready or not. But there was no way he could get his stuff, not with Roberts watching him. Which meant he had to finish this first, catch whoever it was that they were chasing, deliver them to the King, get his stuff, and only then could he make his escape.

After that he'd make his way to LA. Maybe stop by the Hollywood sign, do the tourist thing, head across to Santa Monica, check out Gold's Gym, then pick a nice spot on the Pier to watch the world end. Or maybe he'd start swimming, he wasn't sure yet.

"The one on the left is ours," said Roberts, pointing to one of the Hummers and jarring Clay from his daydream.

"We're taking it as far as Lyons. A car matching the description you gave was found abandoned just north of Sterling twenty minutes ago. Out of gas and pretty shot up. They have a three-hour head start on us, but they're on foot, going cross-country, which means they'll be going slow."

"Why Lyons?" asked Clay.

"Ah, the monkey talks," said Roberts, turning to look at him before sharing a look with the two soldiers. He ignored the King's men completely.

"Why Lyons? Because in Lyons we're picking up a tracker, his dogs, and some horses."

"Horses?" asked Clay, not following.

Roberts shot him another look. "Yes, horses. Are you retarded? How else you gonna catch them? You gonna run? We'll head back south to the car on horseback and pick up their trail from there. I reckon we'll have them tonight, tomorrow at the latest."

Clay nodded. It sounded like a good plan. Except for the horses part. But he didn't think it would be too hard to catch whoever it was they were after either. Not easy, but between the Commander and the King, they had this whole corner of Kansas locked down. The line was thin in parts; they were spread out over a wide area. But like a net or a noose, they could tighten it real quick when they needed to. And whereas their prey would have to take it slow, take the backroads, they wouldn't have that same problem. They could simply call ahead and punch straight through, roadblocks opening up to let them pass and closing again once they had gone.

Clay nodded again. This was going to be over in no time, and it wasn't going to end well for whoever they were after. No, sir.

This time it was personal.

DAY
2

Route Nationale 83 (D1083)
Thirty klicks southeast of Bourg-en-Bresse
France

LEVI

The L-ATV, or Light Combat Tactical All-Terrain Vehicle, was a solid machine, big and ugly. Like the unfortunate result of a one-night stand between a light tank and a Ford 750.

Made by OshKosh Defense, the same company that made the MRAP, the L-ATV was the Humvee's long overdue replacement, and this one was so new that Levi could swear the desert camo paint was still drying.

Externally, it looked nothing like its predecessor. More like a truck than a jeep. Sitting twice as high, with twice the ground clearance, coming standard with back passenger suicide doors, smaller windows, and thicker doors. It rode heavy on honeycomb-run flat tires, with a windshield slanted to deflect small caliber projectiles. All good things in Levi's opinion.

The original Hummer had never been designed with IEDs in mind; it had never even been meant for combat in the first place. They were too low to the ground for one, with flat bottoms and no real armor. Add-on kits didn't count; they barely made a difference.

But with the L-ATV, they'd gone back to the drawing board, taken what they'd learned in Iraq and Afghanistan and started again.

Survivability had been the end goal, so they'd built it with an armored crew capsule, self-sealing fuel tanks, inbuilt fire extinguishers, and an underbody shaped to deflect blasts away from the vehicle. They'd made it into a bombproof pod on wheels.

Problem was there was no such thing, and saying different was just wishful thinking. Political bullshit. Because they already made IEDs big enough to take out tanks. And tanks weigh seventy tons, L-ATVs only seven.

He didn't need to be a genius to work out the rest, and Levi knew too many guys missing legs and arms and dicks. He didn't want to join them. He liked his dick.

So Levi tried not to think about it. Sometimes the worst thing a soldier can do is think. Thinking about what *might* happen was pointless, a distraction. He'd learned long ago it was much more important to concentrate on the moment.

"See anything, Briggs?" Gunner James Colter asked as he leaned forward, his face obscured by his M50 gas mask while his eyes followed the blinding beams of their headlights out into the dark. Headlights that glinted off abandoned cars and falling snow. Cars that lay on their sides, upside down, wrapped around trees, or torn to pieces.

"Negative," said Briggs as hydraulics purred in the roof above their heads.

That was another one of their toys—the CROWS turret, a remote-operated terrorist killer. Its .50-cal machine gun attachment followed every motion of Briggs's hand. Which meant there was no longer the need for someone to stick their head out of the top of the car like an idiot. But it also meant poorer visibility, less situational awareness, slower reaction times. And they jammed. Constantly. Which meant some sucker still had to climb outside to fix the damn thing, and seeing as how neither the gunner nor the driver ever left the car, and Colter sure as shit wouldn't be the one sent out to fix a jam, guess which sucker was left?

This guy.

But Levi had to admit, the CROWS was ten times more tacticool than the manually operated .50, with fifteen times more zoom, twenty times more freedom, and 100 times more infrared.

Just one of the many perks of a bigger defense budget and unending war: better toys.

The L-ATV version they were in also had the ProPulse diesel-electric powertrain, able to extend their range by another 150 miles, or function as a mobile generator that pumped out 120 kW of power. Enough to supply a small airfield, or a hospital, or your mom's vibrator.

"Levi?" Gunner Colter asked.

"Huh?"

"Pull your thumb out your ass. I said, did you *see* anything?"

"Fuck all… sir," mumbled Levi as an afterthought, flinching as the darkness was stripped bare in a flickering flash of light. To Levi, for a brief moment, it looked like the surface of the moon out there. It looked flat and gray and dead. Ground covered in a layer of dirty snow, thin trees cloaked in white.

Thunder boomed in the darkness that rushed back in, and Levi looked out of his window, through the four-inch-thick bulletproof glass, and he wondered again at the darkness that seemed to have swallowed up every sign of life and light and people.

The only lights they had seen in the last hour, since driving through Lyon, were from the abandoned cars they passed along the way. But he hadn't seen a single living person. All that remained were red smears of snow and bits of shredded metal, and he didn't know how to process that bit of information. It didn't make any sense, and it was creeping the shit out of him. Even more than the Cloud, visible from space, 360 miles across, and looking like the biggest hurricane Levi had ever seen.

On the ground it was something else entirely. A black mass that stretched across the sky as far as the eye could see, crawling with lightning and bucketing down rain and hail and snow and ash.

And as their convoy had driven in under it, Levi had watched the world outside grow dark and cold. He had watched the sun become paler than the moon, then paler still. He had watched the world change color, stained blood red, turning a dirty brown, fading to gray, then finally a deep black that only the blind could understand.

Since then, the only view he had of the world was a dim one. And strangely, through the goggles of his gas mask, and in the brief flashes of lightning that jumped through the sky above, in here, under the Cloud, light just didn't seem to travel as far as it should. It just seemed to peter out and stop, and nobody had the slightest idea what was causing it or where all the ash in the air was coming from.

Fingers were being pointed at the Russians. But Ivan was denying it. As usual.

Colter didn't seem to have a clue, either. He just looked worried, and one lesson Levi had learned from his time with the old man was that if Colter was worried, then you fuckin' better be too.

Not that thirty-seven was old, but Levi was only twenty-two, and that made Colter ancient in his books, like a living dinosaur. He couldn't imagine being a marine for as long as Colter. *Eighteen fucking years!* It did Levi's head in. Colter was a career marine, in for the long haul. Levi was here because he didn't have much of a choice, but mostly thanks to the ginger idiot sitting here next to him, Lance Corporal Briggs. His ugly brother from another mother.

It had been his "genius" idea to enlist in the first place. "Bitches love uniforms," Briggs had said.

Levi hadn't necessarily agreed, but there weren't exactly many options for two poor white kids from Southie. And seeing how they'd had each other's backs since they were five years old, he'd followed Briggs's lead and tagged along. Besides, he couldn't just leave the carrot to fend for himself. No survival skills, and he'd never have forgiven himself if something happened. Briggs was the closest thing to family he had; Briggs's parents had basically raised him as their own. His own dad walked out when he was three, and his mom had taken it out on him, like it was somehow his fault for being born. Never mind the constant string of useless boyfriends she kept bringing home, especially the ones that thought he needed to learn some discipline. All they'd really taught him was how to take a beating.

So at the wiseass age of eighteen, they'd joined the Marines. For the money and the pussy and a clean break.

At nineteen, he knew better. At twenty, he already had one tour in Iraq under his belt, and at twenty-two he was on his way back for his third. Or at least he had been until this little detour… But Levi kept telling himself that when this was all over, he was pulling the pin and getting out. His five years would be up. The war didn't look like it was ever going to end; the Taliban controlled more territory than it did pre 9/11, pulling out of Syria had come back to bite them on the ass, Israel and Iran were at each other's throats, the civil wars and ethnic cleansings in Iraq and Syria raged on, and Yemen was quickly heading the same direction as Afghanistan.

Frankly, he'd had enough. And if Briggs tried to talk him into enlisting again, then he was gonna shoot him in the foot and carry him home himself while he still had both his legs.

He didn't know what he'd do when he got back home though. When he had to fit in, when he had to take off the uniform and be "normal" again. No doubt he'd burn that bridge when he got to it. He could already imagine the civilian job applications. No college qualifications. No work experience. Country in the middle of a recession. He could already imagine the interview questions.

Are you capable of standing and walking for long periods of time?

Yes.

What did you like most about your last job?

Working as part of a team to overcome obstacles.

What did you like least?

Improvised Explosive Devices…

He'd end up packing shelves, flipping burgers, or digging pools. Something manual and labor intensive.

He just wished he'd done it sooner, or somehow talked Briggs out of enlisting in the first place, because now they were in France. Not off the coast, running drills with the French navy like they were supposed to be, and Levi's Spidey sense was tingling worse than that time he'd got the clap.

They weren't prepared for this, whatever *this* was. One look outside was more than enough to tell him that, but the shit was hitting the fan, and the French were screaming for help. So here they were, boots on the ground, Operation Human Shield. Forward recon. *Fucked as usual.*

Marine Gunner Colter, Sergeant Miller, Briggs, Weeks, himself, and eight other marines from 1st Platoon, Alpha Company, 2nd Reconnaissance, sent on some wild goose chase. Aiming for Bourg-en-Bresse with no intel, the wrong equipment, and decked out in full MOPP gear because no one had the slightest idea what all the black shit in the air was.

The MOPP gear, or Mission Oriented Protective Posture, would keep them safe. *At least in theory*, Levi reminded himself for the thousandth time. It was designed to be used by military personnel in toxic environments, kinda like hazmat suits, only better.

He also had M9 Detector Paper taped to his right bicep, on his left wrist, and on his right leg. The paper contained an agent-sensitive dye, which would turn pink, red, or a reddish-brown purple color depending on what he ran into. So if he ran into something nasty, he'd know pretty quick, and if it was *really* nasty then none of them would live long enough to worry about it. Not that it made him feel any better.

The main problem with the MOPP was comfort and ventilation, or the lack of it. It was like wearing a wetsuit on land. The rubber was pinching his balls, the collar was chafing the back of his neck, and he was sweating his ass off. But whatever was causing this darkness, whatever this ash was, they weren't taking any chances. So they would wear their MOPP until told otherwise, and that was perfectly okay with him.

"Command, this is Alpha One-Zero, Actual. Copy? Over," Colter said, taking his finger off the button.

The radio crackled, the channel hissing with static. Static that was getting worse with every mile.

"Alpha, this is Command, that's a good copy. Send it," came the response.

Levi was looking at *it* on the infrared monitor. *It* being three stationary cars, two with glowing white hot spots indicating their engines were still running.

"Command, we have visual on a possible squad-sized convoy coming in from the northeast via Bourg-en-Bresse. Over," Colter said.

Possible being the operative word, thought Levi. They wouldn't really know until they got closer.

Aside from their headlights and the CROWS searchlight, IR was the only way they could see anything out here, but it didn't give them a whole lot of the finer details, and the ash in the air was degrading the range significantly. Their night vision goggles didn't help much, either; they only worked by amplifying ambient light, and in darkness like this they were completely useless.

The radio hissed. "Alpha, interrogative, can you confirm whether they are an armored mechanized convoy? We've lost contact with Bravo Two-Zero."

Shit.

Levi twisted around, looking back the way they had come, seeing the two L-ATVs following close behind. He shaded his eyes against the glare of their headlights, trying to see that sliver of yellow light somewhere far behind them. Daylight. But that was gone now, too. All he could see was the L-ATVs kicking up plumes of snow and ash in their wake, billowing clouds that glowed red in their taillights, and he felt a terrible sense of foreboding. A childish fear that if they went in any deeper under the Cloud, he may never see the sun again.

"This is bullshit," Levi said, turning back to face the front.

As it was, they were supposed to be looking for ten French Gendarmerie units that had gone missing somewhere between Lyon and Meyrin, but, after three hours of playing hide and seek, they hadn't seen jack shit. It was like all those men had simply vanished into thin air.

And now our own units are dropping off the map?

Levi didn't understand it. That many men couldn't just disappear, but they had, and for the thousandth time he wished for some air support, or a clue as to what the fuck was going on.

But that cloud above them was like a physical shield. Nothing got through it from above, not even radio waves, and anything that tried to fly through it suffered so many lightning strikes that it came out the other end looking like charcoal with all the aerodynamics of a brick. Even flying below the Cloud was dangerous.

Apparently the ash was abrasive; it was having some sort of sandblasting effect, turning canopies opaque, stripping the paint off, getting sucked in the air intakes, causing combustion failures and flameouts. Planes had literally been falling out of the sky.

So, for now, their entire air support was grounded. And if that didn't scream area denial weapon, then Levi didn't know what did. Because without air support they had no idea what was around the next corner, never mind over the next hill. They were sitting ducks out here.

"Copy that, Command. Negative on armored convoy," Colter replied. "I'm counting three stationary POVs. Got them on the thermals. Over."

The POVs, or privately owned vehicles, practically glowed on the monitor. Two hot white and one a warm gray, and, just like all the other civilian cars they had seen so far, going nowhere.

The radio hissed. "Alpha One-Zero, what is their proximity to your current position?"

"Command, reporting two klicks and closing. POVs stationary, no movement spotted. Over."

They passed a truck, a blue semi parked in the middle of the road with a ragged three-foot-wide hole in the windshield, cage bars bent and twisted as though something had forced its way in.

In, Levi noted, *not out.*

There was blood, too. A lot of blood, about the amount an adult would contain if they were wrung out like a wet rag. Dark red splashes across the interior, long brown smears down the hood where the driver had been dragged out.

Levi stared at the truck until it was lost in the dark behind them, like it was nothing but a bad dream.

Holeeee shit. He turned back to the front, his eyes a little wider than they were before. He even considered giving himself a slap, but he didn't want the others to think he was losing it. *Not yet.*

Even Briggs was quiet for a change. Normally you couldn't get the guy to shut up, but he just sat there, his eyelids peeled back, watching the monitor in front of him, pivoting the CROWS turret with small movements of the joystick in his hand, looking for anything that moved out there. Anything he might need to shoot before it shot them.

Levi shuffled uncomfortably in his seat, swaying from side to side as the L-ATV climbed over the curb. Again.

Weeks, their driver, was being forced to weave between all the abandoned cars that littered the highway, driving on the shoulder more often than the road, which made for a bumpy ride. It also slowed them down, and that made Levi nervous.

Going slow went against everything he'd learned in Iraq. In Iraq, there was no such thing as a red light; you drove fast, you didn't let yourself get penned in. You didn't stop. Not even for kids. Because nine times out of ten, when kids stopped convoys, there was an ambush in play and everyone died. So you kept going. You closed your eyes if you had to, but you kept your foot on the gas, you drove straight, and you told yourself those bumps you felt in the road were just potholes.

But as for Weeks... he almost looked like he was enjoying himself, like it was a Sunday drive, humming some tune that Levi couldn't place, tapping a beat on the steering wheel. Completely out of time, and oblivious to it.

Bastard.

If there was ever an epitome of a MARINE, it was Weeks. Muscles Are Required Intelligence Not Essential.

He liked Weeks. Big, affable guy. Friendly. Just not the brightest. And high-fiving him was like surviving a car wreck. But if Weeks was worried about their speed, he didn't show it, and Levi sure as shit wasn't going to give him the satisfaction of complaining first. So he kept his mouth shut and went back to suffering in silence, watching as their headlights reflected back off a road sign.

Bourg-en-Bresse. Twenty kilometers, Levi read. Maybe fifteen minutes away under normal conditions, but now? Maybe double that. All up, maybe an eight-hour round trip from Toulon. They'd already had to stop once and refuel at Lyon. They'd probably have to stop again on the way back, too, otherwise they'd be crawling back to base on fumes, diesel hybrid or not.

That's if we don't get stuck out here first, an increasingly worried part of him added.

It was another minute before the cars they had seen on the IR were close enough for Briggs to pin them in the glare of their searchlight and for Levi to see them with his own eyes.

One of the cars was in a ditch, a white 2010 BMW X1, maybe a

2011. Levi knew his cars, but it was a bit banged up, so it was hard to tell. Just beyond it was a blue Mercedes, a 2016 GLA, lying on its side, its windshield missing and its engine dead. Its hood was a mottled gray on the IR, and slowly getting darker as the car's engine cooled in the freezing air, which told Levi this was recent.

He didn't think a car could keep running if it was on its side. Either the oil or the fuel didn't flow, he couldn't remember which. Either way, it meant it couldn't have been too long since they were hit. But hit by what?

Because the last car was in pieces, he didn't even know what make it was, never mind what color it used to be. It didn't even look like a car anymore. It looked like a bomb had gone off inside, all twisted metal and gaping holes, windows smashed and tires shredded. He had no idea what kind of rounds left holes like that, with long serrated edges, metal peeled back like it had been attacked with a can opener. IED?

But where was the explosive damage? Where was the burning? And even more worryingly, *where are the bodies?*

Levi leaned forward when he realized the BMW sat on rims that looked to have been ridden on for some time, their edges dulled, blunted, and bent, like they had started to melt.

"Gunny?" Weeks asked, giving Colter a nervous glance.

"Stop us here, Weeks. Look awake, marines," Colter said.

The convoy came to a grinding halt twenty meters out.

Ambush? Levi wondered, his head on a swivel, looking left, looking right, seeing only darkness to either side.

Briggs brought the turret around, concentrating his searchlight on the mess inside one of the cars, and, like a microscope being brought to bear, it made it so much easier to see all the things better left alone.

Briggs whistled in amazement.

The inside of the car looked like the floor of a slaughterhouse. Levi could see flashlights wedged between chairs, their batteries almost dead. He saw a small child's shoe in the back seat; he saw bits of clothing, but still no people. No bodies. Not even bits.

"What the fuck?" Levi said.

"Command, this is Alpha One-Zero," said Colter. "POVs are empty. No sign of friendlies or mechanized unit Bravo Two-Zero. We're seeing heavy weapons damage, heavy casualties suspected. Requesting air support. Over."

Seconds ticked by with nothing but the hiss of static to fill them.

"Alpha One-Zero, this is Command. That's a negative on air support. Continue on."

Continue on? Levi wanted to scream. *Continue on to what?* There wasn't a single light shining out there, their GPS was useless, and sending them further into the dark, with no air support, when they had no idea what they were driving into was just bullshit. Perfect conditions for an ambush.

Fucking orders, my ass.

Some fobbit back at Command was working on one hell of a brain fart.

"Sir?" asked Briggs, sounding as worried as Levi felt.

Colter picked up the mic and pressed down on the transmit button. "Ten-four, Command. Alpha One-Zero, Oscar Mike, ETA to Bourg-en-Bresse..." Colter looked at his watch. "Thirty minutes. Over." Colter nodded at Weeks. "Drive on."

"Sure. Keep going," Briggs muttered under his breath as he made a gun out of his left hand and put it to his own head.

Weeks grunted, and the convoy started moving again, giving the crumpled POVs a wide berth, the two L-ATVs behind following in their tracks as they accelerated away from the mess. "Continue on," muttered Levi in his best impression of Command. "Dumbest idea of the century."

"Shut it, Levi."

"Come on, Gunny, you have to admit this is a load of bullshit."

Colter shrugged. "What's your point? We have a job to do. The quicker we do it, the sooner we can get back. I don't like being under here any more than you do, but someone has to do it, and right now that someone is us. So in the meantime… stop being a bitch and shut up unless you see something. Oorah?"

"Oorah!" shouted Weeks.

"Fucking oorah," answered Levi, sharing none of the enthusiasm.

The L-ATV went off the edge of the road again, dropping with a sickening lurch before it bottomed out.

Levi winced, adding another bruise to his growing collection.

"Any way we can hurry this up, sir?" grumbled Briggs.

"Not unless Weeks here has any tricks up his sleeve that he hasn't shared with us yet," said Colter.

Weeks stopped humming to himself and started talking instead, as though they were sitting at a bar somewhere on shore leave, like they were trading stories instead of watching hell freeze over outside.

"I had a buddy," Weeks said, which was pretty much how every one of his stories started.

Levi groaned.

Weeks didn't seem to hear him. "See, this guy grew up in my town, eight years older than me. Enlisted twenty-four hours after the first plane hit. Anyway, he was in the 4th Tanks, Delta Co."

"And?" interrupted Briggs, rolling his eyes and trading a look with Levi. *Seriously?*

"And fucking patience!" Weeks bellowed. "Anyway. He was a driver in an Abrams. Anyway, fuck!" Still annoyed. "So this guy, he used to love telling me this story whenever we caught up for drinks stateside."

Levi grunted as Weeks gathered momentum. *And here we go again.*

"See, the ragheads over there, they used to have these stands where they'd sell kebabs, motor oil, gas and shit, you know. Anyway, my buddy said that one day he got bored, so he just got off the road. Mounted the curb in his tank, and he just plowed through a whole row of these things." Weeks even added the sound effects like he was a kid and it was show-and-tell. "He said they would just cruise through, demolish the place, and make everybody run away. He said that one time, he saw a really shiny silver Mercedes. And my buddy asked his tank commander, 'Sir, can I crush that car?'"

There was a pause.

"Now, see, the tank commander didn't say yes. But he did say, 'What car?'"

Weeks laughed, Briggs sniggered. Even Levi smiled.

"That's what we need here, my friends," said Weeks. "A fucking tank and my buddy driving. Then we'd get there in no time. Straight through. None of this slow ass slalom shit." He turned to look at Colter. "Hey, Gunner, what you think? Any chance of you getting us a tank?"

More laughter, Colter just shook his head, looking worried again, and Levi went quiet.

Weeks made a good point, though. A tank was sounding like a good idea about now, and least of all because of the traffic.

CASS

Cass held the square of metal up against the side of the bus while the man with the welding torch stepped in next to him. He turned his face away, closed his eyes. The welding torch turned on with a sputtering hiss, and he could see the blood in his eyelids.

"Good."

The light went out, red faded to black, and Cass blinked in the darkness that followed.

He held his breath, and he let go. But the panel held. Job done, another window sealed shut. The plan was working; they were making progress.

Cass knew he should have been pleased, should have felt happy, but he didn't. He felt sick. His head was pounding, his hands wouldn't stop shaking, and he was having trouble focusing. One thought flowed into the next, and the whole room seemed to vibrate in time to the generator's hum.

Closing his eyes helped. But that left him in the dark and made the world spin, which made him want to be sick. So Cass kept his eyes open. He barely blinked, eyes burning as he looked down at the bruise on his arm. A bruise that was particularly dark, as though his skin was stained with ink. And the stain was spreading, crawling into his hand, beneath his insulating gloves, black tendrils where his veins should be, and the same uneasy thought slithered through his mind again.

Something is very wrong.

If it was just him, it would make more sense. Classic signs of Acute Radiation Exposure. He could almost accept that. Massive cell death and internal hemorrhaging. After all, he'd been the closest to Meyrin. He'd been exposed to the highest levels of radiation for the longest time, more than anyone else here. Especially if he had been walking downwind all that time.

But it wasn't just him.

Everyone was sick, and that didn't make any sense. The radiation levels in the fallout shouldn't be this bad. Not this far out from Meyrin, even accounting for wind direction. That's just not how it worked. The levels in the air around them would be harmful, of course, but low, relatively speaking. Symptoms shouldn't show up for years, maybe decades. Just like Chernobyl.

But that wasn't what he was seeing.

Cass looked in the corner of the garage. At the old couple laid out next to each other, their bodies tucked out of the way, out of sight of the kids. The old-timer with his jacket draped across his face, and a dirty piece of plastic tarp for his wife. He could see their hands poking out of the bottom. Old age, weak hearts, and too much stress. He could almost accept their deaths. But next to them was a man in his mid-forties. Externally he looked perfectly healthy, except he'd had some sort of coughing fit, and next to him was his son, thirteen years old. Same deal, both dead, skin tinged blue, growing cold. Which didn't make any sense. Unless it was genetic. A defect, maybe. Like asthma. Some kind of faulty immune response passed down from father to son? But then what was the trigger? The ash?

He had no idea. He was clutching at straws, trying to make the pieces fit.

Cass looked away, and sour bile swam in the back of his throat. He turned his head so most of the mess went on the floor instead of himself.

Another surge of vomit followed the first, waves of nausea crashing down on him, dragging him under as he leaned on his knees, stomach heaving, staring at the mess he'd made on the floor. Concrete splattered with yellow bile dotted with dark beads of red that began to dilute and fade.

Well, that's not good.

He leaned over to spit, shaking his head and wiping his mouth with the back of his hand.

The man with the welding torch flipped up his visor and looked at him.

"You okay?" he asked.

Cass just grunted at him. Stupid question. He waved him away and stood up straight, leaning against the bus as white spots swam in his vision.

"You sure?" the man asked, his accent rolling the *R*.

Cass didn't answer. What was the point? He just bent down to pick up another piece of metal that looked like it used to be one of the workshop's tool chests. Diamond steel plate, spray painted bright red, hammered out until it was a flat sheet. They would have been expensive. Not that anyone cared anymore. They'd already picked the two cars in the garage clean. All that was left of them were their frames, and now they were cannibalizing everything else they could find: the Steelflex roll-up covers from the inspection pits, the stainless-steel workbenches, the lockers in the kitchen, the legs of chairs. Doors, even.

Cass lifted the heavy square of metal up against the side of the bus, and someone else came up on his right to help him hold it flush across the window.

The man with the welding torch stepped in between them and flipped his visor down.

"Ready?" he asked.

Cass nodded. He didn't have much of a choice. They were running out of time, and some small part of him wondered if maybe they already had. But he turned his face away anyway and closed his eyes.

The arc welder turned on with a sputtering hiss, the lights above his head dimmed, and the process started all over again.

LEVI

They hadn't moved in five minutes.

They just sat there. Out on the southwest edge of Bourg-en-Bresse.

Parked on a slight rise where the extra altitude gave them a shallow view of the city and the buildings directly in front of them. An industrial area, maybe retail, or a bit of both, judging by the empty parking lots and bare concrete.

Nobody spoke. Even Weeks had stopped humming. The big guy barely breathed, and he kept both hands on the steering wheel, watching Colter out of the corner of his eye. Waiting for him to make a decision: turn back or keep going.

Levi knew which one he'd vote for, if it was up to a vote—not that it ever was—because going much further was plain retarded. Their fuel was sitting on half a tank, their communications were completely cut off, all calls to Command were going unanswered. So either no one could hear them or no one was listening anymore, and they hadn't come across a single French unit or Bravo Two-Zero either. They weren't here, and they hadn't passed them on the road.

This is ridiculous! Bravo Two-Zero couldn't have gotten this far without us seeing some sign of them, and there's no way they could have pushed on to Meyrin. They'd be running low on gas, just like us... unless they filled up somewhere and kept going?

Levi nodded to himself. They might have to do the same just to make it back to Command, but even finding a gas station in all this darkness was going to take some luck. He couldn't see anything on the IR. No people. No signs of life. No hot spots except an enormous fire to the north and one solitary light shining all the way across to the east.

The city in front of them looked dead. Nothing but cold, empty spaces surrounded by cold, dark buildings that looked almost black on the monitor. It looked like an easy place to get lost in. Full of streets with odd names he couldn't even begin to pronounce, with no landmarks and no navigation cues. Even Colter's compass was acting up, the little red needle spinning and twitching like it was possessed. And if they took a wrong turn in there, Levi could just imagine them driving around in circles until they ran out of gas. And then what? They'd be stranded. At least until the next fucked fact-finding mission came looking for them.

He was starting to wonder if that's what had happened to Bravo Two-Zero. At least, he hoped that's what had happened. The alternative was worse, and with that thought he remembered all those cars they had driven past, all those smears of red snow.

Colter turned to look back at them, and Levi felt the butterflies in his stomach flutter.

"Ready, marines?"

"I'm ready to go home if that's what you're asking," replied Levi, knowing everyone else was thinking the same thing.

Colter shook his head, so Levi knew what he was going to say next. Not hard, considering the options.

Option number one: they go in.

Or option number two: they turn back now, with enough gas to make it back to base, and they come back again later when they're better prepared. That's what normal people would do. It's what smart, sane people would do.

Unfortunately, option two would mean going back without any questions answered, which added delay and would only risk more lives later, and Colter wouldn't accept that. You couldn't get to his level if you turned tail every time a situation went to shit, and in Levi's experience there were two types of NCOs. The type that played it safe, more interested in climbing the ladder than winning the war. And then there was the other type, the type that got shit done.

So Levi knew they weren't going to do the smart thing. They were going to do the other thing. What marines do.

Fucking wonderful.

Colter tried the radio again.

"Command, this is Alpha One-Zero. Radio check. Over."

They heard nothing but static.

"Command, this is Alpha One-Zero, radio check. Over."

Still nothing. Levi didn't like that. He added it to the growing list.

"Command, this is Alpha One-Zero, we've reached Bourg-en-Bresse, currently in the southwest quadrant. Grid coordinates Four-Quebec-Foxtrot-Juliet-One-Five. Possible LNs located. Copy?"

Nothing.

Colter almost threw the mic at the dash. Almost. Instead it was just his left eye that twitched, and Levi watched Colter strongly resist the urge to brain an inanimate object.

Colter breathed out slowly and put the mic down. Then he pressed the push-to-talk button on his chest, clutching it in his hand like it was a cross and he was praying, but it wasn't for talking to God. It was much better than that.

Every marine in their squad was equipped with a Bowman radio pack, a line-of-sight terrestrial network able to extend its range as long as one marine could electronically "see" the next. Meaning that in such close range it was unaffected by the interference in the air, but, more importantly, once they left the cars it was the only link they would have to each other.

The L-ATV's radio wasn't so lucky. Either they were too far away from Command, or their radio was being jammed, or—

"Okay, boys, show time," Colter said. "We're going in, and we're going to aim for that light."

He nodded at the light burning in the distance. A steady white against the black, like the Star of David guiding them in.

"I reckon that if we can see that, then Bravo Two-Zero would have, too. So that's where we'll look for them first. If we don't find them between here and there, we turn around, and we leave. No heroics. No fucking around. Ten minutes, in and out. We're balls deep already, and I'm not going to risk us getting stuck out here without comms."

Levi nodded, feeling his heart starting to thump a little harder in his chest, that first drip of adrenaline in his blood like a bump of speed.

"My car has point. When we reach that light, I want Car Two to take the south corner. Car Three, the east. Cover your quadrants. I don't want anyone sneaking up on us."

Colter looked at Weeks briefly before turning back to the front. "Weeks is going to park us out front. Briggs will provide cover with the CROWS while Sergeant Miller takes teams One and Two in on foot. I want visual contact of the man to either side of you at all times. We're in a highly populated area, so confirm your targets. We don't need any civilian casualties. Copy?"

"Copy," came the group response.

"Once we've secured the area, and if it looks friendly—I repeat, *if*—then Levi has kindly volunteered to play knock-knock and see who's home."

Fuck, I should have kept my damn mouth shut.

Briggs sniggered. Levi gave him the finger.

"Get ready to move, marines. We're gonna do this fast."

"Yes, sir," grumbled Levi. He patted his helmet down, pushed his gas mask back against his face, and checked the fit, feeling the airtight seal pull against his skin as he turned his head left to right. His ears filled with the hiss of his breath.

Colter took his finger off the button, nodded once, and pointed ahead. "Go."

Weeks stamped his foot down on the gas. The tires spun against the snow for a second before digging in, and the L-ATV surged ahead with a roar.

The acceleration shoved Levi back in his seat, pressing his stomach against his spine, a sick feeling churning in his guts that was one-third adrenaline, one-third car sickness, and one-third pure fear.

The suspension kicked, the rattle loud in the cab as Weeks drove them over the median, crossing the road to avoid a snarl of wrecked cars and downed telephone lines that blocked the whole left side.

The road straightened out again, abandoned cars blurring past to either side, and suddenly Levi could see the light again. All the way at the end of the road, bright and beckoning, and getting bigger, fast. A building appeared out of the dark, and he started making out the details. A gas station with lights on inside and a big blue sign out front. *Norauto,* Levi read as they raced toward it.

Weeks spun the wheel to the right and aimed them straight at the gas station. Their L-ATV mounted the curb with a bang, its fat tires kicking them up into the air, car shuddering and swaying as they raced through the parking lot and straight at a line of cars blocking their path.

Some looked like they'd been abandoned, doors flung open, lights still on inside. Others looked like they had been booked in for repairs, covered in plastic, missing bumpers, lights, and doors.

Weeks mashed the brakes, the wheels locked, and the L-ATV's tail kicked out as they skidded to a stop.

"GO, GO, GO!" shouted Colter, but Levi was already gone, cold air pouring in through his open door.

Levi ran through the dark, the faint outlines of Sergeant Miller and González running alongside him. He ran with smooth, quick movements, keeping his upper body still, knees bent, rifle up, letting his legs do all the work.

"I got movement," he said between hissed breaths.

"Where?" Colter barked in his left ear, while a strange noise drilled into his right. A metallic click.

"Southeast corner, far-left window," said Levi, closer now.

"Briggs, give me a light on that," ordered Colter.

Briggs obliged, and the CROWS spun left, its searchlight burning through the dark, stabbing through the window and into their observer's eyes.

Levi watched the face disappear, no doubt blinded. Probably swearing.

"Two more. Right side," added Levi, still trying to identify the noise. It was coming from all around them now, clicks growing louder, starting to hum, like they'd pissed off a hive of bees.

Briggs moved the searchlight from window to window, across the building, illuminating a dozen faces pressed up against the glass, eyes peering through the gaps in what looked like steel shelves and bits of furniture. *Barricades?*

Levi kept moving, slipping from cover to cover, trying to make as small a target as possible while Briggs kept his searchlight pointed at the building.

"Clear ahead!" Levi hissed as he slipped between the last row of gas pumps, feeling exposed and vulnerable.

"Clear left!" shouted Miller.

"Clear right!" echoed González.

Levi could hear the people inside screaming, he could hear

his breath echoing in his ears, his boots smacking on the concrete, crunching through ice. Then there was nothing but empty space between him and the building.

He started sprinting, his shadow extending before him like a giant's as he stepped into the light, rushing forward to bang on the door. Three hard knocks before he stepped back and to the side. Just in case some trigger-happy idiot on the other side decided to put a few bullets through it.

Something raced past his leg, close enough that he felt it graze his shin.

"Shit!" Levi stumbled back a step.

He scanned the ground, turning in the direction the blur had gone.

"Anyone see that?"

All he saw was a floating cloud of black dust and disturbed snow.

"Sarge, you see that?" Levi asked, ignoring the people banging on the window next to his head.

Miller looked at him and shook his head before turning back to scrutinize the dark.

"Problem?" asked Colter in his ear.

"Thought I saw something, must have been a dog."

He turned to bang on the door again.

"Shut up!" Levi shouted back as the people inside continued to scream. "One at a time! I can't fucking understand you! English! Anyone in there speak English? *Comprende?*"

"That's Spanish, you idiot," someone said over the channel.

Levi raised his fist to bang on the door again and stopped.

A pair of blue eyes were staring back at him.

A girl, Levi realized. Her face pale and drawn, eyes wide and terrified. He watched as more and more people started appearing behind her, frantically pulling things away from the door, pushing each other out of the way in the rush.

Just how many people are in there?

The girl pointed at something behind him.

Levi glanced over his shoulder before looking back at her.

"What?" Levi shouted.

He saw her mouth open, lips peeling back, the flash of teeth as she shouted something.

"I can't hear you!" he mimed back, shaking his head and cupping his ear.

She pointed again, getting desperate, so Levi leaned closer, hearing her screaming what sounded like the same word over and over.

"MONSTRE!"

Then the clicks stopped.

COLTER

Colter was an observant man. He was like his old man in that way. A learned trait, or a genetic thing, maybe. Something passed down from father to son, along with his bad knees, high blood pressure, and blind hatred of the Mets.

It's probably why they couldn't be in the same room together. They were just too alike. Mirror images separated by thirty years, too much pride, and a stubborn streak a mile wide.

But at least he could recognize it. He got that from his mom, he supposed. Some humility and self-awareness. Perhaps the only traits he'd inherited from her because all Colter saw when he looked in the mirror was a younger, stronger, fitter version of his old man staring back. And that was all the incentive he needed to be different.

He didn't want to turn out like that. All alone and bitter and borderline alcoholic, living in the ass-end of nowhere, just killing time until he died from cirrhosis or boredom or a trigger-happy redneck.

Colter couldn't even remember the last time they'd spoken on the phone. Couldn't even remember the last time he'd been home. *Not since Mom died,* he realized. With her out of the picture, Colter didn't see much of a point. She'd been the glue desperately trying to hold them together. And when she'd died, the gap between them had only widened.

Colter blamed his old man for that. Not even burying Mom had been enough to bury the axe between them. Worse, it had only reminded him of why he'd left in the first place. Made him wonder why he hadn't done it sooner.

Living with his old man had been hard. Living up to his expectations had been harder still. Like having a constant migraine. *Could do better* had defined the whole first eighteen years of his life.

So at twenty, he'd stopped trying. He realized his old man was never going to change. He didn't even know there was a problem to begin with. Like there was some bug in his code. It just didn't compute, and arguing about it had been pointless. Arguing with his old man was like trying to move a mountain. Keep pushing and all that would happen is he would come down on you like an avalanche.

So he'd cut his losses, he'd dropped out of college, packed his bags, kissed his mom goodbye, and caught the first bus into LA. He'd walked the last two blocks to the recruitment office on Hollywood Boulevard, shown them his ID, signed on the dotted line. They'd shaken hands, and, just like that, he'd joined the Marines.

His old man didn't talk to him for six months. Colter didn't give a shit. Two could play that game.

A year later, the first plane hit; seventeen minutes later, the second. Six years later, Mom was dead, and the rest was history. And he'd never looked back. Not once, not even after that mess in Helmand.

His old man had called him a fool when he'd first found out. Still did. Called it a waste. Only more often as the years went by. Said it was an unwinnable war. Said you couldn't kill an idea. Said they were doing more harm than good. Said that he'd come home in a body bag, or in bits, or not at all. Colter didn't care. Not anymore. He'd made his peace with death long ago. He was where he belonged, and at least here his decisions were his own. So he'd tuned his old man out.

Another set of traits he'd inherited, he supposed. Self-confidence and selective hearing.

And as with all introspection, the first step toward making a change was admitting when you'd fucked up. Like now.

Coming into Bourg-en-Bresse had been a mistake. Maybe a bad one, too, because something was very wrong here. And Colter trusted his gut. It had kept him alive this long, but right now he was drawing a blank.

He didn't know what to make of the people inside the gas station or the barricades he could see across the windows. Because that begged the obvious question: *What were they hiding from?* Barricades wouldn't do shit against an armor-piercing round, never mind a .50 cal or RPG.

And where is everyone else? Where is Bravo Two-Zero, where are the French ground units, the police?

Nothing. They weren't here. They hadn't passed them on the road, and he'd never heard of a weapon that could just make that many people disappear. But the people inside the gas station seemed to be all that were left of a city that was once home to 40,000.

But that's why they were here in the first place. They needed information, and half a recon marine's job was to go places no one else would. To go poke a stick into a dark hole and see what crawled out.

So when Colter saw movement, a tiny blur in the corner of his eye, some part of his brain screamed *threat,* and his head turned on instinct.

That's not right, he thought when the rest of his brain caught up. *There should be a man there.*

But Colter saw nothing but darkness outside his window.

He pushed the button on his chest. "Olson. Come in."

Another blur. Colter turned again. Nothing. He was jumping at shadows.

"Olson, report."

Silence.

"Marcus, you got a visual on Olson?"

He frowned. "Marcus?"

A flashlight spun through the dark, pointing up, pointing down, cartwheeling, then it was snuffed out.

Colter heard a muffled thump. The sound of air being driven from lungs.

"Contact! Contact! Lff—"

Another grunt in his earpiece. Then screams.

"In the cars! They're in the cars!"

And then there was light, three-foot tongues of flame punching into the air as Briggs pulled the trigger and the CROWS opened up.

Glass shattered, tires exploded, and the cars in front of them began to dissolve in a shower of shredded metal and sparks as the .50 caliber rounds tore them apart.

"Where are they?" Colter bellowed. "Someone give me a visual!"

Briggs tracked the CROWS right, across the cars, and he caught a shape in the searchlight.

"Gunner!" Briggs screamed.

Colter saw it too, like a blind spot suddenly revealed. One that was already starting to fade away before hot lead met an invisible wall, detonating in puffs of blue mist and a howling shriek. And for a split second, he could see it again. All of it. As though it had been wearing a disguise and the bullets had torn it away.

Camouflage! Colter realized, his eyes widening as he saw mottled gray flesh and massive arms, a hunched and twisted shape that shuddered as the bullets ate into it.

"What the fuck is that?" shrieked Briggs.

Colter had no idea. Then it was gone, merging back with the darkness.

"Where'd it go?" Colter shouted. "Briggs, you got a visual?"

"Negative!" screamed Briggs, his voice shrill.

Colter looked right. One of his marines was on his back, being dragged away, screaming, his finger locked on the trigger, firing wildly. His mag ran dry, and he disappeared.

"HELP ME! HELP ME!" someone howled in his ear.

Colter had no idea who it was or where they were. It was all happening too fast.

"Left side! LefFTUNngggghhh."

He had to do something. "Weeks, on me!"

Colter pushed his door open. He stepped away from his car and straight into a shitstorm. The air was filled with clicks and screams, the CROWS continued to spew hate and noise into the night above his head, orange tracer rounds burned through the dark, and concussion waves threatened to scramble his brains.

Colter tuned it all out.

His whole world narrowed to a single point, and he let his training take over.

He took a step forward. Something big landed on the L-ATV to his right, and muscle memory did the rest. He'd already aimed and pulled the trigger before his brain caught up.

He kept his finger depressed, and he took a step forward, then another, walking it in, riding the recoil, the stock punching into his shoulder with a stuttering kick. He let out a satisfied grunt as puffs of blue mist burst into existence, and for a split second he could see it again. Gray flesh spasming beneath his assault before his mag ran dry.

Colter kept moving. He pulled a new mag from his webbing, and he looked up to find the thing watching him. Bloodied jaws spread wide. Blue blood oozing from a dozen holes, flesh staining from gray to deep black, a pulse of darkness radiating outward.

What are you?

Then it was moving.

"BRIGGS!" Colter shouted. "Moving left!"

The L-ATV bounced on its suspension as it jumped off, kicking up a puff of dirty snow when it landed between him and the last of his men. Miller and González, their rifles held across their chests, legs pumping, flashlights waving through the dark as they sprinted toward him. He couldn't see Levi.

"Miller, incoming!" Colter screamed as the blur swam toward them, seven feet tall and weaving from side to side. God, it was fast.

Miller stopped. His rifle came up, tracking left, then right, trying to get a bead on it.

He didn't stand a chance.

And even from twenty feet away Colter heard Miller's bones snap like twigs when it hit him. Then it kept going, straight at the building, surging up the wall with Miller folded over its shoulder before disappearing over the edge.

Colter looked back to see González on her knees now, tripped by something on the ground and taking too long to get back to her feet.

She's not going to make it.

He started moving toward her, seeing Weeks out of the corner of his eye laying down covering fire to their left.

González stood up, and something hit her from behind. It wrapped around her leg, thick and black. González spun, screaming as it slithered up higher, curling around her thigh. She tried to kick it off, but another one hit her in the chest. She staggered back from the impact, grunting as it wrapped around her ribs. She grabbed it with both hands, tried to pull it off, and González exploded like she'd been wearing a suicide vest.

Colter blinked.

Something was wrong. He was on the ground. He didn't know how he got there. He didn't remember lying down. There was simply a gap, and a hollow ringing in his ears, and something on his face, a dull heat slowly sinking its claws into his flesh.

It melted through his mind, and the world came back into focus with a lurch.

Colter blinked again. Confused. His gas mask was splattered with red, the visor bubbling and melting as steam boiled from the ground around him. Pain flared across the back of his left hand, it thundered up his arm and into his brain. He turned his head to look at it.

The back of his glove was completely burnt away, pink foam bubbling where drops of dark, sticky fluid stuck to his skin, while small yellow flames licked at his arms like napalm.

"Shit."

Colter wiped his hand on his pants, swearing more when strips of skin peeled off and he did nothing but spread the dark fluid around.

"Shit."

A hole appeared in his visor, an inch away from his eye. Smoke and fumes flooded in, and with it, the smell of burning plastic and cooked meat. The hole grew bigger, and he realized the cooked meat was him.

Colter pulled the ruined gas mask from his face, swearing as his flesh tore away with it. He rolled over with a groan, pushing himself onto all fours, his thoughts sluggish, his hand still burning.

Not good.

Out of the corner of his eye, he saw something weaving across the ground like a snake, coming straight at him, fast, so he rolled again, bringing his M-4 around. He saw hard black flesh and hundreds of legs. Like some giant centipede with teeth. He didn't have time to think, he didn't have time to aim. It was pure reflex that put his rifle between *it* and him as it launched itself off the ground.

The weight of it took him by surprise. It knocked him over, so he rolled again, dropping his rifle, using the momentum to get away from the tangled, twitching mess on the ground.

Move, James. Move!

He pushed himself to his feet, looking up to see the L-ATV in front of him. Its back door wide open and its suspension squeaking as it bounced on its wheels. He could hear the men inside screaming before the driver's window splashed red.

He took a half-step toward it before the thing squirming on the ground spasmed and snapped his rifle in half.

Fuck that.

He didn't bother going for his sidearm. It was useless fighting this thing. He just wanted something solid between it and himself.

He lunged for his own L-ATV, got his foot on the step, fumbling for the handle before he managed to get the door open and pull himself in.

"Gunner!" screamed Briggs as Colter threw himself across the front seat, hauling the door shut behind him just as a heavy thud cracked against the armor plating.

"Where's Weeks?" Colter yelled.

"Don't know," Briggs shouted back.

"Levi?"

Briggs didn't answer.

"Briggs! Where's Levi?"

"I don't fucking know! What the fuck do I do, sir?"

Sorry, marines.

He slammed his fist down on the lock, a satisfying crunch echoing all around him as the doors clamped shut.

Safe, he told himself. *It can't get in.* Not through armor plating and four-inch-thick bulletproof glass.

Something much bigger smashed into his door, and he had to rethink that assumption. It hit them again, and his window cracked. It hit them again, glass clouding under the blows, L-ATV rocking from the impacts. But his window held. So the thing outside stopped; it changed tack, and a harsh squeal sang in Colter's ears as it clawed at his door.

His eyes widened as it pulled at the handle.

OH, HELL NO.

"Sir, what do I do? Do I shoot?" asked Briggs, his voice frantic.

It let go of the handle, and Colter held his breath.

"Sir! What do I do?"

"Hold your fire, Briggs. Wait until you can see it."

"See it? I can't see shit! There's nothing on the fucking monitor."

Colter pressed the push-to-talk button on his chest. "Squad, sound off."

"Hicks."

"Duval!"

The car behind them.

"Hicks, lock your doors! These things know how to open them."

"Way ahead of you. We've got Weeks in here too. He's a little banged up, but he'll live."

"Levi, too?"

"Negative."

What the hell just happened?

Colter looked at his ruined hand, at the dark fluid that continued to sizzle and burn, smoke curling from his MOPP. He needed to do something about that. Now.

He pulled out his water bottle, twisted the lid off, poured it out on his hand, and nearly blacked out as the water touched whatever was still burning him, filling the cab with a spitting hiss.

"Who you got with you?" Hicks asked from far away.

Colter couldn't answer. He could barely think. Spots danced in the air in front of him.

"Gunner?" asked Hicks again, his voice echoing in Colter's ear.

Colter let out a ragged sigh as some of the heat went away.

"Briggs and myself," he said.

"And?"

"Just us. González is dead," said Colter, shaking his head to clear it. "Something took Miller. I don't know where the others are."

Hicks didn't say anything after that.

"Briggs, you see anything?" Colter asked.

"Negative."

"Hicks?" asked Colter.

"Nothing, they don't show up on the thermals. What are they?"

Effective. But he didn't say that. Some things you keep to yourself, and one thing was crystal clear: he'd driven them straight into an ambush, and eight of his marines were dead because of it.

Colter glanced at Briggs, his finger hovering on the trigger, his eyes wide and glistening. He didn't mention Levi. Now wasn't the time.

He turned back to look at the L-ATV in front of them, watching Briggs's searchlight playing across the blood-splattered windows.

"Sir?" came an uncertain voice over the radio.

Briggs swore in relief.

"Levi?"

Colter would recognize that accent anywhere. He leaned forward, peering out into the parking lot. "Levi! Where the fuck are you? You okay?"

"Uh... you're not gonna like it."

Colter looked to his left, to the building glowing with light, and through a crack in one small window he saw a flashlight blink twice, then someone waved.

"Now what?" asked Briggs. "How do we get him out of there?"

Colter didn't have the faintest idea. But he didn't say that either.

LEVI

Colter's L-ATV sat in the middle of the road, with Car Three just behind it, their engines turned off but their lights still on. Car Two stayed right where it was. Back passenger door slightly ajar, engine still running, exhaust turned to a white cloud behind it, and nothing but dead men and one of those things inside.

Levi didn't want to know what it was still doing in there. He tried not to think about it. But every now and then, he heard a loud snap, like someone cracking open bones to suck out the marrow.

He suppressed a shiver and pressed the push-to-talk button on his chest. "Sir?"

He could see dim shapes moving around inside Colter's car, the occasional turn of a head, the wave of an arm. He could just make out Colter in the driver's seat, and he wasn't wearing his gas mask.

"We're pretty much ready to go, sir."

"Pretty much ready, or ready?" asked Colter, sounding pissed. "They're two different things, and we're out of time."

Levi had to give him that one, but he'd taken one look at the bus and all the hillbilly armor the civilians were adding to it, and he'd realized just how fucked they all were. So he was happy with the delay; anything that increased their chances of staying alive was fine with him. And with the snow that continued to fall, someone had made the genius suggestion of adding chains to the tires on the bus. Only problem was the idea had come a bit late, and the men working in the garage had to remove the steel plates covering the wheel wells, install the chains, then weld the plates back on, and that had cost them time. Time Levi knew they didn't have.

"No. They're ready. The last of the civis are getting on now."

Or attempting to.

The line out the door to the garage had jammed, a human bottleneck, and there was grunting and cursing as the people at the back started to push, long past desperate and on the edge of panic, and that wasn't a good thing. Panic made people even more stupid and unpredictable.

"You got a head count? I'll need numbers for Command when we make contact," said Colter.

"Forty-six," answered Levi. *Way too many.*

The idea of all those people crammed in that sardine can of a bus made him nervous. There were a lot of them, and only one of him. It was going to be cramped. He'd already had to break up two fights, and things were only going to get worse. Six hours on the road if they were lucky, if nothing went wrong.

Plus, there was that other thing...

He glanced at Cass. He wasn't looking good; none of the civis were. There was something wrong with them. Like physically.

They looked like shit, all pale and sweating, sick and vomiting, some were bleeding from their noses with bloodshot eyes, and they were all coughing like a dog choking on a bone.

Levi pushed the button on his chest. "Sir... That other problem we spoke about? It's getting worse."

"Copy that, Levi. As soon as we make contact with Command I'll have them prep a med team for our arrival. They'll take care of it.

There's nothing we can do about it until then, you just concentrate on *the package*. He's the priority, got that?"

"Yes, sir," Levi said with a nod, but he didn't share Colter's confidence. He didn't think a med team was going to make a difference. Not anymore.

Cass, or "the package" as they'd started calling him, had shown him the growing row of bodies in the garage—four of them—lined up shoulder to shoulder as if they were sleeping. And in the three hours he'd been there, he'd already seen two more people die. One just up and stopped breathing, like a bad asthma attack, the other had some sort of fit, twitching on the floor and foaming at the mouth. Both male and in their mid-twenties. It didn't take a genius to work out the rest.

There was something in the air, some kind of toxin. But it didn't seem to affect everyone equally, and none of the M9 detector paper taped to him indicated the presence of anything harmful, and he could only think of two reasons for that. Either the detector paper was faulty—which was possible, but unlikely—or they were dealing with some other kind of airborne agent. Something biological, maybe. Something new, something it had never been designed for in the first place. Levi didn't like the thought of that. He didn't even know if his gas mask was filtering the stuff out.

Either way, Gunner had definitely been exposed.

He shook his head. This whole mission had turned into a giant clusterfuck. Cass was the only good thing to come out of it. If you could even call it that... Someone who'd been at Meyrin. One of the pointy-heads. Someone who might actually have some real intel. Someone who might have even caused this.

And it only cost us seven marines to find him...

Levi pushed the thought from his mind. The blame would come later. If there was a later. It wasn't entirely Colter's fault, either, but someone at Command had fucked up real bad. And if he ever found the asshole who sent them in here without air support, he'd put a bullet in them himself.

"Let's go," Levi said, gesturing for Cass to lead the way. He took one last look out the window before turning to follow Cass into the garage, joining the tail end of the line slowly feeding into the bus. Kids crying, people coughing, a ragged, dejected group of people shuffling forward. Levi felt his spirits sink even further.

Back home he would have compared it to the "short bus," good for seating perhaps twenty people. They were trying to squeeze in a little over double that now. Add in the oil drum in the back and space was limited, but Cass said they needed it. The drum was filled with what was left of the gas, and with the amount of extra weight the bus was carrying, it was going to burn through fuel fast. The drum was their reserve. It had a hole drilled in its side with a simple valve connected to a fat, clear tube at its base that snaked through a hole cut in the floor and fed straight into the bus's gas tank.

Clever, as long as no one lights a match...

And in the gloom and fumes of the garage, Levi was struck by how the bus looked like some strange disco ball, or as though a tornado had torn through a junkyard and somehow assembled a car. Light was leaking from a thousand small holes, slipping through tiny gaps in dirty welds, long, wide beams shining out of the mesh-covered lights that decorated the outside of the bus like glowing warts. Every window was covered in steel plating and bits of reworked metal.

Only the driver and front passenger-side windows had small cutouts in them, two-by-four-inch eye slots. Not really big enough to see anything out of, more as backups in case Cass's "invention" failed.

Levi had to give it to the guy. Cass was a genius. The kind of guy he used to pick on in high school. All he was missing was the glasses.

The clever bastard had stripped out the gas station's security system. He'd pulled the cameras from the ceiling and installed them at the front of the bus behind a mess of mesh cages. He'd run all the wiring, powering them to car batteries strapped underneath the front row of passenger seats, and he'd plugged the camera's video feeds into a pair of computer monitors bolted to the dash. One in front of the driver, and one next to the door. And as with most security cameras, they were infrared. Nothing like the tech they had in the L-ATVs. Pretty basic, poor resolution, no zoom, which limited the range, and it had a slight fish-eye effect going on, but it meant they could actually see where they were going without having a giant gaping hole at the front of the bus, and holes were bad.

The cutouts were the backup in case the cameras were destroyed. They were as small as they could make them while still being usable, with metal panels they could slide across the cutouts if something tried to come through. Levi just hoped it didn't come to that.

Five long minutes later it was his turn to climb the two steps into the bus, squeezing in beside Cass and the police officer standing next to the driver's seat. The bald one built like a fridge. Michael.

Levi turned until he could see the other cop at the back of the bus. Luke or Lenny or something. Whatever his name was, Levi could see he was done. He was sitting on the floor, his back against the wall with his head in his hands, his shoulders shaking, and Levi knew he wouldn't be able to count on him for anything. He might just have to take his weapons away and give them to someone who still had some fight left. Cass, maybe?

"Hurry up, Levi," Colter barked in Levi's ear. "Clock's ticking."

"Two minutes," Levi said, glancing over his shoulder at all the terrified faces staring back at him.

"Okay, here's the plan," said Colter. "I want you to tell the driver to follow my lead. Tell him to hang back ten meters off my tail, no closer. And tell him to go exactly where we go. You guys go off the road, and you're on your own. You got that?"

Levi nodded, forgetting Colter couldn't see him.

"Levi?"

"Got it, sir," replied Levi.

"Relax, soldier," said Colter. "You're doing well. Weeks, Hicks, and Duval are going to swing in behind you and bring up the rear. They'll cover you back to base. Keep your cool, stick to the plan, and we'll be home in no time."

"Yes, sir," Levi said, before taking his finger off the button.

"We're all fucked," Levi mumbled to himself.

"What?" asked Cass.

"Nothing."

He leaned over to relay Colter's instructions to the driver. One of the mechanics poked his head through the door. He said something in French. Michael said something back.

"We're good to go," said Michael, seeing Levi's confusion.

"Time to get this shit show on the road, then."

The driver nodded once. He turned the key in the ignition, and the bus's engine coughed to life.

Levi gave the mechanic a double thumbs-up.

The mechanic gave him an odd look before he turned on his heel and hurried across to the generator rumbling in the corner, his feet kicking up little puffs of black dust in his wake.

Levi watched him pull out a plug from the distribution board, watched him pick up another one from the ground. He paused. Levi saw him suck in a breath. Then he rammed the new plug home and started running for the bus.

The mechanic jumped on board with a shout, slamming the door shut behind him as the garage door motor came to life and a grating rumble filled the air. Someone pushed past Levi to help the mechanic seal the door from the inside, the two men working as fast as they could.

Levi turned to watch the computer screens in front of him, seeing the garage door opening. First an inch, then two, chain rattling, metal roller doors shuddering as a flurry of snow and mist flooded in. He turned back to watch the mechanics slotting heavy pieces of beaten metal against the door before dropping several steel pipes into place across them, their ends fitting in brackets welded to the frame, barring the door shut. Then they picked up bolts and impact drivers and began firing bolt after bolt into the layers of overlapping steel, metal on metal sounding like gunshots in the enclosed space.

The rumbling in the garage stopped, the crying and screaming in the bus got louder, and the men working on the door finished. They took a hesitant step back. Levi pushed in front of them, he held his breath, and he waited, heart pounding.

Nothing happened.

"So far, so good," Cass whispered next to him after a minute.

"Don't jinx it," Levi hissed back at him, not taking his eyes off the door.

"Sorry," said Cass with a soft shrug.

"Levi?" asked Colter in his ear.

Levi pushed the button on his chest. "Coming."

"So is Christmas."

"Go," said Levi softly, turning to tap the driver on the shoulder. Then he pointed at the computer screen and the faint gray blob out on the road that was Colter's L-ATV.

The driver nodded. He put the bus in gear, tapped the gas, and they edged forward, out of the garage and into the dark, bus swaying on overloaded suspension as its tires found small dips in the concrete parking lot.

The driver spun the wheel to the left, pulling them out onto the road, chains digging through the snow and ice, grinding against the asphalt beneath.

Someone started clapping. Levi turned to see people hugging, smiling, talking, their mouths moving. He shook his head. He didn't get it. Like those idiots that clapped at the end of a movie. What for? Not like they can hear you.

And it was far too early to be celebrating. In fact, he was pretty sure it was about to get a whole lot worse.

CASS

They were all dying. Cass didn't even need his two PhDs in nuclear physics to come to that conclusion. Just two eyes and half a brain. It was a simple observation. A case of cause and effect.

The result of which told him he'd been right—it wasn't radiation. It was the air, or something in it. Something corrosive and highly reactive. One of the halogens, maybe chlorine, maybe fluorine. Either could explain the symptoms he was seeing. His money was on chlorine.

Levi said that wasn't it. Pointed to a band on his arm that he said would have changed color if it was. But he might be lying, and the air had a smell to it. Acrid and burnt, sour almost. Like a public swimming pool. Or it had.

Cass couldn't smell anything but blood anymore, a sharp sting in his nose, and the scientist in him knew the chlorine was attacking the mucus membranes of his throat, nasal cavity, and lungs, stripping out the electrons, separating the hydrogen from the water, and creating hydrochloric acid that would be causing tissue damage. It was basic chemistry, combined with human biology. And there was nothing he could do about it. It's not like he could stop breathing, and there was only one gas mask in the bus, and Levi didn't look like he was interested in sharing.

So Cass took another slow breath, and he tried to stay ahead of the panic. But it didn't help. He was too drained to feel anything but terror anymore. Four hours on the road, and all he could think about was the gurgle in his chest and the thing above his head. Watching the metal dent and pop beneath its weight as it clambered across the roof, looking for a way in.

He gripped his flashlight a little tighter and dragged his eyes away, glancing at the two bodies lying next to him. Another heart attack, another seizure, both young, mid-thirties at least, both male, and both dead in the last hour, slack bodies swaying with each dip and bump of the road.

Cass looked away. He flicked on his flashlight, and he shined it down the middle of the bus, seeing ice sparkle and flash where the misted breath of the forty-three people had frozen to every cold, hard surface, turning the inside of the bus into a shimmering cave.

Or a tomb, he thought, seeing all the still shapes slumped in their seats, nothing but white puffs above their heads to give any indication they were still breathing.

Those with respiratory diseases seemed to go first—the asthma sufferers and smokers. After that it was luck of the draw, and no one was immune, not even Elayne. She was sitting two rows back from him. Eyes closed, her head resting on the shoulder of the man next to her. She wasn't talking anymore. She wasn't helping anyone anymore. She couldn't even help herself.

And as if things weren't bad enough already, one of the passengers had some sort of breakdown. He'd thrown himself at the sealed-up windows, screaming to be let out, tearing his nails off trying to pry them open before he'd turned on the woman sitting next to him.

It had taken three of them to pull him off her. Cass had caught an elbow to the face for his trouble before Michael put the guy in a headlock. And when that didn't calm him down, he'd choked him out. Then he'd cuffed his limp body to a bench and tied his legs together with duct tape before using a torn-off shirt sleeve to gag him.

Cass watched him now. Awake again, grunting and straining against his bonds, his eyes wide and vacant, a huge vein pulsing in his forehead. And Cass knew it was only a matter of time before someone else lost it. He just didn't know what would get them first—the air, each other, or the things outside.

Nothing the marines did seemed to keep them away for long either. They'd fire off a few rounds, and for a while those things would go away. But never for long. They just kept coming back, more and more of them.

He knew the marines had to be running low on ammo, and there were small holes everywhere now, grunts and clicks slipping through the widening gaps, claws and teeth flashing on the other side, like dogs digging under a fence.

Cass turned off his flashlight and forced himself to his feet, his legs shaking with the effort as he leaned forward to peer out of the small cut-out in the armor covering the windshield, sliding the metal plate across so he could see outside.

He could see the car in front of them clear as day on the monitors, but he liked to check with his own eyes every now and then. Make sure it was still there. Watch its taillights blink and flicker as things moved between them. Big things that blocked out the light.

"Close it," Levi hissed at him.

Cass ignored him. He glanced at the driver.

"Closer," Cass said with a wet cough, pointing at the car as it started to pull away from them.

"Closer," he said again, closing an imaginary gap with his hands, and the driver nodded once before the bus accelerated, correcting the momentary slip.

"Dammit, keep that fucking thing shut!"

Levi pushed him out of the way.

"Sorry," Cass offered in apology as he stumbled back. He glanced over his shoulder as he trod on someone's foot.

"Sorry," he said again.

Michael just grunted back at him, and Cass could see he was feeling it too. His eyes were glassy, his skin was turning blue, he was breathing too fast, and even holding on to the passenger bar above their heads seemed to be a struggle.

Classic signs of hypoxia, thought Cass. Not enough oxygen in their blood, too much lactic acid in their muscles. Unconsciousness and coma would come next.

Levi didn't say anything, he just went back to watching the monitors in front of them, his feet spread wide, left hand gripping the back of the driver's seat, looking young and fit and strong. Cass felt a small stab of envy as he had to lean against the center console, relying more on the hard plastic for support than his legs.

The driver, on the other hand, had the best seat in the house, soft foam, big armrests, and back support. It meant comfort, and rest. But the strain was evident elsewhere. In the tension of his arms, in the tendons standing up like cords in the back of his hands. His sweat-soaked clothes, the bags under his eyes, and the single trail of blood that curled from his nose.

That was another problem they hadn't expected. There were meant to be three of them taking turns driving. Local men, men familiar with the roads, experienced in driving through snow, and there was a lot of it now. But something had happened to the other two, and Cass glanced again at the bodies lying on the floor next to him.

So now they were down to just one driver, and he was tired and sick like the rest of them.

It didn't help that it was getting worse outside, snowing more and more as the hours dragged by. Powder softer than Cass had ever seen in his life, like falling sheets of satin. It was probably the only thing they had going in their favor: the fact that the snow wasn't wet enough to clump together and become ice. So even with the depth, the car in front was able to barrel through it, pushing a wall of glowing snow out to either side like a wave, plowing the way clear. Which meant the bus only occasionally slipped. It only threatened to stop, just a little tease. Shuddering as it lost traction, engine roaring before the wheels dug in with a crunch and they started moving again.

"Any idea how long?" Cass asked.

Levi glanced back at him with wide eyes, and Cass was reminded that behind his gas mask, beneath his suit and body armor, Levi was just a kid. He didn't even look old enough to drink.

"Have you guys made contact?" Cass asked when Levi didn't answer.

Levi shook his head, his eyes lingering on the blood on Cass's face before he gripped the button on his chest and turned away, and Cass knew he was talking to the soldiers outside again.

For the most part, Levi ignored him. He ignored all of them. They'd barely spoken since they'd left the gas station, and when they did it was all one-way traffic. An interrogation, a game of twenty questions passed down the line from whoever was in charge. What was CERN? What happened there? What had they been doing? Where had these things come from? Why, why, why? And yet Cass hadn't gotten much out of Levi except his name.

Cass got the impression that Levi resented being in here, blamed him especially, like this was all his fault somehow. And he had to admit that maybe it was, at least partly. Not that he understood how. He had a theory. But that was it, and a theory without data is just bullshit. Without more information, it would never be more than guesswork, and there was only one way to fix that: CERN's off-site data storage center.

CERN generated an enormous amount of data—about one

petabyte every day, the equivalent of around 210,000 DVDs. But it didn't have the resources to crunch all of the data on site. So in 2002 it had turned to grid computing to share the burden.

The data storage center was just the first point of contact between the LHC and the Grid, and it was enormous, nearly three square miles of server farms located three stories underground. And it was four miles away from Meyrin, in Geneva. Which meant the data might still be okay; it might have been far enough away from the explosion to have come through unscathed.

If he could just get to it. If he could get a look at the numbers, the recordings taken before the explosion. Then maybe he could make more sense of it? Maybe he could see what they had all missed? What Reese had seen at the end, the "numbers" he'd been rambling about.

Cass felt the bus slow, the driver tapped the brakes a little too hard, and he had to catch himself from falling over.

"What's happening?" he asked Levi as they came to a juddering halt.

The driver leaned forward, squinting at the monitor in front of him.

The car in front of them had stopped.

Levi grabbed the push-to-talk button on his chest.

"Levi?" asked Cass. "What's happening?"

People started talking, heads lifted from seatbacks. Their voices grew louder, and so did the coughing.

"Levi?"

The voices rose in pitch. People were looking around, waking up, and starting to panic.

"Shhhh," said Levi, flinching when one of the things outside threw itself against the bus, his eyes tracking the dents in the metal as it climbed onto the roof before moving to their right.

Someone at the back of the bus started shouting. A man. He

sounded angry, like he wanted something, but Cass had no idea what. Someone tried to calm him down.

Something else nudged up against the bus, something big enough to lift it an inch or two, rocking it slightly.

Then it did it again and metal groaned.

"Levi?"

The bus jerked forward as the car in front started moving again, and Cass had to catch himself for the second time.

"Something's happening up ahead," Levi said, not taking his eyes off the roof. "Gunner says it looks like Lyon is burning."

"Burning? How?" asked Cass, trying to be heard above the voices behind him.

Levi shrugged.

"Is that a problem?"

Levi shrugged again. "That's where we were aiming."

"So what are we going to do?" he asked.

"Dunno. Go around it, maybe… Push on to Toulon and hope the L-ATVs have enough gas left to make it, or one of us is going to have to get out and push."

COLTER

W hat are you idiots on about now?" asked Colter. He forced himself to pay attention, but it was hard. His face hurt. His hand hurt worse. He might have broken a rib, too. And he had no idea what to do about it. He was eating Motrin like they were Tic Tacs. He'd already used all of his burn gel, and he knew he wasn't supposed to cover the burns with anything else, but he had nothing else for the pain.

There was morphine in the car, of course, but driving and operating heavy machinery while high on opiates were pretty much a no-go, and driving the L-ATV counted as both. So no morphine. Which meant he had to do it the old-school way. He just had to suck it up and ignore it. Put up walls around it and tell himself that it was nothing.

But it wasn't working.

The pain was winning, tearing through his walls, pissing on his self-control, and that was bad. It was a distraction, and he couldn't afford to be distracted. He'd already lost too many men.

"Uh. What these things are, sir," said Hicks. "Happy clapper Duval here says these things are demons and this is the Rapture..."

A pause. "We all think he's fucking nuts. No offense… Yeah, yeah, fuck you too, choir boy. Anyway, Weeks has a hundred bucks riding on zombies. Briggs reckons it's the Chinese, some new type of combat drone, maybe, and Levi's money is on little green men with an attitude problem."

"And you?" asked Colter, blinking the sweat from his eyes.

"Me? Me, well… I reckon I've just taken a tab of acid and none of this is really happening, you know? Like those lizards from the bar scene in *Fear and Loathing in Las Vegas*. I reckon I'm just tripping balls right now."

"Hicks…" said Colter slowly. "I'm going to pretend I didn't hear any of that. In the meantime, shut up and keep the channel clear."

"Yes, Mr. Figment of My Imagination, sir!" signed off Hicks, and Colter looked in his rearview mirror just in time to see the bus swerve. He saw it rock the other way as the driver lost control. The bus bounced off an abandoned car in an explosion of glass.

Colter stamped on the brakes. He heard the muffled crack of a single gunshot, and he watched as the bus plowed into the back of a small sedan, grinding along for another ten yards before it came to a halt in a cloud of snow.

"What the hell is happening back there?" Colter shouted, turning to get a better look out his window. His earpiece crackled, and something big smashed into his door.

"Levi, report!"

"Sir! Some crazy bastard stabbed the driver in the neck!"

Colter could hear Levi breathing hard, he could hear people screaming in the background. He could hear panic and confusion.

"What about the attacker?"

"He's down, sir. I put one in him."

"Is everyone else okay?"

"Negative, Gunn— I SAID SIT DOWN! Sit the fuck back down!" A burst of static.

"Levi?"

A gap. "Levi?"

"We've got a major problem here, sir. They're acting weird. I think it's the air."

"Copy that, Levi. Nothing we can do about it. Now concentrate. Is the situation secure?"

"Yes, sir, I think…"

"Good. Is the bus okay? Damage? Will it still drive?"

"I dunno."

"Check, Levi. Now."

A pause. "I think we're wedged on something, and we lost one of the cameras."

Colter turned to look at Briggs's monitor.

"Levi. You have a Toyota wrapped around your grill. You're going to have back up off it."

He could hear Levi talking to someone, his finger still pressed on the button.

"The driver's gone," Levi said, his voice trailing away.

"Not important now," said Colter.

"Not important? Fuck that! These—"

"I don't give a shit, soldier! Your job is to get that bus back on the road! Nothing else matters. You hear me?"

Levi didn't say anything, and something smashed into Colter's door again.

"Now, Levi, we can't sit here!"

"We're working on it!"

He nodded. "Hicks. Duval. Keep your eyes open."

"On it."

"Briggs, keep them covered. I don't want anything getting near that bus." Colter turned to stab his finger at it.

"I'm all over it like herpes, sir," said Briggs.

The bus didn't move. Colter looked at his watch.

"Hurry it up, Levi."

He glanced at the fuel gauge, at the warning light that had been on for the last ten miles. Not good. Even with the hybrid they were going to be pushing it. He looked back at the bus. The bus didn't move. He was just about to start yelling when the bus shuddered, the back wheels spinning for a second before they dug in. It reversed with a lurch, dragging the crumpled Toyota with it.

"Give it some gas, Levi."

"Copy that."

Colter could hear the tires whirr and grip as the chains dug in and the bus left the Toyota behind in a crumpled mess.

"Hold it there, you're clear. Turn hard right and go around it."

He put his foot back down on the gas pedal, waiting for the bus to catch up, waiting for the glare of its headlights to fill his rearview mirror like they had for the last four hours.

They didn't. Colter saw nothing but darkness behind him.

"Levi, you've lost your headlights. Can you still see?"

"Affirmative, one camera still works. If we lose that we're fucked, though. The cutouts have filled with snow, and we can't get out to clear them."

"That'll have to do, then." Colter pulled his eyes back to the road in front of him and the enormous orange glow to the north, seeing pulses of light that looked like lightning but could only be bombs. Something had gone very wrong while they'd been away, and it wasn't isolated.

Just what the hell is happening?

He pulled the mic from its cradle and tried the radio. "Command, this is Alpha One-Zero. Radio check. Are you reading me? Over."

Static poured out of the speaker, filling the cab with white noise and disappointment. One of those things smashed against his door again, and Colter eyed it warily. He hated it when they did that. He couldn't even see out of his window anymore, all he saw was cracks, and the windshield was almost as bad.

"Command, this is Alpha One-Zero, radio check. Are you reading me? Over."

He looked at the fuel gauge again. He needed to stop doing that. It wasn't going to change anything.

"Command, this is Alpha One-Zero, radio check. Are you reading me?"

He had been going like this for the last four hours, every five minutes. All he got was silence.

"Command, this is Alpha One-Zero. Are you reading me? Over."

What he heard next was almost as good as if God spoke to him directly.

"Alpha One-Zero. This is Command, reading you three by three."

Briggs swore. Colter leaned forward, speaking louder. "Command, this is Alpha One-Zero, inbound to Toulon. We're under attack! Contact made with unknown hostiles. Heavy casualties, four MIA, three KIA. Requesting immediate air escort back to base and a medical team standing by on our arrival. We have approximately forty civilians in tow, multiple fatalities. Chemical weapons suspected. Copy?"

He had to shout as Briggs fired at something behind them, explosions stuttering above his head.

"Alpha One-Zero, that's a good copy. Re-tasking gunship to you. What is your current location? Can you designate targets?"

Oh, thank God. He was worried all their birds would still be grounded.

"Negative on targets, Command. Hostiles are using some kind of active camouflage, invisible on thermals. We are currently fifty-five klicks out of Toulon, traveling south. Two cars, escorting a civilian bus. Watch for lights. Over."

"Copy that, Alpha One-Zero. Stand by now."

Colter waited.

"Alpha One-Zero. This is Command. Two Blackhawks en route. ETA, ten minutes."

Colter looked at his watch. "Copy that."

"About time those limp sticks did something," muttered Briggs.

Colter nodded, but he couldn't relax. Ten minutes was a long time, and there was still that other problem. The one he'd been trying very hard not to think about: The air, or whatever was in it. And whatever it was, it wasn't sarin. If it was, he'd be dead already. But it wasn't GA, either, or GB, or VX, or anything else that he could name for that matter. The M9 detector paper on him remained black and inert, and the symptoms Levi were describing in the bus didn't seem to match anything he'd ever heard of.

This stuff was slow, inefficient. Sarin killed in minutes, VX in seconds, and he'd been breathing the air for hours, which was good. It meant they still had a chance. He hoped. But he didn't know what constituted a fatal dose, or how it interacted with the body. Was it biological or chemical? He'd already taken his 2-PAM chloride kit, stabbing the needles into the meat of his thigh and pushing down hard on the plungers, but he didn't know if it had made the slightest difference.

In the meantime, they were crawling along. There were just too many cars in the way, and he couldn't weave around them like Weeks had on the way in. The bus would get stuck if they went off the road, and he didn't know what he would do if that happened. Leave it? Abandon Levi? Sit there and watch all those people die?

So he had to clear a path, and it was taking a toll on his car.

The CROWS thumped as Briggs pulled the trigger, and the flash of light illuminated something running alongside his window, something the size of a horse doing thirty miles an hour.

The turret spat again.

"Hit!" roared Briggs. "Fuckin' get some!"

Colter didn't see it. He was watching the road ahead, watching as a mess of mangled cars appeared out of the dark. Cars stacked three deep like they'd driven into the back of each other at a hundred miles an hour.

He pushed the button on his chest. "Hold up, Levi, tell the driver to give us some space. We got another roadblock. I'm gonna have to punch a hole."

"Copy that."

Colter mashed his foot flat on the gas, and the L-ATV shot forward with a growl.

"Hold on to something, Briggs," Colter shouted, cars coming up fast.

He aimed for the biggest gap, maybe three feet wide. He lined the L-ATV up like a 7-ton battering ram, and they hit the wall of cars at forty miles an hour, making the three-foot gap into an eight-foot one. Then they hit the next car, and the next, and the L-ATV slowed, its engine roaring, metal groaning, glass shattering as they tunneled their way through, shoving cars aside until there was nothing but open road in front of them.

Colter looked in his rearview mirror to see the bus following his lead.

He glanced at the fuel warning light again, and the steering wheel that was starting to shudder in his hands. *Great.*

He'd damaged something, one of the wheels or maybe the steering column. He was going to have to drop back and let Car Three take point, let their car soak up some of the damage before his broke down. Problem was he needed Car Three at the back. Three pairs of eyes were better than two, and they were doing most of the work keeping those things from getting inside the bus, and with—

The radio crackled. Full of static and scratchy like an old record.

"Alpha One-Zero, this is Phantom One. Someone said you jarheads needed a hand?"

Briggs made a sound behind him, something halfway between a laugh and a strangled sob.

"Phantom One, you have no idea, we're operating in the dark here."

He turned his head left and right, peering through the clouded and cracked windshield, scanning the dark ahead, trying to spot some sign of the Blackhawks, the literal flying cavalry coming to the rescue.

He saw nothing.

Static hissed.

"Copy that, Alpha One. Two mikes out, we have you on thermals." A gap, then a list of instructions. "Take the next left. You're going through Valence. We'll cover you as far as that. There you'll meet up with an armored French unit pulling back from Lyon. They'll get you the rest of the way home. Over."

"Copy that, Phantom One. Why? What happened to Lyon?" asked Colter.

"It's not there anymore," came the short answer.

Toulon came on like a migraine, slowly, painfully. A faint light on the horizon grew until it was nearly blinding amidst the darkness, and as they got closer Colter saw a city gone mad. Everywhere he looked, he saw panic and confusion. He saw a sky full of helicopters and jets screaming past low overhead, a constant stream of them coming in off the aircraft carriers anchored out in the bay.

He could just make out the USS *Zumwalt*, the guided missile destroyer looking like something from a science fiction movie, all sharp angles and flat edges. Beyond it, Colter could see the USS *Gerald R. Ford*, the world's biggest and most advanced aircraft carrier, dwarfing everything around it. A floating city surrounded by a ring of destroyers, its flight deck lit up like daylight. He wondered if the USS *Bataan* was with them. It had to be; it looked like the whole 5th Fleet and half the French navy were out there.

He could see a thousand smaller ships too; ferries and barges, cruise ships and tug boats, all leaving at the same time. So many of them they looked like paper lanterns. *Civilians running away.* Not that he could blame them. This wasn't an evacuation, it was pure chaos. Every man for himself.

The road in to Command was even worse; only the far-left lane was still open, and to military traffic only. The right-hand side was a parking lot, choked with cars, people on foot flowing around them like boulders in a stream, all running downhill to the boats leaving without them.

Closer, and Colter could see that not even Command was immune from the panic, but Command was a different beast entirely. It was madness and terror, but they were soldiers. There was still discipline, and with it control and purpose. Besides, if a soldier ran away it was called desertion, and they used to shoot you for that.

Command had changed since he'd been gone, though. It had grown, and Colter watched as ten construction cranes rose into view, their frames covered in lights, huge blocks of cement swinging beneath their outstretched arms.

He gazed at it all with wide eyes, looking up as they drove into the Toulon Naval Base through a bunkered checkpoint. A razor wire fence towered on either side of them, fifteen feet tall and still growing, and behind that a wall of concrete that looked like it was going to be even higher.

Colter let out a slow whistle. None of this had been here before. Hell, it had still been daylight here less than twelve hours ago. He'd never seen engineering teams move this fast before. He didn't know they could.

It looked like the French were reinforcing the whole base, surrounding themselves in light and concrete and sentry guns and missile launchers, and Colter could tell they weren't planning on running away. They were digging in.

They passed between a wall of tanks and APCs. He saw French vehicles parked next to British and American, row after row of them.

The armored convoy they were following split off left, and they were shunted down another side road. Past a building blazing with light, through another checkpoint, and into a narrow passage that spat them out into a fenced-off area next to a huge warehouse and a bunch of glowing white tents the size of marquees.

A soldier in full MOPP stepped out in front of them. He raised his hand, and, after twelve hours of terror, Colter brought the L-ATV to a stop for the last time. He put it in park, gas tank empty, battery nearly dead. He slumped back in his seat, and the two of them sat there, watching all the activity outside, watching the soldier walk toward them before he convinced himself it was safe enough to get out and join him.

Even then, when he opened his door and his boots hit asphalt, he froze. Unable to let go, waiting for those clicks, the screams.

The bus pulled in next to him, its engine dying with a throaty wheeze, and he snapped out of it.

Someone began hammering on the door from the inside before it burst open to disgorge a man onto the ground, quickly followed by another. Coughing and grunting as they bent over to grab their knees.

Levi followed them out a little more slowly. Colter looked past him, counting as people stepped off the bus, twenty-three sick men, women, and children. Then they stopped.

"Where is everyone else?" he asked, looking at the people leaning against the side of the bus or sitting on the ground, their heads between their knees, sucking in huge, wheezing lungfuls of air.

"Sir…"

Colter took a step toward the bus. Levi put out an arm to stop him. Colter brushed him aside. He climbed into the bus, stood still, let his eyes adjust to the gloom, and his frown deepened.

The inside of the bus was dark. Like being inside a cardboard box. The only light came seeping in through narrow cracks and tears in the roof. Ragged holes letting in narrow white beams of light that cut through the stale and misty air.

Colter saw bodies on the floor, and the shapes in the seats were just as still, like statues covered in frost. He turned on his flashlight and shined it in their faces, his little circle of light revealing sick and sleeping people wherever he looked, eyelashes crusted with ice, red stains running down their chins, half frozen, half wet.

"Shit," Colter said, the word sliding out between his teeth.

It was worse than he'd imagined.

Then there were the other two. Men, both tied down, their hands in cuffs behind their backs, strips of cloth and duct tape binding their legs together. One of the men was unconscious or dead, Colter couldn't tell. He didn't seem to be breathing. The other one had a hole in his gut, and it looked like he'd bled out.

Colter turned on his heel, taking the two steps at once, back outside, away from the sickness, his eyes drawn to the pale and bloodied faces that turned toward his.

"Cass?" he asked.

Levi answered. "Here, sir."

Colter turned.

"Colter, I presume?" said one of the men leaning against the bus.

"That's me."

"I suppose I should say thanks," Cass said, extending a shaking hand, waiting for Colter to take it. A man trying to put a brave face on. One who seemed to know it was already long past that.

Colter looked at his hand, he hesitated, worried about catching whatever he had. Worried it might already be too late. And men in yellow hazmat suits swooped down on them like vultures.

One of them grabbed his left arm and started dragging him away. Colter was just about to yell at him when another one shoved a gas mask over his face, ignoring his shout as they tugged the straps down over his burns.

"Easy!"

The one on his left jabbed him in the neck with a hypodermic needle.

"Ow! Jesus, what was that?"

"How are you feeling, sir? How long have you been exposed?" asked the one on his right.

"What the hell did you just stab me with?"

"How are you feeling?" asked the one on his right again, pulling harder.

"Where the hell are you taking me?" Colter demanded, looking over his shoulder to see more men in hazmat suits lifting Cass onto a stretcher.

"Answer the question, sir. How long have you been breathing the air?" asked the one on his left. "Did you take your 2-PAM kit? Are you feeling sick? Any dizziness, coughing, eye irritation?"

Colter shrugged. "I dunno, six, seven hours, maybe. Yes. No. And I feel fine, or I did until you monkeys showed up. What the hell did you just give me, and will someone please tell me what the *fuck* is going on?"

"We're at war, sir," said the one on his right, dragging him toward a warehouse with a red cross hastily painted on the side.

"No shit, Sherlock," replied Colter. "Where do you think I've been? I'm asking *who* are we at war with?"

The men in the yellow suits looked at each other.

"Isn't it obvious, sir?" they both asked.

Colter nearly hit them. "No, it's not fucking obvious!"

"Uh…" said the man on his left. "It's aliens, sir."

Colter heard Levi pipe up somewhere behind him.

"You guys hear that? You fuckers all owe me a hundred bucks!"

"Shut the fuck up, Levi!" shouted Colter over his shoulder.

"What? Just saying…" said Levi, managing to sound hurt.

"This way, sir," said the man on Colter's left, guiding him toward a door in the side of the building guarded by two men, but not marines, and not French soldiers, either.

He recognized the badge on their chests from ten yards away. *Mercenaries.* Academi to be specific, formerly Xe Services, formerly Blackwater, and still just as dirty. You couldn't polish a turd, and changing a name didn't change what a thing was.

One of the mercs stepped forward to block what was left of Colter's squad from following him in.

"Not you lot. This is a quarantine zone. You'll get your boss back when he's cleared," he said. "The rest of you are to report to C-Block for debriefing."

"Just try and stop me," growled Hicks, getting up in the merc's face.

"It's fine, Hicks." Colter shrugged off the medics and pulled Hicks away before he did something stupid. "I'll come find you when they're done patching me up. In the meantime, get what gear you need, get some chow, and try to get some rest. Something tells me this isn't over yet."

"Chow? How are we gonna eat with our stupid masks on?" asked Levi, his voice faint as Colter turned to follow the medics into the building.

They walked down a long hall, down a set of stairs, bare concrete to either side, a mess of piping, plumbing, and wiring running above them, the building's guts hanging from the ceiling. They turned a corner and came to a stop in front of another door, this one manned by two more Academi. The one to Colter's right punched a code into a keypad lock, and he opened the door. The medics passed through, and one of the mercs stepped in Colter's way.

"No weapons inside."

Colter felt a hand on his back.

"Don't move," said someone behind him, and Colter felt something in his armpit. The merc's handgun, its barrel aimed in through the gaping hole in his body armor.

"You give everyone this treatment?" Colter asked over his shoulder.

"Precautions," said the one in front of him, his rifle aimed at Colter's chest.

So Colter stood still. He let them pull his handgun from its holster, then they took his bayonet and his Ka-Bar. They lifted his extra ammo and stripped the grenades from his chest. He grunted as the one behind him holstered his handgun and started patting him down, obviously convinced Colter was smuggling a bazooka up his ass.

"Find anything you like?" Colter asked.

"Something that feels like a dick. Only smaller."

Colter shrugged like he was used to it, and on the outside he looked calm enough, but on the inside he was fuming. This wasn't quarantine. They weren't Academi. They weren't mercenaries. Not even mercenaries were dumb enough to point a gun at a marine.

They were CIA, which meant this was a black site, and he'd just walked into shit right up to his eyeballs.

"He's clear," said the man behind him.

The one on the left nodded, lowering his rifle back to a ready position.

"First door on the left," he said, nodding for Colter to walk in front. "Your wounds will be tended to while our medics run some tests. And don't try anything stupid. We'll shoot first and ask questions later."

Colter started moving again. He didn't have a choice.

The guns pointed at his back made sure of it.

CASS

Cass couldn't breathe.

There was something sitting on his chest, something heavy, suffocating him.

He opened his mouth, desperate for air, and sucked in water instead. He coughed and sucked in more. He started choking. His lungs tried to breathe liquid, and Cass panicked. He nearly screamed, but some small flicker of self-control made him kick instead, and then he pulled, and he fought, and he started clawing his way out of the dark. He tore at the water with his hands until he couldn't feel his arms anymore, kicked until his legs barely moved, swimming toward the pale shimmering light high above. His diaphragm spasmed, and his whole world shrank to a single pinprick of white. His ears filled with a hollow whine, and Cass realized he wasn't going to make it. It was too far. He was drowning.

No!

So he kicked again, one last time. His leg barely twitched. His chest heaved, he sucked in water, his eyes rolled back in his head, and he started sinking. The whine in his ears grew louder, stuttering, louder. It started beeping. The sound echoed in his head, and Cass woke up gasping.

Just a dream.

He felt relief crash down on him like a wave.

I'm alive.

He felt his heart pounding in his chest. He felt the ground dip and sway beneath him, and for a while he just concentrated on breathing, listening to his lungs wheeze, feeling cold air on his face and something wet on his cheeks.

And as much as he didn't want to, as much as he just wanted to go back to sleep, his brain wouldn't let him. It started working again, putting things back together, remembering. The bus, those things. His dead friends. The men in hazmat suits and the needle they jammed in his arm. Then nothing.

Except the sound. An annoying repetitive beep right next to his head.

He tried to ignore it, he tried to tune it out, but there was noise all around him now. People moaning and coughing, and far away someone was screaming. He heard a door slam. Its hollow boom echoed down from high above, and Cass got the impression of nothing but empty space above him, like he was in a warehouse or a cave deep underground.

Voices washed in and out of his ears.

"…will this give us?"

The floor tilted beneath him. It felt like he was drifting at sea again.

"…inutes? An hour? Depends."

Cass's left eyelid twitched.

"He's your guy, all right. He was at Ground Zero, or a hell of a lot closer than anyone else. He's got the highest blood count we've…"

Cass knew he wasn't dreaming anymore. He could hear their voices, three separate people talking. But none of what they were saying was making any sense, and he kept missing bits, losing time, drifting in and out of consciousness.

There was another long, loud beep. He moved his head toward it, and the talking stopped.

"He's waking up."

"Good," someone else said, like they were relieved, like it had been 50/50.

Cass got one eye open, but even that was hard.

"Doctor Taylor? Cass? Can you hear me? My name is Carolyn, I'm a doctor, the medical kind. How do you feel? Can you talk?"

Cass looked down, trying to focus on two yellow blurs at the end of his bed.

There was something on his face. It clung to his cheeks and sat over his nose. He grunted with the effort of lifting his arm to try to take it off.

"Please don't touch that. You need to leave it on, okay?"

He felt a gloved hand take his, pressing it back down to the bed, and Cass was alarmed to find he couldn't fight her.

"That's better, good. Relax, just breathe, good. That's it, Cass. You're doing well. Blink if you can hear me."

Cass blinked, still trying to work out what the hell was going on, and why he couldn't see. He blinked again, but it didn't make a difference. Something was wrong with his eyes.

"Everything's going to be okay now, you're safe here."

Cass didn't know where *here* was, but it wasn't a hospital. It felt temporary, and basic. He could just make out blurred crossbeams zigzagging across the ceiling high above, and he was lying on a low, hard bed, or a stretcher. He could feel the struts digging into his back, and there was nothing but a thin sheet thrown across him. And things were far from okay because beneath it he was naked and drenched in sweat, freezing cold and burning up at the same time. Shivering so hard he could hear his teeth rattling in his head.

"Where am—," Cass wheezed, his words unraveling into a wet cough as the room spun around him.

"Just try to take it easy, Cass, okay?" Dr. Sawyer said, like she was talking to a child, trying to keep him calm.

Cass realized he could see through the thing on his face. An oxygen mask.

"What's wr—" Cass coughed again. He felt something wet on his lips as the mask flecked with red.

Dr. Sawyer turned to the two yellow blurs still standing at the end of his bed.

"Hello, Cass," said the blur on the right. "You don't mind if I call you Cass, do you?" They didn't wait for an answer. "My name is Ms. David, and this gentleman to my right is Mr. Alan. I'm sorry for waking you. I know you must be tired. But we have some questions we need to ask, and we don't have much time."

Cass wasn't paying attention. The whole left side of his body was numb, and something was biting the back of his right hand. He could feel its teeth sinking into his flesh as its venom leaked into his veins. He rolled his head to see an IV going in the back.

IV and oxygen. *Not good.*

He tried to sit up. Dr. Sawyer put a hand on his shoulder and pushed him back down.

"Please, Cass. You need to stay still."

Cass started coughing, terrible racking coughs that left him trembling.

"What's wrong with me?" He coughed again.

His bed rolled beneath him, the world spun. He closed his eyes and simply tried to hold on.

"That's it, good. Just relax, Cass," Dr. Sawyer said.

"What's wrong with me?" he asked again, his voice not much more than a whisper.

"Thank you, Dr. Sawyer, we'll take it from here," said Ms. David.

Cass listened to Dr. Sawyer leave, her clothes swishing like she was dressed in garbage bags.

There was a moment of silence.

"I'm not getting better, am I?" Cass asked, looking at the two blurs at the end of his bed and fighting the exhaustion that threatened to suck him back under.

Ms. David looked like she was about to shrug. Then she thought better of it and started talking instead. "No, Cass, you aren't."

Cass closed his eyes, and a small part of him died early.

"You're a smart man. I think you deserve better than a lie, but…"

"What is it?" asked Cass, his mouth still somehow moving while his mind got stuck. "What's wrong with me? Is it chlorine?"

"Chlorine?" Ms. David glanced at the man standing next to her before shaking her head. "No. It's not chlorine. But close. It's the air. It's toxic."

"What?"

"It's the Cloud, Cass, it's killing us."

"The cloud? What are you talking about?"

"We've detected harmful concentrations of known carcinogens and organic solvents in the air: erionite, dioxin, nitrogen oxide, benzene, phosgene, hydrogen fluoride, hydrogen cyanide, methyl bromide, and propene, just to name a few. The kind of stuff we normally only see in pesticides and heavy industry. The dioxin in the air is causing direct damage to your DNA, the methyl bromide and benzene are attacking the ganglia in your brain. As for the erionite, it's 800 times more carcinogenic than asbestos."

"What? Why am I still here?" Cass tried to sit up again.

He got as far as lifting his head.

"Because it's too late."

Cass shook his head, and something next to him made another long, loud beep.

He turned to look at it. A machine covered in buttons and

blinking lights. With tubes feeding into it. Tubes that seemed to be pumping blood.

"I don't understand," said Cass.

"This is taking too long," said the blur on the left. He sounded frustrated, like he had a schedule to stick to. Places to go. Somewhere better to be.

Ms. David started talking again. "There's no easy way of saying this, so I'll just say it. There's nothing we can do. The air is poison. Think biological weapon and broad-spectrum pesticide combined. And you've been breathing it for three days. The damage is done. And to be blunt, the air is what's making you sick, but septicemia and organ failure from the bacterial infection are what's going to kill you first."

Cass frowned at her, thinking he'd misheard. "Bacteria?"

Ms. David nodded. "In technical terms—and I'm using terrestrial classifications here—it's parasitic, aerobic, spore forming, and coccal, as well as being beta-hemolytic. In plain English, it's anthrax on steroids, and it's airborne." Ms. David dipped her head toward him. "It's why your lungs are filling with fluid, and it's the cause of all the fasciitis and purpura… uh, the blotching and bruising of your skin," she added at his confusion. "Right now, the bacteria is attacking the platelets in your blood, stripping out the iron in the hemoglobin and releasing an endotoxin when it lyses. That's the kicker, you see? It's why your liver failed, it's the reason for the dialysis machine, and it's why you have a drainage tube in your chest."

"A what?"

Cass dragged the sheet off him, leaving himself exposed, but he didn't care. There was a tube sticking out between his ribs, taped and bandaged in place, full of blood and twitching in time to his heartbeat. He moved to touch it and stopped.

His fingers were black. He pressed them against his chest and felt nothing. Not even cold.

Gangrene, the scientist in him recognized. *Localized death and decomposition of body tissue, resulting from obstructed circulation or bacterial infection.* His fingers were dead. They were going to have to cut them off, maybe his whole hand, or it would spread.

My hands?

"I know this must be hard. But please try to understand, we can't move you, moving you would just kill you faster."

"Can't you stop it?" Cass begged.

Ms. David shook her head. "I'm sorry, but no. This bacteria is resistant to every antibiotic we've tried, and, believe me, we're trying everything. Besides, we can't actually give you any more colistin without killing you."

"How long?" demanded Cass. Then he noticed the skin on his chest was dotted with the same purple blotches and black veins, and he realized he didn't have to worry about his hands. It was already too late. He started crying. He couldn't hold it in anymore.

This can't be happening.

Ms. David shrugged in apology, but she didn't look away either. "How long? We don't know. It varies, two to three days from infection seems to be the average. But once infected, the disease incubates quickly. Even faster in the immunocompromised."

"And there's no cure?"

Ms. David shook her head again. "Cass, you aren't listening. We're cutting corners as it is, but coming up with an effective treatment will take months, maybe even years. We're still learning about this disease, and we're a long way from knowing how to kill it without killing the patient in the process. In the meantime, the only precaution we've found are these." Ms. David tapped her gas mask. "And our filters will only last so long."

"So that's it?"

"Once you've breathed it in..." She shook her head. "No, the best we can do now is make you comfortable." Ms. David spread her hands again, like that meant anything.

"How is this even possible?"

"That's why we're here, Cass. We were hoping you could tell us. You were at CERN, and we know this started there. Whatever you were doing there somehow brought these things here, caused the Cloud, the disease, all of this. And you're the only eyewitness we have."

Cass grunted, then he started coughing. His mask speckled red again, and the machine next to him started bleating for attention.

Ms. David stepped to the door quickly. She raised her arm like she was hailing a cab, and the next thing he knew Dr. Sawyer was leaning over him, doing something to the IV bag hanging above his head.

The machine next to him stopped beeping, and sunlight washed through his veins.

It started in his hand, warm and wonderful, before it traveled up his arm and into his chest. His heart sucked it up and pumped it into his brain, and Cass let out a happy groan as all the pain and worry in the world went away.

"Thank you, Dr. Sawyer. You can leave us again."

The words echoed in his ears. Like angels singing. He blinked as the two yellow blurs at the end of his bed became four, then ten.

"Cass?"

Cass sighed. Whatever they gave him was good, better than good, it was amazing. He felt warm, he felt free, he felt—

"Cass?"

He didn't remember closing his eyes, but when he opened them Dr. Sawyer was standing next to him again, doing something else to the IV bag.

The machine made another long, loud beep, and Cass let out a grunt as ten thousand volts blasted through his veins.

"Cass? Cass, can you hear me?"

He couldn't speak, he couldn't breathe, he couldn't even scream. It felt like he was having a heart attack.

"Cass?"

His hands balled into fists, his teeth ground to dust, he felt something warm between his legs, and he realized he'd shit himself.

"I'm sorry we have to do it this way, Cass, but we need your help. And that means I need you awake," Ms. David said, coming closer. "Cass?"

He didn't respond. He turned his face and spat blood into his mask instead.

"We're running out of time, Cass. The Cloud will be above the East Coast in three weeks. Do you understand what I'm saying?"

Just leave me alone.

"This is pointless," said Mr. Alan, turning to leave.

"Cass? I need to know what happened at CERN. A lot of people are going to die unless we do something."

He closed his eyes and tuned her out, listening to the machine beeping instead.

A shadow fell across his face.

He opened his eyes to find Ms. David standing next to him, close enough that her face swam into focus. Thin, with pinched cheeks and pale skin, with cold eyes and pupils so brown they were almost black.

"Cass, please? I'm sorry about what's happening to you. I wish there was another way. But…"

And for a second there, he almost believed her, almost, but he saw nothing in her eyes but his own reflection. He meant nothing to her. She was just using him, a means to an end.

Cass nodded anyway. *What difference did it make?* Nothing he had done had mattered. It had all been pointless. *A fucking waste.* So after three days of fighting just to stay alive, he let out a slow breath, and he gave up. He quit.

"What do you want to know?" he said.

Ms. David nodded. She pulled out a pen and a brown notepad from a white pouch around her waist. She took out a small voice recorder, pressed a button, and she rested it on the bed between them. She took another step closer, and she leaned in until there was only a foot between them.

"When did you first know there was a problem?"

DAY
100

Off the beaten path
Fifteen miles northeast of Dodge City
Kansas, USA

TRACE

W e have a problem," Trace said.
"Bad?" Drew asked.

Trace shrugged. "Depends who's following us."

Besides, there was no such thing as a good problem, and they had problems every day. Ever since they had to ditch their car and start walking.

They'd tried to plan for that, just as they'd tried to plan for everything. They had enough ammo to start a small war, as much food and water as they could physically carry, and their police-issue gas masks for when the Cloud caught them. They had a heavily modified one to fit Peter's small face, and spares just in case. They were originally meant for crowd control and tear gas, but their filters were good enough; Trace knew they would do the job. And he had his gun for when they stopped.

He wondered if Sara and Ian had figured that out yet.

Probably not. Those two live on another planet. But right now Trace had a much more pressing concern than the Cloud and getting sick, and this one walked on two legs.

"Where?" asked Drew.

"Three o'clock, in the trees, about a mile back," Trace said, his binoculars held to his eyes as he gazed out into the shallow valley behind them.

"Stupid piece of crap," grumbled Drew.

Trace turned to watch Drew fumbling with his binoculars with one hand while his left arm hung in a sling.

Lucky that, Trace thought for the thousandth time. *Lucky he's even alive.*

The way Drew had been facing when the bullet hit him meant that an inch or two to the left, and it would have taken him in the armpit, gone through the hole in his bulletproof vest and into his chest. An inch or two to the right, on the other hand, and the bullet would have severed the artery in his arm. Either injury would have been beyond them to treat, and a tourniquet would have done nothing but stall the inevitable.

Instead, the bullet had gone straight through Drew's bicep and out the other side. A flesh wound. A perfect wound, really, through and through, while the rest of them had walked away without even a scratch, and a small part of Trace almost wanted to believe they had a guardian angel watching over them. A small part that was quickly mocked and silenced.

Luck. That's all it was. Stupid. Dumb. Luck.

But it meant Drew couldn't use his AR-15 anymore, not properly. Not until his arm healed, and Trace didn't think that would be anytime soon. *Plus, there's always infection to worry about.* And one glance at Drew had told Trace all he needed to know. Drew had a fever. He was burning up. Not that there was anything they could do about that, either. Drew had already taken the last of their antibiotics, and it didn't seem to have worked. It hadn't done much more than slow the infection down, and they couldn't exactly go looking for more.

They didn't have time, not while they were on foot and being followed by someone faster than them. Besides, last time Trace checked, there was no such thing as pharmacies anymore.

One thing at a time, he told himself, turning back to squint through his binoculars, watching as their tail dropped out of the tree line behind them. Walking fast and suddenly exposed on the hill.

"You see him?" Trace asked, his breath misting in air far too cold for summer as water dripped from the branches above their heads.

Drew's head swiveled right, binoculars turning in a slow arc until they stopped and tracked back. "Got him."

Trace watched their tail closing the gap, a mile between them, and apparently oblivious that anyone might be observing him. Naive even.

"You think it's them?" Drew asked, adjusting the focus one-handed. He sounded worried.

"Could be," said Trace. "Maybe… I don't know." He shrugged. "It would mean one of them circled back, which is unlikely. But…"

Trace doubted it was them, at least he hoped it wasn't. The killers whose roadblock they'd narrowly avoided, who were leaving bodies behind them like breadcrumbs, going for the soft targets, the small groups and families.

Like us. Which is why Trace was worried it was one of them coming up behind them now, and coming up fast. And thanks to the endless rain, the ground was far too soft to ride their bikes on, at least this far away from the road. Which is why they were currently pushing them, up to their ankles in mud and leaving footprints behind like road signs.

Still, Trace didn't think it was them; it didn't seem right.

They know we're armed. So why chase us? And why only send one man? It didn't fit.

"What do you want to do?" Drew asked, turning to look at him.

"We push on," said Trace. "But change our heading slightly. Take us northwest for a mile, but make it obvious. If he goes on straight, then it's all good, he's probably no one. But if he turns to follow… well, that will tell us a bit more."

"And?" asked Drew.

Trace shrugged. "I'll hang back to see what he does."

Drew's eyes narrowed, thinking it through, thinking loudly.

"You going to be okay?" he asked finally.

Trace nodded. "I'll be fine. I'll catch up in a bit. Just keep everyone moving. And get them to shut Peter up. I can hear him crying from here."

"Be careful, Trace," Drew said slowly.

Trace nodded back before Drew turned to pick up his bike from the ground. He jogged back up to where the others were waiting.

Trace turned to watch their tail. *Who are you, my friend?*

Sure, their tail could be no one. There could be a completely innocent explanation for him being there. This was a well-worn path already, a path taken by hundreds of people before them, all heading west and keen to avoid Dodge City by going the long way around. Their tail could be nothing more than pure coincidence, just stupid luck at work again. But he was definitely following them, and Trace didn't believe in coincidences.

He'd seen way too much shit in his life for that.

He waited another minute just to make sure their tail didn't change direction before he got up and followed Drew. Just not as quick. He wasn't a young man anymore, and even with his fever Drew still had a good twenty-year head start on him. Besides, his bike with all his gear strapped to it was heavy, and the footing treacherous, his feet occasionally slipping and sliding on the incline that was more mud pile than hill.

He looked up at the trees overhead, their branches heavy and dripping wet, seeing fat gray clouds poking through the gaps, and he wondered when they would open up again and wash the rest of the hill away.

It had been raining for four days straight, almost torrential, and Trace was sick of it. Sick of being wet, sick of being cold, sick of the mud. And he stank.

Not that he was complaining.

They had no shortage of fresh water, and they'd gone much farther in the car than he could have ever hoped, finally running out of gas on an empty stretch of the 14, just twenty miles north of Sterling, Kansas.

But Colorado was still 340 miles away, and with days like today, to Trace, sometimes even the moon felt closer.

It felt like he was trapped in an endless triathlon, or a nightmare. He imagined they were much the same, walking and riding from sunup to sunset, day after day after day.

And thanks to the rain, but mostly the mud, he'd quickly come to learn that 340 miles in these conditions was an impossible distance.

They weren't going to make it. He wasn't being a pessimist; it was simple math. Because after five days of it, they'd hardly made a dent. 100 miles. That was it, and they kept running into problems. The biggest so far being the Arkansas River, engorged with rain, full of debris, and stained a dark brown as the countryside washed away.

With no other option, they'd been forced to swim across it. Because as they came to discover, the only bridge for thirty miles had been blocked by a wall of cars and a giant red spray-painted sign telling them to "Fuck off or die."

Seeing as how they hadn't been too keen on finding out who wrote it, they'd backtracked, picked a spot about a mile downstream where the river was a little wider, and the water seemed calmer. Then they'd stripped down to their underwear, strapped all their gear and bikes to a log, and Sara and himself had paddled it across, ending up half frozen, half drowned, and a mile downstream from where they'd started. Then Ian had swum Stacey over before swimming back to help Drew and Peter.

It had been beyond stupid, and bitterly cold, but, as Drew had pointed out, it wasn't exactly like they were spoiled for choice. And it would probably happen again, so they may as well get used to it.

It's also probably when Drew's arm got infected.

But that was just the beginning. Every day since had been worse than the last, and when Trace rolled into his sleeping bag at night he didn't even remember closing his eyes. The next thing he knew, it was still dark, still cold, still raining, and he was being woken for his turn on watch. But as bad as the rain was, the wind was worse. It felt like it was blowing straight in from the Arctic, and even now, in the middle of September, and two in the afternoon, Trace's lips were tinged blue, and his breath turned to mist in front of his face.

And there could only be one reason for that: the Cloud getting closer. He could feel it, an ache in his bones as it sucked the last of the heat from the air. *And now we're being followed.*

He wanted to laugh, he wanted to scream, but mostly he wanted a break. His back hurt, his feet were destroyed, his knees felt like they were coming apart, and yet, thanks to their tail, they needed to move even faster. At least for a bit.

Just to be safe.

After all, he didn't want them to join the poor dead bastards they kept finding along the way.

Not that bodies were anything unusual. They came across bodies all the time. The forests and fields were littered with them. Well, what was left of them, once the pet dogs gone feral had found them.

They were suicides, mostly. Sad, lonely deaths. Single gunshot wounds to the head or half-starved bodies dangling from trees. And then there were those that had simply succumbed to injury or exposure.

Death was common out here. You couldn't walk a mile without smelling it. A smell he and Drew had learned to follow in the hope of finding something useful. Breathing through their mouths as they picked through dead men's pockets, looking for food, clean socks, matches, batteries, or medicine. Bodies coming apart as they turned them over to check underneath, feeling envious of Sara, Ian, and the kids, waiting just out of sight and upwind.

But Stacey and Peter were struggling as it was. Peter didn't do much except cry these days, and Stacey was losing her hair. So the fewer bodies they saw the better. And besides, he was used to them. After forty years of seeing dead people, he was almost immune to them, and they were just kids. They should have been in school, playing with their friends, learning how to read and write. Not slowly starving to death.

Sometimes they got lucky, though. Sometimes they found food, and clean clothes, but it was never enough. Every day they expended more energy than they took in, and Trace didn't know how he was going to protect them from this new threat, this person following them, and whoever was still ahead of them. Because the last three times they had followed their noses, they had found something else entirely.

They had come across crime scenes. Men with their hands tied behind their backs and bullet holes in their heads.

Trace had only seen two that had tried to run, but the line of bullet holes stitched into their backs had brought them up short. And from a distance they almost looked like flowers, like confused Fire Pinks. Little red star-shaped holes of bloodstained fabric wriggling with maggots.

Trace almost would have said it was deliberate, that the killer had been playing with them, giving them a head start. That was until he examined the clusters and couldn't find any. There were no groupings. The killer's aim was terrible. Trace doubted he could hit a barn door if he was standing a foot in front of it, and, as for his victims, he'd shot one of the guys in the ass first, from about four feet away. At least it made more sense that way when Trace looked at the powder burns on his clothes.

The ass first, then the middle of his back. Recoil lifting the gun higher with each shot.

The headshot came last. A lucky shot. More recoil than aim, before he switched to the next poor bastard. It looked like he almost made it too. Except a bullet had caught him in his side, spinning him around, and another had gone into his shoulder, just behind his heart. The third had clipped his elbow.

The extra shells Trace had counted meant the killer had also missed a few. At least four by his count, maybe more. All of which told Trace several things.

The killer had been relying on the element of surprise, and in this instance they'd ballsed it up spectacularly. But they were also learning. The two most recent scenes, judging by the states of bodies, were better, at least in terms of execution. Pun intended. Being a cop fucks with your sense of humor.

The men were still in their sleeping bags, probably woken up with a gun to their heads. Then they'd been shot, point blank. They were contact shots, and the flesh around the entry wounds had bubbled and ruptured in neat little patterns called tattooing, while the backs of their heads were simply missing.

And then it got bad, because there had been a girl in the group, and whoever had killed her liked to get up close and personal, but this time it had nothing to do with overcoming bad aim.

They'd left her there, naked and spread eagled with her throat slit. And beneath the abuse heaped on her at the end, Trace could see she had been young, and pretty, maybe. Her face was too broken to tell, and by the time he found her the rot had taken hold.

Why did he think all three crime scenes were connected?

Simple. All three had women in the group. All blonde with similar builds. Like they were the target from the start. Like the killer had a type and a few issues to work out. All three had been beaten to a pulp, probably raped, then had their throats slit.

Trace had seen it before. There was even a name for it. "Projecting."

He also found the same bullet shells at each site, their brass casings glinting like dull gold in the overcast light.

Blazer Brass, it had read when he picked one up and turned it around to see the stamp on the bottom. Nothing special in that, a standard FMJ round. A cheap round, really. It dirtied up your gun pretty quick. You got a lot of sparks out of the barrel when you shot, like fireworks. Accurate enough, just not the greatest. Basically a bottom-shelf bullet, probably fired from a bottom-shelf gun. No way for him to tell if they were fired by the same gun though, not unless he sent them to a ballistics lab, and that wasn't going to happen.

But it let him build up a profile of the shooter, make some guesses as to the weapon used.

A handgun, most likely, a cheap one, too. General rule, you don't put shit bullets in a nice gun.

So probably a Sig Pro 2022, a CZ P-07, or a Stoeger Cougar, Trace reasoned. All 9mm handguns you could get for about $400. A handgun for someone who wasn't a professional but wanted a gun. Someone that had never done a lot of shooting. Someone that had never had a gun jam on them in a pinch. A novice, or two of them, maybe.

That was the one thing he couldn't work out, just how many people they were dealing with. It looked like the work of a group, but there only ever seemed to be one shooter, and there was too much contamination at the scenes, too many track marks in the disturbed dirt to be sure of numbers. Who was victim, who was killer?

And Trace didn't know the timing. Had all the traffic come at once or had others already been through here before them?

Whatever the case, two things were certain: whoever these dead men were, they hadn't seen it coming, not in a million years, and it had happened quickly. Trace figured they hadn't posted a sentry. The other alternative was that they knew their killer. But that was unlikely, and he hadn't seen any other shells, either. There had been no exchange of gunfire, no evidence the men had put up a fight. They'd been executed like it was a game.

Trace had forced them to move on pretty quickly after that.

Just not fast enough, he thought bitterly, glancing over his shoulder and catching a flash of movement behind him. Their tail was still there, not dropping his pace for a moment. Trace could swear he'd even gained some ground. *Quick little fucker, aren't you?*

He looked ahead, seeing the others ahead of him, dark figures moving between the trees, moving faster now that Drew had caught up. They turned right, and he lost sight of them.

Good, Trace thought when he reached the same spot. Their footprints suddenly veered off the path, cutting straight through some vegetation and up the hill, leaving scuff marks on the gravel and rocks, smudges where their footing had slipped. They'd even broken some twigs.

To Trace, the new direction looked as though they were making for the top of the hill, aiming for high ground. As though they'd lost their reference point and were trying to get their bearings back. It was painfully obvious in the mud too, like a drunk driver through a brick wall. You'd have to be blind not to see it.

So he followed it, and after another hundred yards he stopped walking. He couldn't see Drew or the rest of the group anymore, and he couldn't see their tail, either. So he stepped off the path, he cut out at ninety degrees to his right, walked another twenty yards, dropped his bike, turned ninety degrees to his right again, and jogged all the way back downhill, ignoring the hot lances of pain and the sound of crunching glass in his knees.

He didn't have to do it for long, so he told himself he could manage, and his little detour meant he wasn't on their path anymore, and he wasn't leaving any new tracks visible from it. It meant that when he got back to the turn they had taken, he did so from a different angle, from behind a screen of trees. Which gave him some cover and a little misdirection, and the high ground. It also meant anyone following them wouldn't expect it; their eyes would be looking ahead of them, and by the time they even thought to look right, Trace would be behind them. It meant he had all the advantage, the element of surprise.

He sank to the ground ten yards out, and he started crawling forward on his elbows, his AR-15 swinging from side to side in his arms until he lined up with the path at a 45-degree angle.

He pulled his hood down over his head, flicked the safety off, and he waited.

It took their tail thirteen minutes to cover the mile. Trace timed him.

Thirteen minutes and twenty-three seconds to be exact, and when their tail caught up with them Trace noticed several things first.

Their tail was male, maybe just shy of six feet, and strong, full of energy, practically bouncing on the balls of his feet, and he was young. Seventeen years old if he was a day, and Trace was good with ages, at least with boys. With girls, he had no idea. Makeup could make a fourteen-year-old look twenty. Or, at least that had been the common excuse when those things still mattered.

But he was definitely in his late teens, that fact becoming even more obvious as he got closer and Trace started picking out the finer details, wide shoulders, long arms, like he was still growing into his frame. Pale face dotted with acne, red cheeks flushed with exertion and stung by the cold. The hair, long, wet, and unkempt, maybe blond, but a dull brown beneath the overcast sky, the barest hint of fuzz on his upper lip. Trace noticed how heavy his backpack was, it almost bulged. Then he spotted a rifle hanging from the kid's shoulder, and his eyes narrowed.

That was a complication, an expected one, but not a problem. *Not yet,* Trace reminded himself as he lined the kid up in his crosshairs.

But more importantly, when their tail neared the turnoff, he wasn't looking anywhere near Trace. His head was tilted down, watching the ground like a hound with a scent.

To Trace's eyes, he looked comfortable, breathing easily, moving with long, even strides, his hands holding the straps of his backpack like he'd been walking hard all day and was still going strong.

Trace guessed he was pretty fit. He guessed the kid could run a hundred yards in twelve seconds. Or at least a lot quicker than he could…

Good thing we aren't racing, then, thought Trace, his finger resting on the trigger guard.

The kid came to a stop in the middle of the path, and not gradually either. He just stopped dead.

This close to him, Trace could see the kid frowning. Brain expecting one thing while his eyes told him something else. Path going right instead of straight like it should have.

Most people hesitate when they see something like that, when expectation differs from reality. It catches them off guard, and they have to think about it for a second, and while they're thinking they don't react, they don't move, they freeze.

It's the same reason you see so many car accidents involving light posts or trees. Sometimes it's the only tree on the road and they still managed to hit it, and not a glancing shot either, not a little to the right or a little to the left, but dead center, right between the headlights. Like people aimed for them deliberately.

Reason being that, in the moment, in that split second before they hit, where they need to make a decision—do I turn left or do I turn right?—most people become paralyzed by the choice. Both are equally valid, so they do nothing.

This kid was one of them. He didn't duck, he didn't turn, he didn't run, he didn't even make a sound. He just stood there.

Trace watched him turn to look back the way they had come, as though making sure he was still on the right path before he turned to look at the deviation their footprints had suddenly taken to his right.

Trace watched him lift his head higher, his eyes following the bent curve of their footprints before they disappeared amongst the trees.

The kid still didn't move. He just stood there. *Thinking*, Trace guessed. Probably thinking the same thing he was.

Going straight made more sense. Going straight was almost directly west, toward Colorado, California, LA, the sea. There was no reason to head north and climb a hill, no reason for the kid to turn right. Not unless he was lost, and to Trace it looked like he knew exactly where he was going. That and his cheeks weren't sunken and gaunt like everyone else's. He looked like he'd been doing well out here. Trace imagined he had plenty to eat. No reason to follow complete strangers. Why take the risk?

"Keep going," Trace whispered to himself, his breathing steady, crosshairs lined up on the kid's chest, center mass. He sucked in a breath, let it out, dropped his finger to the trigger. And it was almost as though someone heard his prayer, their imaginary guardian angel stepping in again, perhaps.

Because the kid shrugged, he resettled his backpack on his shoulders with a little hop, and he started walking again, and he went straight, almost directly west, toward Colorado, California, LA, the sea.

Trace took his finger off the trigger. He watched the kid walk out of sight, and he let his head sink to the ground with a relieved sigh.

He waited another minute before he pushed himself up and began walking back uphill, first to pick up his bike, and then to catch up with the others.

Trace took the walkie-talkie from his jacket pocket and held it to his mouth.

"We're clear," he said, taking his finger off the button. He realized his hands were shaking.

"Problem?" answered Drew.

"No problem, see you in a bit," Trace said, trying to put more cheer into his voice than he really felt, not sure if he was more relieved that their tail had turned out to be harmless or shaken by just how close he'd come to shooting a kid.

The real problems started when he spotted the kid again the next day.

And the next.

When shooting a kid in cold blood started to sound like a good idea. Because no matter which way they turned, they couldn't seem to shake him. Not for long. Not with Drew's slowing pace.

So Trace made a decision, even if the others wouldn't like it. Next time he saw the kid, he'd get a warning shot.

If he saw him again after that, he'd get one in the head.

SARA

Sara peeled the bandage off Drew's arm.

"Oh..."

"Just so you know," offered Drew.

Sara looked up at him.

"You would have made a terrible doctor. No poker face."

He even tried to smile. But his sunken eyes were just as concerned as her own, and this time his normally contagious smile didn't catch.

"It's not working," Sara said, trying to keep the worry out of her voice.

"So it appears."

She turned his arm over so she could see both sides, the entry wound as well as the messy exit. She noted the swelling, and the redness, and the pain. She looked at the yellow pus that had come away with the strips of cloth. She pushed on the wound and ignored Drew's hiss as more pus oozed out. All indications an infection was present, and a bad one, despite all their best efforts at keeping it clean.

They were giving Drew's gunshot wound the "open treatment."

No stitches, no sutures, nothing but butterfly tape to draw the edges together. It had to be open so it could *breathe*.

"The safest way to manage wounds in survival situations," Drew had said.

It meant applying a warm, moist compress to the wound four times a day, wiping away the clotted blood and pus before reopening the wound. And it meant more pain for Drew as she poked and prodded at it with a sterile instrument. And once she was done, she would have to dress it and bandage it up again. She would have to do it twice more today alone.

In short, it meant a lot of work, and a lot of time going nowhere. Problem was it wasn't working. The last two days had only seen it get worse, and she knew they couldn't keep going like this.

They needed antibiotics, or next Drew would have sepsis, and if it got that far he was as good as dead. So Drew figured it was time for maggots, despite the hazards, but that was the other problem. They hadn't seen a single blowfly in days.

Trace said the rain and the cold were keeping them down, and they couldn't use the maggots wriggling around in the corpses they passed, either. The cross-contamination would kill Drew faster than the original infection, and they had no way of sterilizing them. After all, you can't exactly boil maggots and expect them to live.

So they had to wait for the rain to stop and for the sun to come out before the current generation of eggs would hatch and swarm. Until then, they were stuck, and Sara could do nothing but keep cleaning away the pus and infected flesh every day, watching Drew slowly grow weaker and weaker.

"Hey, how's it look?" Ian asked, his voice dying away as he came to stand over her shoulder. "Oh..."

Sara ignored him, wiping the pus away until she could see the gray, wrinkled flesh beneath that stank so bad.

Definitely worse.

"Uh, I'll go check on Peter," said Ian, backing away. "Give Trace a hand, maybe…"

"Whatever," said Sara, trying not to sound frustrated.

Funny thing with Ian, he had no problem getting his hands dirty. He was practical and down to earth. But with this kind of thing—blood—he couldn't handle it. He got squeamish and light-headed. Just the sight of it was enough to undo him. The irony wasn't lost on anyone. Good old Ian, six-foot-two and scared of a pinprick.

It had become something of a running joke in the family. Apparently the first time Ian saw a calf being born he fainted. Out cold for a whole minute. It had taken a bucket of water to bring him around, and after that, whenever there was work to be done around his dad's farm, especially if it was calving season, Ian was mysteriously absent. Ian's dad used to tease him about it at the Thanksgiving table every year. Right up until he died.

Two years ago next month, Sara realized with a start.

She shook her head. It all felt like a lifetime ago. A different life with different problems, when Ian's issue with blood used to be amusing. Not so much anymore. She could have done with some help.

"You okay?" Drew asked, when her hand stopped moving for a little too long.

"Fine," Sara said, "just thinking."

"Good things?" asked Drew.

"A bit of both," she said a little too quickly, pressing on his arm a bit harder than she needed to. Feeling grateful when he hissed and got the message to shut up, then guilty for hurting him. "Sorry."

Drew shrugged like it was nothing.

It's going to be okay, she told herself, taking a deep breath and trying to clamp down on her rising panic. *It's going to be okay.* She had to believe it, she had faith. Something would come along. *He* would provide. Besides, she simply couldn't imagine life without

Drew around. He was their foundation, their rock. He kept their spirits up, he kept them going. He was their little engine that could. Which meant he couldn't just up and die on them; they'd never make it without him. And every day he taught them something new: This berry you could eat, this one you couldn't. How to set traps for rabbits, what roots contained water. That you could eat the weeds that grew by the side of the road if you were desperate, and they were especially good now that the councils hadn't been spraying them with pesticides for the last three months.

He even shot a stray dog that came too near camp one night. A chocolate lab, someone's unwanted family pet. Too much of a burden to feed, too much of a memory to kill, and far too friendly for its own good.

It still had its collar on when Drew put a bullet through its head, but if it had a name Drew didn't say, and Sara didn't ask. She just watched as he skinned it and gutted it and cooked it over the fire like he'd been doing it his whole life.

They hadn't eaten that well in weeks, and, given their dwindling supplies, they might not eat that well again. Not unless another dog made the same mistake.

Sara dropped the soiled compress in a bowl of boiled water at her side, watching the blood and filth stain it a reddish brown.

"Trace, I need more water!" she called, picking up a fresh compress and starting again.

"Coming," answered Trace from behind her, walking toward them while Stacey pegged questions at his back. Forcing Trace to think, talk, and walk while he held a pot of boiling hot water in his hands. He put it down next to Sara and made his escape while Stacey stayed behind to watch.

It had almost become a ritual between the three of them.

Sara cleaned while Drew tried not to complain too much, and Stacey gradually shuffled closer and closer, seeming both equally fascinated and disgusted by the process. At least that's what it sounded like by the noises she made.

"So what have you and Trace been talking about?" Sara asked after one particularly long outburst.

"I was asking where the monsters came from."

Sara turned on her. "I told you not to talk about that."

"Peter's with Dad. He's too far away to hear."

Sara waved a finger at her.

"What?" asked Stacey. "I wanted to know, I thought Uncle Trace might. His son died fighting them, right?"

Sara grabbed Stacey by the arm and pulled her close.

"Please tell me you haven't asked him about that."

Stacey's eyes widened, and she shook her head.

Sara let out a relieved sigh. That's the last thing they needed, the last thing Trace needed, especially. Another reminder.

"Stace, you're not allowed to ask Trace about his son. Okay?"

Stacey looked at the ground.

Sara shook her gently. "You listening?"

Stacey nodded again, still studying her feet.

"Stacey, I'm asking you a question. What are you not allowed to do?"

"I'm not allowed to ask Uncle Trace about his son," mumbled Stacey, sounding chastised.

"Good. You can ask him anything else, just not that. Promise?"

Stacey nodded again.

"Good." Sara let go of her arm, gave her a quick kiss on the forehead, and pointed at the first-aid kit with her chin. "Now make yourself useful and hand me that."

Stacey had only started calling Trace "Uncle" a few days ago. It had taken a while for Sara to work out why, but it turned out half of Stacey's earlier shyness had been due to her not knowing what she should call him.

Trace wasn't Stacey's grandfather. Her grandfather was dead, but he was an adult, like her dad, but old, mom's boss, a friend of the family, but still something of a stranger to her. And he looked like a grandfather, and adults always had titles, but he wasn't a Mr. or a Sir—that was too formal—and he wasn't a Dr. either.

Uncle was the closest Stacey could get, and ever since then she'd been talking Trace's ear off, and that was a good thing because it was forcing Trace to talk back, and he'd gone quiet the last few days. Quieter than Sara was used to, and, in the time she'd spent with him, Sara had come to learn that was a bad thing. Trace wasn't exactly the type to ask for help if there was a problem. He was more the old-school type, raised in an era when men didn't have emotions. So if there was a problem, Trace kept it to himself. He buried it deep, and he let it fester.

Bullheaded is how she would describe him, and brash, and a few other names that were less polite.

And whereas Drew always had a smile on his face, Trace was all right angles and hard edges. He was cold and distant. He never laughed, he barely smiled, and he had this way of staring at you when you talked. His eyes focused somewhere behind you, like he was looking through you, or reading something written on the back of your head. It was unnerving and disconcerting. You couldn't help but look away. Most normal people would. Not Trace.

Sometimes she wondered if he'd always been this way or if being a cop in LA had messed with his head, rewired his brain, broken something, maybe. But it wasn't just that. Even before the Cloud, long before James had died, whenever Trace walked into a new place, it was always the same deal. He would scope it out, check the corners and the exits, looking for threats. And when they had to choose a table, he'd choose one right at the back, in the corner, with his back to the wall so he could watch everyone and everything. Like some nervous tic.

It made him hard to be around. The longer she'd gotten to know him, the less surprised she was that James had run away to join the Marines. She probably would have done the same thing, just sooner, and probably screaming. She imagined growing up with Trace for a dad must have been hard; just being around him for a few hours was exhausting. But maybe that's why Trace had been so hard on himself when James died. She figured he blamed himself, realized too late what he'd done. Pushed his only son away.

But that's the problem with people like him, she supposed. Trace was so used to getting his own way that he'd never learned to deal with losing, or how to compromise. And he'd never learned how to cope when things went badly. Not properly. So she was worried about him. But at least he wasn't drinking anymore. Not from lack of desire; she just didn't think he had any left, which might explain the bad mood.

The tail they'd picked up for the last three days didn't help. It was like a wet stone on Trace's raw nerves, grinding them away to a sharp edge, and that's what worried her. She didn't know what would happen when he finally snapped. Something bad, she could feel it.

"I think we're done here," said Sara after a while.

She couldn't see any more pus, and the wound was bleeding freely again, clear, bright red blood. Healthy blood.

Drew shrugged. "Looks good to me."

"Just let it dry for a bit. I'm going to go wash these. Stacey, stay here with Drew, okay?"

Stacey nodded and shuffled closer to Drew, her nose crinkling up like it always did.

Sara picked up the bowl of dirty bandages and stood up. She turned to see Ian sitting by the fire, his back against a tree with Peter in his lap, her little boy clinging to his dad like a barnacle as Ian stroked his head. She turned to see Trace walking laps through the trees. Like he was patrolling or keeping guard or running from his demons.

She looked back down at Drew and Stacey, with so many worries and doubts crowding her head. They were already falling apart, and she didn't know what would happen when they ran out of food. What happened if the Cloud caught them first? What if there was nothing in Colorado when they got there? What if they never even made it? But there was nothing else she could do about any of them. She was doing everything she could, she just had to have faith and trust there was a plan. A reason for all of *this*.

"Back in ten," she said.

Drew nodded. Sara turned her back on them and started walking downhill, trudging through the mud, stepping on broken twigs and shredded leaves, winding her way between the trees. The voices behind her faded away, replaced with the sound of running water.

It wasn't until a minute later that she saw the actual river. More of a stream, really, maybe six feet across, two feet deep, but it was flowing quickly, and the water was crystal clear and ice cold. No fish, though. That would be asking too much. But at least it was fresh. That was the one good thing about all the rain—they had more than enough to drink. She glared up at the dark clouds overhead.

Seriously, more than enough.

She knelt down at the stream's edge, taking the soiled bandages out one at a time and cleaning them in the water, scrunching and bunching them up before wringing them out. She did it again and again until the water barely turned pink anymore.

She was almost done when she heard something snap.

Sara kept cleaning, her pace didn't change, she didn't pause. Her mind, on the other hand, was running a million miles an hour. Her heart was pounding, and inside she was kicking herself. The sound had come from her right, maybe fifteen yards out, and her gun was back at camp, next to her rifle, with all her gear.

Rookie mistake, Sara.

She heard it again, something moving in the trees, coming closer.

Then silence.

Sara held her breath, then she looked up.

There was a boy on the other side of the stream, watching her.

No. Not a boy. A young man. Almost six foot. He had a rifle slung over his right shoulder, but his hands were empty. He was wearing gloves. His eyes darted left and right, over her shoulder and up the hill before looking back to her face.

"Hi," he said, and he smiled. "I'm Mick."

TRACE

Trace was pissed.

"Trace," implored Sara.

"No fucking way."

"Stop acting like a child," said Ian.

"Fuck that, Ian. He is not coming with."

"Shhh. He's going to hear you," hushed Sara, risking a glance to where Mick waited at the edge of camp. His shoulders hunched as he stared at the dirt and fiddled with his hands.

"Do you think I care?"

"So what? You're just going to chase him off?" asked Ian.

"Yes, Ian, that's exactly what I propose we do."

"Don't be such an ass."

"He's fifteen, Trace. He's just a kid," Sara said. "He's asking for help, I say he can stay."

"Mom?" asked Peter, tugging on Sara's arm.

"Not now, Pete."

"He's coming with us, Trace," said Ian. "He's in trouble, and I won't turn my back on him."

"Mom?"

"Stace, come take Peter, please."

"Do you know how stupid this is?" Trace said. "That's the kid who's been following us for three days, and now you want to let him tag along? Are you mad? We've already changed direction twice, and he keeps coming. You don't think that's odd?"

Trace sure did. Something about the whole situation stank.

Ian crossed his arms, and his eyes glazed over. "We're done talking, Trace. Walk behind us if you don't like the idea. Go jump in a lake. I don't care."

Sonofabitch. Trace wanted to strangle him.

He counted to ten instead.

"Fine, have it your way, Ian," said Trace. "But just to be clear, I don't give a shit how young or helpless you think he is. There's something not right with him." He looked between Ian and Sara. "And just so we're especially clear, he doesn't go on watch, not ever. And you keep one fucking eye on him the whole time. You hear me? You watch him every waking second. Especially round the kids."

"Don't you think you're being a little dramatic?" Sara asked.

"No, Sara, I'm being cautious. You should, too. Let's just hope this thing doesn't blow up in our face."

"This *thing* has a name, Trace, it's Mick. You should practice using it."

"Everyone has a fucking name, Sara. And you think his youth doesn't make him a risk?"

"Now you're just being paranoid," chided Ian.

"And you're being an idiot."

Ian took a step toward him, and Trace forced himself to walk away before he punched Ian in the face.

Nobody spoke the rest of the day.

At least not to him, not that Trace cared. He was glad, in fact. He had nothing but abuse left to give. So in aid of morale, and in an attempt to cool off, he stayed as far away from Ian as possible. He walked at the back of the line, pushing his bike with his left hand while his right hand stayed near his Glock.

And when they got back on the road and started riding, he stayed at the back, peddling slowly, not talking, just watching. His eyes boring twin holes into the back of the kid's head as he jogged alongside Ian, easily keeping up with Drew's slowing pace.

Trace could tell it unnerved him. Not that he was worried about offending him; that was half the point. He wanted the kid unsettled, he wanted to keep him off balance, keep him guessing. And silence worked wonders for loosening people's tongues, especially when they're nervous. Especially when they're trying to establish themselves in a new group. Basic Psych 101: In any group dynamic based off hierarchy, the best thing you can do when you're in a position of power is to say nothing. Silence is a weapon. People hate silence. They talk just to fill the gap, and when they do they let things slip.

The kid was no different. But it wasn't until Drew fell off his bike and they decided to make camp early for the night that he finally cracked.

"Hi," the kid said, poking his head into their tent and letting the wind in. He frowned when he noticed Drew lying on the ground, then hesitated when he saw the bloodstained bandage on Drew's arm and the sheen of sweat that covered his face.

"What happened to him?" the kid asked.

"He got shot," Trace said.

"How?"

"With a gun," Drew said, smiling weakly.

Trace heard the kid grunt. Not quite a laugh. Not quite a cough. Nervous.

Good.

"Do you have any antibiotics?" Trace asked.

The kid looked at Trace quickly. He looked away, his eyes skipping right, then down. He shook his head.

"Is he going to be okay?" the kid asked, pointing at Drew with his chin.

Trace shrugged. He didn't turn to look at Drew; he didn't need to. He knew what Drew looked like. He was much more interested in the kid.

"If we find some antibiotics soon, then yes," he said.

"Oh."

The kid looked back at Trace, holding out his hand.

"Uh, sorry. Hi, I'm Mick, you must be Trace," the kid said with a hesitant smile.

Trace didn't smile back; he didn't take Mick's hand. He let it hang there. He watched the kid's face fall, he watched Mick swallow, he watched his smile crumble as his hand dropped to his side and his cheeks flushed red. Embarrassed or afraid. Hard to tell which, since both cause the capillaries in the cheeks to dilate.

Mick tried again, but he sounded less certain now. Older too. "Look, I know you don't want me here."

Trace shrugged. "Nothing personal, kid, but we've been doing well so far on our own. I would have preferred to keep it that way."

"Well, I just wanted to say I'm sorry, or whatever."

Mick looked away, rubbing the back of his neck.

"Sorry?" asked Trace.

"I heard you all arguing earlier. I just wanted to say I'm sorry, and I get it, and I just wanted to say thanks. For letting me come with…"

"Why have you been following us?"

Mick froze. "Uh…"

"The last three days. You've been following us. Why?"

"I wasn't sure who you were."

"That's beside the point," said Trace. "I asked *why*."

"I needed to know if you were safe."

"Safe?"

"Safe. I've been out here on my own." His voice wobbled, rising a whole octave before dropping. He coughed to try to cover it. "I figured a group is safer. I just wasn't sure who you were."

He smiled again, but the smile didn't reach his eyes, and he held himself perfectly still.

Trace nodded, and Mick relaxed. He swallowed, Adam's apple bobbing. Some of the tension went out of his frame. His smile was wider this time, a little more genuine too. Trace wasn't so easily convinced.

People are liars by nature. Lies are easy. They're just words, and words are empty, they're just noise, and on average people lie three times per every ten minutes of conversation. So Trace had learned long ago that you have to ignore what people say. You have to listen to how they say it. You have to watch their hands. How they hold themselves, where they look, how often they blink, who they look at. Even how they breathe can tell you a lot. Lies are easy, but body language is much harder to fake. Not that it's impossible, just harder, and it takes training and practice.

Trace doubted Mick had either, and he had decades' worth. Still, body language is unreliable, full of false positives and idiosyncrasies. The best way to catch a liar is to get them talking. You get them to relax, you ask open-ended questions, you watch for inconsistencies and contradictions, and you give them just enough rope to hang themselves.

"Where did you come from, Mick? What town?" Trace asked, just getting started.

"Leave him alone, Trace," interrupted Ian from the trees on their left. "Mick, come here. We need to get a fire going, and you can help me find some wood."

"Uh. Sure," Mick said, giving Trace one last nervous glance before backing away.

"He's hiding something," Trace said to Drew.

"Seriously?" asked Sara as she ducked into the shelter behind him and began rummaging through one of their bags. "You need to relax."

"How's the arm, Drew?" Trace asked, changing subjects and ignoring her. It wasn't worth having another fight. Not yet.

"Growing cheese," Drew replied, looking at it with a tired sigh.

"Cheddar or Camembert?" asked Trace.

Drew lifted his arm to sniff. "More like bleu."

Trace grimaced. He had always hated bleu cheese, reminded him of vomit.

"I'll leave you boys to it," Sara said with a disgusted groan before she lifted the tent flap and stepped back outside.

They made camp for the night just like they did most nights, away from the road, beneath some trees, and on the westward side of a small hill. Out of the worst of the wind and on a slight slope.

They had draped a tarp above their tent, suspended by a rope tied between two trees, its corners pegged out and weighed down with rocks so that it made a waterproof barrier above their heads. The most basic A-frame you could get. Angled for the runoff and closed to the wind except for the two ends. They had also dug a trench in the ground around them to funnel the water flowing downhill to either side.

It created a relatively dry patch for them to sit on and, in a couple of hours, sleep. It gave Sara a dry place to work on Drew, and it gave their gear a chance to go from soaked to damp by the morning.

Home sweet home, thought Trace sadly as he looked around the dark interior.

It did a pretty good job of retaining the heat, too, except when the wind was particularly bad. And with the way the temperature was going, the wind was quickly becoming their biggest threat, especially at night. The cold breath of it. The cold that got even worse once the sun slipped below the horizon.

Last night had been the worst yet, the six of them crammed in the little space, practically on top of each other, huddled together for warmth, wrapped in their sleeping bags as a frozen wind tore at the tarp and the heavens pelted them with hail.

Trace had spent a miserable six hours waiting for the storm to break, a miserable six hours listening to Peter and Stacey cry. The adults on the outside and the kids in the center, Sara pressed against him on his right, Drew on his left, and he hadn't slept a wink. So he had been looking forward to sleep. Had, as in past tense, because sure as shit Ian wouldn't watch Mick when it was his turn to stand guard tonight.

That was Ian's failing. One of many. He liked to see the good in people, even when they didn't have any, and he let good intentions get in the way of common sense.

Ian trusted Mick simply because of his age, and the fact he was a good-looking white kid. Prejudice and stereotypes at work again. But Trace knew that didn't mean a thing. So it was up to him, which meant another long, sleepless night waiting for something to happen, but hoping it didn't.

He better have his own tent, Trace thought as he looked up at the darkening sky. Space was already limited, and he wasn't in the mood to share.

He glanced at his watch again. They had maybe another hour of light left, and Ian didn't seem to be having much luck getting a fire going, even with Mick's help. Not surprising, considering how wet everything was, and even if they did find something that would burn, it would do so fitfully, spitting out more smoke than heat. But they needed that fire. Drew needed that fire, especially.

"Trace?"

He turned at Drew's voice.

"We need to talk about what happens next."

"How so?"

"I'm done, Trace."

Trace only hesitated a second. "Bullshit, you're doing fine."

"Liar," Drew responded with a faint smile. He glanced toward the tent flap, and his smile faded. "You can lie to them, but don't lie to yourself, or me. I'm done. You know it. I know it. Deep down I think they know it, too." Drew shrugged. "Shit happens."

Trace opened his mouth, and Drew cut him off.

"Answer me this before you try and argue with me. How far have we gone in the last two days? Twenty miles, twenty-five, thirty, maybe?"

"Twenty-four," Trace said reluctantly.

Drew nodded. "We'll never make it at that rate. Sara and Ian aren't thinking straight, but I can't ride that bike anymore. Fuck it, I can barely stand, and the Cloud is less than two weeks behind us now. Face it, Trace, all I'm doing is slowing us down." Drew closed his eyes, and he kept talking, his eyes moving on the other side of his eyelids, like he was dreaming, or thinking it through, imagining the scene, maybe, and Trace knew he'd already given up in his head. "So tomorrow, when I start to fall behind again, and I will, I want you to do me a favor. I want you to look the other way, and I want you to keep going. Before it's too late."

Trace opened his mouth to interrupt again.

"Shut up, Trace, let me finish…"

Trace closed his mouth and kept his thoughts to himself.

"It's the only way this works, Trace. The longer you wait for me, the worse it's going to get. And I don't want you or anyone else wasting any more time on me. It's not working. I'm not getting better. Right now I'm nothing but a liability, so tomorrow, when I fall behind, I want you to keep pushing the others before they catch on."

Trace didn't say anything.

Drew looked up at him. "Deal?"

Trace shrugged. "Your plan has a flaw."

Drew frowned. "How so?"

"I'm just talking hypothetically here, but have you looked around? Where are you going to hide? There's nothing here. And as soon as Ian and Sara work out that you're missing, they'll turn right around and come looking for you. I give it five minutes tops before the penny drops, maybe longer for Ian…"

Drew smiled again. Like he'd already thought of that. Like he had it all covered, and Trace was still playing catch-up.

"Won't work. They'll just be wasting their time, and that's where you come in again. Sorry, but you're going to have to stop them. Because as soon as I've lost sight of you, I'm going to change direction. And a little later, I'll change direction again. I'll keep going until I can't. I don't even have to go that far. All I need to do is lie down. I know y'all can't track worth a damn. So you can tell Ian and Sara they'll just be wasting their time. They'll hate you for it. But it's the only way you'll stay ahead of the Cloud, and you know it."

Trace was silent for a while. Drew didn't say anything else.

"You done feeling sorry for yourself?" Trace asked.

"What?" said Drew, his eyes snapping open. "Wake up, Trace. This isn't a game, you can't fix this, the best thing you can do is leave me behind before I get us all killed."

Trace shook his head. "Over my dead body. You're in this with me to the end. After all, someone has to stop me from killing Ian."

Drew made a sound, like he wanted to laugh, or cry. "What are you going to do, Trace? Strap me to your handlebars? Tie a rope to my body and drag me?" He shook his head. "Just let it go already."

Trace opened his mouth to say something, and he stopped. "That's a great idea. Why didn't I think of that earlier?"

"You're an idiot," muttered Drew.

"No, I'm a genius. Back in a bit."

Drew closed his eyes again, like he didn't care anymore.

Trace pushed the tent flap open. He stepped out into the cold, and he made a beeline straight for Ian and the kid.

"I need your axe," said Trace.

"Why?" Ian asked, taking a step back, his eyes bouncing between Trace and Mick.

Trace just shook his head. Ian had it all ass-backward. Trace wasn't the threat here, but he didn't bother going into it. "I need to cut down a tree, Ian. Why do you think?"

"Oh…" Ian laughed. He extended the handle toward Trace. "Here."

Trace shook his head. *Naive tit.* He swung the axe over his shoulder, picked a spot at random, and started walking.

"Wait!" Ian called after him. "None of those are good for firewood."

"Good thing I'm not cutting down a tree for the fire, then, isn't it?"

Trace didn't go far. He couldn't, he needed to keep an eye on the kid, which limited his options somewhat. But after ten minutes of searching he eventually found what he was looking for. A sapling, ten feet tall and still going, its trunk a little thinner than his wrist, tapering only slightly toward the top, full of wet green wood, which meant flexibility and strength. Terrible for fires, but great for making things.

Trace slung the axe off his shoulder. He widened his stance, checked to either side to make sure he was clear, but mostly to make sure that Peter hadn't followed him. Kids and axes didn't mix well. He shifted his grip, wrapped his fingers around the shaft, wound back, and he aimed for a spot on the trunk a foot above the ground. Then he let all that pent-up anger and frustration out, and he swung through with an explosive grunt, burying the head of the axe with a satisfying *thunk*.

Drew had brought a machete as well, but the axe was Trace's tool of choice. An axe was all about weight and momentum. It was all about power, multiplied by distance. And it felt good in his hands. Heavy and solid, a little old, a little banged up, but it still had its edge. It could still get the job done, and it could do it all day if it had to.

He barely even worked up a sweat, using smooth and efficient blows. Three to either side, hacking out a little wedge before he stepped back, gave it a nudge, and watched as gravity did the rest.

He cut down two more trees after that, one about the same size, and one a little smaller. He trimmed off all the branches, shortened the two bigger trunks into seven-foot lengths of wood. The other tree he divided into four pieces, each about two feet across, before he carried them back to camp, dumping them next to the fire. Next he grabbed Drew's backpack and started rummaging through it, pulling out a length of nylon rope and cable ties.

Then he made himself comfortable, and he got to work, seeing only by the dim flickering light of Ian's fire as night stole across the sky, the logs spitting and hissing next to him while everyone else went to bed and Sara took the first watch.

"What are you making?" she asked when he was halfway through.

Trace looked up at her, her face full of shadows and questions in her eyes. He held up one hand, signaling for her to wait. He pushed himself to his feet with a groan, his knees popping and cracking, and he hobbled across to their bikes.

He grabbed the trailer attached to the back of his bike, unhooked it, wheeled it back to the fire, and parked it next to the thing slowly taking shape on the ground. Nothing special to look at. A basic rectangle of wood, seven feet long, two feet wide, braced at the ends and in the middle, and lashed together with cable ties and rope.

That was another trick Drew had clued them into. Cable ties. Great if you don't plan on undoing them. They don't stretch when they get wet, they're light and incredibly strong.

Sara was confused at first, then it all fell into place in her head.

"You're a genius, Trace," she said, her smile beaming at him in the dark.

Trace nodded back at her. "I know, right?"

The next morning came cold and wet. More sleet than rain, and Trace knew the weather was changing for the worse. He hadn't slept either; Mick had been moving around during the night. It kept him awake and on guard. So he was tired before the day had even begun, but the look on Drew's face more than made up for it.

"What the hell is that?" Drew asked, leaning on Sara and staring at the contraption hooked up behind Trace's bike.

"Your new wheels," Trace said, flinging his arm wide, like he was a performer on stage or a cheap car salesman.

Trace turned to look at his handiwork, the trailer for their gear that he had turned into a stretcher on wheels, a sleeping mat for padding, long enough for Drew to lie on. A makeshift litter, really.

"Like you said, you can't ride. So we're just gonna have to drag your sorry ass behind us instead."

Drew just grunted, and Ian nodded, pleased. Even the kid seemed to like the idea.

Trace just figured it was because he realized it meant he got Drew's bike and wouldn't have to run anymore.

They broke camp as soon as it was light enough, walking out on foot, pushing their bikes until they stepped from the mud and onto an old farm track. They rode that until the track merged with a country road and their pace picked up, and soon they were moving faster than they had in days. The miles blurred by with no sound but the whirr of tires on asphalt.

Mick rode out in front, next to Sara. His rifle slung across his back, his bag strapped to his bike. He moved easily, he breathed well, and he kept a steady rhythm, standing up in the pedals when they hit an incline, dropping back into the saddle when it leveled out, his legs pumping like pistons as he powered ahead, and a gap opened up between them. A gap that reminded Trace just how young and fit Mick was, and just how much he wasn't.

They didn't talk as they rode, Trace didn't have the breath to spare anyway. He was finding just keeping up with someone fifty-one years younger than him a bit of a challenge.

Age is a bitch, especially dragging Drew's heavy ass behind him.

After two hours of riding, Trace couldn't do it anymore. He started falling behind. After another hour, he was doing even worse. He was breathing hard, his lungs were on fire, his legs were numb pieces of meat, and he was pretty certain he was headed for a heart attack. So he called a timeout and swapped with Ian. It still meant he had to tow Peter, but a four-year-old is a lot lighter than a forty-five-year-old man. He got some of his wind back. He caught up to Mick, fell in behind him, and Trace turned his attention to their other problem, while keeping both eyes on the one in front of him.

Drew was right. He was only slowing them down, and it didn't matter how well Trace made a litter or how far they dragged him. Unless they found some antibiotics in the next couple of days, it was all pointless.

So when they came to a fork in the road later that afternoon, one curving south and hitting Garden City in another eighty miles, a two-day detour if nothing else went wrong, and the other going north and around it—the more direct route—Trace took a risk, and he turned them left, and he aimed them at people.

Half because they needed to. Garden City might have medical supplies, and food if they were lucky. And half because if anyone else was following them, Trace just hoped they were right-handed.

CLAY

"How long?" asked Sergeant Roberts.

The tracker looked at the ground. He crabbed forward, his eyes jumping between the footprints and the bike treads, glancing back over his shoulder at the cold fire, a ring of rocks and bare dirt full of ash and blackened ends of wood.

"A day, day and a half, tops," he said, turning back to look at Roberts with something in his hand. A bloody bandage, stained with mud and something else.

"Dogs will have the scent now." He squinted up at the sky. "Until it rains again." He leaned over and spat on the ground.

Roberts nodded. "Good. Mount up, boys, we're moving out."

Clay sighed. He'd been hoping they would call it quits for the day. He was hungry and wet. Tired of riding, and he hated horses.

Nasty, smelly animals with minds of their own and shit for brains. But Roberts had been right, it's not like the Commander was gonna just let them drive off with one of his trucks and half *his* gas. So horses it was. Horses were free—well… not these ones, these ones were stolen—but they ran on grass, so they were free in that sense, and Clay smiled at his own cleverness.

He'd never ridden a horse before. He'd never even touched one until six days ago, but in the time since he had come to hate the experience. The end of every day was agony, like his ass and his balls had been used as a punching bag, and his smile slipped.

Apparently there was a way to avoid that, apparently there was a rhythm to riding a horse, a way to match their gait. But the fucking *how* of it eluded him. He tried to copy the others, but he couldn't seem to get it right, and after six days of torture Clay's mood was as foul as the weather. After six days in the saddle, he could barely walk, and with that thought the smile fell right off his face.

So Clay hated horses. As far as he was concerned, horses were good for two things: glue and dog food. And they shit constantly, too. He'd never seen so much crap come out of an animal before, and he finally understood what it meant to piss like one. It's like they had a fire hose under there attached to a swimming pool, and every now and then it just decided to empty itself.

Nothing odder than having a chat with a man while a stream of urine drilled into the ground beneath him. Killed the conversation dead.

Clay sighed again before pulling himself into the saddle with a groan. At least he was getting better at that. He hadn't fallen off today. And he smiled again. He was learning. It just took him a little longer than most people. But part of him was also glad that they were moving again, now that they'd picked up their trail, whoever *they* were. Not that it mattered. He'd been told to bring them back, and that was that. He would do as he was told. It was easier that way, less confusing. Less chance of ending up dead, too.

It didn't mean he liked what they were doing, but, the way Clay saw it, the sooner they caught them, the sooner he could drag them back to the Commander and the White Trash King, and the sooner he could get down off this walking shit factory and make his escape.

But as Clay had come to learn, tracking was slow going. Because once they hit the road, the dogs lost the scent, insulated by tires and whisked away by the wind. So they were reduced to relying on track marks and scuffs in the dirt, broken twigs, and common sense.

Their prey was heading directly west, avoiding the towns, sticking to the backroads, moving during the day and camping at night. And when they did make camp, it was always on high ground. In the trees and out of the wind. Had been for six days. So why change now?

It made them predictable. But even so, they lost the trail twice before noon, which meant they had to spread out and look for any recent signs of traffic. Not that Clay knew what to look for. One patch of mud looked exactly like another. Their prey was moving faster, too. Like they'd strapped a rocket to their ass or gotten rid of some dead weight.

The tracker said as much when he lost the trail for the third time, when he claimed the rain, which was more like icy slush, had washed away any remaining tracks there might have been.

After that it was guesswork and blind luck. So when they came to a fork in the road late in the afternoon, both roads heading west, one heading north, the other slightly south and into Garden City, Clay flipped a coin in his head and said they should go left. Roberts sneered at him and turned them right instead. Clay figured he did it just to spite him.

Clay didn't care. He was used to it. His opinion had never counted much. Besides, he preferred to stay at the back of the line. If he did that, then the others left him alone, and his horse followed the one in front without too much input from him. Easier that way, and being at the front wasn't going to make them catch these people any faster either, and being at the back meant that if they ran into trouble, he'd be the last person to ride into it. Like sitting in the tail of an airplane. Safest place, he had been told. More likely to survive if you went into a mountain, and, if not, then you had one hell of a ride for the last second of your life. Plus it meant he was farther away from the tracker and his stinking dogs, and Clay hated dogs even more than he hated horses. Dogs were like one giant angry muscle with teeth.

So Clay sat at the back of the line. He kept his eyes open and admired the view. After all, he'd expected to spend the next twelve years of his life rotting away in a cell, and prison had taught him to appreciate the little things in life. Like quiet and freedom, and wide-open spaces and shitting in privacy, and that there is nothing like a sunset, especially after not seeing the sun for three years. Exercise yards didn't count; the idiots staring at the sky were the ones that got whacked. You kept your eyes on the inmates next to you, you watched their hands, you watched their eyes. Nothing worse than coming out of a daydream to find a shiv in your side.

And even with the Cloud bearing down on him, Clay was going to make the most of the time left. Not like one of those pussies that put a gun in their mouth and ate a bullet. Not his style, no, sir. Clay liked living, and he wanted to keep it that way. Didn't matter what he had to do. Didn't matter how much longer he had to do it for. Longer than the people they were chasing, that much he was certain of.

It was already growing dark when they came to a halt.

"They didn't come this way," the tracker said, glancing back at Roberts.

"What do you mean?" asked Roberts, kneeing his horse closer.

They'd stopped in the middle of the road, sun sinking toward the horizon as shadows stretched across the land. Clay took the halt as a chance to stand in his stirrups, trying to ease the cramps in his legs.

"Wrong road," said the tracker. "We should have seen some sign of them by now. They must have gone south, through to Garden City instead."

"You mean we just wasted half a day?"

The tracker shrugged.

"Fuck!"

The tracker whistled to his dogs and started leading his horse off the road and into the trees.

"Where are you going?" shouted Roberts at his back.

"Sun's setting," said the tracker. "Making camp here for the night. Catch them tomorrow."

"Fuck that, get back on your horse. We're catching these bastards today!"

"Really?" the tracker asked, not looking back. "You soldier boys see in the dark? Coz I sure as shit can't. But if you want to break your horse's leg and your own neck, then please, go right ahead."

Roberts's face went bright red, and Clay chuckled, but he hid it quickly, covering it with a yawn when Roberts spun to look at him.

"Fuck!" spat Roberts again. He kicked his horse into a trot and left the rest of them behind.

The other two soldiers didn't follow him. Clay figured they knew better. They just climbed down off their mounts and followed the tracker and his dogs into the trees.

Clay watched Roberts ride another half a mile down the road before he stopped, staring almost directly west, outlined against the horizon like some old western.

Tomorrow, Clay thought. The tracker was right. Their prey had gotten lucky today, but that luck was about to run out. Clay nodded. *Tomorrow.*

That's when the killing would start.

DAY 3
D-DAY

US F.O.B. Lightning
Toulon Naval Base
Toulon, France

LEVI

Soldiers can't sleep, not when it's war.

Enter a little yellow pill, the Go Pill as it's called.

One pill down. Thirty hours awake, and Levi was still going strong. He knew he was tired, but he couldn't feel it. Instead he felt focused and rested, like he could run a marathon, and Levi knew the Modafinil in his veins was doing its job.

Sold in Canada as Alertec and in the US as Provigil, he knew it would buy him at least forty hours without sleep, without the impaired judgment and side effects the old-fashioned uppers like Dexedrine and Ritalin gave you. None of the jumpiness or confusion, no high blood pressure or that wired feeling. None of the normal effects that are part of the nervous system's fight-or-flight reflex.

He wouldn't fall asleep as soon as he stopped taking it either. That's where the No-Go Pill came in. And as long as he got eight hours of sleep sometime in the next twenty, US military studies had found that he'd be able to do it all over again. Apparently the stuff was a hit on Wall Street too. Go figure.

"Where do you reckon they're from?" whispered Briggs on his left.

"Don't know," said Levi, wedged in between Hicks and the ginger idiot. Weeks and Duval were right behind them, Weeks standing half a foot taller than everyone else, the five of them at the back of the briefing room crammed full with over four hundred unhappy marines, all dressed in MOPP, and all watching it unfold like a train wreck on the screen in front of them.

"Don't care," he added. "As long as we can send them back."

"This is the Cloud," bellowed General Marsh, a two-star general straight in from Iraq who was handling the ground operations in France.

The image onscreen changed to a satellite feed. Half the world hidden in night, cities and roads burning with light, and a black flickering mass slowly snuffing them out. The Cloud, swallowing up Spain, rolling across Germany, heading for Italy and Ukraine.

"This is the Cloud as of 0200," the general barked, and the image onscreen changed again, the satellite picture replaced by a computer simulation—a bird's-eye view of France. Neighboring countries outlined in white, lakes and oceans filled in with black, and a bright red circle hovering over their heads. The Cloud, looking nothing at all like the darkness outside.

"Where's Gunner?" whispered Briggs, scanning the room. "He should be here for this."

Levi just shrugged.

"Shhhh," hushed Weeks, poking them both in the back. "I'm listening."

"For those of you dumb fucks that haven't worked it out yet," the general said, "the Cloud is not a natural occurrence."

Levi could see the UK, the tip of Africa, Turkey, the North Atlantic, and a clock running at the bottom of the screen, the minutes a blur as the hours spun by.

"This is the Cloud in 12 hours, 24, 48, 72…"

General Marsh let the image do the rest of the talking. The clock sped up, days turned into weeks, the view zoomed out, and Levi watched the Cloud grow like a cancer. Circular outlines tracking its growth like the rings of a tree, a new one made every day.

Two weeks and it covered half the world. Three and it was at the East Coast of the United States, coming down from the northeast. Hitting Boston first, then New York, Philadelphia, and Washington before rolling out to claim the Midwest.

Four weeks and LA was gone. Five and it was sweeping out across the Pacific, heading for Hawaii. There wasn't much point watching after that; there wasn't much left.

"I'm not paid enough to sugarcoat shit, marines, but the black stuff the Cloud is dropping is a bioweapon that makes Ebola look like a runny nose. Some of you have seen its effects, the rest of you will learn soon enough." General Marsh pointed at the screen, at the world covered in a sea of red. "But believe me when I say that if you breathe this stuff, you're dead. So unless we stop this here, now, then in three weeks it will be your family back home. Your wife, your girlfriend, your kids, even your pet dog bleeding out their assholes while they choke to death on their own lungs."

He turned his head slowly, taking in the whole room. "It's our job to see to it that doesn't happen. So we're going to go out there. And we're going to do what we have to do, and if you don't know what that means for us, then I have neither the time nor the crayons to explain it to you again."

"We're all going to die," murmured Briggs, almost too softly for Levi to hear.

"And this ugly son of a bitch," said General Marsh, changing topics, "is the enemy."

The image changed again, and the whole room leaned forward to see a mess of mangled gray flesh and body parts spread out on a sheet of blue plastic. There wasn't much left to look at. These things were proving hard to kill, like cockroaches. You could stomp down hard and they just kept going, trailing yellow guts and purple gore. The one splayed out onscreen looked like it had taken an RPG to the chest. At least Levi thought it was its chest; all he saw was cooked meat and splintered bone.

But someone had collected the leftover pieces and brought them back to Command, where someone else had tried to put it back together. Built something that looked like it might work. Some macabre puzzle assembled without the instructions. Levi wasn't even sure how many legs the thing actually had, or were they arms? But it was huge, easily seven feet tall, fifteen feet from nose to tail. Mouth overflowing with teeth, huge arms splayed out to either side, claws on its hands like eight-inch knives, and they were definitely hands, fingers and opposable thumbs and all. But no eyes, just six holes on top of its fucked-up head.

It almost reminded Levi of a dinosaur, but hunched and twisted, skin so pale he could see the veins beneath, as though it had lived its entire life in a cave.

"We don't know where they're from," said General Marsh. "We don't know what they want. We don't care. Our job is not to care. Our job is to kill every fucking one of these things. Oorah?"

The room roared in agreement.

"That's what I like to hear, marines!" General Marsh bellowed back. "Now, while we wait for the powers that be to compare the size of their dicks… Dr. Larsen, the floor is yours."

Levi watched as General Marsh stepped aside and a small man in an oversized hazmat suit shuffled forward, making quick, nervous little strides.

Civilian. A civilian with an armed escort, Levi figured, noting the soldiers that flanked him to either side. *A high-profile civilian, maybe.* One of the scientists they kept talking about. Flown in from God knows where, probably operating on less sleep than himself, but probably paid a shitload more too.

"What's he talking about?" Briggs asked.

"What you think, numbnuts?" grunted Hicks. "We're going to war. Those libtards over at the White House will want to make a statement first."

Levi watched Dr. Larsen try to push back the glasses on his nose. His hand bumped against his gas mask and he paused, as though he'd somehow forgotten he was wearing it in the first place, and Levi imagined he didn't get out much. Or get laid much. Probably still lived with his mom. Probably spoke fluent Klingon.

"We think the EBEs hunt using echolocation, and possibly infrared," Dr. Larsen said.

"Speak louder!" shouted someone from the back.

"What's an eebee?" murmured Briggs.

Levi just shrugged.

"We think the EBEs hunt using echolocation and infrared," Dr. Larsen repeated, leaning closer to the mic.

"You think?" shouted someone to Levi's left. "Fuck kinda answer is that?"

Levi turned to look at the speaker. Boyd, maybe? It was hard to tell underneath all the gear, but it sounded like Boyd. The South was strong with that one.

"Uh, well, we think those clicks they make are just the part of the frequency range that falls within human hearing." Dr. Larsen aimed a laser pointer at the screen. "The holes on the sides of their heads appear to be resonance chambers. Ears, basically. And the holes on top of their heads aren't eyes, but perhaps more comparable to pit organs."

"To fucking whats?" Boyd shouted.

"Pit organs, they can see temperature variat—"

"You mean infrared?"

"Yes, that's what I said. Techni—"

"How do they do that Predator shit?"

"The what?" said Dr. Larsen, sounding flustered.

"Go invisible!"

"They don't." He frowned. "I mean, not really. The closest terrestrial analogy we have is cephalopods... uh, octopus," he added, when he was met with a room full of blank stares. "We've found chromatophores and pigment proteins in their skin cells."

Levi felt his eyes glaze over. He knew mitochondria were the powerhouses of the cell, but that was it. He'd flunked bio, and math, and just about everything else except PE.

"We think they see through their skin," Dr. Larsen elaborated, like he was talking to idiots.

"Ah," grunted Levi.

"Their skin detects a change in light intensity and wavelength, feels it, like heat. It automatically alters its texture and pigment to match, and they just kind of... blend in. To them, changing color might even be as easy as breathing, automatic, simple reflex."

Levi stuck his hand up. "Sir? How do we see them, then? They don't show up on the thermals."

Dr. Larsen nodded. "We think there might be a lag, a short delay between a change in ambient light levels and their camouflage adapting to match. A reaction time, basically. Some constraint due to their nervous systems perhaps, we aren't sure yet. But a sudden bright light or a constantly changing light source might reveal them for short periods."

"How long?" shouted Levi, murmurs growing louder.

Dr. Larsen paused. "We don't know. A second, two? Maybe longer..." He shrugged, his voice uncertain. "As for the thermal issue, we're working on it. We think it's just a question of calibration. Their core temperatures are much colder than ours, and, given the temperatures recorded beneath the Cloud, we think the only reason they don't freeze solid is because their blood contains a beta-helical protein."

More blank stares.

"Natural antifreeze, basically," he said. "So wherever these things are from, we know it's cold, much colder than here. Their blood also contains the copper-containing protein Hemocyanin, possibly another cold environment adaption. It's why their blood is blue, by the way. It's actually quite remarkable when yo—"

"Nobody fucking cares, just tell us how we kill 'em!" shouted Boyd. And for once, Levi actually agreed with the village idiot.

"Right. Yes, that," Dr. Larsen said, deflated. "Well, that's why they aren't showing up on the thermals. Upping the sensitivity might fix that. As for killing them, aim for the body or take off a limb. Don't bother with the head, it's too well protected, the skull is four to five inches thick in parts. But if you have to, then armor-piercing rounds or .50 caliber might work."

"Might?" spat Hicks.

Levi felt the mood start to change. The last thing any marine wanted to hear was a bunch of "we thinks" and "maybes." They'd heard enough of them as it was.

Dr. Larsen shrugged again. He looked at General Marsh for support before turning back to the increasingly pissed-off audience.

"You have to understand," he said, "these are theories, based off dead tissue samples and reports from those who've come in contact with these things in the field. To make a more certain analysis, we'd need to capture one of these things alive, run a few tests…"

"Screw that," Briggs said as the room dissolved into a hundred small arguments. "Who's the dumb shmuck they're gonna send out on that suicide mission?"

"Probably you," quipped Levi, leaning in and giving him a nudge. "You've always had a talent for picking up the ugliest bitch in the bar. I reckon that makes you uniquely qualified to act as bait. I say we tie a rope to you, dangle you out the back of a chopper, sit back, and see what latches onto your dick."

Briggs elbowed him in the side and Levi grunted, rubbing his ribs and smiling to himself. But in all seriousness, he'd never known the carrot to do better than a solid four, and that got downgraded to a hard three in daylight. But he supposed that's what happens when you're ugly, five-foot-three, and your pubes look like an out-of-control brushfire. It's why they called him Captain Redbeard behind his back, but more often to his face.

"Thank you, Dr. Larsen…" said General Marsh, rescuing him and dismissing him at the same time.

The general glanced at his watch. "Okay, listen up, marines! I'm now officially authorized to tell you what all of us already know, but as of 2:15 AM local time, the rest of the world knows it, too. ET is real, and he ain't here to phone home."

The image onscreen changed again. Mangled body parts and blue plastic were replaced by a satellite image.

"You are now all part of Operation Daylight, a coordinated offensive with NATO to retake France, destroy the Cloud, and burn these fucking things off the face of the earth."

A name appeared on the map.

"This is our target, marines: Meyrin, Switzerland. Or to be precise, this is where Meyrin used to be. Because as you can see, there ain't much left."

Several more windows appeared on the display, some showing video footage on repeat, others showing an array of black and white photographs. Images taken from the air, images washed out and grainy. Saturation dialed all the way down, contrast ramped all the way up, all capturing a lake of fire and a black cloud vomiting into the sky from an enormous hole in the ground like some sunken volcano.

"These images were taken approximately eighty-three hours ago. We believe there was an accident at CERN, a civilian research facility located here." An icon started flashing on the map. "We think—or the physicists think—that somehow those geniuses at CERN made an Einstein-Rosen bridge."

"Huh?"

"A wormhole for all you Trekkies in the room."

"Ah." Levi nodded. He understood that reference.

"We don't know where this wormhole goes. We don't know how it was made. You don't need to know. We have the greatest minds in the world working on it, and they don't even know. All you need to worry about right now is that it's getting bigger, and it's our job to close it."

"How the hell are we supposed to do that?" balked Hicks on Levi's right.

"Hundred bucks says they nuke it," said Levi.

"Nuke it? What good would that do?" Hicks shot back, pointing at the screen. "There's nothing left to nuke. And besides, the Swiss and French would have a fit."

Levi shrugged like he didn't care either way. "Hundred bucks."

"Fine, then, I'll see your stupid hundred."

The general turned to nod at the screen and dozens of flashing icons appeared in quick succession, arranged around the edge of the Cloud in a loose circle, and some deep within.

Levi identified Paris easily enough, and the forces gathering at Toulon, and a whole bunch he didn't know. He saw several more way out in the Pacific. The 6th Fleet, he assumed, sailing at full speed toward them, and closer still, the 5th Fleet, with French and British Naval forces sitting just off the south coast. Nearly 50,000 armed and pissed-off personnel already, with more arriving every minute.

The general pointed at the three large icons sitting off the coast. "The British *HMS Queen Elizabeth*, the French *Charles De Gaulle*, and the Italian *Giuseppe Garibaldi* aircraft carriers arrived off-shore approximately two hours ago." His hand traced right. "Russia's Black Sea Fleet and the *Admiral Kuznetsov* are en route from Syria, while their airborne units will be over France in the next fourteen hours." His hand moved back to the left. "As for our boys, the 82nd Airborne is somewhere over the North Atlantic, and the 6th Fleet will be here by 0800."

Levi saw nodding heads, and a low murmur filled the room.

"However…" General Marsh didn't bother hiding his frustration with the next part. "The Russian armored units pushing in from the east will be operating under their own directives, with American attachés to coordinate our movements."

Murmurs turned to groans. Levi wasn't surprised. Ivan was never going to follow American orders. Cooperate? Levi didn't even think there was such a word in Russian. No, Putin would do things his own way, like always.

"The 82nd Airborne will be going in first."

Levi just shook his head. *Poor bastards.*

"It's their job to secure the Lyon–Saint-Exupéry Airport so the rest of our forces can follow. Once retaken, the airport will serve as F.O.B. Thunder for close air support missions and refueling. American, French, British, and Swiss armored units will push in from the south, establishing a secure corridor between here and Lyon. Once our supply lines are in place, we'll—"

"Sir?" one of the marines interrupted.

General Marsh turned to glare at him, but the marine either had zero fucks to give or nothing between his ears because he kept talking. "Just to be clear, you want us to go up against these things on foot, in the dark, with no air support, and no comms?"

General Marsh shook his head. "Good question, marine, but no. You're all going in broad daylight."

Briggs shared a confused look with Levi. "What's he talking about?"

Levi shrugged. "No idea. I just work here."

An aide came up on the general's left, stepped in close, and said something in the general's ear.

The general stopped talking and listened.

He nodded once. The aide stepped back, and the general glanced at the screen behind him. He looked back at the room. "You'll have to excuse me, marines. Apparently, I'm needed elsewhere. But to answer your question."

He looked at his watch.

"We're a little early, but I want you all to watch the screen. I want you all to watch what happens next. I think you'll like it. I know I will." He snapped a salute at the room. "Make me proud, marines."

Then he walked off stage, aides and attachés falling in behind him. His own private entourage.

Levi turned to watch the screen once he'd left. He saw the Cloud, its huge swirling arms extending out like tentacles, lightning bouncing through its insides, and a bulging black eye hovering over Meyrin, bubbling up like it was under pressure.

A minute passed by and nothing happened.

Briggs turned to him. "What are w—"

Levi saw a flash, and he watched it grow, watched as a small sun was born on the planet far below, light blossoming, growing brighter, blinding. It overloaded the satellite's filters, and the feed cut out.

"Told you," said Levi, watching as the image came back online, screen filled with static, glitching and shaking, shockwave racing outward, pushing the Cloud away and exposing the ground beneath.

"Clever," said Briggs.

Levi held his hand out and turned to look at Hicks, waiting.

"What?" asked Hicks. "I don't owe you shit. The deal was Meyrin, remember?" He pointed at the screen. "That's not even close. Besides, does it look like I have my damn wallet on me right now?"

"Uh, guys…" said Briggs.

Levi turned back in time to see another flash, then another, a whole series of them. Detonations racing out in an expanding spiral, coming faster and faster before the screen blacked out completely.

"Holy shit," whispered Levi, his hand still extended, bet forgotten. Because, even from four hundred miles away, he swore he could feel the ground trembling beneath his feet.

COLTER

Colter slept like a dead man.

When they finally let him.

After they'd treated his wounds and stuck him with needles, taking so many vials of his blood he'd gotten light-headed.

And when they were done patching him up and pumping him full of fluids, they'd debriefed him. Asking him every question ten different ways until he had nothing new to add. The details hadn't changed, and he couldn't keep his eyes open anymore. Then they'd dosed him up on painkillers, locked him in an empty, windowless room, and left him.

After fifteen minutes of watching the door, he'd given up waiting. Escape was impossible. The door didn't even have a handle, the hinges were on the wrong side, and he figured the only way he was getting out of here was if they let him.

Seeing how there was no point stressing about when that might be, he'd tried to make himself comfortable. He'd laid down on the floor, tucked his right arm under his head, rested his bandaged left arm on his chest, and then he'd stared up at the ceiling. Because as tired as he was, as heavy as his eyes felt, he couldn't stop hearing that disappointed voice in his head.

Could've done better, James.

He knew that. No denial, no excuses. He'd screwed up. Seven men were dead because of him, and now that the danger was over, the distractions absent, he couldn't think about anything else. Like some scab he couldn't stop picking at, going over the things he'd missed, the mistakes he'd made, and the letters he'd have to write because of them. The families he'd destroy starting with two little words. *I regret…*

But after ten minutes of wallowing in guilt and self-pity, he'd stopped beating himself up.

What's done is done, his old man would have said. Hindsight is 20/20, and he couldn't change the past. He'd just have to live with it, make his peace with it. And with that, he breathed in once, closed his eyes, and let the darkness drag him down.

The most important lesson anyone learned in the Corps: sleep when you can.

His old man would have said something different. Sleep is a defense mechanism, a cop-out. It's what people do when they're scared, when the adrenaline wears off and the shock sets in.

Colter was too tired to give a shit. Besides, he hadn't listened to his old man in years.

He woke up feeling like crap. Feeling hot and closed in, with lights like daggers in his eyes and something burning in his throat. He coughed, then he frowned. He didn't know where he was. He raised a hand to block out the glare, turned his head to take in the concrete walls, the concrete floor, the locked door, his bandaged hand, and it all came rushing back.

Right… He let his head thump back against the floor. *Now what?*

It didn't feel like he'd slept long, more than an hour, less than three. He couldn't be sure. They'd taken his watch along with his shoelaces, but he was still tired, and whatever painkiller they'd given him was still doing its job because he couldn't feel anything below his left elbow.

He closed his eyes and tried to fall asleep again.

After five minutes of counting sheep, he gave up. So he just lay there, his throat dry and itching. Hearing the rumbling roar of aircraft flying overhead, trucks coming and going, diesel engines revving, hearing the booming thump and scrape of metal on concrete, doors slamming, footsteps echoing. And faintly, muffled by walls and distance, crying and coughing, sad sounds filtered through the air vents above his head. Then he heard voices growing louder, clearer.

Voices coming toward him.

Colter heard footsteps outside. He heard the scrape of a key in the lock. The talking stopped. The door opened, and one of the CIA agents stepped into the room.

"On your feet, soldier boy," he said.

Colter didn't move.

"Now, sunshine, someone wants to see you."

"Or what?" asked Colter.

"Or I tase you, and we drag you there." The agent patted the stun gun strapped to his chest. Like it was a dare, like he wanted nothing better in the world than to see Colter twitch.

Colter looked at the distance between them. He looked at the open door and the two agents waiting in the corridor beyond. He looked at the MP5s slung across their bodies, thought it over, and decided against it. He was unarmed and injured. It was three against one, and the only way he knew out of this place was through them. But mostly, he just didn't feel like adding being electrocuted to his already shitty day.

"Whatever you say, princess," Colter said instead, pushing himself to his feet and gesturing for the agent to lead the way.

They walked down a long passage, an agent in front, two behind, boxing him in. Like it was routine. Like they'd done it a thousand times before. They passed through a door into another hallway, this one a little dirtier and less well lit.

"In here," the agent in front said, coming to a stop in front of another plain, unmarked door. He knocked once, waited a beat.

"Come in," came a muffled response from the other side.

The agent opened the door and poked his head inside. "Marine Gunner Colter to see you, ma'am."

"Good. Send him in."

The agent turned to look at Colter. "Behave yours—"

Colter shouldered past him and walked into a small room, this one with no windows either, the same bare concrete floor and exposed halogen tubes in the ceiling, but it wasn't completely empty.

A man in a hazmat suit leaned against the wall to his left, and there were two white plastic lawn chairs in front of him with a small figure in a hazmat suit sitting in one of them on the other side of a desk. A woman, Colter realized, but so thin she looked like a skeleton wrapped in yellow plastic.

"Marine Gunner Colter," she said, "have a seat."

Colter eyed her warily. The door closed behind him. He didn't hear it lock.

"Please," she said, gesturing to the empty chair across from her. "Sit." She didn't get up. No handshake was offered.

Colter shrugged. He pulled the chair back from the desk, sat down, and she nodded, like she was pleased. Like he was some old dog and she'd just taught him a new trick.

"My name is Ms. David, and the man of few words to my right is Mr. Alan."

"Lovely to meet you both," said Colter, his voice dripping with sarcasm. "Now how about telling me what the fuck is going on?"

"All in due time, Gunner Colter." Ms. David tilted her head to the door. "I do apologize for the rough treatment. I hope Wilkins wasn't too hard on you, but it's been a trying time for everyone, and we've had to take precautions. Too many green-on-blues to be a coincidence. Something in the air, I believe…"

Colter just sat there.

"How's the hand?" Ms. David asked.

Colter shrugged. He didn't look at his hand. He knew it was a mess. Besides, there was nothing to see. There was so much gauze and bandaging it looked like he was wearing an oven mitt. And he was much more interested in the two people in front of him.

He put Ms. David in her late forties, maybe early fifties. It was hard to tell. She had the pale, unlined skin of a shift worker or someone who never saw the sun, while the man leaning against the wall looked like he'd spent too much time in it. He looked old and weathered, squint lines so deep they looked like scars.

Colter recognized the look. A souvenir of an unforgiving sun and too much worry. Something he'd seen on every marine that had ever served in Iraq or Afghanistan. But there was something wrong with him, with his right side, in the way he held himself. Like he'd been hit by a bus or suffered a stroke. Something that should have killed him but didn't.

Colter turned back to find Ms. David studying him just as intently. Pinched features visible through her full-face gas mask, pupils so brown they were almost black, with deep bags under her eyes like she hadn't slept in years.

She picked up a manila folder from a pile to her left and placed it on the desk in front of her. She leaned forward as if to speak, but hesitated. She looked down at the folder, reached forward, put her fingers on it, both hands, and she moved it forward an inch, and then an inch to the left. She squared it off, two inches from the edge, until there was a perfect border between it and her. She picked up her pen and placed it down next to the folder, on the right-hand side. Nothing special about the pen, a plain black Bic, but Ms. David went through the same process, like it was a ritual and he was the sacrifice.

Then she leaned back, put her hands to either side of the folder, palms down, body still.

"I'm going to be uncharacteristically frank with you, Gunner Colter," she said. "Ms. David is not my real name."

"No shit," he said. "What do you want?"

"Good." Ms. David nodded. "Straight to the point, I like that. In short, we want you, Gunner, and your squad. Well, what's left of it, really."

"For what?"

"We're getting to that. A few formalities first. I've read your file. Awarded the Silver Star, the Soldier's Medal, the Bronze Star. Even the Navy Cross for that mess in al-Qaryatayn."

"Those records are classified."

Ms. David shrugged as though that meant nothing. "What I'm saying is that you have a reputation for getting things done. You're a survivor, you're adaptive, and you're smart. You have a cool head under fire, you follow orders, and you're experienced. Three tours in Iraq, two in Afghanistan, one in Syria, and on your way back for more." She paused. "Or you were until this little hiccup. But even so, you made it as far as Bourg-en-Bresse, you came in direct contact with the EBEs, and y—"

"EBEs?" Colter cut her off, ignoring the flicker of annoyance that crossed her face.

"Extraterrestrial Biological Entities."

"You mean those big fucking things that killed all my men?"

Ms. David frowned at him and continued. "What I'm trying to say is that you have a particular set of skills and experience. That makes you valuable. But more importantly, you've come up against these things once before, and you made it back out alive, and that makes you rare. Believe me. Under normal circumstances you'd probably have gotten another medal fo—"

"Don't talk to me about medals," Colter growled, losing his patience. "I lost seven men today, so cut the bullshit and get to the fucking point!"

Mr. Alan shifted slightly, moving from one foot to the other. Colter glanced at him, at the handgun he wore on his left hip, at the distance between them.

"As you wish," Ms. David said, drawing his attention back. "You're sick, Gunner. You're going to die, and sooner rather than later."

She must have seen Colter's shock.

"Come now." Ms. David frowned at him. "You must have known that. All the blood samples we've taken, all those tests? You've breathed the air. You saw what was happening to the civilians you brought back, and you're a smart man, otherwise we wouldn't be talking… My guess is you're already starting to feel the first symptoms. Sore throat, headache, sensitivity to bright light, perhaps? It will get worse, you know. And before you ask, yes, I'm sure. No, there isn't a cure. No, we can't stop it. And yes, I'm sorry. But you don't strike me as the type of person who cries over spilt milk, or are you?"

Colter didn't say anything; he didn't know how to at first. It felt like he was teetering on the edge of a deep, dark hole with nothing at the bottom but despair and panic and screaming.

But Colter had never been the type to panic. *Panic is pointless*, his old man would have said. It wouldn't change anything, and Ms. David was right, in a way. Dying had always been a possibility, ever since he'd seen the inside of the bus, ever since he'd seen Cass's face. Ever since he'd joined the Marines, really. He'd made his peace with death long ago, but still… a man can hope.

"How long?" Colter asked, his voice flat, hopes crushed.

"How long? Hard to tell, we're still trying to understand how this thing works."

"How fucking long?" Colter demanded, trying to regain some composure. Some control.

Ms. David shook her head at him. "We don't know. I'd be lying if I gave you a timeframe. We can only base our estimates off the civilians flooding in, and their mortality rates vary. But two to three days on average." She shrugged like it was a minor detail. "But your case is different. You were only exposed for a few hours, not days like the rest of them have been. We don't know what impact that will have on the progression of the disease. You might have longer, or you might not." She lifted her hands up in a helpless gesture. "At this point, your guess is as good as mine."

"What about the others... the civilians we brought back?" Colter pressed.

Ms. David shook her head.

"All of them?"

"I believe a couple are still alive, but I wouldn't go holding my breath."

"Cass?"

Ms. David didn't answer, and Colter went silent, trying to get his thoughts in order, feeling his heart pounding in his chest. Feeling like he wanted to be sick.

"So what do you want from me?" he asked, proud his voice didn't waver.

Ms. David shared a look with Mr. Alan.

"It's simple, really," she said, turning back, leaning in. "Thanks to you, and thereby Cass, we now know there's a building in Geneva, a very important building: CERN's off-site data storage center. And if what Cass told us is correct, then I might go so far as to say it's the most important building on Earth right now. If it's still standing, and we think it is, then it may hold some highly valuable information. Which, if we're really lucky, might just tell us how to undo all of this." She raised her hand, pointing at the roof above her head, the darkness outside, the air between them.

"If we're lucky?" Colter frowned at her.

"We're clutching at straws, Gunner. At this point, any intel is good intel. But Geneva might at least tell us where to start looking, point us in the right direction. There's just one catch…"

There always is.

"Thanks to the Cloud, we're having to bounce all communications off unsecured ground networks, which means we have to assume the Russians are listening, which means they know everything we do. Which means this just became a race. That's where you come in. We want you to go back in there, find what we're looking for, and bring it back. And we need it done fast. So we'll be inserting you by air, and we'll be sending a Navy SEAL retrieval team in with you. It's your job to secure the area, then cover the SEALs' backs while they retrieve the tapes."

Colter just stared at her. "Are you nuts?"

"Don't worry," Ms. David said, "you won't be alone. We'll be doing the same with two Army Ranger armored units. Each at different approach points to Geneva. That way if you fail, we still have redundancies. But once the tapes are secure, you're to link up with the Army Rangers. They'll escort you back to Lyon."

"You're fucking with me, right?" Colter looked at Mr. Alan. "That's your plan? Throw us out a plane and hope for the best?" Colter's eyes bounced between them. "Do you even know what you're talking about? No, stupid question." Colter shook his head. "Let me spell it out for you then, make it real clear. Your plan won't work, not in a million years. What you're proposing is suicide, plain and fucking simple."

Ms. David shrugged. "If that's what it takes."

"Easy for you to say. It's not your ass on the line."

"Oh, I wouldn't say that. We screw this up and we all die. You'd just get to die sooner than the rest of us. And don't take it so personally. This isn't about you. This is bigger than one man. We're trying to save seven billion lives here, and I'd gladly sacrifice a million of you if it meant winning."

"You're a piece of work, aren't you?"

Ms. David shook her head, put both hands on the folder in front of her, pressing it flat. "You misunderstand me, Gunner. I'm not here to worry about your feelings. I couldn't give a shit what you think about me, it's not in my job description to care. I'm here to do what needs to be done, and we don't have time for subtlety. This is triage, we cut off the foot before we lose the leg. But I digress." She leaned back, lifted her hands off the folder, and let them hover an inch above it, fingers splayed, palms open, like she was going to do a magic trick and make it disappear.

Colter shook his head.

"What if I say no?"

"I'm saying you can't. I'm giving you an order." Ms. David leaned forward until she was halfway across the desk. "But in the interest of full disclosure, say no, and we'll be done here. I won't send you to Geneva. But you'll never set foot outside of this building again. Not now that you're infected. We can't send you back to the USS *Bataan*, you see, and we can't let you leave France. What will happen is that Wilkins will escort you to a bed upstairs, willingly or not. And once there you'll spend what time you have left as one of my lab rats. I'm sure there are some drugs we haven't tried yet. You can be our first human trial. We'll tie you down if we have to. Would you like that?" She paused, staring at him. "Or you can say yes, we keep talking, and maybe, just maybe, your death will actually mean something. Because whether we win or lose, you're still going to be dead, and there is nothing you or I or anyone else can do about it." She cocked her head to the side. "You want your options laid out for you? You want them in black and white? There they are. And just in case there's any confusion remaining, with or without you, we'll still be

sending your squad. The choice is yours, the door is right there…"
She nodded over his shoulder.

Colter didn't know what to say to that. He wanted to say she couldn't do that. He wanted to tell her to go fuck herself. He wanted to reach across the table and snap her scrawny little neck. But he knew what his old man would have said to that.

There is no such thing as fair in life, James. Accept that, or you will always be a victim.

Colter took a deep breath, counted to three, and let it out.

"What about all those ships in the harbor?" he asked.

"What about them?"

"They're leaving. Aren't you worried about it spreading?"

Ms. David waved his question away. "Unavoidable. We couldn't possibly stop them all, and, besides, in a few days' time they'll all be nothing but ghost ships anyway. And once they're away from the cameras, a torpedo from one of our subs will take care of the rest. Take my word, Gunner, nothing is getting away from the Cloud without us knowing about it, and nothing is heading anywhere near the US. The only planes in the sky are ours. Anything else, and our pilots have orders to shoot it down on sight. We can't let something like this reach the mainland."

Colter grunted.

"So, what's it gonna be? Clock's ticking."

Colter didn't answer. He asked her a question instead. "You ever heard of a folding defense?"

Ms. David shook her head, but Mr. Alan nodded.

Colter glanced at him. "Good, someone with half a brain in his head." He turned back to look at Ms. David, and he hunched forward, using his hands to map it out for her. "A folding defense is when a small force retreats in the face of a far larger one, inflicting heavy losses on the attacker for each foot gained. It's incredibly effective if done well. Done really well, and the attacking force doesn't even know they're at war. Troops go in, none come out. The losses aren't noted. All that happens from a command perspective is that you go blind; no good news, but no bad news either. It's a communication black hole. You follow?"

"What's your point?"

"My *point* is that it's been used on us since day one. My *point* is that I drove 400 miles without so much as a flat tire, and these things were there the whole time. My point is that they could have hit us any time they wanted. But they didn't, they waited, and they let us keep pushing until we were cut off and isolated, and, with that bastard cloud, I just thought there was a problem with our comms. I mean, no one can take out a whole army without someone getting word out, right? Wrong. That's exactly what happened, and I drove us straight into an ambush. And now you want me to do it again? Fuck you." Colter would have spat except for the mess it would have made inside his mask.

"My point, *Ms. David*, is that these things are smart, real smart. They're strategic, coordinated, and so far they're winning. So I'm saying that unless you come up with something better than throwing us out of a plane and hoping for the best, then no matter how many boots you put on the ground, they'll be dead inside of a minute. And in the interest of *full disclosure,* if that's the best plan you have, then we're done here. I'm leaving, and if you try to stop me, I'll take that bed of yours and shove it up your ass."

Ms. David raised an eyebrow, and Colter couldn't tell if she was amused by his outburst or if she wanted to wash his mouth out.

Colter decided he didn't care.

"We know all that, Gunner," Ms. David said slowly, sounding tired. "But a lot has happened since you've been away, and we know what we're up against now. As for a plan, if we had all the answers we wouldn't be here. This is your area of expertise; you have operational control. I don't care how you do it, just get it done, and fast. As for the Cloud, we have the best minds in the world working on a permanent solution. In the meantime, we have nukes."

"Nukes?" Colter thought he'd misheard her. "What good is a nuke going to do? How are you even going to find these things to drop a bomb on them?"

Ms. David leaned back in her chair with a tired sigh. "You ever throw rocks in a pond as a kid? One of those covered in pond scum and green algae?"

Colter nodded slowly, confused at the change in direction.

"What happened when you did?" she asked.

"It made a splash."

"Yes, and ripples. And ripples radiate outwards. Make a big enough splash or throw enough rocks in, and you make a hole."

Colter's eyes widened as he caught on. "You're going to nuke the Cloud."

Ms. David smiled. "What did I tell you, Mr. Alan? I knew I picked the right man for the job. But no, Gunner Colter, we aren't going to nuke the Cloud."

Colter frowned.

"We already did, an hour ago." She took a folder from the pile on her right and pushed it in front of him. "We've made ourselves an opening. Several, actually, but they're closing fast. Current simulations give us a day, maybe a day and half, of clear skies before we're back to where we were."

"And the French are okay with this?"

Ms. David gave a soft shrug. "It's not like they have a choice. The French are done. What's left of their forces are here and in Paris. The Swiss aren't far behind either. We have to worry about ourselves now."

"But the fallout…"

"Will be minimal, and irrelevant anyway. You aren't thinking about the big picture here. Let our grandchildren worry about the fallout. If we even have grandchildren, I'll consider it a success. Right now, our only job is to stop the Cloud. Everything else is secondary."

"You don't ask for much, do you?"

Ms. David didn't say anything.

"How much time do I have?"

Ms. David looked at her watch. "Twenty-six hours before Stage Two. You're wheels up in seven. Right now, we're just waiting for dawn and for the dust to settle."

"Stage Two?"

"Stage One was us nuking the Cloud. It allows our units to move up in daylight. Stage Two, we nuke Meyrin and everything within a hundred miles. Then we move up again, we go for the source, and we end this."

"Cutting it pretty fine, aren't you?"

"Time is a luxury none of us have, Gunner. I'm sure you can appreciate that."

"What about Stage Three?"

"There is no Stage Three. We get one shot at this; we don't have the resources or time for another attempt."

Colter was quiet for a moment, thinking hard, running through his options, looking for a way out and finding none. He sighed.

A man knows when he's beaten.

A marine knows that's when he's just getting started.

"If I'm going to do this, then we're going to do it my way," he said.

"I already said that, didn't I? Just tell us what you need."

"I want full access to the USS *Bataan*'s armory."

"Done," Ms. David said.

"I want air support, full mission coverage, no gaps."

"Difficult, but possible, and the longer we sit here, the more the Cloud grows back and the less coverage you'll get. Conditions aren't exactly ideal for flying that close to Meyrin. Anything else?"

"We'll need vehicles, something with tracks, armor, a big gun, and a troop compartment. A couple of Bradleys will do."

"We can't get you those," said Mr. Alan. "Too heavy to lift

for where you're going, but I can get you a couple of IFVs and something else."

"Like what?"

Mr. Alan pushed away from the wall. "You familiar with the X0S4?"

"Those pieces of junk?"

"Prototype is the word you're after."

"Million-dollar paperweights, you mean."

"Take it or leave it."

"Do I have a choice?"

"I can always give them to someone else."

"I want six."

"You'll get three," Mr. Alan said with a grunt. "But I can get as many TALOS suits as you want to plug the gaps."

Ms. David cut in. "These are your orders, Gunner Colter." She picked up another folder and added it to the pile growing in front of him. "And everything we know about the Cloud and EBEs."

Colter looked at it like it had teeth.

"One more thing," he said, still not picking them up.

"Yes?"

"I want you to deliver a letter."

"A letter?" Ms. David asked with a puzzled expression. "Do I look like a postman to you?"

"I don't care who you are. I couldn't give two shits who you send in your place. But if you want me to do this, then you're going to get a letter to my old man, and you're going to make sure they put it in his hand. Otherwise you're just wasting my time."

Ms. David stuck out her hand. "Deal."

Colter leaned forward to grip it hard, feeling the delicate bones grate beneath, imagining the popping sounds they'd make if he just squeezed.

"You do realize we will have to read whatever you write first though, and he won't get the original. It will be a scanned copy. Nothing contaminated can leave France."

"Whatever, just make sure he gets it."

"I give you my word."

Colter didn't think that meant much, but it would have to do. He was trying to be realistic. He supposed dead men walking had to be.

LEVI

Levi didn't think things could get any worse. He thought he'd seen the worst of it. He thought he'd live through this.

Boy, had he been wrong.

He was almost tempted to shoot Briggs in the ass because of it. Briggs in the ass, then himself in the head. Foot wouldn't cut it anymore, and he figured that if he was going to die on Colter's stupid suicide mission anyway, then he'd rather it was quick, and now.

Why wait?

But he'd at least make Briggs pay for it first. *Dickhead.* He should have never listened to him. He shouldn't be here. He should have been back home instead, working at McDonald's, watching this all on the news, watching it happen to someone else, from somewhere warm and dry and safe and 4,000 miles away.

Instead, here he was, standing in the pouring rain. Ash and snow turned to black mud at his feet, his MOPP glistening and dripping wet.

"Showtime," Colter shouted, and for once Levi didn't have a

smartass comment ready. It felt like he hadn't said a word in years. Couldn't. Nerves do that, he supposed.

He just bowed his head as two Super Stallions came in to land, navigation lights strobing in the dark, downdraft blasting the rain sideways and into his face, and visibility dropped to zero. He couldn't see a thing, couldn't hear anything except the wind tearing at his mask, screaming in his ears, pushing him back on his heels.

He turned his face away and waited for the whine of the Super Stallions' jet turbines to drop in pitch, for the gale force winds and sideways rain to cease. Waited until he could see the Super Stallions sitting on the tarmac in front of him, their rotors a blur of darker air and spray. He saw the pilots in the cockpits, heads pivoting, hands moving, running through their post-flight checks. And since those things were 100-feet-long, 28-feet-tall, and weighed in at 33,000 pounds when empty, Levi imagined it was quite a list. The Super Stallion was the largest and heaviest helicopter in the United States military. "Shitters," as they were affectionately known, because apparently piloting one was like sitting on your toilet and flying your house.

Levi watched as a soldier in MOPP jumped off the rear loading ramp and hurried toward them.

"Gunner Colter?" the man shouted when he was a few feet away, using his arm to shield his face.

"That's me," Colter shouted back.

The soldier saluted, his eyes skipping over Colter's shoulder to Levi, then bouncing back.

"Where do you want us to set up?"

Colter jerked his thumb over his shoulder at the hangar behind them.

The soldier nodded and turned to shout instructions as a line of men in MOPP appeared behind him, pushing trolleys loaded with gear and weapons crates.

Colter turned and started walking, the soldier keeping pace

alongside, and Levi fell in behind, following the two men across the tarmac toward the light spilling from the hangar's wide-open doors. Away from the noise, out of the rain.

"I'm Lieutenant Dan," the soldier said when he didn't have to scream anymore.

"Lieutenant Dan!" said Levi, finding his voice again. He couldn't help it. "You got new legs!"

Colter turned to glare at him, and Levi suddenly found his boots to be far more interesting than he first realized.

"You get everything I asked for, Lieutenant?" asked Colter, turning his back on Levi and ignoring him. "I want my boys kitted up and ready to go in three hours."

Lieutenant Dan stopped walking. "Three?"

Colter turned to look at him. "Two would be better, but we're wheels up in six, and I still need time to drill. Can you do it?"

Say no.

The lieutenant sucked in a breath, and Levi could see him thinking, gears turning, cogs spinning, taking shortcuts in his head. He nodded.

Shit.

"We'll get it done, sir. But I have to make it clear, these units haven't been tested yet. Not for what you want them for, and we still haven't worked out all the bugs."

"I don't care how pretty it is, Lieutenant, just make it happen. I…"

Levi tuned them out, turning to watch as a row of metal skeletons hanging in steel frames were wheeled past him. Wicked, brutal-looking things, brown armor plating layered over black metal struts, with integrated helmets and armored faceplates. The TALOS Exo-suit, the pinnacle of the Future Soldier Program, and a cool million bucks apiece.

But right after that came three of the Raytheon X0S4s. Four times the size, five times the price, and painted a dull desert brown, part of the same program as the TALOS. But whereas the TALOS was all about speed, moving light, hitting hard, and getting out without being seen, the X0S4 was the exact opposite.

It looked like a fridge on legs, or one of those metal diving suits from the 1900s. Big, heavy, and ugly. Designed for narrow alleys and close quarters combat, meant for high-risk breach-and-enter roles. Meant to go where tanks couldn't. Meant to draw fire and take the hits. Shit magnets, basically.

Its predecessor, the X0S3, had first been deployed in Iraq in 2019, but only for logistical support, munitions, and supply roles. Never off-base, never in combat. They were too slow, too heavy, with no battery life, which meant they had to operate on a tether.

The X0S4, on the other hand, was the bigger, badder, faster, stronger model, and their petrol-hybrid engines meant they could run at fifteen mph, carrying 400 pounds of gear without the user even feeling it. At least in theory, Levi reminded himself. The USS *Bataan* had been carrying them to Iraq for their first combat trials, and he supposed he'd find out soon enough if the hype lived up to reality. If it didn't, well, then he wouldn't live long enough to write a negative user review on Amazon.

"Well, at least we get to go out in style," said Hicks, coming to stand next to Levi.

"Who's first?" Lieutenant Dan asked, dragging Levi's attention back. "We'll get them fitted, go through a basic how-to while we continue to mate the weapons systems you wanted."

"Levi, Duval, you're up. Hicks, you're next," Colter said, turning to nod at them.

"Fuck yes, come to Daddy."

Colter groaned. Levi turned to see Weeks had cracked open one of the weapons crates.

"This one, I want this one," Weeks said, bending down to lift out a Dillon M134D Minigun.

"We all get one, Weeks," Colter said. "Duval, Hicks, and Levi get the GAU-19/Bs."

"We do?" asked Briggs, sounding like a kid at Christmas, moving across to join Weeks in admiring the new toy. Six barrels, electrically driven, belt fed, forty-three pounds carry weight, and capable of putting out anywhere between 2,000 to 6,000 rounds of freedom a minute. You could literally cut down trees with them.

"Man, whose dick did you have to suck to get all this stuff?" asked Weeks, opening another crate to peer inside.

Levi thought Colter was about to explode when they were interrupted by a cough.

They all turned to find one of the CIA agents that Colter had warned them about standing at the entrance to the hangar, just out of the rain, with a black Humvee waiting just beyond him. Lights on, engine running, windshield wipers a blur, and two dim shapes sitting inside.

The agent jerked his head at the car, and Colter sighed.

"Start getting them ready, Lieutenant. There's something I need to take care of first."

COLTER

Colter climbed into the waiting Hummer and out of the pouring rain.

"Close the door," Ms. David said. "It's wet out there."

You think? But Colter didn't say that, he just pulled the door shut and turned to face her, water coming off him in rivers, drenching the seat, pooling at his feet.

"Speaking of," he said. "Any idea when it's going to stop?"

"Not for a few hours," Mr. Alan answered, sitting in the front passenger seat, typing away on a laptop with his left hand. But he didn't turn around or look up. Better things to do than make eye contact, Colter supposed.

"Hours?"

Mr. Alan chuckled. "You sound surprised, Gunner. We nuked half of France, and there's a lot of moisture in the air with nowhere else to go but down. So I hope you like mud."

"Like a pig in shit."

He didn't, really; mud made a marine's miserable life even worse. Weapons jammed, men slipped, accidents happened.

"How are your men?" Ms. David asked.

Straight to business, then. "As good as can be expected."

And what more was there to say? He'd told them the truth. They deserved to know what they were in for. That this was probably a one-way trip, and they were all handling it in their own way.

Weeks had been humming the same tuneless song for hours. Duval kept reaching for the cross he wore around his neck. Levi kept making bad jokes, blowing off steam and pissing people off, while Briggs had his earphones in, nose buried in one of the user manuals like he was studying for a test.

As for Hicks... He'd found a magazine somewhere, and he'd been doing the crossword at the back, and Colter didn't know if he was struggling the hardest or not at all. But that was Hicks; he'd always been a little touched in the head.

"Do you have something for me?" asked Ms. David.

Colter pulled a folded piece of paper from his left breast pocket, saw his cramped and rushed handwriting, lines crossed out, smudged ink, and he hesitated.

There were a lot of things he'd needed to say to his old man, things he should have said long ago, things he never should have said in the first place. But hindsight is 20/20, what was done was done. He could only move on. So he'd written what he could, and to an outsider it would look like nothing, but his old man would be able to read between the lines. It's what he was good at, maybe the only thing.

He handed it to Ms. David, sat back, and waited.

"Odd," she mumbled when she was done reading. "I was expecting something a little more..."

"More?"

She shrugged as if it wasn't important, then passed the letter to Mr. Alan.

He skimmed over it himself, made a noise at the back of his throat before placing it face down on a small scanner next to him. He closed the lid and pressed a button. There was a pulse of light.

He typed a few more commands on the keyboard and hit enter.

"Done."

Colter frowned. That had been easy. Too easy. He'd expected some resistance; the CIA never just said yes. There was always a catch.

"You get what I asked for?" he asked.

"Of course." She handed Colter a stack of black and white photographs.

He flicked through them. Geneva was laid out before him, a tangled mess of collapsed buildings, blocked roads, and burnt out ruins covered in snow and ice. He paused on the Aérodrome d'Annemasse, a small domestic airport. Mangled wreckage that used to be aircraft and vehicles scattered across the ground, its single runway covered in a blanket of snow, only 1,300 meters long. Too short to land a C-17 Globemaster, but perfect for their needs, and much clearer in these new images. No obstructions that he could see. The snow was a problem, but he'd already planned for that. And just like that, the mission was still on.

Ms. David cleared her throat. "Last but not least, I have a gift."

"A gift?"

"Don't get excited. It's a transponder, low tech, non-directional. Turn it on when you have the tapes, and it will transmit a low-frequency signal that we'll be listening for."

"What for?"

"Why, so we can find you, even if you're all dead. The battery will last a couple of months, but you're to activate it if and only if you're successful in locating the tapes. I can't emphasize that enough. We don't have the manpower or resources to waste if you fail. Are we clear?"

"Crystal."

"Good. Wilkins will give you the device when you get out."

Colter nodded to himself. The conversation was over. He was being dismissed.

He reached across to open the door.

"Oh, and Gunner?" she said like she'd just remembered something.

Colter paused.

"Good luck and Godspeed."

He just frowned at her before he climbed back out into the rain.

"You think he can pull it off?" Mr. Alan asked when they were alone again.

Ms. David didn't say anything at first.

"Do you believe in miracles, Mr. Alan?"

Mr. Alan didn't answer.

"Me neither."

Ms. David watched Colter walk away, transponder slung over his shoulder, folders clutched to his chest, back bent and hunched over like he had the world crushing him flat.

"What should I do with this, then?" Mr. Alan tilted his head at the image on the screen. A page of cramped writing and smudged ink, lines crossed out. A dying man's last wish and confession all rolled into one.

Colter turned a corner, disappeared from view, and Ms. David knew she'd never see him again.

"Delete it," she said, turning back to face the front. "We were never here, and what he doesn't know won't hurt him."

Mr. Alan seemed to hesitate. Wilkins opened the driver's door and climbed in.

"You're going to like this," he said, letting go of the push-to-talk button on his chest and pulling the door shut. "They caught one."

"About time. Who has possession?"

"The French."

"Not for long. Mr. Alan, make a call, would you? And Wilkins, prep the *Kono* for our guest."

"Yes, ma'am."

"And Wilkins, I want to put to sea the moment the EBE is secured, not a second after. We're done here."

"Yes, ma'am."

LEVI

Levi frowned at the PlayStation-shaped controller in his hands, Boston Dynamics embossed on it in big, bold letters.

"So, what's this button do?"

"Don't worry about that," the technician said.

"And this?"

"Not important."

"Right... so how do you drive this thing, then?"

The tech shook his head. "You don't, Barf drives himself."

"Barf?"

Levi looked at Barf. A four-legged robot the size of a horse with a barrel-shaped chest four feet wide, a triangular-shaped head covered in sensors and antennas, and a series of metal poles sprouting from its body like some cyborg hedgehog.

"I'll leave you two to it," Lieutenant Dan said, tired of listening, or too busy to stay. Either way, he aimed for the Navy SEALs in the corner and didn't look back. The men were already suited up and going through final weapons checks, looking calm and collected, like they did this every day, like they weren't all going to die out there. Their TALOS suits a dull gray instead of the desert brown units Colter had sold his soul for.

Levi turned his attention to the two canines sitting at their feet, some breed he didn't recognize, similar to a German shepherd but smaller, more compact—Colter's low-tech solution to an invisible enemy. Each fitted with their own special gas mask, boots, Kevlar vest, and doggles—specially designed goggles with night vision and infrared.

Levi was glad the Frogs and their dogs were coming though, especially given the shitstorm they were heading for, and the boys from SEAL Team 4 were good, some of the best, maybe. But Team 4 specialized in operations in Latin America, and they'd spent the last year training the Afghan Police in Uruzgan. From what Levi had seen of the conditions under the Cloud, speaking Spanish and making friends with the locals were going to be about as useful as tits on a nun.

"Can he fetch?" asked Levi, turning back to study Barf.

"No, he—"

"Can he play dead?"

"No, dammit, Barf's a pack mule. It's his job is to carry all your gear and ammo, that's it. You want a toy, get a poodle."

"So, what's that do, then?" Levi asked, pointing at something that looked like a garbage can on tank tracks, three feet tall, three feet wide, four feet long, but sprouting a M240L medium machine gun, robotic arm, and a side-by-side grenade launcher.

"Oh, that's R2-FU, he shoots things."

"That's more like it. Wait. And Barf doesn't?"

"No, Barf follows you, goes where you go." The tech yanked the controller out of Levi's hands. "This," he said, waving it in front of Levi's face, "is simply there in case he gets stuck, or you need him to do something that's not on the list."

"What li—"

"Do you ever shut up?" The technician cut him off, holding

up an orange laminated A5 card. "This list, these are his voice commands. I suggest you learn them. But if you remember nothing else—and I wouldn't be surprised—" Levi's eyes narrowed. "Then just remember to tell him to 'Follow tight,' and he'll walk on your heels. 'Engine on' wakes him up. 'Engine off' puts him to sleep. By the way, that's a good one if you need him to be quiet."

"Why? How loud is he?"

"Let's just say stealth is not his best feature."

"Wonderful."

"Don't worry. You'll be making enough noise of your own in this bad boy."

Levi and the technician both turned to look up at the X0S4.

"You ever used one of these before?" the tech asked.

"You're kidding, right?"

It looked like an emptied-out robot, eight feet tall, four feet wide, oval-shaped chestplate folded up, brown armor plates folded out, exposing a human-shaped hole in the middle.

The technician shrugged. "I suppose there's no time like the present, then. Get in."

Levi nodded nervously. He ducked under the suit's raised arms, a three-barrel Gatling gun on its right, and a grenade launcher and the biggest shotgun he'd ever seen on its left. He climbed in backward, sliding his feet into the clamps, putting his arms though the holes like he was putting on a jacket. He pressed his back into the padding and pushed up into the shoulder braces, his hands sliding deeper until he gripped what felt like handlebars covered in buttons and triggers.

The technician climbed up after him, standing on the suit's feet. He grabbed a buckle and clasp on the side of Levi's waist and started clipping him in.

"First lesson," he said, looking him in the eye. "You've just gotten two feet taller, three feet wider, and 2,000 pounds heavier. That means you have to change how you move. You're also going to

want to swing your arms when you move. That's normal, but don't."
The technician glanced to either side. "With your loadout, each
arm is going to weigh nearly 170 pounds, not counting ammo. You
swing your arms at the wrong time and you're going to be eating
dirt. You understand?"

Levi nodded. Things were moving too fast to do anything else.

"Good." The technician pantomimed a boxer's stance. "Keep
your arms up, elbows out, knees bent. Having your arms out wide
will help with the balance, and bending your knees lowers your
center of gravity. It means you won't fall over as much, and you'll be
able to turn around faster. Also, try to keep one foot on the ground
at all times. It helps with the not falling over part."

"Anything else?" asked Levi, already feeling overwhelmed.

"Yes. You have a top speed of fifteen mph, and you can't jump
for shit. But anything else you do, the suit will do. You kick, it kicks.
You hit, it hits. Just ten times harder. You sacrifice speed for power
though. You're also in Rig Two, that's good. She's one of the least
buggy."

"Great," mumbled Levi.

The technician pulled down a crossbar over Levi's head, like he
was strapping him into a rollercoaster. Or an electric chair. Neither
mental image helped the sick feeling churning in his guts.

The technician started fiddling with something to the left of
Levi's head.

"Water," he explained, attaching a hose to the left port of Levi's
gas mask. He fitted an attachment over Levi's goggles like sunglasses,
but bigger and bulkier, with cords leading into them. He turned
Levi's head from side to side, checking the fit before feeding the
cords down behind his head.

"Polarized," he said, like that explained anything. Levi didn't
even bother asking this time.

The technician turned to point at the touchpad on the suit's left
arm and Levi followed his finger. "Green button is *GO*. You hold

it for three seconds. You do that before you get in, by the way…"

He went to press it with his thumb.

"Wait!"

The tech paused.

"How do I piss in this thing?"

"The same way you've been doing all day. Anything else?"

Levi shook his head, not sure what he'd been expecting, and he supposed pissing himself would soon be the least of his problems.

"Oh, one last thing," the tech added. "You don't get claustrophobic, do you?"

"No. Why?" answered Levi.

"No reason," he said, then he jammed his thumb down and stepped back.

Levi heard a solid thump, and somewhere behind him something started to hum, an electric whine, growing louder.

"Now what?"

"Now the magic happens," the tech said.

Levi heard a loud hiss, he felt another thump, then a whole series of them, compressed air venting, like a rocket getting ready for liftoff. He felt a pressure on his chest, against his back, felt it travel down his spine to his waist, felt it grip his thighs and squeeze his legs from his hips down to his feet, and, with a start, Levi watched as the suit came alive, armor plates moving, sliding, closing in. The visor snapped down over his head, and Levi was plunged into complete darkness.

"Son of a bitch."

"What?" the technician called, his voice muffled, faint.

"Nothing," Levi lied, but for one brief second he panicked. He couldn't move, he couldn't see, he couldn't even breathe. He was trapped, and the suit continued to squeeze, tighter and tighter.

"Boot-up takes fifteen seconds," the technician continued from somewhere far away, his voice calm and completely oblivious. "Right now, the suit is adjusting to your body shape, the tighter the better."

There was a joke in there somewhere, but Levi missed it.

"The onboard computer is also calculating your weight distribution and the suit's total loadout. It will use that information to calibrate the suit's range of moti—"

A loading icon appeared in the dark in front of him, and Levi remembered to breathe.

"Huh?" He hadn't heard a word the technician had said.

"You're carrying a lot of extra weight," the technician said, louder, slower. "That's going to affect your sense of balance. You follow? Momentum is the enemy. The suit will try its best to stop you from falling over, but it has its limits. Just think of her as good old American muscle. Lots of power. Great in a straight line, but she can't corner for shit. It's why we call them wrecking balls."

"What?"

"You know… great at going through walls."

"Wonderful," Levi mumbled, watching as the spinning circle stopped spinning.

A page of glowing green icons and acronyms appeared in the dark before him.

"Fuck!"

"Easy," the technician scolded, his voice as clear as if he was talking in Levi's ear. "No need to shout, the suit is fitted with directional microphones and a front-mounted loudspeaker. Just talk normally, or we'll all go deaf."

"Right, sorry."

"Never mind. As for the menu system, this part was actually designed by one of you jarheads, so any idiot can use it. Grunt proof. At least, that was the idea…"

Levi turned his head, and the green icons followed him, soft and out of focus in the corner of his eye, barely visible until he looked at them. Then they bloomed out, big, clear, and vibrant. "What the?"

"Like I said, this part was designed by one of you jarheads. The goggles you're wearing have tiny built-in infrared cameras that track your eye movement and sensors that monitor your head position, tilt, and rotation. Ever use a HoloLens? Same idea. Now, you highlight an icon by focusing on it, wink to expand, then hit the button by your left thumb to select."

"Which one?" He could feel at least three, like the joystick of a fighter jet.

"The small one on top. It also doubles as your radio, just push to talk. The two bigger triggers are your secondary and tertiary weapons. You don't want to be pushing those just yet... besides, they won't actually do anything until they're loaded. Got it?"

"Got it."

"Good, do you see the icon that says ENG? Top left, a little bigger than the rest. I want you to select it."

Levi did as he was told, and an enormous wraparound screen powered on, so clear it was like looking through glass.

"How's it look, marine?"

"I can see you." But not much else, and no matter how far he turned his head he couldn't see over his shoulder, the screen just ended in strange little black hexagons.

Not good. This thing had more blind spots than Stevie Wonder. He'd have to turn the whole suit if he wanted to look behind him.

"This thing not have a rearview mirror?"

"Patience, marine, I'm getting to that. See those other icons? LT is light." He reached up to pat Levi's right shoulder and pointed to both arms. "They're 500-watt LED searchlights, that's around 50,000 lumens, or about half as bright as the sun. So careful where you point them. Aim them at someone wearing NVGs and you'll blind them. Next we have FLR, that's your infrared. NVG is night vision, obviously. LDR is LiDAR, the same tech Barf uses to see." He pointed to something above Levi's head. "It's also the one that will take the most getting used to. I want you to turn it on now, and I want you to leave it on."

Levi looked at the button, watched it expand. He pressed down with his thumb, and a 3D image appeared beneath his chin. A black circle surrounded by thousands of multicolored lines, hard edges, and moving gaps. Levi frowned. At first, he didn't know what he was looking at. The technician stepped back a few feet, and suddenly it all clicked in his head.

"That's your LiDAR map," the tech said, "the black circle in the middle is you." The orange human shape in front of him waved. "That's me. Now for the science lesson, the LiDAR system uses a pulsed laser to measure distance, the colors relate to height. Green-blue is ground, red is anything above eight feet, yellow through orange is anything in the middle. It's a line-of-sight system, so while you have a 360-degree field of view, you still can't see around corners. But the system can see through smoke, dust, and in complete darkness."

Levi grinned. "Now we're talking."

It was like third-person view in a computer game. He could see the whole hangar, even what was happening behind him. He could see the tables loaded with gear to his left and people moving between them.

He looked up to try to match what he was seeing on the screen with his own eyes. Hicks was directly across from him, being strapped into his suit and going through the same rushed tutorial. He saw Briggs in the corner, being fitted with his TALOS suit, black and brown metal skeleton fitted over his MOPP. He saw technicians swarming over the two M113A4 Infantry Fighting Vehicles parked to his right—stretched, more heavily armed versions of APCs. They looked like lopsided boxes on tank tracks, sloped at the front, sporting two pairs of round headlights, armed with 25mm Bushmaster cannons and independent CROWS turrets, with clusters of smoke grenade dischargers fitted to the upper glacis plate. On the rear end was the ramp, which had a door in the left side that was hinged on the right, while the sides were flat, bare, and totally featureless.

Levi watched the technicians tying the IFVs down to their special pallets with mesh and chains, fitting parachutes to their backs, and he looked away before he followed that thought any further. Then Colter walked back in from the rain, carrying something heavy on his back and clutching something close to his chest. Levi leaned forward, trying to see what it was, and to his surprise the image zoomed in.

"I think I'm going to like this," he said. And for the first time, he felt like they might actually stand a chance. A slim one, but better than none. Provided they didn't all die trying to get there...

"Okay, now for your weapons," the tech said. "I want you to take a hold of the right-hand grip. You feel the button by your thumb? There's only one on this arm. That's your trigger, there is no safety. This is your safety." The tech gave him the thumbs-up. "Press the button, and the GAU will take 0.4 seconds to spool up. It's set to fire 1,000 Raufoss MK 211 rounds a minute. Hit something with this and you'll turn it into mush. But you're only carrying 1,500 rounds. You follow?"

Levi followed. At $500 a pop, the MK 211 round was a 0.50 caliber armor-piercing bullet, incendiary, and bomb all rolled into one. Pulling the trigger would be like firing an anti-aircraft gun on fast-forward. Expensive too.

He started humming the Team America theme song.

"I'm serious, marine. You'll have to manage your ammo and reload while still in the suit, and reloading it is a bitch. You're also going to be firing from the hip, and recoil is going to be an even bigger bitch. That means you're going to have to fire in short bursts. You hear me?"

Levi nodded.

"You have to say yes or no, marine, I can't see you. We clear?"

"As mud," said Levi.

"Good enough."

The technician nodded to the suit's left arm. "This is where it gets a bit more up close and personal. Grip the left handle, and remember those two other buttons from earlier?"

"Yes."

"You'll also feel a pressure bar just in front of your fingers. That controls the articulated claw. You wanna pick something up? Pump it like the brakes on a bike."

Levi did as he was told, and the claws at the end of the left arm closed like crab pincers.

"Congratulations," said the technician. "You're now left-handed. You'll be able to lift up to 250 pounds without falling over, and it has a crush strength of 3,000 psi. Just don't try to do anything that requires a light touch or fine motor control. Use that to undo your fly and you'll rip your dick off. Got it?"

"Roger that, no robot handjobs."

"Lastly, the two buttons you can feel are for your XM307 grenade launcher and something we like to call the Judge. XM307 on the bottom, Judge on the top. The XM fires 40mm airburst grenades with an effective range of 1,600 yards."

"And the Judge?"

"The Judge is special, basically a sawed-off punt gun, semi-automatic, gas operated, only it fires half a pound of triple-zero buckshot. You wanna kill everything in front of you without aiming? Use him."

Levi smiled. "Can I call you Q?"

The technician ignored him. "You have thirty-one rounds for the XM. Belt fed. The Judge uses six-shot drums. But when you run out—and you will—you'll have to reload manually from Barf. And do you remember what I told you about reloading?"

"Reloading is a bitch."

"That's right, reloading is a bitch, and it's a team effort. So go easy on them. But we'll have you and Lance Corporal Briggs practice that next; he's going to be your support. And while I would love to explain what every button does, we don't have a week." The technician took the orange laminated card from his pocket and taped it to the suit's left arm, next to the touchpad screen. He took out another white card, and he taped it to Levi's right arm.

The technician pointed at the orange card. "Barf." He pointed at the white one. "Everything else." The same three- and four-letter acronyms were displayed, but with the full text meaning next to them. "I hope you're a fast learner, kid."

"I can tie my shoelaces."

"That will have to do. Well, that's pretty much it in terms of your loadout. All your ammo is going to be with Barf. Remember, Barf is your new best friend. You lose Barf, you're dead."

"What else do I need to know?" asked Levi.

"Too much, you're going to have to pick it up on the go. But the most important thing is that you only have nine hours of battery life, the hybrid buys you another three. After that the suit will shut down unless you can find more gas. And refueling isn't like reloading, it's not something you can do from inside the suit. But to be honest, if you're still running around out there after twelve hours, then you have other issues."

"Thanks, Captain Obvious."

The tech shrugged. "That's pretty much all I can tell you, the rest is on you." The tech took another step back, putting some distance between them. "When you're ready, I'll take the suit out of lock, and you can take your first step. Just take it slow, okay? It's going to feel a little weird to start." He held up a touchpad, his finger hovering over the screen. "Ready?"

"Ready."

The tech pushed down, and Levi felt a soft thud. He sucked in a breath, pulled back on the handles, and was surprised when the arms responded instantly. He'd expected them to be heavy, but he couldn't feel anything except a slight lag, as though the air was a little thicker than normal.

Levi took a tentative step forward, then another, confidence growing, his feet falling like anvils, metal on concrete singing, and for one brief moment he felt unstoppable, like nothing could touch him. Like he was the fucking Juggernaut. Levi smiled. He couldn't help it. Because whatever came next, Hicks had been right. At least they got to go out in style.

COLTER

Colter was a gambling man.

Just not the kind that played with money. Instead, when he made the wrong decision, people paid with their lives. And now he had six marines, six Navy SEALs, two M113A4 IFVs, and their three-man crews all depending on him. And he was going to let them down.

It wasn't a maybe, he wasn't being paranoid, just realistic. This was war, men were going to die, and there was nothing he could do about it.

He had a plan, of course, but things never played out how you're expecting. Something always goes wrong, and there were a million things that could wrong between here and Geneva. Too many moving pieces, too many uncertainties. Number one: just getting there.

As the crow flies, Geneva was almost a straight shot north from Toulon. 400 miles by air, 500 by road. But they couldn't drive, they didn't have the time. They had to fly, and in something big enough to carry eighteen men and all their gear and vehicles. So that meant two Lockheed C-130Js. Big, slow, four-engine turboprop military transports that had been around in one form or another since the 1950s.

But they had to fly low, beneath the Cloud, and low was dangerous. Terrain strikes in Afghanistan killed more pilots and soldiers than bullets ever did. And flying beneath the Cloud in planes that big, and on instruments alone, made Afghanistan look like a walk in the park.

The only visual reference they had was the convoy of lights below them. An unbroken chain of military traffic making the A51 glow like a river of fire as it snaked its way through the French countryside. And if they didn't somehow lose an engine or fly into a mountain along the way, there was the landing to worry about.

Geneva's international airport was gone; not even the runway was left. The only viable option was the Aérodrome d'Annemasse five miles east of the city, and landing wasn't possible there either. The snow was too deep, the runway too short. And even if they could put the planes down in the dark without them all dying in the process, there wasn't enough space to taxi, turn around, and take off again. Choppers weren't an option either. It was too far, would take too long, and they had too much gear. And a paradrop was out of the question; they'd hit the ground with nothing but what they could carry, scattered over a mile, alone and on foot, and Colter knew they'd all be dead inside of a minute.

It was time and distance and simple math working against them.

So they were going to use something called LAPES, a low-altitude parachute extraction system, or as Levi called it: Operation Human Pancake.

It involved the C-130Js flying ten feet off the ground at 150 miles an hour, ramps lowered, while the loadmaster pushed a button and their IFVs and all their gear got yanked out the back by a parachute with them strapped inside.

Admittedly not the smartest idea he'd ever had. But it was the best he could do given the time constraints, and technically it should be survivable. There had been a lot of interest in the concept over the years, patents had been lodged, papers written, but they were going to be the first human trials, and Colter knew they were either going down in history as the men with the biggest balls in the universe or complete shit for brains.

Hicks reckoned it was 50/50. Levi said even that was being optimistic, and Colter was pretty sure those two had a bet going. They always did.

"How're we looking?" Colter asked, leaning forward to peer over the pilot's shoulder. His right hand was clamped on the back of the pilot's seat, his knees bent as the plane bucked and swayed beneath him, airframe shuddering as they hit another patch of turbulence.

"Engine four is running a little hot," the pilot said, not taking his eyes off the hundreds of glowing dials and buttons in front of him. "But we're keeping an eye on it."

Colter nodded, seeing nothing but darkness and lightning and rain hammering against the windshield, thick drops flattened to streaking trails before the wind tore them away.

He knew they could fly on one engine if they had to, but if that happened they'd have to turn back, and they didn't have the time to try this again later.

"How long?" Colter asked, looking at his watch.

"Soon. We should be seeing the edge of this right about—"

"Now," Colter finished his sentence, seeing a yellow crack in the darkness. A horizontal line stretching east to west, crack widening, growing brighter, world slowly coming into focus below them. Ridges and hills rising from the gloom, the tips of trees reaching up, the straight lines and curving loops of towns laid out like chalk outlines.

They burst out into daylight, into dirty brown air full of ash and radioactive dust, rays of light stabbing down, black walls of cloud to either side, and blue sky peeking down from high above as though they were in the eye of a hurricane or at the bottom of an enormous grave, and Colter had to look away. His eyes watering, a purple afterimage floating in front of him, and he realized it was the first time he'd seen the sun in two days. Probably the last time, too, if he was honest with himself.

"Hold on," the copilot warned before he pushed forward on the throttles and pulled back on the yoke. Colter felt his stomach drop as the floor tilted beneath him, but thanks to his TALOS suit he just tightened his grip, his hand closed like a vice, and the only stress he felt was on his internal organs.

"What you see, Gunner?" Hicks asked in his earpiece.

"A mess," Colter said, peering at the ground far below.

Nothing was left, it was scorched earth as far as the eye could see. He saw fires and rain clouds and rivers of black mud, towns and forests burning, gutted ruins vomiting up plumes of smoke, roads clogged with the husks of burnt out cars. He saw mile-wide craters and convoys of military vehicles kicking up black dust clouds in their wake, and then he saw the Cloud, a towering mass of darkness rising up all around them, a near-vertical wall so tall it seemed to touch the stratosphere.

"Holy shit," the pilot said.

Colter could only murmur in agreement. It looked like the end of the world. A churning, swirling mass of black ash crawling with lighting, pulsing and moving like something alive.

"And?" pushed Levi. "Details, Gunner, details. In case you haven't noticed, it's not like we can just get up and have a look."

"Remind me to send you a postcard, then."

"Dick," muttered Levi.

"What was that?" demanded Colter.

"I said I feel sick. Sir."

Colter let it slide. The kid nervous, probably shitting himself, and he had a point. Duval, Hicks, and Levi had been trapped in their X0S4 suits for the last five hours. And Colter was pretty sure Levi had ADHD. The kid wasn't an idiot. Lazy, yes, with the attention span of a goldfish, but he was also one of the best soldiers Colter ever had serve under him. But sitting still for that long with only himself for company must be as close to torture as Levi had ever known, and Colter grinned. Maybe karma did exist after all.

They leveled out at 11,000 feet. Nowhere near the aircraft's ceiling, but airspace was congested, communications patchy, and visibility horrendous, making a mid-air collision a real risk. But at least this high up the view was better, the air clearer. At least that's what Colter told himself, trying to look on the bright side.

"Let me know when we start to descend," Colter said.

The pilot nodded. "Yes, sir."

Colter took one last look out the window, seeing their sister C-130J sitting off their left wing with Duval, R2-FU, and the Navy boys inside, and he left the pilots to it. There was nothing more to see, nothing for him to do. He couldn't fly the plane; the conditions on the ground weren't his problem. The only thing he needed to worry about was the mission and his men.

He made his way off the flight deck, ducking through the cabin door, his bulky TALOS suit making it hard to fit down the narrow stairs, managing to squeeze himself into the cargo hold. And if he'd felt cramped before, in here it was worse.

The IFV filled the eight-foot-wide space from wall to wall, sitting high on its special pallet, half sled, half shock absorber, strapped down with cargo mesh and chains. And behind it, closest to the ramp, were Hicks and Levi, locked in their X0S4s. Their suits were suspended in steel frames, surrounded by gear and wrapped in layers of padding and cardboard. Barf was crammed in behind them, and their parachute was a solid brick of fabric sitting between them and the way out.

Colter poked his head through the rear hatch of the IFV and

looked at Weeks, hunched over, head touching the ceiling, his knees almost level with his ears, bags of gear and bricks of foam packed in all around him. He looked at Briggs wedged in on his left, then at the transponder strapped into the seat on his right.

He had no idea where Ms. David had dug it up from. It reminded him of those old radio packs from the Vietnam War: analog, no GPS positioning, no LCD screen, big and bulky and heavy.

You could buy a better device in a boating store for fifty dollars and have it fit in your hand. But he understood the reasoning: GPS wasn't going to work under the Cloud, and this was the only alternative—technology that had been obsolete for twenty years.

Briggs turned to look at him, his eyes pleading. "Please, sir, they won't shut up."

Colter could hear Levi's and Hicks's voices being piped through the IFV's speakers, filling the air with insults and moans.

He looked at Captain Green, the IFV Commander, at the gunner manning his station, then at the back of the driver's head. There was nothing Levi and Hicks loved more than a captive audience. Shit stirrers the both of them. But the IFV crew seemed more amused than anything else.

He grabbed the push-to-talk button on his chest.

"What are you girls on about now?" he asked.

Bitching was expected. Banter was healthy. Par for the course. It's how soldiers blew off steam. The only time you needed to worry about a marine was when he stopped complaining.

"Well, sir," Hicks answered matter-of-factly, "we're just trying to decide what movie we're in and which characters we all are."

"And?" asked Colter, wondering where this was going.

"And Levi reckons he's Iron Man, you're Captain America, Duval is Vision. Weeks is the Hulk.

"Hulk smash," Weeks declared.

Hicks kept talking. "I'm War Machine, and Briggs is a shorter, uglier, trans version of Black Widow."

"Ass," muttered Briggs.

"And you, Hicks?" Colter asked, playing along.

"Me? Well, sir, I figure this is a lot like *Lord of the Rings*, we're all on a suicidal quest to take the One Ring to Mordor. But that would mean Briggs is Gollum, you're Frodo, Duval is Gandalf the Gay. And Lev—"

"What the hell is that supposed to mean?" demanded Duval.

"It means you're so far in the closet you couldn't find your way out if you had a map and your tiny dick was the compass."

"Up yours, Hicks."

"In your wet dreams."

Colter sighed. "Give it a rest, Hicks. We have a long way to go still, and I'd prefer if everyone didn't want to kill you before we got there."

"Yeah, speaking of, any way we can hurry this up? I have an itch I can't reach."

"More like crabs," Duval fired back.

Colter shook his head. "No, Hicks, I can't *hurry this up*. Not unless Weeks has any tricks up his sleeve that he hasn't shared with us yet."

"Oh, God," Levi groaned.

There was a moment's silence.

"I had a buddy…" Weeks said, which is pretty much how every one of his stories started.

Levi groaned again. Weeks didn't seem to hear.

Mission accomplished, Colter took his earpiece out, replaced it with an earplug, and pushed it in deep. Then, blissfully deaf, he climbed into the back of the IFV, head ducked low, he reversed himself into a seat opposite Briggs, and he strapped himself in. Then he leaned back in his chair and let out a slow breath.

But he couldn't rest. He needed time to think. He needed to go through the folder stuffed into his left leg pocket one last time. The folder full of hazy photos taken from 3,000 feet, full of maps of their flight path and ground routes, radio call signs for sister units and air support. A whole battle plan that would fall apart as soon as they hit the ground. If they got there, he reminded himself. Because in less than an hour they'd fly back in under the Cloud, somewhere just north of Chambéry, and everything would turn to shit.

Their GPS would lose connection, their compass would become useless, visibility would drop to zero, and the pilots would have to fly off instruments, seeing the world in black and white, FLIR overlaid with computer-generated LiDAR images. Flying above rainbow-colored hills and mountains. Using towns as waypoints and roads as arrows, following the A41 to Annecy, then hugging the A410 to La-Roche-sur-Foron before tracking along the D903 to Bonne, where the D907 would spit them out right next to the airport. All while dodging power lines and radio towers and buildings, a whole obstacle course just waiting to kill them.

And just like that, Colter was back to square one. A plan only gets you so far, and no plan survives first contact with the enemy. Something was going to go wrong. It wasn't a maybe, he wasn't being paranoid, just realistic.

They had too much riding on dumb luck, and if being a marine had taught him anything, it's that eventually luck runs out.

LEVI

"TWO MINUTES."

The plane dropped, invisible downdrafts and updrafts throwing them around with sudden violent changes in direction that left him breathless and bruised.

The plane dropped again, yawing from side to side, and Levi groaned, his stomach in the back of his throat, sour bile coating his tongue.

"NINETY SECONDS."

It was all happening so fast.

The rear loading ramp started to open, hydraulics whining, frozen wind howling through the widening gap, and Levi squeezed his eyes shut, imagining them plowing into the ground at 200 miles an hour, then wondering if he'd die on impact or be burnt alive. The roar of the engines drowned out the terrified voice in his head.

Fuck. Fuck. Fuck. Fuck.

"ONE MINUTE."

He forced his eyes open, just in time to see the drone chute deploy, guide rope snapping taut, chute kicking and twitching like something possessed.

"Screw this!" Levi screamed, seeing nothing but pure darkness outside.

"THIRTY SECONDS."

Already?

Someone started praying, maybe Duval. "Yea, though I walk through the valley of the shadow of death, I will fear no evil."

A pause.

"For I'm the evilest son of a bitch in the valley!"

"Amen!" shouted Weeks.

Not Duval, then. Hicks, definitely Hicks.

"TEN SECONDS."

Lightning flashed, and Levi saw trees. He saw the ground, a white blur beneath them, coming up fast.

"Oh, God." Levi's eyes widened, his chest heaving, hyperventilating.

"BRACE! BRACE!"

The drone chute disappeared into the dark, hauling the main chutes out with it, and Levi went from 150 miles an hour to 60 in one tenth of a second. Like driving into a brick wall, and ten G's of deceleration crushed his chest flat, forcing the air out of his lungs in a strangled wheeze, and then he was falling, hurtling through empty space.

They hit the ground so hard they bounced. He saw stars, his vision a blur, teeth chattering in his head, skidding and bouncing and grinding across the ground, hearing someone laughing like they'd lost their mind before they shuddered to an exhausted halt. Brown parachutes slowly drifted down to settle on top of them.

Levi just sat there, body numb, tasting blood, wondering if he'd broken his spine or just bitten off his tongue.

"Everyone okay?" Colter asked.

"Holeeee shit," answered Hicks. "Can we do that again?"

"I'll take that as a yes. Levi?"

Levi shook his head to try to clear it.

"Define okay," he said, working his jaw, licking his teeth and feeling a flap of loose skin where he'd bitten clean through.

"Are you breathing?" Colter asked.

"Yeah," Levi said, wiggling his toes just to make sure they still worked.

"Then you're okay. Now get a move on, we need to clear the runway."

Levi opened a private channel to Hicks. "I'm starting to hate that guy."

"What do you mean starting?"

Levi snorted. He flicked through his menu, turned on his searchlights, took the suit out of lock, reached down with his left hand, grabbed the eight-inch steel pin holding everything in place, and ripped it out like he was pulling up weeds.

The frame holding up his suit came apart, chains and ropes falling away. He shrugged out of it and stepped out onto snow, turned to his left, his searchlights washing across frozen ice, snow-draped shapes, and misshapen lumps that could have been anything. He spun right, eyes flicking through his menu, switched to infrared. He saw nothing, no movement, no bright spots. Nothing warm-blooded. And that was the problem, wasn't it?

"Hurry up, you two," Colter pushed. "They can't fly in a circle jerk forever."

Levi looked up at the plane flying in a holding pattern above his head, Duval and the Navy boys still strapped inside and waiting their turn to play Russian roulette with the ground.

"Yes, sir," he said, grabbing the edge of the sled with his left hand, claws clamping shut, and he started dragging Barf and their gear off to the side while Hicks walked ahead of him, the exhaust on the back of his suit burning bright white on infrared. And beyond him lay the airport terminal, a series of squat low buildings and sheds, dark inside, cold and empty.

"See anything?" Colter asked, his IFV surging through the snow to Levi's right.

"Negative," Hicks said.

Levi dropped the sled. "We're clear."

"Copy that. Putting up flares."

The IFV spat twice and streaks of hot white spiraled high into the sky until they stopped dead a thousand feet above the ground, small chutes opening, flares suddenly yanked to the left by the wind.

Levi switched to the visible spectrum, seeing a world bathed in red, his shadow stretching in front of him as the flares drifted south.

"Eyes open, boys, they know we're here," Colter ordered.

Levi started moving, aiming for the terminal, his arms up, elbows out, his suit powering through the three feet of snow like it was nothing.

He risked another glance at the C-130J as it came in to land, its landing lights on, its tail kicking out, plane slewing to the left as it got caught in a crosswind.

Maybe it was a sudden gust or engine failure. Maybe it was fatigue or pilot error, or maybe it was just plain bad luck. But the second C-130J completely fucked up the drop. They hit the ground so hard Levi felt the shockwave beneath his feet, so hard it tore the left wing off on impact, and Levi could do nothing but watch as the right wing continued to do its job, still trying to lift all that weight into the air, and seventy-four tons of metal and men began to roll. Slowly at first, then faster, its left side engulfed in flames as it slid across the runway, coming straight at them.

"MOVE!" screamed Colter.

Levi didn't have to be told, he was already running. Just not fast enough. It felt like he was walking on the moon or running in a dream, taking huge lumbering steps, unable to move his feet any faster.

He didn't get more than ten yards before the scream of metal and death crashed down on top of him, roar deafening, earth shaking.

Hicks's scream was cut off as the flaming wreckage steamrolled him into the earth and something hit Levi from behind. It lifted him off the ground, sending him spinning. He saw snow, he saw sky, and he saw a single parachute thundering past before he crashed back down to earth and a wave of white buried him in darkness.

DAY 103

Home Sweet Home
Ten miles south of Garden City
Kansas, USA

SARA

Y ou sure about this, Trace?" asked Sara.

"Drew won't approve," said Ian, glancing at their tent and the dying man inside.

"What's your point?"

Ian shook his head. "It's too risky, Trace. What if you run into trouble?"

"Then I'll try my hardest to get out of it, won't I?"

"You better, because I'm sure as hell not coming in after you."

Trace frowned at Ian from across the fire. "Ian, I couldn't think of anything worse than you coming to *rescue* me."

"What's that supposed to mean?"

"It means you don't know what you're doing."

"What? And you do?" Ian shot back, his voice dripping with scorn.

"Enough!" Sara said, louder than she meant to. She held up a hand to try to calm the situation. "That's enough."

Ian opened his mouth to protest.

"You too, hun, it's not helping. We need to think about how we're going to do this."

"There is no *we*," Trace said, not even looking at Ian anymore. "I'm going alone."

"Not an option," said Sara.

"No, think about it, Sara. For once, Ian is actually right."

Ian gave Trace the finger.

Sara sighed, pinching the bridge of her nose and trying very hard not to scream.

"You can't go by yourself, Trace," she said, letting out a slow breath, trying to stay calm. "It's not safe."

"Noted," Trace muttered, pulling his hood over his head as a gust of cold wind stirred the branches above. "But Drew needs antibiotics, and he needs them now, and that means I need to go into town and hope I find something. Even if I have to steal it. And while I'm gone, someone has to watch over Drew. That means you. And someone needs to keep watch on the camp, and that means Ian. And that means you both have to stay here."

Sara opened her mouth to poke a hole in his argument.

"It's okay, Sara, I'll do this quick. In and out. Nobody will even know I'm there."

"I still don't like it," she said. "There has to be another way. You can't do this on your own."

Trace paused. "What about the kid, then?" he asked, almost like an afterthought, and everyone turned to look at Mick, like they'd forgotten he was even there.

"Him?" asked Ian.

"Me?"

"You," said Trace. "You want to be part of this group? This is how." Trace looked at his watch. "We wait for it to go dark. Then we go in, just the two of us, quietly."

Ian shook his head. "No way, too dangerous."

"We don't have a choice, remember?" Trace said. "You don't want me to go alone, you can't come with, and we can't all stay here. This is the only solution, and you know it."

And, if Sara hadn't already been looking at Trace, she just might have missed it, something on his tired face, something cold and calculating, gone so fast she thought she imagined it. And just like that, she knew what he was up to.

Still?

Sara shook her head. Mick was a good kid, and his heart was in the right place. She just wished Trace could see it, but Trace saw what he wanted to, mind already made up. So damn suspicious he wasn't even sleeping anymore. Claimed he couldn't, but that was a lie. It was a choice, just like everything else in his life. Simple reason was Trace didn't trust Mick, didn't like him, not since the moment he saw him, and Sara knew Trace was keeping an eye on him, like he was waiting for something. God knows what. But the lack of sleep was slowly killing him. He looked like a cancer patient, with deep bags under his eyes, skin like wax, and the amount of weight he'd lost in the last week was frightening, and Sara knew something had to give before Trace gave himself a heart attack.

"He's right, I can help," Mick said slowly.

Sara turned to frown at him.

"Not happening," said Ian.

"Why not?" Trace said. "Let him pull his own weight for a change. All he's done so far is eat."

Mick looked at Ian, he looked at her, he looked at the tent with Drew inside, he looked at the sky overhead, the dirt between his feet, anywhere but Trace.

Sara glanced at Trace, his face a mask, eyes blank, wrinkles carved into his forehead like it was stone. Nobody said anything.

Sara pursed her lips. She had a problem. Having Mick and Trace by themselves was a terrible idea. It could only end badly. But Trace was right, Drew was fading fast, someone needed to go into Garden City, and two of them needed to stay here, and that gave her an idea.

"I vote yes," she said.

Ian looked at her like he couldn't believe his ears. "What?"

"What, you didn't hear me?" Sara replied, getting annoyed. They didn't have time for this. Drew was dying, Trace was so damn paranoid he wasn't thinking straight, and all Ian did anymore was complain. Sara's patience was worn thin. She had one little boy to look after already, she sure as hell didn't need two more. But they couldn't continue like this either. They were coming apart, self-destructing, turning on each other. Which meant it was up to her to fix it, as always.

"Trace is right," she said slowly. "Four eyes are better than two. Mick goes with him, and we wait here. Like he said, we don't have a choice."

Ian didn't say anything. She had to raise one eyebrow at him before he sighed and nodded.

"Are you sure about this, Mick? It's a lot to ask…" Ian said.

"Drew's going to die if we don't do something, right?"

"Yes."

"Then why are we still sitting here talking?" Mick said, suddenly looking a lot older than his fifteen years.

He smiled at her, his cheeks turning red, but the look in his eyes told Sara it had nothing to do with the cold.

Mick had a crush on her, a bad one. She'd have to be blind not to see it. Ian found it amusing, said he remembered the feeling, that awkward teenage lust confused with true love. So she tried to cut him some slack. She almost felt sorry for him, and it wasn't like the end of the world suddenly stopped the raging hormones of puberty.

It was also probably why he was so quiet most of the time. He was shy. Standoffish. Awkward around the men. His voice was still in that terrible and unpredictable stage of breaking. It made him self-conscious, like a crack in his armor, and that was a bad thing to have around Trace.

"Good, that's settled, then," said Trace. "But we do this my way, kid. You listen to what I say. If I say drop to the dirt and crawl, you drop to the dirt and crawl. You don't ask why, you don't argue. You just do it. Got it?"

Mick saluted him. "Yes, sir."

Trace pointed a finger at him. "Don't get smart with me. This isn't a game."

"Sorry."

Trace waved him off, his eyes swinging from Mick's face to his rifle, where it rested against a tree.

"You know how to use that?" Trace asked.

Sara followed his gaze.

Mick glanced over his shoulder. "Yeah, why?"

"Mind if I see it?"

"Uh… sure."

Sara's frown deepened, confused at the change of direction.

Mick pushed himself to his feet, picked up his rifle, and walked around the fire before handing it to Trace.

"Is it loaded?"

"No."

Trace nodded like he didn't believe him, holding the rifle gently, barrel pointed at the sky.

"Cricket?" Trace asked, looking closer, then nodding to himself.

Crickets were learners' rifles, the kind of rifle you might buy a child. Good for target training and getting children used to handling a weapon. A long barrel for accuracy, slim, light, single action, .22 caliber, with low enough recoil that it didn't take their shoulder off. Not something a fifteen-year-old would normally have.

Sara figured he must have been using it to shoot birds or small game, or however he'd been surviving out here; she still wasn't sure. He got defensive and flustered when she asked him. She'd tried to be gentle, but Mick didn't seem to want to talk about the past.

Trace slid the bolt action back, checked for a round in the breach, worked the mechanism a couple of times before he lifted the rifle to his shoulder. Aimed at the branches overhead and pulled the trigger. There was a loud click as the hammer struck home on an empty chamber.

Trace lowered it again, shook his head, and passed it back to Mick. "You got anything else?"

"Like what?"

"Something bigger, caliber-wise. Shoot someone wearing body armor with this and the most you'll do is annoy them. Why do you have it, anyway? You know this is a kid's rifle, right?"

"It was my stepbrother's," Mick said quietly, pulling it to his chest.

Sara's ears perked up. He'd never mentioned a brother before.

"Your stepbrother? Where's he now?" Trace asked.

Mick shook his head, looked away.

Sara managed to catch Trace's eye. *Don't*, she mouthed. He frowned at her. She shook her head softly. *Just don't.*

She'd tried asking Mick about his family already, a couple of times, actually. But each time his eyes went blank, and it was like he dropped a wall between them, and the most she could get out of him afterward was grunts. It had taken hours just to drag him back into a conversation.

She didn't need to be a cop to know something bad had happened, and the only way Mick had of dealing with it was to ignore it, push it deep, and bury it. She thought he might open up to her eventually, but in the meantime the topic was strictly off limits. He needed time to process, time to heal, time to forget. Or start to, but confronting him about it now would only reopen the wound and drive him further away.

Trace sighed. "Show me what else you've got, then."

Sara saw the look of relief on Mick's face as he turned his back on Trace and hurried over to their tent, glad to escape another interrogation.

"Go easy on him, Trace," Sara said, when Mick was out of

earshot. "He's been through enough without you busting his balls all the time."

"Whatever," mumbled Trace, barely paying attention to her. His eyes focused on their tent instead, body tensing as Mick re-emerged carrying something in his hand, and Sara saw Trace's right hand drop to his hip.

"Here," said Mick, walking up to them, oblivious, carrying a small handgun still in its holster.

"Loaded?" Trace asked again, and Mick nodded.

Trace took it from him like it was a snake and he was scared it would bite. He checked the safety before he removed the gun from its holster, then his movements became fluid and easy. He thumbed the release and ejected the mag, catching it in his hand before racking back the slider to make sure there wasn't one in the chamber.

"A Rami," Trace said, turning the gun over in his hand. "A good gun," he added as an afterthought. Almost like he'd been expecting something else and didn't know what to make of it.

He worked the mechanism backward and forward a few times. "Dirty," he mumbled to himself when it seemed to catch. "A concealed carry? Yours?" Trace asked Mick, the tiny gun almost swallowed up by Trace's hand.

"Huh?"

Trace shook his head. "Never mind."

Sara leaned closer, trying to get a better look.

Trace dropped the mag in his lap and lifted the gun closer to his face, almost like he was trying to read the serial number, but Sara knew he was smelling it to see if it had been fired recently.

"When was the last time you cleaned this?" Trace asked, passing the gun to her so she could have a look, his attention on the magazine in his lap while everyone else looked at her.

It fit much better in her hand than his. Like it was made for her. But it was dirty, like Trace said. There was mud on the grip, residue buildup on the breach, and the mechanism didn't slide as easily as it should have. She wiped some of it off with her thumb and it came away black.

"Uh, I haven't." Mick shrugged. "I don't have anything to clean it with."

Sara handed the gun back to Trace, but she had to hold it under his nose before he noticed.

"Hmmm," said Trace, taking the gun from her. He turned his attention back to the round he had thumbed out, turning it around to read the stamp, brass shell glinting like gold.

"Not yours, I take it?"

Mick looked away. "Mom's."

Trace didn't say anything, didn't move, he just kept watching Mick, like he was waiting for more.

"My stepdad believed she should be able to defend herself…" Mick's voice trailed away.

Sara tried to catch Trace's eye again.

"You any good with it?" Trace asked.

Mick shook his head. "I'm okay. But—"

"But not amazing, hard to hit anything, I imagine."

Mick nodded.

"Not really your fault, 9mm and a short barrel like this." Trace dipped his head at a tree just outside their camp. "From here to there you'd be lucky to hit it one time in ten. But if you have to…" He hefted the handgun in his left hand. "Then make sure you're within six feet, and aim for the chest."

Mick nodded like he knew that already.

"How much ammo you got for it, anyway?" He nodded at Mick's backpack, and everyone turned to follow his eyes.

When Sara looked back, Trace had reloaded Mick's gun and was holding it out to him grip first.

"I got enough," said Mick. "Why?"

Trace shrugged like it didn't matter.

"Okay, so now that show-and-tell is over, how do we do this?" asked Sara, confused by Trace's behavior.

Trace rubbed his face, looking even more tired than before, his eyes faraway and darker than she'd ever seen them, not dangerous or worrying, just grim. Like he'd made a decision and knew no one else would like it.

"We wait for sunset, move down later while it's still light enough to see. We find a spot with a view of the city, sit tight for a couple of hours, wait for it to get dark. I figure we'll have more chance of getting in without being spotted, and hopefully less people are moving around that late. We'll try to find a hospital first, or a pharmacy, maybe a CVS, somewhere with medical supplies. Even a vet will do. And if all that fails, then we'll go door to door in one of the nicer neighborhoods, do some good old breaking and entering. Who knows, maybe we'll get lucky."

"How long?"

"Twenty-four hours, maybe? It depends. Hour or so to ride there, hour or so to ride back. That gives us at least twenty hours to have a look around."

"That's too long," said Sara.

"I know." Trace shrugged. "But that's all I got. This might be pointless, the odds of us finding anything... I think we need to be prepared for that."

Sara shook her head. "I refuse to accept that."

Trace held up both hands, palms open. "Just saying, Sara, I can't promise miracles."

"Good thing that's not up to you, then," said Ian.

Sara glared at him.

"What? I'm just saying. It's not like he believes anyway."

"Ian, I love you... But please shut up. Now is not the time." She turned her attention back to Trace, ignoring the hurt look on Ian's face.

"Twenty-four hours?" she said.

Trace nodded. "Max. We'll move light, weapons and backpacks only."

"What about our sleeping bags?" asked Mick.

Trace glanced at him.

"Who said anything about sleeping, kid? We have a lot of ground to cover and not much time. Take only what you need. I want us to be able to move quickly if we need to."

Sara could see Mick was starting to have second thoughts, saw him hesitate.

Trace must have seen it too.

"You still up for this?" he asked.

Mick nodded.

"You sure? No shame in backing out if you're scared."

But the way he said it meant the complete opposite, and, whether Trace had meant to be an asshole or he was just being his usual self, it got a reaction. Mick's hands balled into fists, his nostrils flared, and the hesitation Sara had seen in Mick's eyes vanished, replaced by a flash of testosterone-fueled teenage anger bordering on hate.

Sara wanted to kick Trace.

"Good," said Trace. "We leave in three hours. Get some sleep if you can, you're going to need it."

Trace pushed himself to his feet, dusting off his pants as he stood up.

"Now, if you'll excuse me, I'm gonna go take a piss, and then I'm gonna have a nap." Trace nodded at Sara. "Wake me in an hour."

TRACE

Taking a nap was the furthest thing from his mind, and he couldn't sleep if he tried. He was way too wired for that.

Instead he propped himself up in the tent, using his bag as a headrest, Drew's still shape lying next to him, his Glock within easy reach, and he kept his eyes on Mick, thinking about opportunity and motive, evidence and selective bias. A thousand conflicting thoughts all bouncing around in his head, trying to make the pieces fit, then trying to convince himself he was wrong. Letting his paranoia get the best of him.

But he trusted his gut, like a sixth sense, and by the end of the day he was going to get his answers, once and for all. No Ian or Sara in the way to run interference, no interruptions, just Mick and himself, and there was too much about Mick that didn't add up, didn't pass the sniff test.

Some alone time would fix that.

Until then, he'd taken what precautions he could. All he could do now was keep an eye open, save his energy, and wait for nightfall.

At some point Sara came to give him his dinner, basically multivitamins and chicken stock dissolved in hot water, half an

MRE, and some trail mix for dessert. She knelt down next to him, put her hand on his shoulder, held his cup under his face, like she wasn't going anywhere until he finished it. Mothering him.

She took his cup when he was done, stood up and walked away without a word, and Trace went back to thinking, listening to Drew breathing, hearing the wind blowing through the trees.

He didn't even remember closing his eyes. It shouldn't have been possible.

But when he opened them again, it was dark outside, and quiet. Too quiet. Sara hadn't come to wake him up, and Trace got a bad feeling.

He glanced at Drew sleeping next to him, gave him a nudge. Then another, harder. Drew blinked one bleary eye open.

Trace held a finger to his lips, pointed two fingers at his eyes, then pointed outside, and Drew nodded, coming awake fast. Trace pushed himself to his knees, feeling groggy and a little unsteady as he climbed to his feet. It felt like he'd been drinking, like he was still drunk. He shook his head, trying to clear the cobwebs.

He pulled his Glock from its holster, and he went out the back of the tent, not the front. He stayed low, crabbed around the side, gun drawn, and he listened, hearing the wind sighing through the trees. And voices.

He poked his head around the side of the tent, saw Ian sitting by the fire. Peter and Stacey's silhouettes to either side of him, his arms holding them close, their hands held out to the flames.

Trace frowned. He didn't see Sara or Mick, Mick's gear was gone, and his bad feeling got worse.

Dammit, Sara. What have you done?

He stepped out from behind the tent.

"Where are they, Ian?" Trace asked, hiding his Glock behind his back as he walked closer.

Ian spun.

"Where are they, Ian?" Trace asked again.

"What?" said Ian, a guilty look on his face.

"How long?" asked Trace.

"How long what?"

"How long have they been gone, you idiot?"

"An hour."

"Fuck!"

Trace put his Glock back in its holster, pulled out his walkie-talkie, flicked it on, and pressed the transmit button. "Sara, you there? Answer me!"

Nothing. He tried again, no answer. He started moving toward the bikes. Sara's and Drew's were missing. Trace undid Drew's stretcher from the back of his bike, kicked it to the side, and started pushing his bike downhill.

"What are you doing?" asked Ian, standing up.

"What does it look like? I'm going after them."

"Relax, Trace, they'll be fine. Sara can look after herself."

"Sara isn't the problem."

Ian stepped in his way. "Trace, this needs to stop."

Trace tried to go around him. Ian sidestepped and blocked him again.

"Move, Ian," growled Trace.

"Mick is a good kid, Trace," he said. "Why can't you see that?"

Trace lost his patience. He didn't have time for this. He dropped his bike, put his palm against Ian's chest, and pushed. Watched as Ian stumbled back, off balance, arms windmilling before he landed on his ass.

Stacey jumped up from the fire, face frightened. Peter's mouth curled down, and his eyes bunched together like he was about to cry. Trace ignored them. He went back to their tent and ducked his head inside.

"Problem?" asked Drew.

"Sara gave me the slip. They've gone into town on their own. I'm going after them."

"Be careful, Trace…"

"Too late for that now." Trace shook his head. "Just keep your radio on you."

He picked up his AR-15 and slung it over his shoulder. He grabbed a flashlight, flicked it on to make sure it worked. He stepped back out, looked for the night vision goggles but couldn't find them. Sara must have taken them.

He picked up his bike and started walking it out.

"What the hell are you going to do, Trace? You won't catch them," Ian shouted behind him. "It's pitch black out there, and they've got an hour head start on you. Just give it a rest!"

Trace ignored him. Hoping for all their sakes that Ian was wrong. He started jogging. He ran until he hit the road. He jumped on the bike and started pedaling as fast as he could, with nothing but half the moon hanging in the sky to light his way, and the sinking feeling that he was already too late.

SARA

Garden City was busy. There were more people in the streets than Sara would have thought, and she realized that maybe she should have listened to Trace on this one. Come in under the cover of darkness instead. But it was too late for that now. They were here, so she decided to put the worry behind her and make the most of the daylight left. Only problem was she didn't know which way to go; one direction looked as good as the next.

So she'd stopped at the edge of town in the middle of a four-way intersection, road littered with garbage, paper and plastic bags swirling in the wind, watching all the people watching her back.

"Now what?" asked Mick.

Sara almost shrugged, but Mick already looked worried. He kept glancing over his shoulder. Probably imagining Trace bearing down on them, already paranoid and now pissed off. Not a good mix.

But she'd deal with Trace later. She knew how to handle him. Besides, a little sleep wouldn't kill him.

God knows, he'd needed it. He was becoming impossible to deal with, a risk to himself and everyone around him, so she'd slipped something into his drink. Something to knock him out for a few hours. Either way, Trace wasn't something Mick needed to worry about.

So she smiled at him instead, trying to calm his nerves. "Now we say hello."

He looked at her like she was mad.

Sara pedaled over to the side of the road, stopped ten feet from the curb and the man she'd seen watching them from the doorway of an abandoned building.

She could tell it was abandoned because someone had lit it on fire, tried to burn it to the ground. Almost succeeded, too. Half was burnt timbers and ash, the other half was almost untouched, the white paint stained with smoke. It looked like it used to be a restaurant or a bar; she could see tables and chairs inside, big glass windows, now just empty holes, and it had a name across the top of the door in big, flowing script. "Rav" something, the rest was missing. But it looked like it might have been expensive once upon a time. Which is why the man sitting in the doorway was something of an oddity.

He was filthy, his face gaunt, cheeks hollowed out, and his beard looked like a bird's nest. Like he hadn't seen a shower in years. His clothes were in tatters and nothing matched. He had at least three layers on that she could count and plastic bags on his hands and feet. And when Sara leaned closer she could smell him. He stank of urine and sweat and neglect.

Homeless, Sara thought. Once a minority and now the majority, but homeless long before the Cloud arrived. She imagined his life hadn't changed much, which was probably why he smiled at her when she got closer. It was just another day to him.

"Hello," Sara said.

"Hello," he answered, voice gravelly, rough, like it hadn't been used much. "New around here, aren't you?"

"That obvious?" she asked.

The man smiled wider, revealing gaps in his yellow teeth. "I can smell it on you."

His eyes swiveled to something behind her, and he frowned.

Sara turned to find Mick watching her with a strange look on his face.

"What?" Mick asked, glancing back down the road behind them, pulling at the strap for his Cricket.

He'd insisted on bringing it, along with all his gear. Like he hadn't trusted them not to steal it. Sara hadn't wanted to risk an argument in case it had woken Trace up, so she'd let him bring whatever he wanted. Didn't see the harm in it.

"You shouldn't be here. You should leave," said the man, all serious now, his hand stroking something next to him. Sara saw it was a small dog. Just as filthy as him, and just as thin, its ribs poking through matted fur.

"Bad place for a lady," he added, almost as an afterthought, glancing at the buildings across the road.

"Good thing I'm not a lady, then," Sara said.

The man paused. He looked her over, like he was seeing her for the first time. His eyes narrowed.

"Cop?" He nodded to himself. "Cop. You smell like a cop. That's even worse. You should go now, before it's too late."

"We're wasting time," Mick said.

The man glanced at Mick, and his frown deepened.

"Don't have a choice," Sara said, dragging his attention back to her. "We're looking for the hospital. Or a pharmacy. Anything, really. Our friend is sick, and unless we can get him some medicine he's going to die."

The man nodded. "Lots of people dying. No pharmacies around here though, no medicine either, but if it's a hospital you're after, missy... you best head that way. About a mile down, can't miss it."

He raised his hand and pointed over her shoulder, left at the intersection, west.

"Just don't hold your breath," he said. "There ain't much left."

"Can't hurt to look," said Sara.

The man shrugged, still stroking the back of his dog's head. "You'd be surprised."

"Well, thanks for your help," Sara said, turning to leave before stopping herself. "I'm sorry… I didn't even ask your name."

"Sam," said the man, having to think about it for a moment, as though he couldn't remember the last time anyone had cared to ask.

"Hi, Sam, I'm Sara. Thanks again."

Sam made eye contact and held it. "You wanna thank me, Sara? Leave. Now."

Sara shook her head sadly. "Can't."

Sam nodded and looked down. He didn't look back up.

Sara put her foot back on the pedal and pushed away, and she followed Sam's directions and turned left at the intersection. West, into the deepening gloom.

Mick pulled in close on her left as they rode.

"You sure about this?" he asked, his voice barely above a whisper. "What if he's lying?"

Sara shook her head. She didn't think so. Sam had struck her as genuine, but it wasn't so much what he had said or how he had said it. It was the dog that had made her mind up for her.

Food was scarce. Sam looked hungry, starving, and a dog was just another mouth to feed. It took a certain type of person to still care about a dog in all of this instead of eat it. And Sara had seen its collar. She'd never seen a homeless man own a dog with a collar before, which meant it probably wasn't even his, probably a stray he'd taken in. So Sara trusted Sam. She had to, she wanted to. It was the only chance Drew had, and sometimes, when you have nothing else, you just had to have faith.

"I believe him," Sara said, her eyes scanning the road and the buildings to either side as darkness fell. She saw faces peering out of windows, she heard a door slam somewhere, and further away she heard dogs barking.

"What are we even looking for out here?" Mick asked.

"A miracle," Sara said easily.

Mick sniggered, and Sara looked at him.

"Sorry," he said, but he didn't sound sorry, and his lips threatened to curl up at the edges.

Sara sighed. She couldn't really blame him. He'd been through hell, lost everything he had ever known. She couldn't begin to understand how that felt. Mick had no reason to believe in miracles. But that's why she was here and Trace wasn't. Trace didn't believe in miracles either. Didn't believe in anything really, not anymore. He just *was*, like he was just going through the motions, killing time, like this whole trip had given him something to do before he died.

Trace didn't think they were going to make it, and that's why he would have failed. That little fuse in his head would have blown long before he made it to Garden City, and he would have turned on Mick, and that would have been the end of it. He wouldn't have made it to the city. He wouldn't have found what they needed, and Drew would have died.

Sara couldn't let that happen.

"Guess this is it," she said, coming to a stop in the middle of the road.

"This?" said Mick, cheeks inflating as he exhaled. "We're going in there?"

Sara had to give him that one. Sam had been telling the truth. The hospital was hard to miss. It was a mess. Like it belonged in a war zone, somewhere in the Middle East, not the middle of the United States. All the windows on the ground floor had been smashed in, and most of the ones on the second. The third floor was a little better, like people's arms had been getting tired, or maybe they'd simply run out of things to throw by then. The rest of it looked even worse. There'd been a fire in the north wing at some point, and someone had driven a car through the entrance to her left. Sara saw bits of clothing and shoes and what she assumed used to be medical equipment scattered across the ground in front of her. And in the middle of the parking lot, between her and the way in, were two burnt out shells that used to be cars.

There had been a lot of anger directed at this place, a lot of hate. Probably when that story came out that there was a vaccine. Something they'd been testing on the soldiers in France toward the end. And true or not, people went insane. There were riots in every city that day, mobs pouring into hospitals and clinics, desperate, frightened people looking for something that didn't exist, then angry when they didn't find it. Like it was Black Friday, but with knives and guns.

A lot of people died that day, and that's what felt so wrong about this place. It felt haunted, as though all that fear and rage had soaked into the ground.

Sara shivered, and, for the first time since they'd set out, she started to have doubts.

What if there's nothing left?

The mob would have picked this place apart. What if she was looking for something that didn't exist?

Then Drew is dead, a little voice in her head said.

Sara shook her head. She refused to accept that. This was where she was meant to be. She could feel it, pulling her on like a magnet.

She turned to Mick. "You ready?"

Mick shrugged.

"Good enough, I guess. Okay, no talking from here on in, and don't turn your flashlight on until we're inside. Point it at the ground, never above knee height, and keep it cupped with your hand. Good?"

Mick swallowed. "If you say so…"

The first floor was a waste of time.

All the rooms had been gutted, cupboards emptied, doors kicked in. There was paper everywhere, and the ground was covered in a layer of glass and dirt and dust and bits of plaster. Someone had even ripped out all the lights and pulled the ceiling down.

They did one lap and gave up. They left their bikes in one of the rooms on the ground floor, tired of carrying them but too worried about punctures to wheel them along either, and they went upstairs.

They came out on the second floor. Sara turned right on a whim and they crept along, their footsteps crunching on glass, loud in the echoing halls.

"What are we even looking for?" Mick whispered, so close he was practically breathing in her ear.

"The dispensary. A supply room. A locker. Anything. Something somebody missed."

"There's nothing here," said Mick. Glancing over his shoulder, breathing fast, and when he turned back his eyes were wide. "Shouldn't we leave? What if someone finds us?"

Sara shook her head. "Not if we're quiet."

"What about Trace?"

Sara looked at him quickly before turning back. "Don't worry about him, Mick. He's harmless. Besides, he's back at camp."

"Good," said Mick.

But there was something wrong with the way he said it.

Sara heard him grunt, and she turned just as Mick smashed a brick into her face. There was pain, a bright light. She lost control of her legs. She slumped to the floor, spitting out blood and teeth. She looked up, and Mick hit her again.

TRACE

He'd stopped at the edge of town, in the middle of a four-way intersection, buildings dark and menacing all around him, roads empty and deserted in front of him, and he found himself at a dead end.

Trace had no idea which way they would have gone. Sara still wasn't answering her walkie-talkie. He had a one-in-three chance of guessing right, or a two-in-three chance of guessing wrong. He didn't like those odds. He could spend hours looking in the wrong place, and he didn't have hours. He might not even have minutes. He might already be too late. But he clamped down on the rising panic, and he tried to work through it.

What would Sara have done?

Trace looked left, litter and glass and bits of crap scattered everywhere. He looked right and saw much of the same. He stared straight ahead, the moon high overhead, peeking through clouds and lighting the world in a soft gray, and Trace came back to a dead end. Nothing. He had no map, no plan, no sign, he couldn't even flip a coin, and he felt the panic start to build again. He'd failed.

Something moved on his right.

Trace spun, his Glock in his hand a second later, and, whatever it was, it went dead still.

"Who's there?" Trace called, opening his eyes as wide as possible, hungry for light, trying to pierce the shadows that filled the doorway.

"Nobody," came the muffled answer, and Trace saw one of the shadows move.

"You alone, Mr. Nobody?" Trace asked, watching for movement in the corner of his eye, ears straining for the slightest sound, the scratch of a footfall, the click of a safety, waiting for a bullet in the back of his head.

"Alone? No, just me and Belle here."

"Belle?"

"My dog."

Trace moved closer, lowering his Glock as his eyes adjusted to the gloom, making out a figure wrapped in rags and the dirty bundle of fur next to him.

"You two seen anyone come through here recently?"

"We see lots of people, mister," the shadow said.

"Fine, then. You seen a blonde woman come through in the last two hours? Blue eyes, five-seven, nice smile. She would have had company, too, a kid. Says he's fifteen but looks older. They would have been on bikes, looking for a hospital or pharmacy."

"Who's asking?" said the shadow, his voice suspicious.

"Her friend."

"If you're her friend, then why ain't you with her?"

"Because I fucked up. I fell asleep, and she thinks the kid is trustworthy, and I think he's a piece of shit."

The shadow went quiet, and Trace could tell he didn't believe him, or maybe he didn't know anything, which meant Trace was just wasting time.

"Did you see them or not?" Trace asked, getting impatient.

The man stayed quiet. "Say I did see something. Why should I believe you? Could be you're the dangerous one."

"Do I look dangerous?" Trace asked.

"You stink of it, man," said the man. "But you also stink of cop."

"So?"

"So did she. You guys stink worse than me. I told her to leave. She didn't listen."

"Which way did they go?"

"You tell me her name, and I might tell you. Call it a trade. Call it proof. Evidence. Your type likes that kind of stuff, huh?"

"Sara. Her name is Sara."

The shadow seemed to think it over, then he lifted his hand, and he pointed to the north, straight through the intersection.

"Thanks," Trace said. He turned to move away, but something made him stop. That little voice in the back of his head that told him something was wrong, that he was being lied to.

Trace turned back to the shadow in the door. He fished in his left pocket, and he felt the shadow stiffen. He pulled out something wrapped in plastic that glinted.

"For you and Belle," Trace said. "It's not much, but it's all I got."

He tossed it to the shadow underhanded and made to move again, put one foot on the pedal, prepared to push off.

"Yo, officer," called the shadow. Just like Trace hoped he would.

"My memory plays tricks on me sometimes, but I think they went that way. You should find what you're looking for about a mile down. Can't miss it, really."

The shadow pointed over Trace's shoulder, and this time he pointed west, left at the intersection, and deeper into the city.

Trace nodded, and then he was moving again.

"You better hurry," the shadow called after him. "Pretty lady like her don't wanna get caught around here at night. Believe me."

Trace found what he was looking for easy enough, just like the stranger had said. A mile down the road and impossible to miss. But by then he was breathing hard, his calves were cramping, and he had a pain in his side like he'd been kicked by a horse, but he kept moving; he didn't have a choice. He rode into the hospital's parking lot, dropped down off his bike, and jogged in the rest of the way. One hand on the handlebar, the other holding his Glock, his AR-15 bouncing up and down on his back while he studied the building in front of him.

Sara had been wasting her time here. One glance was enough to tell him that whatever had been here was long gone; the building was nothing but an empty shell. It looked like parts of Detroit. Like it had been abandoned ten years ago, not three months. There wasn't a pane of glass left in any of the downstairs windows, and there was graffiti all over the walls. He saw dark rooms and empty halls. He saw no lights, no sign of life.

But in front of him, under the pale moonlight and in the patches of mud and dirt blown in by the wind, he saw tire marks and footprints. Two pairs going in, and none coming out. So he followed them across the parking lot, through where the front doors used to be, past the tail end of a car, its nose buried in ruined furniture and drywall, and Trace stopped. He leaned his bike against the wall and went still, trying to control his breathing, trying to stop his legs from shaking. He closed his eyes and listened. Nothing, quiet.

He took his flashlight out, cupped it in his palm, and he turned it on. Opened his hand a crack, his fingers glowing red, and Trace shined a sliver of light on the floor.

He saw footprints in the dust, and bike treads leading deeper into the darkness, so he followed them, flashlight in his left hand, holding it like an icepick, his left arm across his body, using the back of his left hand as a brace for his Glock.

He found their bikes two doors down, hidden around the corner, and Trace knew they were still here. He was getting close.

He was about to hurry after them when he heard a noise, but it came from the wrong direction. It came from behind him, out in the street, and Trace spun, flattening himself against the wall. He turned his flashlight off and waited.

It wasn't long until he heard it again. Voices, growing louder. And Trace realized he'd been followed.

"Give me a fucking break," Trace muttered, then he heard another sound, but this one came from above him. A solid thump, something heavy being dropped on concrete.

Trace looked back at the door outside. He looked at the ceiling, hearing the voices growing louder, and for a second he didn't know what to do. He couldn't go forward, he couldn't go back, but he couldn't stay here either.

He was trapped, and he couldn't allow that.

Trace turned his flashlight on again, and he started moving, deeper into the hospital, glass crunching with every step as he ducked beneath hanging wires. He no longer worried about being quiet. What he needed now was speed and distance and a little misdirection.

Trace rounded a corner, saw a long hallway stretching ahead of him, empty doorways to either side. He looked behind him and saw more of the same, and what looked like a nurse's office at the far end.

He looked at the room to his right, beds moved, blankets strewn across the floor, wires hanging from the ceiling like exposed roots.

He looked in the next room and saw the same, and he had an idea.

He ducked inside, grabbed a hanging wire, tied it around his flashlight. And then he sent it swinging like he was playing tetherball.

Decoy made, he exited the room and turned left, hurrying back the way he'd come, feeling his way along in the dark. He passed the intersection and kept going.

He made it to the nurse's office and slipped inside, holstered his Glock, slung his AR off his shoulder, dropped to his knees, and crawled under a desk. Then he turned around, lay down on the floor, and aimed his AR down the hallway and waited.

Trace didn't have to wait long.

He heard them coming. They were trying to be quiet, moving slowly, no more talking, but there was nothing they could do about the glass that covered the floor.

He saw the beam of their flashlight first. It came in from the right, a dim red circle sweeping across the wall. Then they stepped out into his line of sight, two of them, big, dark clothes, wide shoulders. Men.

They stopped moving. Trace saw them tense. They'd spotted his decoy, flashlight still swinging, but slower now, momentum almost gone, like someone was moving around inside. He could see them look at each other, some unspoken agreement passing between them.

They turned off their flashlight and crept forward single file, weapons raised.

Trace sighted down the barrel, his finger on the trigger, and he breathed out. He didn't shout freeze. Didn't yell police. That world was gone, and something told him they weren't here to say hello. So he didn't aim for center mass—they might be wearing body armor, there were two of them and one of him, and he needed them dead. So he aimed for their heads and squeezed the trigger.

His rifle kicked and the one at the back pitched forward.

Trace tracked left, less than an inch; he squeezed again and the second one went down same as the first. Two seconds start to finish.

Trace didn't move for another minute. He stayed perfectly still, blinking, his ears ringing, his heart racing.

But nothing happened, no one else came. It went quiet. So he crawled out from under the desk, got to his feet, and left the nurse's office on shaky legs. He walked toward the two men on the ground, his rifle at the ready. But they didn't move; their heads were in too many pieces to be a threat.

He retrieved his flashlight, slung his AR over his shoulder. Then he picked up their weapons: a Remington Model 870 pump-action shotgun and an M&P15—Smith & Wesson's version of the AR.

He pumped the shotgun, caught the shells—those went in his left jacket pocket. He thumbed the release for the Smith & Wesson, ejected the mag, and put it in his back pocket.

He hid the weapons in a cupboard in one of the empty rooms. Then he leaned against the wall, his heart beating like a drum, his face pouring with sweat. He bent over, grabbed his knees to stop his hands from shaking, and tried to slow his breathing.

Adrenaline was a bitch. It came on fast, and it came on hard. But he knew he couldn't wait, he couldn't rest; he wasn't done yet, he still had to get to Sara, and he'd just lost his one advantage: the element of surprise. So he pushed himself away from the wall and started moving, following the footprints down the hall before they disappeared under the door to the fire stairs.

Trace pushed the door open, and he started climbing, legs heavy, breath hissing between his teeth, hands still shaking. He reached the second floor, looked at the stairs to the third but didn't see anything; the footprints ended here. He turned his flashlight off, grabbed the door handle, eased it open an inch. And he waited.

Silence.

He stepped out into the hallway. He closed the door behind him just as quietly and looked to his right. He saw dark rooms and empty doorways and footprints. He looked to his left, saw a desk and bits of bedding strewn across the floor, but no footprints.

So he turned right, following the footprints until they ended at a closed door, and from the other side Trace heard a grunt and a muffled groan. Then came Mick's voice, and Trace knew he'd found them.

A minute later, and he still hadn't moved. He stood outside the door, thinking.

He didn't bother to check if it was locked. He wasn't worried about getting in. It was a hospital, not a prison.

It's what was waiting for him on the other side that was the problem. Mick was armed, and he'd have to be deaf to have missed the gunshots downstairs, and now he had Sara's weapons as well. Trace kicked himself for the thousandth time for not acting sooner.

But it was too late for that now. What was done was done, hindsight was 20/20. Now he was trying to think of a better way of doing this short of kicking the door in and going in guns blazing, but he came up blank.

This wasn't a movie. He couldn't come in through the ceiling or rappel down the side of the building, and he was on his own. Screw this up and they were both dead. So he took his time, and he brought his breathing back under control, trying to still the tremor in his hand, a tremor that would throw off his aim, and he couldn't afford to miss. He'd get one shot at this, and that was another problem. He didn't know where Sara was; he was going in blind, and all he needed was for her to get caught in the crossfire, but he couldn't wait any longer.

It's now or never, old man.

Trace aimed his Glock at the door. He brought his left hand underneath his right, flashlight gripped tight, left thumb on the switch. He sucked in a breath, flicked on his flashlight, and launched himself at the door. Left foot anchored, right heel driving through, he nearly kicked the door off its hinges.

Then it all went to shit.

Mick wasn't where he was supposed to be; he wasn't where Trace needed him to be. He'd put Sara between them, her hands in cuffs behind her back, her body pulled against him, his left arm around her neck, using her as a shield. And from around her waist, he had a gun pointed straight at Trace. Trace looked at it—short barrel, 9mm, a Rami, a good gun.

"Trace!" Mick said, blinking in the glare of Trace's flashlight. "I thought that might be you."

Trace kept his flashlight pointed in Mick's face. The kid was only half dressed. Pants on, only wearing one shoe. He didn't need to look at what was left of Sara's clothes on the floor to know the rest.

Sara blinked at Trace, her face a pulped mess. Her left eye was swollen shut, blood bubbling from her ruined nose.

Fractured cheekbone, Trace figured. *Broken jaw, maybe, definitely missing some teeth.*

Mick blinked, eyes scrunching up. "Turn that off."

He tried to duck away.

Trace hesitated. He didn't have a clear shot. Couldn't take the risk, not with Mick moving so much. He might hit Sara by accident.

"Now. I'm not going to ask again!" He jabbed the gun at Trace, then put it to Sara's head.

Trace let his flashlight drop until it was pointed at their knees.

Mick said, "That's better. Isn't it, Sara?"

Sara made a noise, something that sounded like a garbled yes.

"What do you want?" Trace asked, not that he cared. They were long past that.

Mick didn't say anything. Trace could see his eyes darting left and right, like a cornered rat looking for a way out.

"Why don't you let her go?" Trace said, trying another tack, stalling for time. Time bought him options.

Mick shook his head, a small movement. "Nah, I think I'm gonna hang on to her for a bit. I'm not stupid. Tell you what though. Why don't you drop the gun and the flashlight?"

"It's okay, Sara," Trace said slowly. "I'll have you out of here soon."

Mick snarled. "Drop it! I'm not going to say it again."

Sara shook her head, her chest heaving.

"Now!" Mick screamed, gripping Sara tighter.

"Okay, okay, whatever you say," Trace said. He held up his gun, turning it away. "Just take it easy."

Trace bent down and put his Glock and his flashlight on the floor.

"The rifle, too," Mick said.

Trace unslung his AR from his shoulder and laid it down next to his Glock. Then he straightened back up, slowly, hands spread wide, palms open.

See, kid. I'm no threat.

Mick looked down at the floor between them. Trace's flashlight cast a flat light against the ground, the reflected glow just bright enough to see the cold smile that split Mick's face like an axe. Like he was enjoying this.

Sara tried to struggle, her one good eye wide and terrified, blood running down her neck onto her chest.

"What was it you said about shooting someone?" Mick asked. "Make sure I'm within six feet, and aim for the chest?"

Mick looked down at the floor again.

"Looks a little far, don't you think?"

Ten feet by Trace's estimate.

"Come closer, slowly," Mick said. "And keep your hands where I can see them!"

Trace took a step forward, over his weapons, and the ten feet narrowed to eight.

"Closer," Mick said.

The gap narrowed to six.

Trace saw his grip on Sara loosen, and he watched Mick relax. In control, everything going to plan, his eyes locked on Trace, already ignoring Sara. She wasn't a threat, but she was still too close. She was in the way, and he needed to change that; he needed to make Mick forget all about her. So Trace kept his hands up and took a step to the left.

"Stop there, old man. That looks like six feet."

"Five, actually," Trace said, and he took another step to his left.

Mick shuffled awkwardly to follow him, and a gap opened up between him and Sara.

"Stop."

Trace stopped. "Take it easy, kid. You're in control now."

"Yes, I am, aren't I?" Mick said, and he gave Sara a shove. She stumbled, lost her balance, and her head slammed into the end of the bed. She went down hard.

Mick brought both hands to the grip, barrel of his gun pointed at Trace's chest.

Trace could hear Sara groaning on the floor, but he didn't take his eyes off Mick.

"Okay, you got what you wanted. You've had your fun. Now why don't you let her go?"

"You must think I'm stupid, old man."

"Stupid? No. I think you're sick," Trace said. "Calling you stupid is an insult to stupid people."

Mick shook his head. "You think you're so smart, don't you? Tell you what, I'm not going to aim for the chest either. I know you have body armor on."

He aimed his gun at Trace's head.

"You watching this, Sara?"

Sara groaned again, trying to get up.

"It's okay, Sara," Trace said. "Stay there."

"Get on your knees."

"No."

Mick blinked. "No?"

"What's wrong, you deaf?"

"Get on your fucking knees!"

"Make me."

He saw Mick's nostrils flare. Saw Mick's jaw clench, his hand tightening on the grip. Saw Mick's eyes close. A flinch, as it was called. Brain anticipating the bright flash and loud noise.

Mick pulled the trigger. There was a loud click.

And nothing else.

Mick blinked, a confused look on his face. There'd been no bright flash, no loud bang, and Trace wasn't dead.

Most people hesitate when they see something like that, when expectation differs from reality. It takes their brain a second to catch up, and Trace already knew what kind of person Mick was, and by then he was moving. He didn't bother going back for his gun—too far away and in the wrong direction. He just stepped forward, weight planted evenly, and pushed off his right heel, twisting from his hips, driving his shoulder around, right arm swinging through, powering a meaty fist broken in on bar fights and crackheads, fist full of hard knuckles and scar tissue.

It was an old man versus a fifteen-year-old kid.

It wasn't even a competition. Trace didn't even have to hit with everything he had. He didn't want to take the kid's head off. He just landed it perfectly, middle of Mick's face, and he felt the kid's nose crunch beneath his fist. He watched Mick's head snap back, watched his eyes roll into the back of his head and his legs turn to jelly. And just like that, it was over.

A ragged cough was the first sign the kid was coming 'round.

His eyes fluttered open, and Trace shuffled back, watching confusion and pain play across Mick's face, watching Mick frown up at the ceiling like he was suffering from some short-term memory loss. A little brain damage, maybe. Like he couldn't work out why his face hurt, or why he was lying down, or why his hands were tied behind his back.

Mick turned his head, saw Trace, and Trace watched it all come back to him.

"Good," said Trace. "You're awake. I was worried I might have hit you too hard."

Mick turned his head, saw his backpack, its contents emptied out on the ground, clothes scattered, cans of food lumped in a pile, and his eyes stopped on a black toiletry bag.

Trace watched the realization sink in, saw a vein pulsing in Mick's neck.

"Sara's just getting dressed, you see," Trace said.

Mick turned back to glare at him.

"And then we need to leave. But I figured you and I could have a little chat in the meantime."

He reached into Mick's pack and took out a glass bottle with a clear liquid inside and a tiny medical script on the label. He held it up in front of him. "You had it all this time?"

Ceftriaxone the label read. A powerful antibiotic and exactly what Drew needed. Used in treating a range of diseases. Bone and joint infections. Pneumonia. Sepsis. He knew this because Jen had been on it when the skin infections didn't respond to anything else. When the cancer had her up against the ropes.

And this little shit had been carrying it on him the whole time.

"So what? I lied," Mick said, his nose blowing red bubbles, eyes watering. "You want a medal?"

Trace shook his head.

People think evil is easy to spot. They think of evil and imagine a monster. They imagine the Devil with horns, something obvious and identifiable.

But sometimes evil looks just like the kid next door.

Trace sighed. "I'd planned on having this chat away from camp, somewhere private. Who knows, maybe things would have worked out differently. Maybe not." He shrugged. "Something tells me this isn't the first time you've done something like this, and something tells me it wouldn't be the last."

And maybe there was a reason why. Maybe the kid had been abused growing up. Maybe he had mommy issues or a couple of screws loose.

Not that it mattered now.

"Anyway, I just wanted you to know a few things before we left," Trace said.

"Oh yeah, what's that?" Mick said, turning to spit out blood at Trace's feet.

Trace shrugged again. "You're nothing, kid. A parasite. By tomorrow you'll be even less. Nobody will miss you, nobody will care when you're gone. Sara is strong, she'll get over this. But you won't, and I'm always going to hate myself for not doing this sooner."

Trace bent down and covered Mick's mouth with his left hand. He put his knee on Mick's chest, put all his weight on it, and he watched Mick's eyes bulge out of his skull, watched Mick try to breathe through his broken nose, blowing snot and blood all over the back of Trace's hand.

"Do you know what comes next?" Trace asked, leaning closer.

Mick's eyes went wide, and Trace pinched his nose shut. Felt Mick scream on the other side of his hand.

It tickled.

Asphyxiation wasn't pretty, but it was relatively quick. Two to three minutes was all you needed. It was quiet, too, and Trace didn't want any more unwelcome guests. So he just sat on Mick's chest and waited, watched Mick's face turn bright red, felt his legs kicking uselessly, heels drumming against the floor, back arching, trying to throw Trace off, trying to bench-press 190 pounds with his arms tied behind his back.

Trace didn't budge. He just pressed down harder. Watched

as Mick's chest heaved, lungs sucking on a vacuum, face turning purple, blood capillaries bursting, petechiae spreading like chicken pox. Watched Mick's struggles grow weaker, eyes glazing over, pupils dilating, body going slack.

Trace counted to sixty, then again. Just to be sure.

Then he stood up, wiped his hand on Mick's shirt, picked up Mick's bag full of medicine and food, slung his AR over his shoulder, and walked out of the room. He collected Sara from next door. He put her arm over his shoulder and helped her down the stairs. They stepped over the bodies, picked up the bikes, leaving Trace's behind, and they went out the back of the hospital, not the front.

Trace went first, walking across the street pushing Drew's bike with his left hand, his Glock back in its holster, his AR held across his chest.

He waited in the shadows of a building, made sure it was clear before he signaled for Sara to come across. He helped her onto her bike, listening to her small grunts of pain, and then they left. They rode back to the intersection, turned right, and headed south, back out of the city.

And from a doorway, a shadow watched them leave. He turned to the smaller shadow beside him and promptly forgot all about the strangers and the fact that there were less of them than before.

After all, he had his own problems to deal with.

It took them longer to get back than it had taken Trace on the way in. Nearly two hours by his watch, which was both good and bad.

Good because it gave them time. Time for Sara to come back to herself. Time to try to put it behind her, to develop some short-term scar tissue, to try to forget. A simple, ingrained, and very human coping mechanism. A survival stress response.

Trace didn't talk. The less he said the better. Anything he said at this point was meaningless, and he figured Sara would talk when she was ready.

It took an hour.

"Trace," Sara began, her voice slurred, mouth misshapen. "I…"

Trace knew what Sara was going to say next, or he had a good idea at least, and he needed to steer her thoughts away from that path. It wouldn't do her any good. Wouldn't do any of them any good.

"Don't. He fooled us all," he said.

He didn't know what else to say. He wasn't good at these things.

Sara went quiet again for a long time, thinking so loud Trace could almost hear it.

"What happened?" Sara asked eventually. "You should be dead."

Trace shrugged. That part was easier to answer.

"I'm a cautious man, so when I reloaded his gun back at camp, I put the round in backwards."

"But what if he'd used mine?"

"Then we wouldn't be talking."

Sara didn't seem to like that answer.

Trace glanced at her sideways as they rode. Dried blood was smeared down her chin, her one eye stared straight ahead. Broken, abused, and beaten half to death.

"Trace," she said softly. "Don't tell Ian. Please?"

Trace didn't say anything. It wasn't his call. He wasn't her therapist. But as much shit as he gave Ian, the guy wasn't a complete idiot. He'd figure it out pretty quick. Trace just hoped he was a big enough man to be there for her when she needed him the most.

So the extra time was good, but also bad. Bad because it was late when they got back. Nearly midnight. No one was responding to his radio calls, and Trace didn't know what to make of that.

And when they finally limped into camp and he found Ian and Drew's slumped shapes sitting in front of the fire, with Stacey and

Peter to either side, wide awake and waiting for them, Trace got another bad feeling.

"Drew?" he said.

Drew didn't move, but Ian shot to his feet. "Sara?" He took a step forward, then stopped himself as men with guns melted out of the trees.

"Oh, good," said one on Trace's left. "We've been waiting for you. Haven't we, kids?"

Trace looked at him. He looked at the men to either side, saw one of them holding the AK-47 he'd taken from the bikers, and something cold wrapped around his heart.

He didn't need to be a cop to know this wasn't going to end well.

CLAY

Nobody had said anything about kids.

The kids complicated things. It was one of his rules, even before he'd gone to prison. Prison had just reinforced it, burnt it into the gray mush between his ears.

The way Clay saw it, everyone has to look down on someone to feel better about themselves, and prison was no different. There's just a whole new set of rules on the inside, a pecking order, a ranking system. And a child molester is about as low as you can get. Even rapists and serial killers found pedophiles repulsive, and there's no rehab inside. Prison spat you out more screwed up than when you went in.

That was why most "tree jumpers" didn't have any balls after their first time in gen pop. They'd get spread-eagled and held down while someone with a strong hand and a dirty razor cut them off. That way there was less chance of them reoffending when they got out. Like no chance at all. That was also why they had some of the highest suicide rates inside. Clay figured most of them couldn't handle being on the receiving end for a change.

So Clay had his rule. No kids.

But the way one of the King's men was looking at the little girl meant his rule was going to be tested, and soon.

He wasn't the only one who'd figured it out either. The old cop had, too. Clay could see it in his eyes. It's how Clay knew he was a cop to begin with. He was too calm, too cold. He just watched, and Clay could see him thinking. Like he was taking notes, remembering their names, like he was waiting for something.

But what that was Clay couldn't figure out. No one was getting away. No one was coming to rescue them. And all the thinking in the world wasn't going to save the old man from what came next. Ray's AK-47 made sure of that.

A literal smoking gun, and Clay smiled at his cleverness.

But then he remembered the kids and his smile faded.

He looked at the line of horses plodding along in front of him, their prisoners stumbling alongside, hands tied together and leashed to a horse.

Clay looked at the mom, third in line, blonde, thin, nice body, great ass, even better in the daylight. But her face looked like she'd run into a door, an angry one. Clay thought she might even be missing some teeth. The dad seemed to be walking fine—at least Clay assumed he was the dad—but he didn't seem to be on planet Earth anymore. His eyes were far away, and he kept squeezing them shut. Like he was counting to three and wishing he was somewhere else.

As for the sick one draped over their packhorse, Clay ignored him. He was half dead already, and the King would take care of the rest soon enough. The only real threat was the old man next to him.

Everyone else ignored him because he was old, but Clay knew different. Old cops are the ones you needed to worry about the most. Not that there was anything he could actually do. They'd taken away his weapons, his hands were tied in front of him, he was on foot, and the leash attaching him to Clay's horse meant he couldn't go far.

Clay turned back to the front, to where the girl was sharing a saddle with the King's man, Hill. Sergeant Roberts had the boy sitting in front of him. Incentive, as he called it.

Clay shook his head. The asshole had been spending too much time around the Commander.

But that wasn't the issue. The issue was that for the last three hours Clay had watched Hill's hands begin to wander, cautious at first. Starting on her waist, moving down to her hips, pulling her against him as he whispered something in her ear, something that made her freeze, too scared to even breathe. Staring straight ahead as he rubbed himself against her, wandering hands becoming more confident as one hour turned into two, then three. Four and his hand slid up under her shirt.

Clay clenched his fists. Heard his knuckles pop, and it was almost as if the old man could read his mind.

"You gonna do something about that?" he said.

Clay turned to look down at him.

The old man dipped his head at the little girl. "Or are you just gonna sit there and watch?"

Clay frowned.

Confidence was good, confidence was fine. In the right place, at the right time. The old guy's wasn't, and Clay didn't like the way he was looking at him, didn't like the way it made him feel. So Clay kicked his horse in the side, and they broke into a short trot. The cop stumbled. He went to a knee, got yanked off his feet and dragged for ten yards before Clay pulled back on the reins.

Clay watched the old guy get up slowly. Watched him dust himself off as best as he could, and Clay wondered if he'd gotten the message.

He wasn't his friend. He wasn't his buddy. He didn't owe him shit. The fact that they'd managed to elude them for so long was pure luck. But that luck had changed, and when they got back to base the King would make an example of the old man, and the husband, and the sick one, and then he'd start in on the woman. And there was nothing Clay could do about it.

But no one had said anything about kids, and Clay didn't know what to do. He knew what he was taking the girl back to. The men didn't care about a messed-up face, or their age. All their attention was focused further south, and the girl would be a beautiful woman one day, a real stunner if the mother was anything to go by, not that she'd live that long.

And Clay knew it would happen tonight, tomorrow morning at the latest. Hill would make his move before they got back to base, because then he'd have to share.

Fucked if he knew what he was going to do about it, though. Because as soon as that happened, all hell would break loose—the cop would do something stupid, Roberts would overreact, and the little boy would pay for it.

They stopped riding at sunset, which was just as well. Clay and the old man had gradually fallen further and further behind as the day wore on. His knees seemed to be a problem, and Clay knew he couldn't go any farther. He could barely stand, never mind walk, and Clay almost felt guilty for dragging him across the ground earlier. Almost.

So by the time they caught up with the rest of the party it was dark, the soldiers had a fire going, and they'd put the prisoners in the middle. Not that they were worried about them running away, but it was cold, and they'd left all their sleeping gear behind. Which meant they'd have to huddle together for warmth or they'd freeze.

Clay climbed down off his horse, his ass one giant bruise, his thighs rubbed raw, and he walked the cop over to the rest of them. Put a hand on the old man's shoulder and pushed him down, made him sit before he walked back to his horse. Then he took his saddle off, slung his rifle over his shoulder, and walked back to the fire. He set his bedroll up for the night, where his saddle became his pillow, and then he stopped, his breath misting before him as it started to snow.

He watched the flakes drift down. He held out his hand, catching them in his palm, watching them melt on his skin. He'd never seen real snow before. The only snow you got in Florida went up your nose.

"What's wrong with you?" asked Roberts, and Clay forgot all about the snow. He turned to watch Roberts poke the sick one with the barrel of his M-16.

"Hey, I'm talking to you."

"He's sick," said the old cop, dragging his head up to look at them.

"Was I talking to you?" Roberts asked. He nudged the man on the ground with his boot. "Hey! Answer me, what's your deal?"

The man mumbled something.

"The fuck you say?" asked Roberts. He turned back to the group. "The fuck he say?"

"He said he needs his insulin shot," the cop said.

Clay saw the dad open his mouth, then close it. A confused look on his face.

The mother didn't seem to care. Not quite all there. She just stared at the fire, her left eye swollen shut, her face an ugly blue in the flickering light. Her kids to either side of her, their heads resting in her lap and pretending to sleep.

At least they aren't crying anymore, Clay thought. But he figured the relief would be short-lived, and he turned to watch Hill leaning against a tree.

"Hey, I'm talking to you," Roberts said, poking the sick one again. "Get up."

"He can't, he's sick" said the old cop. "He needs his shot. He's going into shock."

Roberts turned around, walked a step, reversed the M-16 in his grip, and hit the old man in the face with the butt of his rifle.

The old man turned his face away at the last second, tried to go with it, lessen the blow. Didn't really do much; it knocked him over, and he collapsed onto his side with a pained gasp.

Roberts grabbed him by the collar and dragged him back upright. "You hard of hearing? I wasn't asking you."

The old cop blinked back at him.

"Sorry," he said, "must be your accent. All that dick you've sucked makes you hard to understand."

Roberts grunted, almost a laugh. Then he hit him again, and this time the old man went down hard. Stunned.

Roberts dragged him upright again, blood running from a cut in his forehead down into his eyes.

"Anything else?" he asked.

The old cop turned his head and spat on Roberts's boots.

Clay frowned.

Confidence was good, confidence was fine. In the right place, at the right time. The old guy's wasn't, and Clay didn't know what he was trying to prove. Goading Roberts wasn't the smartest thing to do.

"Have it your way, then," Roberts said, and he wound the rifle back.

"Stop! Just stop! Please," the woman cried.

Everyone turned to look at her. Even Roberts, his rifle pulled back, frozen mid-swing.

"He's telling the truth," she slurred, talking like she had rocks in her mouth. "Please. He needs it. He'll die if he doesn't get it."

Roberts let his rifle down slowly. He stepped away from the cop and walked toward her.

"How long?" he asked.

"I don't know." She shrugged, hesitated, looked at the old cop, like she was looking for direction, then back at Roberts, looking up at him with her one good eye. "Tonight, maybe sooner."

Clay frowned. Something didn't smell right, he just couldn't work out what.

Roberts scratched his chin, and Clay could see him thinking. It didn't take him long. Wasn't much of a choice, really.

The sick man was a dead man either way, but Roberts had promised to deliver them to the King alive, and four was better than three.

Clay didn't know where the kids figured in there though. Roberts didn't seem to have thought that far. Or he didn't care.

"Where is it?" Roberts asked.

"My bag," the old cop said, leaning forward and spitting out blood. "The green one."

Clay looked at the gear next to the horses, some of it theirs, most of it belonging to the King's men. The weapons and spare ammo they'd lifted off the group, anything that looked valuable, the rest of it had been left behind. Except for the food; that was the first thing they'd taken. Not quite enough to feed six men, but better than nothing. And Clay burned through food fast. Any ounce of fat he'd once carried had long since melted off; there was nothing left under his clothes but muscle.

Clay realized everyone was looking at him.

"What?" he said.

"I said go get it, you moron." Roberts jerked his head at the pile of gear.

Clay shrugged and walked over to the horses. They'd picketed them in a line. *Picketed.* Another word he'd learned, like bridle, and stirrup, and canter.

"Like talking to a brick sometimes," Roberts said to his back, and the soldiers laughed.

Clay ignored him.

Sticks and stones. Besides, he had his fists. He didn't need much more to break bones, and words were empty. *Let people think you're dumb and you'll always surprise them,* someone had once said. He didn't know who, and he might not have much of an education, but that one lesson had stuck.

Clay picked up the bag.

"Left side," said the cop.

Clay opened it up and peered inside.

"It's a little glass bottle."

"I see it," Clay said. It was like a small pharmacy in there, bandages, some tape, gauze, some needles, disinfectant, painkillers—the good kind. Clay pocketed those. He took the bottle out and turned it toward the fire, trying to read the label in the flickering light.

"Sef...sefet...seftry, ax on?"

Clay gave up.

"Ceftriaxone," said the cop.

"Now what?" Clay asked.

"Now you give him a fucking shot, you idiot," said Roberts, shaking his head.

Clay walked over to the sick one, bottle in one hand, a needle in the other.

"How much?"

There was a slight pause.

"The whole syringe," the old cop said.

Clay frowned; something was definitely wrong, but he didn't see what difference a single needle could make. So he crouched on his heels, unscrewed the bottle, placed it on the ground next to him, dipped the needle in and pulled back on the plunger until it was full. He pulled it out, closed the bottle, and shuffled closer.

"Wait, you need—" started the cop.

"I know what I'm doing," Clay said, cutting him off.

Growing up where he did, you learn a lot of things, like how not to shoot up. And injecting air was a good way to kill yourself, painful, too. So he held the needle up to his face, pushed down on the plunger until a bead of liquid formed on the end.

"Where?" he asked.

"The ass."

Clay nodded. Always the ass. The guys that juiced up in prison took two shots a day. Steroids meant for horses. But the principle was the same. Same dirty needle passed between them. Clay never touched the shit. Didn't need to. Gaining muscle had never been a problem. And there was such a thing as too big. But he knew the ass was good for heavy doses. Lots of dense muscle, lots of blood flow, good place for drugs to be absorbed into the body.

"Wait!" said Roberts. "Better give him two just to be sure."

Clay frowned at him. "That's not how it works."

"I'm not gonna have him die before we get back to base. Give him two shots." Roberts came to stand over him. "That's an order."

Clay shook his head. *Idiot.* He rolled the guy on his side, pulled his pants down, and jabbed the needle into the pale white flesh. Harder than he needed to, but the guy didn't even twitch. He was out of it.

Clay pushed down on the plunger, pulled the needle out, put the cap back on, pulled the guy's pants back up over his hips, picked the bottle up, and he got back to his feet.

"What you doing?" asked Roberts, taking an involuntary step back as Clay turned to tower over him. "I said give him another one."

"Another one will kill him."

"What the fuck do you know? Give him another one."

Clay frowned. He took a step forward, and Roberts shrank back, lifting the barrel of his M-16.

"Careful where you point that next," Clay said. "We don't want an accident, lots of kids around here." But the way he said it, he made sure Roberts knew exactly who would be having the accident.

Roberts glanced over his shoulder, and Clay saw the soldiers watching them. He turned back to look at Clay, and he puffed out his chest.

"I said give him another one."

Clay grunted. "He'll get another shot in the morning. You give him another one now and he's dead. And I'll let the Commander know exactly whose decision that was."

He watched Roberts deflate, he watched Roberts glance over his shoulder again, trying to save face in front of his men.

"You better hope he doesn't die during the night, then. If he does, it's on you." Roberts poked him in the chest to drive the point home.

Clay looked down at his finger, he looked back at Roberts, and Roberts pulled it back like he'd been stung.

"I'll take my chances," Clay said.

He pushed past Roberts, sat down in front of the fire, lay back, rested his head on his saddle, crossed his feet, and he got himself comfortable, waiting for the fun to start.

TRACE

It happened in the middle of the night. Just like he knew it would. Opportunistic behavior combined with some evolutionary thing, that low point in human circadian rhythms, when people are at their most tired or fast asleep.

Not that Trace was surprised. If you look at the number of robberies as a rate, its highest was during the day, ramping up steadily from nine a.m. before dropping off a cliff at five. Why? Common sense, mostly, because that was when most people were at work. No point robbing a house if everyone is home, not unless you want to go to prison.

Shootings, murders, assaults, and rapes were different. They occurred at their highest rates under the cover of darkness, between two and five a.m., generally, especially the premeditated ones. Why?

Common sense again. Less chance of witnesses that way, and then there's that evolutionary thing. Humans weren't meant to be awake at those hours. Our senses evolved for daylight and open grasslands, not complete darkness and sprawling cities. Most people are asleep at that time of night for that very reason, and sleeping people are vulnerable, and another kind of person takes advantage of that. Especially if he wants to get away with it.

But Trace was awake, which is why he heard the footsteps first. Footsteps crunching through snow, soft sounds slipping through the trees on his left, and Trace waited, his breathing steady, his body still, his hood pulled down around his face, listening as the fire popped and crackled, logs burnt down to red coals that pumped out heat and a soft orange glow.

The footsteps came closer, and Trace could feel his heart pounding. But he didn't move, he just kept his hands tucked under his chin, wrists rubbed raw.

But he was ready. He'd gotten his right wrist free using his own blood and spit as lubrication, his teeth as pliers, gnawing at the knots that had bound them together. He didn't bother with the left, and he ignored the pain. Pain was temporary, skin grew back, and he'd already fucked up once. He wasn't going to do that again. He wasn't going to let something happen to Stacey. Not while he was still breathing.

So he waited, snow continuing to fall, an inch deep and still going, smothering the world in a cold white blanket and filling the air with a soft hush, and Trace watched as the problem stepped into the light. The one who was supposed to be standing guard. The creepy one with the pinched face and the wandering hands. He stood at the edge of the light, his head turning slowly until he was looking directly at Trace.

Trace saw him pause, then the man's eyes moved on, coming to rest on Stacey. Tucked up against Sara, her arms around Peter, the three of them huddled together for warmth.

Trace watched the man slink forward, snow crunching beneath his boots, a little unsteady on his feet, like he'd been drinking, and Trace waited, pretending to be asleep.

The man came closer. He slung his rifle off his shoulder and laid it down on his pack. He pulled a knife from its sheath, a long, wicked thing, and Trace sucked in a breath, his hands tightening around the rock in his grip, rehearsing the moves in his head.

The man came closer, crouched down low, left hand extended toward Stace, knife tucked close to his chest.

Wait.

He'd only get one chance at this.

Trace saw the knife flash, cold steel glinting gold in the flickering light.

Wait.

He didn't even see where the other one came from. He didn't know someone so big could move that quietly. He was just there. A dark shadow the size of a bear looming over them.

"What you doing, Hill?" the shadow asked.

The man with the knife spun. "Fuck me!" he spat in surprise.

"What are you doing?" the big one asked, stepping closer.

"Fuck off, Clay, this ain't none of your business!" he hissed. Loud enough that Sara woke up, and her scream woke up everyone else.

Ian came awake fast, blinking in confusion before his eyes cleared. Drew didn't budge, but Trace was already moving, all his desperate plans gone to shit. Now he was just reacting, scrambling across the ground on his hands and knees, putting himself in front of Sara and the kids.

"Stay behind me," he hissed as Peter started screaming.

The man took a step toward them, annoyed now, his lips pulled back in a snarl.

"Get out the way!" he said, pointing the knife at Trace.

"Leave them alone," the big one said, stepping sideways and putting himself between them.

"Fuck off, Clay, this got nothing to do with you."

"What the fuck is going on?" shouted one of the soldiers, the one who seemed to be in charge. The runt of the litter who talked too much.

One of the dogs started barking. That set off the rest of them.

"Fuck me! What the fuck are you two doing? I'm trying to sleep here. And will someone please shut those dumb things up!"

"Why don't you ask Hill?" the big one said. "Ask him why he isn't out standing watch, like he's s'posed to."

"Hill?"

The dogs kept barking, harsh sounds echoing in the dark.

"Ask him why he's got his knife."

Hill didn't say anything.

"Hill?"

"He wants the girl," the big one said.

"That's it? Shit, man, let him have her. I don't care what you two idiots do. Just do it quietly."

The one with the knife smiled, and he took another step forward, braver now.

"Hear that, Clay? Soldier boy says it's okay."

"I heard."

"Good, so now you're in my way."

"Am I?" the big one asked, letting out a slow breath, and Trace noticed his legs were spread wide, knees bent, weight on the balls of his feet.

"You're some kind of dumb, aren't you, Clay?"

The big one shrugged, huge shoulders rising and falling as he spread his hands wide.

"Let me spell it out for you, then. Move, or I'll make you."

"You can try."

The guy with the knife glanced at Clay's empty hands, and he smiled.

"Have it your way, then," he said, and he feinted left.

The big guy moved right, and they met somewhere in the middle.

In Trace's experience, there were two types of big guys.

There was the dumb kind, and then there was the dangerous kind. Neither of which has anything to do with IQ.

People associate size with stupidity, they equate slow movement and overdeveloped physiques with low intelligence. Stereotypes. Just as they equate attractive people with higher IQs.

Difference being that the dumb ones didn't develop as fighters. They never had to. Born big. They'd had a natural advantage their entire lives, and then they kept going. They hit the gym and wrapped their big bones in even more dense muscle. They went for power at the cost of speed. They became one-sided fighters, and they tried to overwhelm their opponent with pure meat. They were brawlers. There was no technique, no stamina, no strategy. Most had never needed one, most had never been in a fight that lasted more than a few seconds.

The dangerous ones were another breed entirely. And they were dangerous exactly because people underestimated them.

One second into the fight and Trace knew what kind of big guy Clay was. Like Muhammad Ali in his prime, pure speed, hands too fast to follow.

Two seconds in, and the guy with the knife was down, screaming, his knee bent entirely the wrong way, arm disabled, twisted around behind his back, forcing his face into the ground.

"Drop the knife," Clay said.

He had to say it twice before the guy on the ground stopped screaming long enough to hear him.

"My leg! You broke my fucking leg!"

Clay twisted his arm and broke his wrist. Trace heard the bones snap like twigs.

The guy on the ground started screaming again, a high-pitched shriek until he ran out of air and sucked in more.

"Told you to drop it," Clay said as he pulled the blade from the guy's useless hand and let go of his wrist.

"I'm gonna fucking kill you, Clay! Just you fucking wait!" the guy howled, sucking in strangled gasps between each sentence.

Clay shook his head. "No, you won't." And he bent down and

pushed the blade into the guy's neck. Buried it to the hilt.

It happened so fast it took a second for Trace's brain to catch up.

It took the guy on the ground even longer. Two for the pain to register, three for the realization to hit, and Trace watched his eyes go wide. He watched him open his mouth like a fish, and he made a sound, something deep in his throat, something wet, before the big guy pulled the knife out, stepping back so the spray of blood didn't get on his boots. The guy on the ground started twitching, gurgling, hot blood spurting into the snow.

"What the fuck, Clay?" shouted one of the soldiers in disbelief.

Ian vomited.

Clay shrugged like it was obvious.

"I warned him," he said, with no more emotion than if he'd stepped on a bug.

Then he bent down, grabbed the guy by the back of his collar, picked him up off the ground with one hand, and he stopped. He looked at Stacey, he looked at Trace, looked at Trace's hands.

"This one's got loose," he said before he turned his back on them and dragged the body off into the trees.

Trace woke up to a boot in his side.

"Rise and shine, old man. Taxi's here," said one of the soldiers.

Trace pushed himself to a sitting position. Hard to do with his hands tied behind his back. He had to roll onto his stomach first, use his head as a crutch, pressing it into the cold snow before he could pull his knees under himself and lean back. But when they'd tied him up again after all the excitement last night, they'd gone for the more is better approach, and the ropes were so tight he'd lost almost all the feeling in his hands.

"Get up!" said the soldier, losing his patience. Then Trace felt rough hands under his armpits, pulling him to his feet before someone gave him a shove from behind.

Trace looked around him as he stumbled forward, seeing the fire snuffed out, smoke curling in the air, and the red smear of snow that disappeared off to his right, and then Trace heard it. The distinct rattle of a diesel engine slipping through the trees.

He looked over his shoulder as Sara and Ian were pulled to their feet. He saw the big guy nudge Drew with the toe of his boot, needle in hand, and then Trace turned right and lost sight of them.

He stepped out from under the trees and stopped. There was a truck in the middle of the road in front of him, big and green, sitting high off the ground on huge tires with a simple canvas-covered back. Army, Trace recognized, the rumble of its engine louder now, its exhaust turning white in the freezing air.

The big guy strode past him with Drew slung over his shoulder like a sack of potatoes. He sat Drew on the back of the truck, lifted his legs, and pushed him in. Trace started walking again.

The one who was in charge turned as Trace got closer.

"Get in," he said with a toss of his head.

Trace looked at the truck, looked at the height from the ground. The first rung on the ladder was above his knee. The tray was level with his chest. There was no way he could jump it. He looked back at the soldier.

"I can't," Trace said, half turning to show him his hands behind his back.

"Get in," the soldier said again.

"Last time I checked I couldn't fly. So how exactly do you expect me to do that?"

"You're a fucking smartass, aren't you?"

"Smarter than most," Trace said.

"You think?"

"All the time, you should try it."

"Old joke, heard it before," said the soldier, taking a step toward him and raising his fist.

"I got this," said a voice from behind him, and Trace felt two huge arms wrap around him in a bear hug. He was lifted in the air like he weighed nothing and carried forward until he could put his feet on the bottom rung. He felt hands at his back holding him up, pushing him forward, then doubling him over so he fell forward onto his chest, half in, half out of the truck before his legs were lifted up and he was rolled inside.

He rolled over onto his stomach and began the process all over again. He pulled his knees under him, using his head as a crutch, his face pressed against the dirty floor, breathing in oil and dust and old sweat, and he pushed himself to a sitting position. Then he shuffled forward on his knees, toward the front of the truck and Drew's still shape.

"Drew?"

Drew didn't answer.

Trace wriggled in next to him. "Drew?"

"Yeah," Drew said.

"How're you feeling?"

"It's too late, Trace," Drew said softly.

"Too late?"

Drew looked at Trace, and for the first time in days he didn't look sick. He wasn't sweating, his breathing was better, some of the color had come back into his cheeks, and Trace could tell his fever had broken. He looked like death, but he was going to live.

"I told you to leave me, and now it's too late. They're going to kill us, Trace. And what do you think they're going to do to the girls?"

Trace didn't know what to say. Leaving Drew behind had never been an option, but neither was giving up. Not now. Not until Peter and Stacey were safe, not until they all were. They had to escape, and that meant he had to keep thinking, wait until an opportunity presented itself.

He just hoped it was soon because Drew was right. These people were monsters, and the big one was the worst of the lot. And the longer he waited, the less options he'd have.

Trace turned as one of the soldiers climbed up into the back of the truck, followed by Stacey and Peter, then Sara.

The soldier came to stand in front of him, then sat down across from him, his rifle across his lap.

Trace looked at him. The soldier winked back and patted his rifle.

"Just in case you get any more clever ideas," he said.

And with that Trace felt his options drop to zero.

SARA

Sara was a mother first. Everything else was secondary. Her face, her missing teeth. The cuts and bruises on her arms and legs. That broken feeling inside her that went deeper. Secondary. Even Ian.

Sara glanced at him again, sitting directly across from her, but he couldn't even look at her, couldn't even make eye contact. Not since he'd seen her face and worked out the rest. He just stared off into space. And to Sara that hurt worse than anything else.

She shook her head and blinked the tears away. *Not now,* she told herself. She couldn't let Stacey and Peter see her cry. They were her everything, and they needed her to be strong. So she pulled them close, breathing in their smell. Peter with his head in her lap, lulled to sleep by the rumble of the engine and the sway of the truck. Stacey on her left, her face buried in Sara's neck, crying softly as they kept driving. East. Back the way they'd come. Toward the Cloud and God knew what else, but Sara had a pretty good idea after last night. That man with the knife and that look in his eyes…

She couldn't even finish the thought; it made her sick, and for the thousandth time Sara prayed for a miracle. *Please God, not like this.*

But if He was listening, He didn't answer. There was no bolt of lightning, no flat tire; the engine didn't fail, they didn't stutter to a stop. The truck drove on, and Sara felt powerless and pathetic and dirty, surrounded by animals, and she had to smother the sob bubbling in her chest, crushing it down until it came out as nothing more than a cough.

She peered down at Stace with her one eye, and part of her was glad that Stacey wasn't looking back, scared Stacey would see the truth in her ruined face, and she didn't know what she'd say to her if she asked what was going to happen next. She wanted to tell her it was going to be alright. That everything was going to be okay, but that would be a lie, and Sara couldn't lie anymore. She didn't have the strength. The best she could do was keep quiet.

Sara looked back up and found Trace watching her with sad, knowing eyes, like he could read her mind. And for the first time in as long as she'd known him, she saw something in his face that she'd never seen before. Guilt, and regret. He thought he'd failed them, and she could see it was tearing him apart. Because they both knew that whatever these men wanted with them, it wasn't good; and as bad as Mick had been, he'd been nothing but a warm-up, and this time she couldn't stop the tears.

She looked away, out the back of the truck, world blurring, the canvas sides of the truck rippling and fluttering in the wind, seeing their tire tracks like twin grooves carved into the white snow behind them.

She didn't know where they were being taken, but they'd been driving east for hours already, pace holding steady, maybe thirty miles an hour, undoing days of travel in just a few hours, and Sara knew that even if they did somehow make it past the soldiers, even if they somehow managed to escape, there was nowhere left to run. They had nowhere to go, they had no gear anymore—no equipment, no weapons, no food, no clothes. And escape on foot into weather like this was a death sentence. But then again, maybe that wasn't such a bad thing...

Sara looked at the big one in the corner. His cheeks red with cold, his eyes dark and dull, staring at his big hands and the blood stains on his fingers, and she remembered how calmly he'd slit that man's throat. Like it had been nothing, like he'd been gutting a fish.

She wanted to believe he'd done it to protect them, that he'd done it for Stacey, but that was a lie. He wanted Stace all to himself, and there was nothing she could do to stop him. She'd seen how he moved, how strong he was. They didn't stand a chance. Not even with Ian and Trace working together, and Sara thought nothing short of a bullet to the head would take him down.

And maybe she was staring, maybe he felt his eyes on her, but he turned to look at her, their eyes met, and Sara looked away. Just not fast enough. *Shit.*

She glanced at him again and found he was still watching her, a frown on his ugly face. Sara looked away again.

She heard him get to his feet, heard the sound his boots made as he shuffled toward them, knees bent, feet spread wide against the sway of the truck, until he was standing right in front of her. Sara didn't look up, she just stared at his mud-stained boots. Too scared to breathe.

Something was pushed into her chest.

She flinched, closing her eye. "Please don—"

"Here."

She didn't move.

"Here," said the voice again, louder.

Sara opened her eye to find his jacket in her lap. Dry, and still warm with his body heat, heavy with his smell, but not sour or rank. Heady. He smelled of earth and dirt and trees and horse.

She made a sound, not a thanks, not even a word, and she kept her head down, too scared to look up in case he wanted something in return. But he just grunted and walked away, slouching back in the corner by the door.

She looked up to see him staring out the back of the truck, watching the freezing wind blow flurries of snow across the road in long streamers like nothing had happened.

Sara looked away, and she pulled the jacket over Peter and Stacey, making a bubble of warmth for the three of them. And somehow in all the cold and the terror and the uncertainty, she fell asleep.

She could have stayed there forever, warm and oblivious. If she did that it meant things wouldn't get worse, nothing would ever change, and nothing bad would ever happen. But as with any dream, at some point you have to wake up.

It was the gear change that did it.

There was a grinding crunch as the truck slowed, and Sara blinked her one eye open, coming awake slowly, and then, all too fast, the engine began revving hard before the driver lifted his foot off the gas. He tapped the brakes, put his foot back down, and the truck shuddered forward, turning off the road and onto a dirt track, and Sara knew they were getting close.

They drove for another ten minutes, truck swaying and bouncing, the giant and the soldier looking more relieved with each passing second. As though their journey was at an end, as though the worst was over instead of just beginning.

They drove through a gate with a small building next to it. A guardhouse, Sara realized. Boom gate pointed at the sky and a ten-foot-tall fence topped with razor wire to either side. They drove past another fence, past army trucks, tanker trailers, and APCs and a helicopter sitting on a clear patch of snow. A dark H beneath it.

The truck turned right, and they stopped, the driver killed the engine, deep rumble dying, and quiet flooded in to replace it.

The big one moved first, walking across to her and taking his jacket without a word. He jumped down off the back of the truck, his boots crunching through snow as he disappeared around the side. The soldier followed him a second later, turning to look back at them once he was on the ground.

"Out," he ordered.

Sara looked at Trace, she looked at Drew. Then she looked at Ian, and for the first time in hours their eyes met. Disgust and self-loathing festering in their depths before he looked away again, and Sara could see he'd been crying. His eyes bloodshot, cheeks wet. She saw his lip tremble. She wanted to reach out and touch him, but she didn't know what he'd do if she did, and she was too scared to try in case he pulled away. Her heart couldn't take that.

"Out!" the soldier shouted, losing his patience.

"Wake up, Peter, we're here," Sara said, not that she knew where *here* was.

Trace struggled to his feet, bracing himself so Drew could lean on him for support.

"Are you fucking deaf? Get out," said the soldier, gesturing for Ian to climb out. "You first, crybaby."

Sara pushed herself to her feet and steered Peter toward the exit, watching Ian climb out backward.

"What's happening?" asked Stacey, clinging to her waist.

Sara shook her head. "I don't know. Just stay close, okay?"

Stacey nodded and hung on even tighter. Trace followed Ian out. He sat down on the edge awkwardly, his hands still tied behind his back, and he shuffled forward on his ass, letting his legs dangle over the edge before he tilted forward and hopped off.

He hit the ground badly, his left knee buckled, and Trace went sprawling face-first into the snow.

"Clumsy old fart, aren't you?" said the soldier, grabbing Trace by the back of the collar and dragging him to his feet.

Sara heard Trace gag as the fabric dug into his throat, snow and ice clinging to his eyelashes and beard.

"You next," the soldier said, pushing Trace away and nodding at Drew.

Drew nodded and followed Trace out, climbing out backward before the soldier grabbed him by the arm and pushed him next to Trace.

"Now you," the soldier said, looking at Sara.

Sara had to pry Stacey's hands off her before she could sit down, and just like Trace had done, she shuffled forward until her legs dangled over the edge. She turned to grab the handle next to her, and she swung herself out until she was facing backward and could drop the last few feet to the ground.

Sara shivered as she stepped away from the truck, freezing wind cutting down to her skin. She hadn't realized it had gotten so cold. The back of the truck had felt warm in comparison. She looked up at Peter and Stacey, tucking her hands to her chest as she shivered.

"How do we get down?" asked Stacey.

Sara didn't know. Stacey could probably do it, but Peter couldn't, and she couldn't reach out to grab him with her hands tied together, and she didn't trust him to do it on his own. She looked at the soldier.

"Not my problem," he said.

"I got it," the giant said, appearing next to Sara so silently it gave her a fright, his long arms reaching in and grabbing Peter and Stacey before they could pull away.

"Thick as pig shit, but at least he's useful," said someone, and Sara turned at the voice.

Her spirits sank when her eye came to rest on the one she pinned as the leader. The short one with something to prove. The one who'd sat up front next to the driver the whole way, out of the wind, where it was nice and warm.

"Let's go," he said. "We're all waiting on you, and the weather looks like it's about to turn."

Sara looked up at the gray sky, dark clouds pressing down, snow growing heavier, like a blizzard was rolling in.

"Go where?" asked Trace, glaring at him. "What do you want with us anyway?"

The soldier didn't even hesitate. He just stabbed the barrel of his rifle into Trace's guts, and Trace sank to his knees, wheezing, mouth moving as he tried to learn how to breathe again.

"Haven't you worked it out yet, old man? You're the entertainment."

He gestured for two soldiers to get Trace back on his feet. "Move."

The soldiers picked Trace up and pushed him ahead of them.

"You too, Kronk."

The giant shrugged and started walking, carrying Peter and Stacey, one on each hip.

"Mom!" Peter screamed, wriggling and twisting in the big man's grip. He screamed again, and Sara ran to catch up, struggling through the snow, knees lifted high, feet sinking in. And as she ran, she saw tents and vehicles and men in camouflage. But they didn't look like soldiers. They looked like the rejects, they looked old and dirty, with long hair and messy beards. And they were all looking at her like she was a piece of meat. She could feel their eyes on her. Their heads turning as she passed. Sly smiles on their faces that made her skin crawl.

"Hey, baby!" shouted one of them as she walked past. "What happened to your face? Your boyfriend not like something you said?"

"Don't worry, sugartits," said someone else. "It don't bother me. I'm an ass man myself, you'll see…" The men around him roared with laughter.

Sara could taste the sour surge of bile in her mouth, like she was going to be sick, feeling growing worse as more and more men came out of their tents to watch them walk past. Then she smelled them, stinking like sour milk, like they hadn't showered in years. Someone felt her up; she didn't see who. She felt hands pawing between her legs, pulling at her clothes, and the air took on a brittle quality, like it was made of glass, like she was watching it happen to someone else.

She heard a grunt of pain behind her and Sara turned to see Ian on his knees, clutching his face, blood streaming from his nose as one of the soldiers drew his rifle back, about to cave his head in.

"Enough," hissed the one in charge. "He got the message. And we're almost there. The Commander will decide what to do with them. Now get out of the way."

The men in front of them parted like a river, and Sara found herself at the edge of a clearing, ground trampled to mud, and beyond it big green tents in perfect rows, and an enormous tent the size of a marquee directly in front of them, and two old men standing in front of it.

"You're late," spat the one on the right, his voice bitter.

The one next to him didn't say anything, didn't move; he just stood there, his back ramrod straight, feet spread wide, his hands behind his back, and a baseball cap on his head.

"This them?" the one on the right asked. "You sure?"

The short soldier stepped to the front.

"Yes, they had this with them." He held out the AK-47. "Thought you'd wan—"

"Shut up."

The short one snapped his mouth shut.

"Down," said the soldier behind her, and Sara felt a rough hand grab the back of her neck and force her to the ground. The soldiers kicked in the back of Trace's and Drew's knees, and they collapsed to the ground next to her. Ian didn't need to be told, he ducked his head beneath his hands, palms open in surrender, and he knelt in the snow, crying again.

The big one came to stand next to her. He put Stacey on the ground, but he didn't let go of her arm, and he didn't put Peter down.

"Mom?" said Stacey, and the look on her face tore Sara in half.

All she wanted to do was go to them, wrap them up in her arms and carry them away. But she couldn't, and Sara felt time slipping through her fingers. She felt everything coming to an end.

"What's with the kids?" the one wearing the baseball cap asked, looking at the big one.

"They belong to these two, I think," he said, tilting his head at Sara and Ian.

The man grunted before turning his attention back to them.

"I would say welcome. But you aren't. I would ask your names, but I don't care, and you won't be here long enough for it to matter."

"What do you want with us?" asked Trace. "We didn't do—"

The soldier standing behind Trace stepped forward and hit him in the back of the head with the butt of his rifle. Hit him a little too hard, and Trace pitched forward into the mud, out cold.

The man wearing the baseball cap glared at the soldier.

"Uh, sorry, sir."

"Just get him up," he said, sounding annoyed. "But let that be a lesson. The next one of you who interrupts me will have their tongue cut out. Understand?"

Sara nodded, her eyes wide. The soldiers dragged Trace upright, his eyes closed, face smeared with mud, mouth hanging open. One of them grabbed a fistful of his hair to stop his head from slumping forward, and Sara could see the back of his head was sticky with blood.

Please, God, Sara begged. *Where are you?*

"Now, where was I?" said the man wearing the baseball cap.

"Payback," said the man next to him.

"Ah yes, eye for an eye," agreed the man with the baseball cap. "You're here to settle a debt. You took from us. So we'll take from you."

"I want the kids," said the big one, pulling everyone's eyes to him.

"No!" shouted Sara.

The man with the baseball cap turned to the big one, a flicker of annoyance on his face as he was interrupted again. But then his eyes fell on Stacey, and his annoyance turned into something else.

"You want them?" he asked.

"Sir, no," said the short soldier. "He killed Hill."

"Is that true?"

"Yes, sir."

"Any particular reason? Or you just didn't like the way he looked at you?"

The big one shrugged his enormous shoulders, and when he spoke his words were slow, as though he had to think about what order they came out in first.

"He wanted the girl. I said no. He came at me with a knife. Tried to kill me. I explained to him that was a bad thing to do."

"You explained?"

"I killed him first."

The man started laughing. "You're a regular comedian, aren't you?"

"No, sir, I just don't like pedophiles."

"You don't like pedophiles?" The man looked from him to the kids and back and laughed even harder. He wiped the corner of his eye. "I like this one, Taimus."

The big one didn't have anything to say to that.

"Fine. You want them? You have to do something for me first."

"Yes, sir."

His smile vanished, and he tilted his head at Drew and Ian. "Kill one of them. Just so we know we're all on the same page. After all, I can't have you killing everyone who doesn't like you, or I'd have to start questioning where your loyalties lie. Wouldn't you agree?"

The big one nodded. He put Peter down next to Stacey, his hands still wrapped around their arms.

"Please, no!" begged Sara. "Don't do this."

The big one looked at her. His eyes like two dead things. He looked at the one in charge. "Sir, not in front of the kids."

The man pursed his lips before he nodded at one of the soldiers behind her.

"Put them in my tent. And make sure they stay there."

"Yes, sir."

The soldier grabbed Stacey and Peter by the back of the neck, spun them around, and started dragging them away.

"Mom!" screamed Stacey.

"No! Please, God, no!" cried Sara. She tried to get up, and one of the soldiers stepped forward and slapped her across the face.

Sara saw stars, she heard a ringing in her ears, and when the darkness cleared Stacey and Peter were gone. The side of her face felt like it was on fire, her cheek pulsed and throbbed, but through her squinted eye she saw the man with the baseball cap turn to the one next to him.

"Any preference, Taimus?"

"Don't care," he said, a cold sneer revealing yellow teeth and dark gaps.

The big one nodded and pressed his gun to Drew's head.

Ian didn't move.

"I'm sorry," the big one said.

Drew just breathed out, his shoulders sagging as all the fight went out of him.

"It's much better this way," he added, and he lifted the gun from Drew's head and swung it right until it was a foot away from Sara's face.

She had just enough time to close her eye before he pulled the trigger.

DUNCAN SWAN

MONSTRE

VOLUME TWO

Coming Winter 2021

Keep reading for a sneak peek.

DAY
4

The *Kono*
Somewhere in the Alboran Sea

MR. ALAN

Mr. Alan gripped the railing with his left hand as the *Kono's* bow plowed into a wall of water. Metal groaned, and the floor shuddered as 10,037 tons of ship became a temporary submarine—momentum, buoyancy, and 27,000 HP the only things standing between them and sinking.

He felt them break free, deck tilting as they crested another wave, bow reaching for the sky before they dropped into the canyon that yawned open on the other side.

In the gap, Mr. Alan started moving again. But it was hard going, like balancing on a seesaw, and he wasn't as mobile as he used to be. Having only one good arm and leg made everything ten times harder, and each step hurt. But five surgeries later, Mr. Alan knew this was as good as it was going to get.

He was okay with that. His line of work required a certain level of innate pragmatism, and he figured a bad limp and chronic pain were a small price to pay for surviving this long.

So he just gritted his teeth. He sucked it up and soldiered on, right leg dragging, his hazmat suit rustling with every awkward step. But his little handicap meant he was struggling to keep up with

Wilkins and Ms. David, and Ms. David wasn't exactly the type to wait. She didn't stop or turn back to check if he was still there.

Mr. Alan didn't hold it against her. It wasn't that she didn't care. It wasn't a choice. She simply couldn't, like being born color-blind. Where most people would feel empathy, Ms. David felt nothing.

"High-functioning" was the term psychologists would use to describe her condition. "Cold-hearted bitch" was the one used by everyone else. It was why she was so good at what she did.

Mr. Alan didn't share the same advantage. He still had a conscience—a liability in their line of work—and a moral compass, as messed up as it was.

It was why he'd ignored Ms. David and hit send on Colter's email. Win or lose, Colter deserved better than to just disappear into thin air. Ms. David would never understand that, what it meant to be a soldier, but Mr. Alan did, which was why he was here.

Ms. David was an intellectual and the "brains" of the operation. She'd spent her life looking through a microscope, learning how to weaponize and counteract every disease known to man. It made her uniquely qualified to study the Cloud and its effects on people, but sometimes she forgot to see the forest for the trees.

That's where he came in. Mr. Alan was the practical side. He understood how things worked in the real world, and he was quite capable of getting his hands dirty when needed. Like a janitor, he dealt with the shit no one else wanted to touch.

They were an odd pairing, admittedly, but one that had served them well for the last five years. They had complementary skill sets, different areas of expertise. That was why they were pulling out of France—their job was done, they had what they wanted. Ms. David had her blood and tissue samples, some stiffs on ice, and a live EBE in the forward hold. One of the big six-legged "grays" Colter's team had run into. No one had been able to catch one of the exploding centipede things alive for obvious reasons...

But the Russians were on their way, Operation Daylight was in full swing, and if Stage Two didn't work, then there wouldn't be a Stage Three. No time. After all, war was complicated. It took weeks, if not months, to work out the logistics and support infrastructure, never mind loading men and machines onto ships and actually getting them from point A to point B.

The only reason they'd been in the area in the first place was thanks to serendipitous timing, en route to Iraq as part of Operation Peacekeeper—a last-ditch attempt to reintroduce some stability to the region. But, thanks to the buildup, by Day 3 they'd had 50,000 boots on the ground in France. Any other day of the year and Mr. Alan would have said that was impossible. It also meant they only had one shot at this. No do-overs. They'd pulled as many forces out of Iraq as they feasibly could, but that left the soldiers remaining behind at risk, over exposed and stretch too thin, and ISIL and the Taliban apparently viewed the Cloud as a "sign"—Allahu Akbar and all that shit—and attacks on US forces had only increased in frequency in the last two days.

Quite simply, they were stuck between Iraq and a very dark place. And while the US still controlled the skies above France, Mr. Alan didn't know how that dynamic would change when the Russians showed up. He didn't want to hang around to find out either.

So they were headed home. A four-, maybe five-day trip, and at a top speed of thirty-two knots it would be another six hours at least before they passed through the Strait of Gibraltar, then another ten before they were clear of the Cloud. Which meant another sixteen hours fighting forty-foot-tall waves, near hurricane-force winds, and an ocean that was trying to kill them.

Not that Mr. Alan was worried about sinking. Externally the *Kono* looked like an antique, destined for the scrap heap or the bottom of the ocean, but under the skin it was a whole other story. Like the *GSF Explorer* before her, the *Kono* was all about deception.

Built in the 1970s as a Norwegian whaling ship, the *Kono* was classed as a long-range fast ice ship. She was built for rough seas. An icebreaker measuring in at 389 feet long, weighing 10,037 tons, with a crew compliment of 175. She was ugly but functional. Bought by the CIA through a shell company in the 1980s, she'd been refitted in Africa, registered under a Dutch flag, then sailed across the North Atlantic, where she'd spent four years in a Philly dry dock being given the Bond treatment.

She'd spent the last thirty-five years going places the US couldn't. A taxi for Spec Ops forces and, more recently, a floating prison for terrorists. Off the books, of course. Some questions needed to be asked in international waters, away from prying eyes and congressional oversight, using a more "hands-on" approach. It was also a handy place for the bodies to disappear after. Plausible deniability was their motto.

But now they were transporting an altogether different type of illegal alien, and Mr. Alan had some reservations. They didn't have the proper facilities to house it, and they still didn't know what it was capable of.

He didn't like that—unknowns worried him. So he tried to catch up, the gray bulkheads before him ending in a watertight door and combination keypad on the right-hand side.

Ms. David was already slipping inside as Wilkins turned to hold the door open for him.

"Sir," he said with a dip of his head.

Mr. Alan squeezed past, bracing himself awkwardly as he stepped over the lip.

He found himself in a dark, cramped room—the ship's nerve center. Technicians and comms specialists were seated all around him, their hands mere blurs on keyboards. They talked on headsets, faces hidden behind gas masks as they watched the radar screens, video feeds, glowing maps, and satellite feeds that filled three of the four walls.

"How's our guest, Dr. Larsen?" Ms. David asked.

A small man in an oversized hazmat suit turned at his name. He shuffled across until he was standing in front of them, his head level with Mr. Alan's chin.

"All settled in," Dr. Larsen said.

"Show me," she said.

Dr. Larsen nodded at three specialists seated at a console to their left. "This way, please." He walked five steps and pointed at a row of black-and-white TV screens.

Mr. Alan went to stand next to him, leaned forward, and squinted. He was looking at high-angle CCTV feeds of the forward hold. The huge area was bathed in light, and an agent in full MOPP stood in each corner. A big metal and concrete box the size of two shipping containers was in the middle.

The forward hold's layout had originally resembled the processing bays from Guantanamo Bay, with small rooms off to the side and a long rectangular cage in the middle made out of steel pylons spanned by barbed wire and chicken fencing, otherwise known as the holding pen. Its design was made famous by pictures of jihadis on their knees, hands in cuffs, wearing orange jumpsuits, black hoods, goggles, and earmuffs pulled down over their heads.

But barbed wire and a little sensory deprivation was never going to hold one of these things, so they'd taken a page out of Cass's book and improvised. They'd called in Army engineers and had them wrap the cage in concrete slabs, steel plates, and cross braces. But improvisation was risky; there was no process, no learned experience. They were making it up as they went, and that left room for mistakes. That made him nervous.

"Wilkins?"

"Sir?"

"What are they carrying?" Mr. Alan pointed, trying to make out the agents' weapons.

"Beowulfs, sir."

Mr. Alan shook his head. The Beowulf was an assault rifle, full auto, chambered for .50 caliber rounds, capable of putting down a full-grown moose, but still not good enough.

"Double the guard, Wilkins. I want eight men in there at all times, and put an M2 Browning on that." He pointed at a metal walkway that spanned the hold at the far end.

"Yes, sir."

Wilkins turned his head to talk into the mic on his shoulder.

"Collins, on screen," Dr. Larsen said.

The specialist sitting in front of them pushed a key. The image on the center screen changed, and Mr. Alan saw an empty room—a camera feed from inside the cage in the center of the hold. He saw the tattered remains of mesh netting and what looked like oil splattered across the floor.

Ms. David frowned. "Where is it?"

"Hiding," Dr. Larsen said.

"Show me."

The specialist moved his hand across a scroll ball on his right, and the camera panned down until it was looking in the corner.

"Impressive," Ms. David said.

Mr. Alan agreed. It looked like the wall was giving birth. Or growing a tumor. He couldn't tell where concrete ended and the creature began.

"It hasn't tried to escape?" Mr. Alan asked.

"Quite the contrary. It gave up trying to get out an hour ago. My compliments to the engineers, by the way. They did a good job. But since then it's been talking to itself."

"Talking?"

Dr. Larsen nodded. "We're picking up minimal ultrasonic vocalizations, but it hasn't shut up in the infrasonic range. Same sequence, lasting exactly thirty-three seconds, repeated on a three-minute interval."

The technician pushed another key on his keyboard, and the speakers in front of them crackled to life.

Mr. Alan listened, trying to ignore the constant chatter and clatter of fingers on keyboards. He closed his eyes and concentrated. Beneath all the background noise and constant thrum of the ship's engines, he heard a deep, sighing wheeze, and he realized he could hear it breathing.

But nothing else.

"What sequence?" Mr. Alan said, opening his eyes to look at Dr. Larsen. "I don't hear anything."

Dr. Larsen grinned, wrinkles bunching in the corners of his eyes. "To us, no. But if you slow it down and boost the audio…"

The technician sitting in front of them pulled up an image on his computer screen, a wide-band spectrograph. Individual pitch periods appeared as vertical lines or striations. Jagged groupings of dark black lines—formants—separated by clear white gaps, periods decreasing as the graph became increasingly noisy.

Dr. Larsen nodded. "Play it, Collins."

The technician hit a button, and the speakers boomed, and a low keening sound filled the room. It almost sounded like a whale singing at first. But choppy, jarring, out of tune, full of sharp spikes and sudden clicks. It made the hairs stand up on the back of his neck.

"What do you make of it?" Ms. David asked.

Dr. Larsen shrugged. "Absolutely nothing. I'm a biologist, not a linguist."

"You really think it's talking?" Mr. Alan looked at the TV screens, watching the images taken from inside the EBE's cage.

"Don't you?" Dr. Larsen answered. "That's not random noise, Mr. Alan. It's structured, repetitive. There's a pattern, and it's incredibly complex, too. But exactly what it means is beyond me."

"We're recording all of this?" Ms. David asked.

Dr. Larsen sneered at the question. "Of course, Ms. David, since the second it came on board." But his annoyance was short lived. "What would you like us to do now? Ideally I would like to get some additional blood and tissue samples. Run some tests..."

"Soon, Dr. Larsen, soon," Ms. David said. "Just observe for now. We'll wait for the seas to calm down before we do anything else."

Mr. Alan turned his back on Ms. David and Dr. Larsen and the wall of TV screens, and he left them to it. He hobbled over to the computer-generated map on the wall, icons and symbols blinking and flashing for attention.

He could see the Cloud spreading out across Europe, its black eye bubbling up like a tar pit over Meyrin, and slowly growing back into the ragged patches of clear air the nukes had opened up— 200 miles wide in some parts, narrower in others. Clear air dotted with mushroom clouds that topped out at 90,000 feet, their shapes slowly distorting in the high-altitude winds. And in the shrinking gaps, there were long, straight clouds of dust as their armored units pushed in toward Ground Zero.

Closer still were three blinking icons deep beneath the Cloud, nearing Geneva, two coming in from the west—the armored Army Ranger units, still ninety klicks out by their last update—and Colter's team coming from the south, only four klicks from CERN's off-site data center.

He frowned. They should have been closer by now.

"How old is this position update?" He tapped it with his finger. Wilkins checked his watch. "Ten minutes, sir."

"What's taking them so long?"

"Last update said resistance into Geneva has been stronger than expected... but air support is inbound. We should know more soon."

"Any sign of the Russians?"

"No, sir," Wilkins answered with a shake of his head. "But in all honesty, they could be moving in an army a million strong from the east and we wouldn't have a clue, not with that cloud in the way."

"What about air units?" Mr. Alan pressed.

Wilkins consulted his notes. "A couple of Berievs, an air tanker, and a squadron of SU-27s escorting their fleet."

"That's it?"

"We also logged a flight of helos leaving the *Admiral Kuznetsov* twenty minutes ago."

Mr. Alan turned on him sharply. "What helos?"

Wilkins consulted his notes again. "Two Mi-35s, a 26, and one 28."

"And I wasn't told because…?"

"They wouldn't have the range to make it to Geneva, sir. Not from that far out. Besides, last contact showed them heading back east."

Mr. Alan clenched his fist, not bothering to hide his annoyance. "No, they weren't. They'll be heading north next. They'll come in over Switzerland. And the Swiss are too busy dying to care about a little unauthorized air traffic."

"Sir?" Wilkins said, not following.

"The 26 is carrying fuel, Wilkins. Has to be. They'll leapfrog their way to Geneva. It's slow, dangerous, too, but if nothing goes wrong they'll get there before the Rangers. Shit." Mr. Alan turned to the communications specialist sitting in the corner. "Get a message to Colter! Tell him he's about to have company. One Havoc and two Hinds inbound from the southeast."

"Orders?"

"Assume inbound units are hostile and be prepared to defend. And contact the Swiss. I want to know if they're tracking any bogies headed west."

"Yes, sir."

Mr. Alan turned back to watch the map with its glowing icons and blinking dots, glaring at Colter's green symbol as though he could make it move through sheer willpower.

Hurry up, marine, clock's ticking.

ACKNOWLEDGMENTS

If you're reading this, having skipped blank pages hoping for more, like sitting through the end credits of a movie for a teaser, and now instead find yourself reading the acknowledgments, then thank you. A lot of time and effort, a lot of blood, sweat, and tears goes into writing a book, but actually getting it into people's hands is a whole new level of difficulty, and very much a team effort.

So while I have your attention, I just want to direct the spotlight to all the people who made *Monstre* a reality. Those vital, precious few who kept me fed and clothed and well hydrated, who kept me moving, improving, and pointed in roughly the right direction. Because without them, *Monstre* and my sanity simply wouldn't have made the journey. This whole mad idea would have died long ago. So, without further ado, and in rough order of appearance:

To my parents, thank you for having me. And thank you for your undying support and patience over the years. This all never would have happened without you. And although it took me a while, I just want to say thank you, Dad. I finally took your advice and became my own boss. Mom, thank you for teaching me the universe has a plan and a place for everyone. I think I finally found mine; it just took a little digging and a little longer than expected. But I think I can finally say the Eagle has landed.

To my brothers, Ryan and Keaton, this book is dedicated to you. You didn't laugh when I said I wanted to do this; quite the opposite, you believed in me, even when I didn't. Love you guys.

To Kristine, my wife and partner in crime, thank you for telling me not to feel guilty about wanting to do something as crazy as write a book. Especially when I went from a pretty good salary to none, when three months turned into six, and six months became a year, when a year became two, then three, then four. I know it wasn't easy, seemingly impossible at points, but you kept the faith, kept us on track, and gave me a kick up the ass when I needed it. Couldn't have done it without you. Wouldn't even have tried.

To Will, who read more crap first drafts than any person should, and for some strange reason kept asking for more. Don't know why you did it, mate, but thank you. Your feedback was invaluable, and although I may not be able to get you that Lamborghini, I'll try my damn best to make it up to you somehow.

To my editors, Crystal Watanabe and Clay Bohle, love you three thousand. Crystal, for being there from the very start, when *Monstre* was barely an idea, to helping me finalize the font selection and final print layout. Wow, what a journey. Holy shit, I'm tired, are you?

And to Clay, for going above and beyond what I ever thought an editor would do for a book. I honestly can't thank you enough, and I can't wait to work on the next project together.

To the creative agency guys at Blow, to March D'Altilia in particular, thank you for your experience and expertise, and for answering all my stupid questions. You turned an idea into a brand. You turned an art piece into a cover, and you helped me learn how to start looking at everything through a creative lens.

And to all my artists (which is a constantly growing list), but in particular Eileen Steinbach, Laurie Greasley, Markus Lovadina, Chris Cold, and Stephen Oakley, thank you! Thank you for taking my ideas and making them real, for breathing life and color into pictures I had in my head. I can't wait to spam your inboxes with more concepts. Volume Two, here we come!

To my publisher, the amazingly gifted team at Super Hoot, thank you for bending over backward and moving heaven and earth to make this happen. Still doesn't feel real.

To the team at Smith Publicity, to Sarah Miniaci and Corrine Moulder, thank you for an amazing campaign! Couldn't have been in safer hands.

To my friends, to those that read rough drafts and my early stumbling attempts, to those who cheered me on, asked how that novel was coming along... To Paulie, who lent me his spare desk and was the best coworker I've ever had, thank you. And thank you to everyone else, too many to name, but you know who you are, and I know where you live... So you better have bought my book.

Last but not least, to anyone who has no idea who I am, to those of you who simply picked up *Monstre* on a whim and liked it, thank you for joining me on this journey. If you'd like to see more, come and find me on the interweb at www.duncanswan.me and say hello. I'd love to hear from you.

ABOUT THE AUTHOR

Duncan Swan was born and raised in Cape Town, South Africa. His family emigrated to New Zealand when he was fifteen, then he moved yet again to Australia as an undergrad in Aerospace Engineering, dreaming of becoming an astronaut. Somehow he ended up working in finance making fancy spreadsheets and writing stories on the side. He lasted five years before pulling the eject lever.

He now lives in Los Angeles with his wife, Kristine, and daughter, Zara, writing full time and finally using both sides of his brain. Yes, he also has a moody cat, because he's a writer. Obviously.

9 781734 574005